A city that's falling apart,
with a secret past who ha
complicates things, compli
that the missing girl is the c
men in America. She just d<

Hong Kong is teetering on the edge of anarchy. Violent street battles are raging between riot police and mobs demanding democracy.

Samuel Tay is a legendary Singapore homicide detective. He's retired, but it was purely involuntary. It seems his legend made a lot of senior officers uneasy and they wanted him gone. John August is an American who has shadowy connections to the intelligence community. He's done Tay a lot of favors in the past, and Tay owes him one.

When August asks Tay to come to Hong Kong to track down the missing girl, Tay doesn't much want to go. August and his friends deal in the fate of nations. Tay deals with personal tragedies, one human being at a time. Even worse, he doesn't like Hong Kong and, to be completely honest, he's not all that fond of Americans either.

But Tay answers August's call for help, regardless. He's a man who honors his debts, his forced retirement really sucks, and there's this woman… well, there's always a woman in there somewhere, isn't there?

August thinks that the triads may have kidnapped the missing girl. Tay doesn't have the sources to get inside the Hong Kong triads so August teams him up with Jack Shepherd, an American lawyer living in Hong Kong who just might be the only white guy on the planet the triads trust.

Tay is considerably less than thrilled by that. Here he is in a city that seems only moments away from going up in flames, everybody is certain the missing girl is dead, and now he's stuck with all these Americans.

Can things get any worse than that? Oh yes, they absolutely can.

Tay has developed symptoms that indicate he may be very seriously ill. For everybody, there is always a last time around the track whether they know it when they make the trip or not. As Tay's symptoms worsen, it begins to dawn on him that this missing girl just might be his own last time around.

But if this really is the end for him, Samuel Tay vows, he's going to go out with one hell of a bang.

WHAT THE CRITICS SAY

ABOUT JAKE NEEDHAM

"Needham deftly morphs 1930's American Sam Spade into Inspector Samuel Tay, a world-weary 21st century Singapore homicide detective." — **Libris Reviews**

"Inspector Tay is an endearing flawed protagonist, and the storyline full of twists and turns kept me up all night." — **Cosmopolitan Magazine**

"Jake Needham is Asia's most stylish and atmospheric writer of crime fiction." — **The Singapore Straits Times**

"Jake Needham's the real deal. His characters are moral men and women struggling in an increasingly immoral world, his plotting is top-notch, and his writing is exquisitely fine. Highly, highly recommended." — **Brendan DuBois, New York Times #1 bestselling author with James Patterson of THE SUMMER HOUSE**

"Needham writes so you can smell the spicy street food mingling with the traffic jams, the sweat, and the garbage." — **Libris Reviews**

"Needham exudes the confidence of a man who has seen it all, done it all, and still bristles with energy and butt-kicking tales well worth writing about." — **Singapore Today**

"Tight and atmospheric, Needham's novels are thrillers of the highest caliber, a perfect combination of suspense and wit." — **The Malaysia Star**

MONGKOK STATION

AN INSPECTOR TAY NOVEL - BOOK 6

JAKE NEEDHAM

Dedicated to those who met the monsters.

This one is for Aey, too.

Of course it is.

Everybody knows that the dice are loaded
Everybody rolls with their fingers crossed
Everybody knows the war is over
Everybody knows the good guys lost

Everybody knows that the boat is leaking
Everybody knows that the captain lied
Everybody got this broken feeling
Like their father or their dog just died

Everybody knows

Everybody Knows
Lyrics by Leonard Cohen

PART 1

NEWTON'S FIRST LAW OF MOTION

Every object will remain at rest or in uniform motion in a straight line unless compelled to change its state by the action of an external force.

ONE

HONG KONG IS a city of splendor and sorrow. It is smooth, sophisticated, and sly, but it is also ruthless, scheming, and cruel. And it's as doomed as Jack Kennedy riding through Dallas in the back of an open car.

Most Americans know next to nothing about Hong Kong. Not many could find the place on a map if you threatened to kill their dog. A few people might remember hearing that the British fled Hong Kong in 1997 and turned over to the People's Republic of China what for a hundred and fifty years had been a colony of Great Britain. But ask them anything else about Hong Kong and all you're likely to get is a blank stare.

If you believe in omens, the ceremony in which Great Britain surrendered Hong Kong to China was a dilly. An unrelenting monsoon hammered the city and the ceremony was moved from the shoreline of the famous harbor to a slightly shabby auditorium inside the Hong Kong Convention Centre. Prince Charles and Tony Blair stood on the stage, emissaries from a threadbare colonial past, and watched stone-faced as China buried the British Empire forever.

When the flag of the once mighty Commonwealth was lowered for the last time, Hong Kong became the Hong Kong

Special Administrative Region of the People's Republic of China. A fractured mishmash of words to describe a fractured mishmash of a city.

The British withdrawal from Hong Kong turned it into the Berlin of the twenty-first century, or maybe the Beirut. It became a patch over two worlds so disparate, so fundamentally at war with each other, that the strains underneath its surface were uncontrollable.

That was why no one was surprised when the riots started.

Just like Berlin and Beirut, Hong Kong always seemed on the verge of coming undone.

This time, maybe it really was.

SAMUEL TAY HAD only been in Hong Kong for ten minutes and he was already thinking about going home.

It certainly wasn't his first trip there. During all those years he had spent as a homicide detective with Singapore CID, more than a few cases had produced leads that took him to Hong Kong. He remembered a flying visit not long ago to interview a woman who had been a witness in a murder case, but he had been in and out then in one day and he didn't even have to stay overnight. For Tay, that was the next best thing to not going to Hong Kong at all.

Tay had never been much of a traveler. He had never found any place he liked more than his colonial-era row house in a quiet and dignified Singapore neighborhood called Emerald Hill. That was why mostly he just stayed home.

When Claire called and asked him to come to Hong Kong, his knee-jerk aversion to going anywhere at all kicked in almost at once, but his lack of enthusiasm went well beyond just his general reluctance to travel. He really didn't like Hong Kong very much.

The city wasn't as attractive as Singapore, and its over-weening sense of self-importance drove him crazy. Hong Kong had a lot of soaring, glitzy buildings, of course, but now every city in Asia had soaring, glitzy buildings, and no matter how many garish buildings Hong Kong constructed, the city still felt trivial to him.

Underneath its façade of snazziness and glamour, there was something insubstantial about Hong Kong. It was all flash and noise, and very little else. Tay hadn't been to Los Angeles and had never seen Hollywood, but he had heard people call Hollywood *Tinseltown*, and that was exactly the expression which came to mind every time he thought about Hong Kong.

If it had just been the summons to Hong Kong, Tay would have refused without a second thought. But there was another consideration.

Spending a few days helping Claire with whatever she was doing seemed quite appealing, even if he had to do it in Hong Kong. Tay didn't mix with very many women like Claire these days. If he were being honest about it, he supposed he never had. He and Claire seemed to get along well. It was a start, maybe, although a start on *what* Tay didn't quite know.

Claire wasn't even her real name. Tay knew that, but he had no idea what her real name actually was and he didn't know her last name either or even if she had one. Well, of course she had a last name. Everyone had a last name, didn't they?

John August had introduced him to Claire since she was one of the people who worked with him. August had simply called her Claire when he did. No other name was mentioned. Tay had gotten used to that. What difference did it make what name was on her birth certificate, anyway?

Claire was interesting, intelligent, and obviously good at her job. Tay understood her job included killing people occasionally, but no job was without at least a few aspects with which you could find fault, was it? Besides, he gathered she only killed people who needed killing so maybe it wasn't such a big deal.

Claire was also very attractive. There was that, too. He

would have liked to tell himself it wasn't a consideration, but it was.

She was tall, lean, and fit with the most glorious dark eyes Tay had ever looked into, and she kept her long, dirty blonde hair pulled back into a no-nonsense ponytail. Tay thought Claire looked like a girl not many years out of school who had played on the college volleyball team. He didn't know where Claire had gone to college, or even if she had gone to college at all, but he doubted she had played on a volleyball team if she had.

He thought she might have spent time in the military, but he wasn't certain about that. Still, she had her special skills and she had to have learned them somewhere. It certainly hadn't been at Miss Porter's School for Young Ladies.

When Claire called him, she hadn't been specific about why she wanted him to meet her in Hong Kong. She only told him it was important and asked him to get there as quickly as possible. A plane was waiting for him at Signature Flight Support, she said, which was at the private terminal across Changi Airport from the commercial terminals.

If Claire had said she wanted his help looking into a murder, he would have been a lot more enthusiastic about making the trip to Hong Kong. He would have gone to Timbuktu for a decent murder case. Well, maybe not Timbuktu, but one hell of a long way.

Still, he doubted Claire needed help investigating a murder case. She worked for John August. She and August didn't investigate murders. They committed them.

WHEN TAY GOT Claire's call that Monday morning, it had been a nice surprise. The part about her wanting him to come to Hong Kong hadn't been so great, but he thought he could get past it. Spending a few days with Claire almost anywhere would be a welcome relief from the boredom that had taken control of his life.

The retirement thing was a pile of warm shit. If it had been entirely his own idea, maybe he would have felt differently, but it hadn't been. He had always known the enemies his independent streak had accumulated for him among the senior ranks of the Singapore Police would get him one day. It had just never occurred to him they would get him quite so soon.

When he had been forced out of CID and into reluctant retirement, it was John August who had hauled him from the scrapheap and put him back in the game. Tay had known August ever since the American ambassador's wife had turned up dead under rather embarrassing circumstances in a suite at the Singapore Marriott.

After that little imbroglio had been quietly resolved through their off-the-books collaboration, Tay had asked for August's help several other times when he was involved in difficult and sensitive investigations. August had asked no questions about any of the favors Tay sought nor had he asked for anything in return.

Not until somebody tried to kill him.

That was when August did ask for Tay's help. He wanted very much to find out who it was who was trying to make him dead, preferably before they succeeded, and he was smart enough to know he needed an investigator of Tay's talent to do it.

Until then, Tay hadn't known for certain who John August really was or who he worked for. He was a man who seemed able to get almost anything done, and he was obviously involved with the highest levels of the American military and intelligence communities, so the natural assumption to make was that August was CIA. But that had never felt right to Tay. He always figured August for being involved in something worse than the CIA.

When he eventually found out who August actually did work

7

for, he realized he had been right all along. August was part of an organization few people even knew existed. Those who did know it existed inevitably referred to it simply as the Band. And the Band was a *lot* worse than the CIA.

Tay was flattered when August asked him to help the Band out with a few things, but he couldn't see any real future in that. He was a homicide cop. Well, he *used* to be a homicide cop. Whatever it was he had turned into now, it wasn't a spy or an international man of mystery.

August and the Band dealt in the rise and fall of nations. Tay dealt in human tragedies, one human being at a time. What was a sophisticated team of international intelligence operators going to do that could possibly require the help of someone like Samuel Tay?

THE FLIGHT FROM Singapore to Hong Kong took a little less than four hours. Since Tay was the only passenger on a luxurious private jet, those four hours passed quite pleasantly.

There was no flight attendant, so one of the two pilots showed him how to find whatever refreshments he might want and where the toilet was. After takeoff, he got a bottle of water from the refrigerator in the galley, tilted his big leather seat all the way back, and looked out the window at the world slipping by below.

Tay didn't know what kind of plane he was flying on. He had thought about asking the pilot when he was pointing out the galley and the toilet, but he decided it would just mark him for the rube he was. Most people who flew on private jets already knew what they were flying on, didn't they? Why expose himself to the pilot as some putz who didn't rate a private plane often enough to know anything about them?

When they landed in Hong Kong, Tay found himself at another private terminal very much like the one they had departed from in Singapore. It was hushed and discreet, and the immigration and customs checks took place so unobtrusively Tay hardly realized they were taking place at all. He felt like he had stepped from the airplane directly into a plush private club which, when he thought about it, he supposed was exactly what he had done.

A chubby, cherub-faced driver was waiting for Tay just outside the terminal. The man was a Chinese of indeterminate age, and he was wearing a black suit and white shirt and holding up a sign that said Samuel Tey.

"It's Tay with an A," Tay said when he walked over. "Not Tey with an E."

The driver was a little puzzled by that, but he didn't see the point in investing any effort in trying to figure out what Tay was talking about. He had long ago realized trying to figure out what foreigners were talking about was almost always a waste of time. He just took the envelope he had been told to give his passenger and thrust it out without a word.

Tay tore open the flap and unfolded the single piece of white paper he found inside. There were two lines written on it in blue ink. There wasn't any signature, but there didn't need to be.

The driver will take you to the Cordis Hotel where you're stay-ing. Meet me in the Garage Bar at six o'clock.

Tay contemplated the message for a moment.

The Cordis Hotel where you're staying.

The name of the hotel sounded familiar, although he couldn't think where he might have heard of it. That wasn't what bothered him.

It was the *where you're staying* part of the message on which he had his attention focused.

9

That had to mean Claire was staying someplace else. Not in the same hotel where he was staying, but someplace else. That was a rather inauspicious beginning to his trip, wasn't it?

He had been in Hong Kong for all of ten minutes and things were already going to shit.

TWO

T HE DRIVE INTO the city didn't make Tay feel any happier. It turned into an up-close look at what was happening on the streets of Hong Kong, and there was absolutely nothing happy about that.

In the beginning, everything was unremarkable. They cruised at speed down an expressway with very little traffic, crossed over the harbor on a soaring suspension bridge which impressed Tay every time he saw it, and didn't slow down until they were in the heart of Kowloon.

Tay had read about the democracy demonstrations that had been sweeping the city for the last few months, demonstrations which more often than not became running battles between the protestors and the riot police. He had assumed the newspapers were simply exaggerating to make their stories more interesting. It wouldn't be the first time they had done something like that, would it?

But when the car came to a dead stop in Kowloon, Tay realized the newspapers had not been exaggerating at all.

. . .

I T HAD ALL begun as nothing more than a minor political demonstration.

Doesn't it always?

Nobody thought much about it then. It was just a group of office workers gathering in Hong Kong's financial district on their lunch hour to voice their unhappiness over something the government was proposing. There were a hundred people there, maybe two hundred. A few people made speeches, everyone cheered, and they all went back to work.

That doubtless would have been that if the government of Hong Kong had made soothing noises and uttered a few platitudes about hearing the voice of the people, but it didn't. Instead, the government responded with disdain and condescension. It made the rules, it reminded everyone, and it would make whatever rules it thought were necessary.

A lot of people in Hong Kong didn't like that very much so the crowd at the next demonstration was bigger, which caused the Hong Kong government to step up its expressions of annoyance and warn people not to demonstrate like that again. On the following weekend, hundreds of thousands of people came out to make their unhappiness with the government clear.

When the police came into the streets to break up the crowds, Hong Kong's course toward anarchy and chaos was fixed. No one knew it then, but the city was only weeks away from pitched battles in the streets between riot-suited police armed with tear gas and water cannons and Hong Kong people armed with bricks and improvised gasoline bombs.

Everyone called the people in the streets demonstrators because no one knew what else to call them. *Rioters* seemed too much, at least it did at the beginning, and *rebels* was way too melodramatic. They were both, of course, even if no one wanted to say it plainly.

They were mostly young. Very young, teenagers mostly, which lured the government into dismissing them as nothing but rebellious students. What the government either didn't know or didn't want to admit was that in the shadows behind the kids in the streets were hundreds of thousands if not millions of older residents of Hong Kong who not only sympathized with those kids, but stood ready to give them whatever support they could.

Within weeks, Hong Kong became a city in open rebellion against itself. There were people in the streets somewhere almost every day chanting slogans about freedom and waving American flags as symbols of freedom. Meanwhile, the faceless monolith of Chinese authoritarianism muttered threats and built up their troops across the border from the city.

That will scare the little buggers off, the old men in Beijing told each other.

It didn't.

The kids in the streets didn't run at China's show of force. The government had been sure they would, but instead the kids fought back with their bare hands against the tear gas, the water cannons, and the armed riot police.

And soon things got worse.

"I SORRY, SIR."

The driver spoke over his shoulder to Tay without taking his eyes off the road.

"Must go long way. Protestors in Kowloon. We take Jordon Road close to harbor tunnel. Try get around."

But they didn't get around anything. When the car exited the expressway, it emerged into a scene so surreal it could have been a painting by Hieronymus Bosch.

Billowing white clouds of tear gas smothered the whole area and caused it to glow with an eerie, unreal light. Off to the right, ranks of riot police had massed four or five deep facing off against a crowd of democracy demonstrators gathered on the southbound approaches to the harbor tunnel, the side used by traffic trying to get from Kowloon to Hong Kong Island. But there was no traffic moving through the tunnel toward Hong Kong Island now.

Broken glass, bricks, pieces of concrete, chunks of wood, old tires, and other debris Tay couldn't identify littered the roadway. Fires burned here and there, and lines of flame sketched geometric patterns across the pavement. The area around the roadway hummed with a blur of formless energy, its precise source indistinct, but the scene itself was so quiet that somewhere off in the distance Tay could hear a single siren howling.

It looked to Tay like there were several hundred demonstrators out there among the fires, most if not all of them very young. Many of them were carrying open umbrellas, which they tilted toward the riot police as if the umbrellas were magical devices which could protect them from evil.

And the riot police did look like evil made flesh.

They might well have been good men, men who were simply doing their duty, but the protective gear they wore made them look like a troop of demonic androids. Black helmets with opaque visors and bulbous gas mask respirators hanging below, black body armor stretching from neck to toe, and heavy plastic protectors strapped around their arms and legs.

Tay couldn't imagine what it would be like for a kid in the street armed with an umbrella and a brick to be facing hundreds of men who looked like that. He would have to feel like he was in a movie about the invasion of earth by faceless, insect-like creatures from somewhere outside the solar system.

"My God, what's going on?" Tay asked the driver.

"Democracy demonstrators. They everywhere in Hong Kong. They show up, block roads, leave when police come."

"It doesn't look to me like they're leaving."

"They try close harbor tunnel."

"I think they've succeeded."

The riot police appeared to have surrendered the southbound lanes of the tunnel to the demonstrators in return for keeping the northbound lanes open, but the young protesters didn't look willing to settle for that. They began scooping bricks and other debris off the pavement and flinging them toward the ranks of riot police.

As the kids edged forward with their bricks, some cops moved out to meet them. Just then Tay noticed a thin figure dressed all in black step in front of the other protestors. It was a woman, he realized, when he saw her long black hair blowing out behind the mask on her face. Or maybe it was just a young girl. He couldn't see enough of her face to tell.

As she lifted her arm and hefted the brick she carried, a cop took two quick steps toward her and swung his riot baton in a long, arcing stroke. It caught her across her ribs and she toppled to the ground, rolling and covering her head with her arms. The cop moved forward another step while she lay there unmoving and hit down at her with two more quick chopping strokes from his baton. The girl stayed down, although Tay couldn't tell whether she wasn't able to get up after absorbing the baton blows or if she was just trying to protect herself.

That was when the cops began firing volleys of tear gas into the protestors. Tay found himself thinking there was a kind of beauty to the long white clouds the gas canisters trailed behind them as they arched over the crowd, but then the wind pushed the gas back toward their car and all at once beauty was less important than escaping the gas.

"I turn off air conditioner," the driver called back over his shoulder. "No pull gas into car."

Tay thought the driver sounded remarkably matter-of-fact about it all. Perhaps people whose daily work took them into the streets of Hong Kong had grown so accustomed to encountering street battles that now they treated them like an inconvenience similar to any other traffic jam.

It was the kind of resilience you learned trying to survive in Hong Kong. Figure it out, suck it up, and get on with it. Hong Kong people were tough little bastards. They had to be.

Tay looked up at the clouds of gas and saw the International

Commercial Center off behind the protestors. The ICC was one of the world's ten tallest buildings, and it presided over Hong Kong with a swagger and haughtiness that underlined its status as the king of the skyline.

Up at the top, on the one hundredth through the one hundred and eighteenth floors, was a Ritz-Carlton Hotel, and Tay had a sudden vision of a group of men gathered somewhere up there in a bar sipping early evening martinis, popping the olives into their mouths, and peering down on the street battle from a third of a mile in the sky as if they were watching a sporting event.

But what they were watching wasn't anything like a football game. It was more like the gladiators slaughtering the Christians in some Roman arena two thousand years ago for the amusement of the ruling class. Maybe, Tay thought, civilization hadn't progressed as much as we would like to think.

The car crawled forward. Off to the right, Tay saw that the harbor tunnel toll takers had abandoned their posts, although it didn't really matter. No traffic was moving through the tunnel, and electronic sensors registered most road tolls in Hong Kong automatically now, anyway. Life went on, administered by invisible electronics, while people fought with each other in the streets.

The driver suddenly spotted an opening in the wall of creeping traffic. He eased the car over one lane and floored the accelerator. The big Mercedes shot ahead, cleared the battleground, and disappeared into the streets of Kowloon. Within a minute or two, they were on Nathan Road cruising north toward Mongkok. All around them, Tay saw people strolling the sidewalks, doing their shopping, and getting on with their lives in all the usual mundane ways.

Only a very short distance away, anger and frustration had exploded into violence on streets which looked just like this one, but here it was almost as if none of those things were happening at all. That was another truism about the world in which we lived now, Tay thought. We had developed an almost limitless capacity not to see what we didn't want to see.

I T WAS IN the early fall that the riots, or protests if you prefer, began in earnest. It was just a coincidence, but the early fall is a part of the year both ripe with symbolism and rich with irony.

It is the time of Hong Kong's annual Festival of the Hungry Ghosts which occurs every year during the seventh month of the Chinese calendar. That is when, so legend has it, the gates of Hell open and the ghosts of everyone's ancestors are set free to roam the earth. And roam it the ghosts do, seeking food and drink and entertainment, which makes them seem a lot like normal folks who are still alive.

Shops are closed to leave the streets open for the ghosts, and during the evening incense burns in front of the doors of many households. Westerners who live in Hong Kong sometimes say the Festival of the Hungry Ghosts is Halloween without the candy.

Many traditional Chinese hold ceremonies to relieve the ghosts from their suffering. They are mostly late in the afternoon or at night because people believe the ghosts are released from Hell only with the sunset. Monks and priests throw items of food into the air to distribute them to the ghosts, and live performances of Chinese opera are often staged at high volume as the sound is supposed to attract and please the ghosts. The first row of seats is always left empty at every performance. Where else would the ghosts be expected to sit?

Family members gather in the streets in front of their houses and apartments to offer prayers to their deceased relatives and they burn joss paper items they believe will have value in the afterlife.

People burn joss paper houses, cars, televisions, furniture, servants, and even mistresses to please the ghosts. But most of all they burn spirit money called Hell Bank Notes as a tribute to the wandering ghosts. All of this is in the hope of enticing these homeless souls from the afterlife not to bring bad luck to the living.

Fourteen days after the festival, people float lanterns in containers filled with water and set them outside their houses. The lanterns are made by folding joss paper into the shape of a paper boat, placing a candle inside, and lighting it. The purpose of the lanterns is to light the way for the ghosts to travel to the underworld. When the candle goes out, it means the ghosts have found their way back to the afterlife.

No doubt all those candles went out this year just as they had for untold generations before, but many people said this time the ghosts only pretended to leave. This year they stayed.

As fall turned to winter and Hong Kong became a city under siege, it became easier with every day to believe that the ghosts really had done what everyone feared they had done. They had refused to return to the underworld.

Instead, they had brought Hell to the streets of Hong Kong.

THREE

W HEN HE GOT to the Cordis Hotel, Tay checked in and exchanged some money at the front desk. Then he went up to his room.

He was on the thirty-seventh floor and the space was quite large for a hotel room. It was furnished in the bland, expensive good taste he had noticed Americans in particular seemed to love. A dark-stained bamboo floor set off the cream, gold, and green upholstered sofa and the matching chair in the seating area, while the king-sized bed sported a blindingly white duvet that looked puffy enough to double as a trampoline.

The room's biggest selling point, however, was its view. A curving wall of floor-to-ceiling glass offered an unobstructed, godlike perspective on Hong Kong. A carpet of buildings of varying sizes, shapes, and shades of white stretched off far below him in every direction. Here and there, towers of fantastical design soared above it, but otherwise the blanket of humanity rolled away until it spilled into the pewter waters of Hong Kong Harbor.

From so far up, the traffic clogging the streets and the mobs of pedestrians fighting for space were invisible. Hong Kong was noisy and it stunk, and somewhere down below kids were choking on tear gas and being beaten to the ground by riot police, but you wouldn't know it up here. Tay felt more like he was examining an enormous scale model of a city rather than looking down on the real thing.

Hong Kong was pretty much like every other big city Tay had ever known. The further away you got, the better it looked.

T URNING AWAY FROM the windows, Tay's eyes fell on something which made him hugely unhappy. In the center of the desk encased in a Lucite block was a white card with a message in elaborate gold script.

He knew what the message was going to say before he even read it, and he was right.

THIS IS A NON-SMOKING HOTEL. ABSOLUTELY NO SMOKING IS PERMITTED IN OUR GUEST ROOMS.

Was there no end to it? The sourpuss killjoys were everywhere. In Singapore, they were close to banning smoking entirely throughout the whole country. In some parts of Singapore, people could already smoke only in seemingly random locations where the government had painted bright yellow boxes on the sidewalks marking authorized smoking zones.

Tay had always believed there couldn't be any other government on earth as nitpicking and persnickety as Singapore, but now he wasn't so sure. If the anti-smoking hysteria had spread even to Hong Kong, a place in which it had always appeared to him most everyone did what they wanted, nowhere was safe.

Smokers hadn't yet been ordered to register and wear badges warning all who saw them of their shame, but Tay was certain that was coming. Soon smokers would be marked with some symbol like the Jews of Nazi Germany and their addresses would be listed in public databases like sex offenders in America. He would bet there was already some little shit in a Singapore government ministry in charge of planning it.

Tay had smoked Marlboros for decades. Smoking wasn't a habit for him, not exactly, but something closer to an act of meditation. He opened the pack and breathed in the content's rich, earthy aroma. He shook out a cigarette and tapped it on the back of his hand to tighten the tobacco. Then he lit it with a wooden match.

The ritual mattered. It was how he focused his thoughts. And when the first flow of nicotine hit his bloodstream, those thoughts took wing and soared.

Tay often wondered how it was permitting, even encouraging, the smoking of marijuana had become the cool cause of the day. Most of the same people pushing for legalizing the smoking of marijuana, he had noticed, were also frothing to ban the smoking of tobacco products. How did that make the slightest sense to anyone? Smoking was bad and should be forbidden, unless you were smoking marijuana instead of tobacco, and then it was admirable. You could only think that was rational if you were stoned.

Tay knew part of the explanation was simply that he was growing old. The habits of people his age were getting the chop, while the habits of the young were being celebrated. He wondered if the little bastards had even the slightest inkling that one of these days somebody would come for them, too, and that the things which gave them pleasure would end up on some future hit list marked for extinction as social evils. Probably not. The young always thought their world would go on forever, didn't they?

Tay picked up the Lucite block and read the card again. He searched the words for a loophole.

He didn't find one.

Crap.

· · ·

A T TEN MINUTES before six o'clock, Tay left his room and went downstairs to find the Garage Bar.

He thought the name was idiotic. A hotel bar should be a refuge, a haven of soft lights and repose. Why in the world would anyone think it was a wonderful idea to name a hotel bar after a place with oil-stained concrete floors where you parked cars?

It had taken him a while to decide what he should wear to a bar called the Garage. Eventually he gave up trying to work it out and put on a dark blue suit, the only suit he had brought with him, and a white shirt with a red and blue striped tie.

Tay called down to the concierge and was told the Garage Bar was on the lobby level of the hotel, which was the fourth floor in this vertically constructed city, so when the elevator doors opened on four he stepped out and looked around. He didn't see anything called the Garage Bar.

Having no clue which way to go, he turned left more or less at random and found nothing in that direction other than the hotel's reception desk and a small shop selling the same junk hotel shops sold everywhere in the world. Reversing direction, he walked the other way across the lobby and discovered himself at the entrance to one of the hotel's restaurants, but it wasn't the Garage Bar.

He wasn't sure what to do after that. Had he misunderstood the concierge? Did the name mean the damn bar was actually *in* the garage?

No, he was certain that couldn't be. It had to be here somewhere even if he couldn't find it. Perhaps he would have to ask someone for directions.

It is never easy for any man to admit he is lost and ask for directions, and in that Tay was no different from the billions of other males with whom he shared the planet, but he didn't see he had any choice. He would have to gird his ego for the humiliation and ask somebody for help since he couldn't see the slightest sign of the bar anywhere.

An impossibly young-looking woman wearing an impossibly short black sheath dress with a white silk scarf draped around her neck stood behind a glass and chrome podium in front of the restaurant. Tay must have had a befuddled expression on his face as he approached because the woman smiled and spoke before he could ask her anything.

"You're looking for the Garage Bar."

Tay noticed she didn't bother to make a question out of it. It made him feel a little better to know this happened often. He nodded.

"This way, please, sir."

Tay followed the woman into the restaurant, all the way across the dining room, and out a door on the other side. There the hostess inclined her head, wished Tay a pleasant evening, and made her way back the way they had come.

He looked around and saw that he was on a very large terrace covered with a huge, open-sided tent which soared at least twenty feet above his head. Inside the tent, brown wicker sofas and chairs with plump white cotton cushions were grouped around low tables. On a scattering of medium-size dining tables, each sheltered by its own red canvas umbrella, candles flickered. Tall trees in big green wooden buckets, each of them festooned with strings of tiny white lights, were positioned throughout the tent.

Two full-sized Citroën vans, vintage models painted black and red, sat parked at opposite ends of the tent. They both looked old enough to have been abandoned during the French retreat from the Maginot Line in World War II, or perhaps they were abandoned during one of France's other retreats since there were quite a few possibilities to choose from. The hotel had turned the vans into food trucks, and waiters in Paris café garb shuttled back and forth from the vans carrying trays piled with bar snacks.

The Garage Bar was an island in a forest of glass-walled skyscrapers. The thousands of mirror-like panels dappling the skin of the surrounding buildings caught the light of the flickering candles and the glow of the white bulbs in the trees, transformed it into a soft white cloud, and showered it over the tent like a mist. Tay had to admit it looked downright romantic. At least it did for a place called the Garage Bar.

The bar wasn't very crowded, no doubt because the street riots had made people reluctant to visit Hong Kong and the hotel was probably half empty. When Tay looked around he didn't see Claire, so he settled himself on one of the sofas in an area as far away from everyone else as he could get without looking too conspicuous.

Right away, he saw something he liked very much. There was an ashtray on the low table in front of the couch. He wondered if he should ask somebody if he could smoke there, but then he decided that was silly. There was an ashtray right in front of him, wasn't there? Why would there be an ashtray on the table unless he could smoke? He had brought his Marlboros out of habit, so he fished the pack and a box of matches out of his jacket and lit up.

He had smoked half the Marlboro before a waiter appeared. When he did, Tay asked for a Bushmills Irish whiskey and water without ice.

Tay had gone out for a few months with an Irish woman who was a banker in Singapore and he had developed a liking both for her and for Irish whiskey. His liking for the banker had passed, as such things always did for him, but he found he had kept his liking for the whiskey.

Of the two, he had no doubt he had picked the right one to hang onto.

FOUR

T AY SMOKED TWO Marlboros and finished half his whiskey before Claire arrived, fashionably late. She slid into a deep-cushioned chair positioned at a right-angle to the sofa where he was sitting.

"There couldn't be another bar this well-hidden anywhere in Hong Kong," Tay said.

"I thought you were a detective."

"I am. I detected a woman working at a restaurant who showed me where the goddamned bar was."

Claire grinned. "How are you, Sam?"

Claire was wearing something which looked vaguely like a man's tuxedo, but probably wasn't. Her hair, no doubt bleached by the sun, was blonder than Tay recalled, but it was pulled back into the same ponytail she had worn ever since he had known her. Her makeup was so subtle he wasn't certain she was wearing any, and she wore no jewelry at all other than a good-sized pair of diamond ear clips. The diamonds sparkled with a light so incandescent Tay gathered they were either very good stones or fantastic fakes. Since Claire wasn't a woman who tried to fake anything, his money was on very good stones.

Claire's appearance was always slightly over to the butch side of the scale, although Tay thought the look suited her. He had never understood how someone could dress like Claire did and still be so feminine, but he knew so little about women he had no hope at all of working out anything so tricky.

When the waiter reappeared, Claire ordered a glass of merlot. Tay ordered another Irish whiskey.

"How do you like the hotel, Sam?"

"It's fine," he said. "Nice view."

"And you're wondering why you're staying here and I'm not, right?"

Tay was frequently amazed at Claire's almost telepathic ability to know what he was thinking about without him saying a word. Was she truly possessed of some kind of psychic ability or was he just that transparent? He really didn't want to think about it.

"Now that you mention it," he said, "the question had crossed my mind."

"You need to be in Mongkok, and this is by far the best hotel around here."

"Why do I need to be in Mongkok?"

Claire hesitated a moment, then continued without answering Tay's question.

"I should be in Mongkok, too, but I don't want to stay here."

None of that made a great deal of sense to Tay. Why did he need to be in Mongkok? And why did Claire not want to stay in the same hotel? Was it because he was staying here? Did she think he might creep into her room one night and attack her? Of course she didn't. Then what *did* she mean?

"You don't recognize the name of the hotel, do you?"

"It sounds familiar, but..." Tay trailed off with a small shrug.

"It's where they tried to kill us last year."

Now Tay remembered.

My God.

The Cordis was the hotel where a few months ago somebody planted the bomb that was meant to cripple the Band. John August and Claire thought they were tracking a CIA case officer who was defecting to China, but it was all a set-up. Claire would have died in the blast if they hadn't realized what was about to happen and gotten out before the bomb exploded.

Tay could understand why Claire was unenthusiastic about staying in a hotel somebody had once blown up in an effort to kill her. Nobody had ever blown up a hotel trying to kill Tay, but if they had, he imagined he would have felt very much the same way.

The attack on August and his people was the reason Tay was working with the Band now. August had asked him to figure out who had tried to kill them. Tay had done that. Soon after he fingered the two men responsible, they both died in an automobile accident. Or so the newspapers said. There had been no automobile accident, of course. August and his people had killed the two men and dressed it up as an accident.

Tay's feelings about that were a little ambivalent. He had been a policeman all his life. He identified and tracked down people who killed other human beings and brought them before the law so justice could be served. That had always been what his life was about.

Criminal charges, an arrest, and a trial weren't in the cards for the men who tried to kill August because of who they were. If August and his people hadn't acted, they would have walked away from what they had done with no consequences.

Tay told himself that identifying the two men to August meant they had faced justice after all, even if it was a different kind of justice than the one he had served before, but wasn't that just sophistry? When Tay identified the two men, he had marked them for death. It was just that simple, wasn't it?

Yes, and just that complicated.

Just move along, Tay admonished himself. *Don't overthink everything.*

When the waiter returned with their drinks, Claire and Tay

clinked glasses and each of them took a sip or two. Then Tay leaned back, folded his arms, and got to the point.

"So, what's this all about?" he asked.

"JOHN ASKED ME to call you."

John August.

Okay, Tay thought, then this wasn't something for which Claire needed his help after all. It was something to do with the Band, which meant it was part of the cloak and dagger world in which the Band operated.

Tay had to admit he was a little disappointed to hear that. He had entertained himself with the fancy he was being asked by Claire to do her a personal favor, and there was something about that which he quite liked.

"We're meeting John at seven."

Tay was even more disappointed to hear *that*. He had been looking forward to an hour or two sitting in a quiet bar with Claire. Now that wasn't happening either.

"Is he coming here?"

"No. We're meeting him at Salisbury Garden down by the harbor. It's a park. Well... more or less. John thinks we should have a lot of space around us when we talk about this."

"Talk about what?"

Claire hesitated, and the way she did it made Tay wonder if he should have made his Bushmills a double.

"I think I should let John explain everything," she said. "I just work here."

She's not certain how much she ought to tell me.

August and Claire trusted him, he had no doubt about that, but secrets defined the world in which they lived. Even when keeping something secret didn't matter much, and Tay couldn't help but notice how little it mattered most of the time, they still kept the secrets. It was a reflex with the Band: tell everyone as little as possible. But Tay was an investigator, not a spy, and he

28

had a reflex, too: keep asking questions until you find out what the fuck is going on.

The two world views seemed irreconcilable, but when they had worked together before, they had managed an accommodation. He would ask all the questions he wanted, and they would avoid answering most of them.

Tay had learned to live with secrets. He didn't have much choice when he was dealing with John August, because the Band was itself about the biggest secret around.

WASHINGTON DC IS a simmering caldron of rumors and fables, and few things stay secret for long. The Band had. There weren't fifty people in the entire world who knew the Band existed. At least not for sure. Of the people who did know for sure, only a handful had any idea how the Band worked or who was part of it.

The origins of the Band stretched all the way back to the days of Ronald Reagan. Reagan's closest advisors had devised a process for undertaking direct presidential action, a mechanism through which actions the president undertook in strictest secrecy were shared among a few trusted people. The group they formed was tucked away within the National Security Council at the White House. One of the very few people who knew it existed nicknamed it the Band, and the nickname stuck.

The federal bureaucracy was smaller then, but it was just as faithless as it is now. The first priority of government officials has always been to protect themselves. Protecting the country came second. Or maybe it was third. Or fourth.

Leaking information to the press about government actions you didn't like had two purposes. The leaker wanted to damage the people who had undertaken those actions, of course, but he also wanted to position himself as the man who had been wise enough to know those actions were wrong.

Leaking was Washington's highest art form, but that didn't

change a harsh truth. Sometimes governments had to do things they could never under any circumstances permit to show up on the front page of *The New York Times.*

That was why the Band existed. Those were the things the Band did.

When Bill Clinton became president, the wise men who directed the Band decided it would be better to remove the Band from government before any of Clinton's people discovered the things it had done and started talking about them to score themselves airtime on CNN. Those wise men quickly organized a company which was presumably an international business consultancy called Red River Consultants and they moved all of the functions of the Band into it.

But one important thing didn't change. There still were only a handful of people who knew the Band existed. The president knew. The vice president knew. And there were perhaps a dozen others in the government who knew. But that was all.

Even among the handful of people who knew the Band existed, it was not necessarily loved. A few months back, two men high up in the government had decided the Band was a threat to them and they had tried to destroy it. The plan they developed was straightforward enough. They set up John August and the people August worked with to be killed and tried to make it look like the Chinese were responsible.

When Tay identified the two men, the White House realized it had a problem. These weren't people you could charge with a crime simply because they had committed one. The positions they held in the government made that unrealistic.

There are many such men, and women, in America, even if Americans didn't understand that, so the president asked John August to solve the problem.

When the president had a certain kind of a problem, he called on John August and the Band to solve it.

Because John August solved problems the old-fashioned way.

He killed them.

FIVE

C LAIRE AND TAY took a taxi to the Kowloon Public Pier where the Star Ferry docked. The little green and white boats had plowed back and forth across the harbor between Hong Kong's central business district and Kowloon hundreds of times every day for well over a century. They were as much a part of the city as the harbor itself.

They got out of the taxi in front of the ferry terminal and lost themselves in the mobs of people going back and forth to the Star Ferry. Tay realized Claire was checking for surveillance, but who in the world did she think might be watching them? He didn't ask. He knew Claire wasn't likely to tell him if he did. He thought she was probably just doing it out of habit anyway. At least, he hoped she was.

When the crowds thinned out, they turned east away from the piers and followed the wide walkway along the harbor toward the Intercontinental Hotel. A little after seven, they stepped off the walkway and entered Salisbury Garden from the west.

· · ·

S ALISBURY GARDEN IS a small park at the foot of the Kowloon Peninsula.

It is a modest space tucked into an odd-shaped plot of ground between busy Salisbury Road and the harbor and sandwiched between tall buildings on the other two sides. Forget grass and trees. Garden is just a name. It's not a description. Salisbury Garden is green-tinted concrete with a few brown-tiled planter boxes jammed with nondescript vegetation. Parks aren't particularly popular in Hong Kong. Parks don't make money, and making money is the only reason Hong Kong exists.

Salisbury Garden may not be much of a garden, but it's a fine place to hold a private conversation. The sight lines are clear in all directions, the space is big enough that no one else is close to you, and the noise of the city makes it difficult for anyone to eavesdrop. It can be done, of course. Anything can be done these days, somehow. But it would require a sophisticated operation and take a while to set up. Meeting in Salisbury Garden with little notice offers as much privacy as you will get anywhere in Hong Kong.

The moment they entered the park, Tay and Claire spotted August sitting on a green wooden bench facing the harbor. They walked over and sat down, one on either side of him. The mist hanging in the air made the lights of the office towers across Hong Kong Harbor blur and ripple in the darkness like wisps of colored smoke.

It was there on a damp and gray Monday evening in October, sitting on a wooden bench in Salisbury Garden, that August and Tay might have had a conversation.

Or perhaps they didn't.

Later on, when it was all over, no one was absolutely sure.

"H ELLO, JOHN."

"Sam. Thanks for coming."

"You could have called me yourself."

"I didn't want to answer a lot of questions on the telephone, and I knew you would ask a lot of questions if I called. I figured you wouldn't if Claire called."

Tay said nothing. August had him there.

"Here's the deal," August said. "A young girl is missing. She's the daughter of someone I know, and I promised him we would find her."

"Missing?" Tay asked. "Here in Hong Kong?"

August nodded.

"How young?"

"Twenty-four."

"Twenty-four? I thought you meant she was just a little kid."

August shrugged. Just a quick up-and-down jerk of his shoulders. "Twenty-four seems pretty young to me."

"Look, John, I don't have much experience with missing persons cases, but my understanding is they're usually pretty simple. People who disappear do it for a reason. When they're finished with whatever the reason is, they come back, and that's the end of the case."

"It's not going to be that easy, Sam. You know somebody like me wouldn't be here if it were that easy."

Tay had been just about to ask August why he *was* here.

August wasn't a guy people sent out to find missing kids. Maybe if your kid went missing, and you found her and got her back and you wanted to erase any evidence she had ever been gone by erasing whoever took her, *then* you might call John August. Erasing things was what August did best.

"We think she may have been taken," August added.

"Taken?"

"Kidnapped."

"When did she disappear?"

"A little over two days ago. Saturday. About noon."

"There's been a ransom demand?"

"No."

"Then why would you think she was kidnapped?"

"That's what the circumstances suggest."

"But if there's been no ransom demand—"

"We don't think she was kidnapped for ransom, Sam. We think she may have been taken for another reason."

"Such as what?"

"We don't know yet, not for sure, but standing around with our thumbs up our asses until we find out doesn't seem to me to be a great plan. We need to find this girl, and we need to do it quickly."

"This isn't making a hell of a lot of sense to me, John. You sent a private jet all the way to Singapore just to get me to help you find this young woman who went missing a couple of days ago?"

August nodded.

"But she's barely been gone forty-eight hours. That's not enough time to declare anyone missing."

"It is in this case."

"Look, John, I don't know what to tell you. I'm an old homicide cop. All my experience is with dead people. I wouldn't even know where to look for a live one."

"Now you're being disingenuous, Sam."

"*Disingenuous*? Have you started reading vocabulary books, John?"

"I need for you and Claire to do this, Sam, and I need for you to do it fast. The man whose daughter is missing is someone who makes the whole situation very tricky."

"I don't care if she's the daughter of the goddamned President of the goddamned United States. I don't do missing persons. You're asking the wrong guy. "

"It's the vice president whose daughter is missing," August said.

"The vice president of what?"

August allowed himself a smile, although it was a very small one.

"The Vice President of the United States," he said.

Tay said nothing. August didn't look like he was joking, but surely...

"I am here because the Vice President of the United States has a daughter," August continued. "She is missing, and the President of the United States called me in and asked me to find her."

"You know the President of the United States?"

August said nothing.

"You never told me that. *The president?* Really?"

"Look," August said, "let's walk. I get twitchy sitting still in public for too long. And there's some stuff I haven't told you yet."

"Wow, John. Stuff you haven't told me? I'm shocked, man. Completely shocked."

"Don't overdo it, Sam."

THEY STOOD AND crossed Salisbury Garden, August slightly in the lead with Tay and Claire walking more or less together behind him.

When they reached the edge of the harbor, August turned left and walked east on what a sign proclaimed to be the Avenue of the Stars, a walkway apparently meant to be a Hong Kong version of the Hollywood Walk of Fame. Tay had never seen the original in Los Angeles, but he doubted the Hong Kong copy measured up very well. There were a few plaques purporting to contain the handprints of Hong Kong movie stars but, except for Bruce Lee, he doubted anyone who wasn't Chinese had ever heard of any of them.

It wasn't the walkway which drew the punters. It was the

view of Hong Kong Harbor, and it was spectacular. Tay's eyes skipped through the turmoil of the water traffic to where a jumble of skyscrapers jammed every piece of level ground on Hong Kong Island across on the other side of the harbor. Rising behind the buildings like a painted theatrical backdrop were the steep, green-forested slopes of Victoria Peak.

The Peak presided solemnly over the chaos of one of the world's great cities with the benign indifference which came from having been there before it all began and the certain knowledge it would be there when it was all over. When all those imposing structures scattered over its slopes had turned back into dust, the Peak would still be there just as it had always been.

The Avenue of the Stars circled around the brown granite and glass clad bulk of the Intercontinental Hotel and skirted the northern edge of Hong Kong Harbor for several hundred yards. All along its length groups of tourists, overwhelmingly Chinese, chattered in excitement and posed for pictures in front of the harbor. The crowds and the noise made it a perfect place to talk without any risk of being overheard.

"I don't understand why you're even talking to me about this, John. The President of the United States is the most powerful man in the world. If the vice president's daughter is missing, he can send in the FBI, the CIA, and the United States Marines. I'm just a retired homicide detective from Singapore."

August snorted. "Fuck the false modesty routine, Sam. You're the most intuitive detective I've ever known."

The wind had risen and a light chop roiled the gray-brown waters of the harbor. A bright red tour boat decked out to look like a traditional fishing junk passed close to shore and the Chinese rushed to take selfies in front of it. August pointed to a Starbucks up ahead on their left.

"Let's go over there," he said. "I just got off an airplane from DC and I need the caffeine."

When August turned toward the Starbucks, Tay took a

careful look at him without being too obvious about it. August was a good-looking man, but he appeared older than the last time Tay had seen him, closer to his mid-fifties than the mid-forties Tay knew he was. Maybe he was just travel weary, or maybe the attempt to kill him had taken a toll in ways August would never tell him.

He was wearing a white button-down shirt with pressed jeans, and he had on stylishly battered brown loafers without socks. He was tall and solid looking and carrying no extra weight, like a runner or a cross-country skier. His face was deeply tanned, and he wore round eyeglasses with what looked like steel frames. His dark brown hair was on the long side and brushed straight back against his head in a way which looked a bit old-fashioned. There was a sense of world-weariness in the way he moved, and Tay had to admit it suited him very well.

August looked like he might be a university professor on vacation. He was anything but that.

THEY WENT INTO Starbucks and bought coffees and took them back outside where a dozen small metal tables with uncomfortable looking green metal chairs sat on a narrow terrace elevated a few steps above the Avenue of the Stars. A breeze was coming in off the harbor and the terrace was deserted. The few coffee drinkers left in the place at this hour had all taken refuge inside.

The two men and Claire sat in silence for a bit. They all sipped their coffee and looked out at the harbor until something occurred to Tay.

"I think I remember seeing the vice president and his family on television once," he said. "They said he had two teenage boys. I don't remember anyone mentioning a daughter."

"With your usual incisiveness, Sam, you have just cut straight to the heart of the problem."

"I don't understand."

"No, I'm sure you don't."

Tay glanced at Claire, but her face was a blank. So, he just nodded, drank his coffee, and waited for John August to tell him the rest of the story.

And after a minute or two, August did.

SIX

"THE VICE PRESIDENT'S daughter wasn't a visitor to Hong Kong. She lives here. Her name is Yu Yan Lau. Everyone calls her Emma."

August fell silent as two women in full burkas strolled past on the Avenue of the Stars about twenty feet away. From the way they moved, they seemed to be young, but with the burkas who could tell? Both women had their faces turned toward the harbor since its panorama of activity and energy was far more interesting than three people drinking coffee in a Starbucks.

"About twenty-five years ago," August continued, "the man who became Vice President William Marsh Rice was a young foreign service officer assigned to the American consulate here in Hong Kong. He had an affair. That affair resulted in the birth of Emma Lau."

"I gather," Tay said, "the woman with whom he had this affair was Chinese."

"Yes. And she was married so they talked about terminating her pregnancy, but neither one of them was comfortable with that. She had the baby and her husband always believed the child was his. She asked the man who became vice president never to contact her again. He honored her wishes."

"Then Rice doesn't spend any time with his daughter?"

"Vice President Rice has never met his daughter, and he has told no one she exists. If this comes out now, it would be a significant problem for him. Both a political problem and a personal one. And therefore, it would be a problem for the president, too."

Tay said nothing.

"The first time the vice president had spoken to Emma's mother in nearly twenty-five years was when she called him to tell him Emma was missing," August continued. "He says Emma's mother has never told anyone he is Emma's real father, not even Emma."

"How can he be sure of that?"

"He can't, but she told him she hasn't and he says he believes her. The woman's position is such that she has at least as big an incentive as he does to keep her daughter's parentage a secret."

"Her position?"

"When the vice president met Emma's mother, she was working for the Bank of China."

"I hope you're not about to tell me this woman is now some big-time executive there."

"No, that's not what I'm about to tell you."

Tay watched August's face. Whatever was coming, Tay could see it wouldn't be good.

"You probably know that recently China forced out the Chief Executive of Hong Kong and most of the senior members of his government," August said.

Tay nodded.

"They didn't think he had been tough enough on the democracy demonstrators, so they manipulated the Hong Kong Basic Law to place a new Chief Executive in charge. They chose a woman who has a no-nonsense reputation for toughness and whose loyalty to China is unquestioned and she appointed

41

people just like her to most of the major government ministries."

Tay waited.

"Her name is Doris Lau," August finished. "Doris Lau is Emma Lau's mother."

Tay's first thought was that August was joking, but he knew he wasn't.

"You're telling me the Vice President of the United States has a secret daughter with the Chief Executive of Hong Kong put into office by China to bring an end to the democracy movement here?"

August nodded.

"Holy shit," Tay murmured.

"Yes," August said. "Exactly."

THEY ALL SAT in silence for a while and watched the ballet of movement in the harbor.

"Spell it out, John," Tay said after a minute or two. "Just tell me what you want from me."

"I want you to find Emma and get her back."

Tay waited. He knew there was more.

"When she's back," August added, "Claire will deal with whoever took her."

Tay had no doubt what *that* meant.

So, there it was. Another one of those issues of moral ambivalence he always seemed to run into when he got involved with John August. August was asking Tay once again to finger some poor chucklehead to be killed. Was that to punish the kidnapper, or to make certain the secret of who Emma's real father was never became public? Tay didn't have to ask. He had no difficulty at all guessing the right answer.

"You're asking me to go running around a city about which I know next to nothing and try to get people to tell me where this girl might be and who has her?"

August nodded.

"That makes no sense at all, John. Detective work requires relationships. I don't have any here in Hong Kong."

"We do. You can use ours."

"It doesn't work that way, John."

"Do you have any idea what's going on right now in Hong Kong, Sam?"

"You mean the democracy demonstrations?"

"It's gone way beyond demonstrations. The city's in chaos. A lot of people say they no longer feel safe in Hong Kong. The place is falling apart."

"What does that have to do with this missing girl?"

"People are scared. Panic buying has even started. Go into a ParknShop and the shelves are half empty. You'll probably find there's no rice. No rice in a Hong Kong supermarket!"

"I still don't see what—"

"Can you imagine the pressure Doris Lau is under? And then, right in the middle of everything, her daughter is taken. We think there may be a connection."

"A connection between what?"

"The girl's disappearance and the riots." August waved a hand toward Kowloon. "All this shit."

"Wait, you're saying the disappearance of the vice president's daughter has something to do with the political upheaval here in Hong Kong?"

"Possibly," August nodded.

"I thought you told me no one knows who this girl's father is."

"They don't. But they know who her mother is."

"So, your theory is the Chinese Ministry of State Security grabbed the girl to put the screws to Mom to crack down on the democracy activists?"

"It's one possibility. Another is the democracy activists grabbed her to put the screws to Mom *not* to crack down on them."

"Which is it?"

"No idea. Maybe it's neither. Maybe her disappearance has nothing to do with what's happening in Hong Kong. Maybe a human trafficking ring grabbed her and she's halfway to Saudi Arabia by now. Whoever has her, we have to get her back."

Tay sat back and folded his arms. He didn't really know what to say to that, so he said nothing at all.

"I THINK YOU can forget the human traffickers, at least for now," August began again. "We've got three far better candidates for the role of villain."

"If there is a villain at all."

August ignored Tay and pushed on. "One of those candidates is the Chinese Ministry of State Security. Maybe they took Emma to put pressure on her mother. The second candidate is the democracy movement. Maybe they took her for the same reason."

"And the third candidate is the triads."

"Right. They have a history of kidnapping prominent people for ransom that goes back a hundred years."

"If one of the triads has her," Tay said, "It's simple enough. Pay, and she comes back. It's not personal with them, just business."

"There's been no ransom demand, but the triads are still at the top of my list. I think that's where we have to start."

"You brought me here to go after the Hong Kong triads? Seriously?"

"I want you to find out if they're involved. If they're not, we'll move on. It's hardly the same thing as *going after* them."

"I'm not sure they'll see it the same way."

August said nothing. He had made his pitch. There was nothing more he could say.

"I think I'm beginning to understand why I'm here," Tay

said after a few moments of silence. "You think you need a Chinese face to do this, don't you?"

"This is a Chinese city, Sam. A Chinese face has a better chance of finding Emma than I do."

"And I guess you figure a Singaporean is the next best thing to a real Chinese."

Tay's mother was a Singaporean, but his father had been an American. His father's parents had both been ethnic Chinese which, he supposed, made his father ethnic Chinese too even if he had been an American by nationality.

Tay had never thought of himself as having a Chinese face. He had been so young when his father died that he barely remembered him, but in the pictures he had seen, he never thought of his father as having a Chinese face either. What did that mean, anyway?

Tay hadn't spent a lot of time contemplating matters of ethnicity and race, but he had never considered himself to be anything other than a Singaporean. Whatever that was.

Now it sounded like August was saying he looked Chinese regardless of how he thought of himself. Was that possible? Maybe white guys thought all Asians looked Chinese.

Tay leaned back and knitted his fingers together behind his neck. His eyes tracked a double-decked green and white ferry as it plowed across the harbor toward Causeway Bay.

"Let me just make sure I've got this straight, John. You want me to mess around with the Hong Kong triads, the Chinese Ministry of State Security, and some angry mobs of street rioters to locate a girl who may have been kidnapped by somebody, but who also may have just taken off with her boyfriend to Macau. Right?"

August offered a small shrug. "That pretty much sums it up."

"Why would you even *think* I'd be willing to do that?"

"Because I know you can't resist," August grinned. "You live for stuff like this, Sam. You know you do, and I know you do. So, cut the crap and let's get to work."

SEVEN

TAY LOOKED AT Claire. "You haven't said a word. What do you think about all this?"

"If I had a daughter and she was missing in Hong Kong, I'd want people exactly like us looking for her."

"What does that mean?"

"It means people who are willing to do whatever it takes to get her back."

"*Whatever* it takes?"

"You already know that, Sam. That's who John is. That's who I am."

"I'm just not sure that's who *I* am," Tay said.

He drained the last of his coffee, leaned back, and folded his arms.

"Is there any reason to think the girl really is in danger, John, or is it just the political careers of the vice president and this woman who's now running Hong Kong that are in danger here?"

August chuckled. "Even by your standards, Sam, don't you think that's a bit cynical?"

"I learned a long time ago that when you're dealing with politicians, you can *never* be too cynical."

"I suppose the completely honest answer," August said, "is we don't know whether or not the girl is in danger. She's not been seen or heard from since she disappeared. We don't know what's going on."

"What *do* you know?"

"The vice president says he was told by Doris Lau that two days ago Emma and a girlfriend went to lunch at a restaurant they go to a lot. They traveled together on the MTR just as always. When the train arrived at their station, the girl Emma was with stopped after they got off to look at messages on her phone. When she looked up again, Emma had disappeared. When she searched and couldn't find her, she called Emma's mobile phone. It was turned off. Emma hasn't been heard from since."

"Where was this she was last seen?"

"She was getting off the MTR at Mongkok Station."

"Mongkok's a stronghold of the triads, John. You do realize that, don't you?"

"Of course I realize that. That's why *you're* here."

"That's what I was afraid of," Tay muttered.

"YOU AND CLAIRE are meeting Doris Lau tonight," August said. "She'll tell you what she knows. It's not much, apparently, but it will give you a place to start."

"You arranged for me to meet this woman before you had even talked to me about doing this?"

"I didn't arrange it. The vice president arranged it."

"That wasn't my point."

"I know," August smiled. "I suggested to the vice president I get you and Claire to do a quiet search for his daughter without involving local law enforcement, and he said he thought that was what we ought to do."

"Why would he think that? He has no idea who I am."

"No, he doesn't know who you are, but the president does.

He told the vice president you were an excellent choice to do this, and the vice president accepted the president's recommendation."

"*The President of the United States knows who I am?*"

"Sure he does. You're the guy who figured out who was trying to destroy the Band. He's very grateful to you."

Tay just looked at August. For once in his life, he was at a loss for words.

"Come on, Sam, get over it. It's not that big a deal."

"Not that big a deal? Finding out the President of the United States knows who I am?"

"The president knows a lot of people," August shrugged. "I doubt he's planning on asking you to play a round of golf or friend you on Facebook."

"I don't play golf and I barely know what Facebook is," Tay grumbled.

"I've got a question," Claire said, and they both looked at her. "Do you know exactly what the vice president told Doris Lau when he arranged this meeting? Did he give her our names?"

"No, of course he didn't give her your names. Doris Lau doesn't know who she's meeting. She just knows the vice president has sent two people to find their daughter and they will be here tonight to talk to her. Give her any names you want."

"What if she asks us for our credentials?"

"She won't. She knows the score. Tell her whatever you like if she does ask who you are. She doesn't care. She just wants you to find her daughter."

"You're not coming with us?" Tay asked.

"I can't since I'm not actually here. In fact, as far as I know, I may not even exist."

.   .   .

AUGUST PRODUCED TWO black iPhones, one out of each of his front pants pockets, and he handed one to Tay and the other to Claire. He did it with a flourish, like a magician producing a rabbit out of a hat.

Tay was annoyed at the flourish. If there was a rabbit around somewhere, he figured he was it.

"These are clean phones," August said. "They're registered in Hong Kong and have never been used, but of course they won't stay clean when you start to use them. So be cautious and sparing."

Tay turned his iPhone over and saw a Hong Kong telephone number written on a piece of tape stuck to the back with a six-digit number below it.

"That's the number and the security code for your phone," August continued. "They've both got the Signal app on them so you can make secure calls and send secure messages. You know how to use Signal, don't you, Sam?"

Tay had no idea what August was talking about, but he would ask Claire later so he just nodded.

"We gave you civilian, off-the-shelf software so it won't compromise you if somebody gets into your phone. If we had put on proprietary stuff that's better than this is, it would compromise you."

"You think somebody might sneak into my room at night and break into my phone?" Tay asked.

"I didn't know there was anyone left on the planet who thought you have to have someone's phone in your hands to break into it. Not even you, Sam. But I see I was wrong."

"I was joking," Tay muttered.

"No, Sam, you weren't."

Tay hadn't been, and he knew August knew, so he kept quiet and said nothing else.

"You'll find two numbers stored in the directory of each phone," August went on. "The one listed first is the number of the other phone so you can call each other, and the second one is the number for Doris Lau's personal cell phone, the number she gave to the vice president."

"Where is this meeting with Mrs. Lau happening?" Claire asked.

"Her instructions are for you to walk out the back door of the Peninsula Hotel at eight o'clock tonight and call her on the number you have."

"I think she's seen too many spy movies," Tay said.

"The back of the Pen's old building is on Middle Road. It's a quiet block, almost no traffic, which I'd guess is the reason she chose it. I assume when you call her she'll give you further instructions. For whatever help it may be, I've messaged you a picture of Doris Lau. I don't see any reason she would try to slip a ringer in on you, but just to be on the safe side I want you to know what she looks like."

Tay powered up his phone and went to the messages. There was only one. He opened the attachment and looked at the picture.

"This is Doris Lau?"

"That's her."

"She looks like a Chinese Meryl Streep."

August bent over and contemplated the picture on the screen of Tay's phone.

Doris Lau appeared to be in her late fifties. Her dirty blonde hair was piled casually on top of her head and held in place by a black stick pushed through it. It looked like, but probably wasn't, a chopstick. It was the sort of offhand, no-effort look women spent hours and paid hundreds of dollars to achieve.

She wore cat-eye shaped eyeglasses with brown plastic frames and a high-necked silk blouse streaked with bright colors that looked unassuming but expensive. Her features were soft. Gentle-looking brown eyes, pink cheeks that just begged to be pinched, and a small, rounded nose. There was something about her face which hinted she could adjust its appearance with a blink and become someone else entirely, which is what had made Tay think of Meryl Streep.

"You know," August said, "you're right. I never thought about it before. Maybe Doris will show up as somebody else and won't look anything like this picture."

"You love all this cloak and dagger bullshit, don't you, John?"

"I don't think Doris Lau considers it bullshit. Can you imagine what her masters in Beijing would say if they knew she was meeting in secret with people sent by the Vice President of the United States who were here to find her daughter?"

"I thought you said no one other than Doris Lau knew this girl's father is the vice president."

"As far as we know they don't, but Beijing knows Emma is Doris Lau's daughter. If they're behind this, they must think they have Mrs. Lau right where they want her. What they don't know is they have just taken a personal shot at the Vice President of the United States of America and now they have the White House on their ass."

"I thought you said Beijing might have nothing to do with this," Claire spoke up.

"Maybe they don't. But regardless of who's behind it, if Doris Lau's bosses find out she's consorting with the White House, it won't do her any good so she's being careful to make sure they don't find out. She's got more at stake here than anyone."

"Except maybe for her daughter," Tay said.

"Yeah," August conceded, "except maybe for her."

EIGHT

C LAIRE AND TAY walked up to Salisbury Road and waited at the light to cross. Just on the other side was the Peninsula Hotel, and it presided over Kowloon with the same solemn dignity it had exhibited for nearly a hundred years.

Tay looked around at the other people waiting with them for the light to change.

"What's with all these surgical masks?" he asked. "It looks like half the people you see on the street now are wearing them."

"It's always been common here in the winter. A lot of Chinese think they can prevent a cold by wearing them."

"They never caught on in Singapore." Tay glanced around again. "I remember seeing people wearing them here before in the winter, but never this many."

"It's not the thing about colds this year, it's the demonstrations. The cops started filming the protests and a lot of the people involved began wearing the masks to prevent being identified. The Hong Kong government made noises about banning them, so people who weren't demonstrators started wearing them every day just to spite the government."

Tay wasn't sure what to make of that, but it did look weird to him to see so many people walking around wearing masks which rendered them all but unidentifiable. If was as if half the city was preparing to rob the other half.

When the light changed, they crossed Salisbury Road and walked up the circular driveway of the Peninsula Hotel. The fountain in the center of the forecourt was bubbling away as it had for as long as anyone now alive could remember and two of the hotel's famous green Rolls-Royces sat nose to nose at the front door.

The Peninsula was a Hong Kong institution. It was East-of-Suez British colonialism at the height of its power. The original structure dated back to the 1920s and its façade had been preserved more or less unchanged since then, although in the mid-1990s a thirty-story tower with a rooftop helipad was added to the back of the property.

Something else was different, too. When the venerable old Pen was built, it faced the harbor across a narrow roadway, but now it was several hundred yards back from the water. Over the last several decades, the Hong Kong government had learned there was money to be made filling in parts of the harbor and then selling the reclaimed land to favored developers. Salisbury Road was now a wide thoroughfare and dozens of large buildings occupied the several hundred yards of new land the government had created between the other side of it and Hong Kong Harbor.

Two white-jacketed doormen swung open the Pen's glass front doors as Claire and Tay approached.

The lobby was massive, rising at least thirty feet to a gilt-accented ceiling supported on square white pillars with golden caps. At one end, a string quartet dressed in black tie played Mozart. Small tables surrounded by leather armchairs filled the space from end to end and well-dressed people lounged, sipped drinks, and conversed at them in those carefully modulated tones associated with wealth, privilege, and standing. The Peninsula's lobby was so deliciously anachronistic Tay wouldn't have been in the least surprised to see Fred Astaire and Ginger Rogers come dancing through.

"I'd offer to buy you a drink," Claire said, "but I don't think we have time."

Tay looked at his watch. "It's still ten minutes before eight," he said. "Let's at least sit down and decide how we're going to do this."

They settled at an empty table off to one side and waved away a white-jacketed waiter when he headed toward them. The man inclined his head deferentially and disappeared.

"I want you to take the lead," Tay said.

"That doesn't make any sense, Sam. You're the investigator here."

"Just lead her through telling us what she knows. If anything occurs to me, I'll speak up. Otherwise, I think it would be better for you to handle the conversation."

"You want me to talk to her because she's a woman and you think talking to another woman would make her feel more comfortable. That's why you want me to lead, because I'm a woman, not because you think I'd handle the conversation better than you would."

Tay cleared his throat and folded his arms.

"Well, not exactly," he said, "but I suppose—"

"Stop trying to explain yourself, Sam. I agree with you."

"You do?"

"Sure. I was going to suggest it myself, but I didn't want to offend you. Now, is there anything else we need to talk about or should we get moving?"

"This is a little embarrassing to ask, but what in the world is this Signal thing John said he put on our phones? He seemed to assume I'd know."

Claire smiled and pulled out the iPhone August had given her, punched in the security code, and opened the home screen.

"You do know how to use an iPhone, don't you, Sam?"

"Very funny."

Claire pointed to an icon on her iPhone's home screen which looked like a speech bubble in an old cartoon.

"This is the Signal app," she said. "You can use it to send encrypted messages and to encrypt telephone conversations. When you use Signal to call somebody, the server that encrypts the conversation produces two words which then appear on the displays of both your phone and the phone you're calling. You say the first word to the caller when you answer. If the caller verifies the same word is on their phone, they say the second word for you to verify. When both words match on both phones, you know you're fully encrypted. If they don't match, you kill the call, switch networks, and try again. Got it?"

"You do understand how funny I think all this spy bullshit is, don't you?"

"There's nothing funny about being two outsiders chasing around Hong Kong asking questions about the triads and the Chinese Ministry of State Security, Sam. This is only technically Hong Kong. It's really China. We're vulnerable here. You need to remember that."

Tay tried to look abashed, but he couldn't quite pull it off.

"Okay, I'll remember, but I'm still not going to crap around with secret agent apps on my iPhone. If I need to call you, I'll call you."

Claire couldn't help smiling. "Somehow I thought you'd say that."

G LASS DOORS AT both ends of the Pen's lobby opened into long corridors which led out to Middle Road at the back of the hotel. They walked along one lined with the kind of exclusive designer shops Tay had never bothered walking into because he didn't have the slightest interest in anything they sold. Tiffany, Hermès, Chanel, and even a Davidoff cigar store.

Tay considered going into the Davidoff shop and asking if

they had Marlboros just so he could tell people he had bought his cigarettes at the Peninsula Hotel, but he didn't. He doubted Davidoff sold anything as down-market as a pack of Marlboros anyway, and even if they did, he couldn't think of anyone he wanted to tell.

They emerged at the end of the corridor onto Middle Road and it was quiet and empty just as August had said it would be. There were several cars and two vans parked along the curb, all of them shiny and expensive, but the sidewalk was empty and Tay saw nothing to suggest what they should do now.

"John said to call her when we get here so let me give it a shot," Claire said.

Claire took out the iPhone August had given her, opened the directory, and selected the second number, the one which August said was Doris Lau's personal cell phone.

She listened for a moment while the call was connecting and then said, "Mrs. Lau, we are waiting at the back of the Peninsula Hotel as you requested, and—"

Claire stopped talking and looked at Tay.

"She hung up on me."

"What did she say?"

"She didn't say anything. She just hung up."

"Huh."

Tay was standing with his back to the street, but then Claire pointed over his shoulder and he glanced around.

The driver's door of a large black van parked about fifty feet up the road from them had opened and the man inside was looking them over. They watched as a man unfolded his enormous body from the driver's seat and walked toward them.

Tay knew next to nothing about cars and vans, but he knew enough to recognize the Mercedes-Benz emblem on the back of the van. He tried to see inside, but the van's windows were tinted so deeply its interior was invisible.

"You wait for Chief Executive?" the driver asked Tay when he got to where they were standing.

He was huge for a Chinese with hands the size of frying pans. In a strange contrast to the hulking threat the man's size conveyed, his face was round and almost cherubic, but there was nothing cherubic about the bulge Tay saw under the left arm of the man's black suit. It announced the presence of a large handgun in a shoulder holster.

"Yes, we are," Claire responded to his question. "Who the hell are you?"

The man shifted his eyes from Tay to Claire. He seemed bemused that she, not Tay, had responded.

"Identification, please," he said to her.

"No."

He didn't seem certain what to say to that, and he stood looking at Claire and tilting his head first left then right like an enormous dog given a command he had never before heard. When Claire said nothing else, he watched her for a moment, then lifted his shoulders and let them drop in a tiny shrug. He stepped closer and gestured with his open hands for Claire to lift her arms so he could pat her down.

"Forget it, fatso," she snapped. "You're not laying a hand on either of us. You can either take us to Mrs. Lau without any more of your bullshit or we're leaving and you can explain to her what happened. Now what's it going to be?"

Fatso didn't look like he was going to back down. His face clouded, he shifted his weight as if preparing for an imminent attack, and he glared at Claire. Tay watched the man's big hands opening and closing. He didn't know what that meant, but he was pretty sure it wasn't anything good.

The standoff continued for a minute or two, neither Claire nor the driver backing down, and then a metallic sound from the black Mercedes van caused them all to look toward it. They watched as the door on the side of the van slid open, but no one emerged.

The driver looked at the van, glanced back at Claire, then looked at the van again. His face was expressionless, but he stepped slowly to one side and nodded his head toward the vehicle's open door.

"Let's go, Sam," Claire said.

She set off for the van, her heels making crisp clicking sounds on the sidewalk.

Tay fell in behind her and the driver followed. They were both afraid to do anything else.

NINE

DORIS LAU DID look like a Chinese version of Meryl Streep. She was no one and everyone at the same time. If Tay had encountered her on the street, he would have had no doubt she was either an actress or a politician.

The man sitting with her was something else altogether. He did *not* look like no one and everyone. He looked like a guy you kept your distance from.

He had broad shoulders, thick arms, and a deeply lined, slightly saggy face. His eyes slanted a little downward, which gave him a menacing air. Tay thought he looked like a Chinese version of Tony Soprano, the New Jersey mafia boss on an American television show a few years back who had people killed, then went to a psychiatrist to talk about his insecurities. That show had been the most American thing Tay had ever seen: violence and self-doubt all rolled up together.

Tay climbed into the van behind Claire and settled into a brown leather captain's chair. The van's side door slid shut with an audible *clunk*. It was apparently operated by remote control, but he couldn't see who was operating it. Fatso had remained outside and was now leaning against the rear fender smoking a cigarette. Tay considered joining him, but he decided it would be unseemly.

The interior of the van was luxurious. It reminded Tay of the private jet that had brought him to Hong Kong. It was all soft brown leather and polished burl wood with four big chairs like first-class airline seats. They were grouped around a small, wood-veneered conference table, two on each side. Between the two chairs in which he and Claire sat, there was a burl wood console with two cup holders and a variety of switches and knobs. Tay didn't have the slightest idea what any of the switches and knobs did so he felt an immediate impulse to play with them and find out. It was an impulse which he defeated.

On the other side of the table, Doris Lau and Tony Soprano sat side by side and regarded them with looks which Tay thought fell somewhere between suspicious and downright hostile.

"Who are you?" Doris Lau asked, looking at Tay.

Again, as he had with the driver, Tay kept his mouth shut and let Claire do the talking.

"My name is Claire," she said. "And his name is Sam."

Mrs. Lau seemed as surprised as the driver had been to find herself talking to Claire rather than to Tay. Tay couldn't help but smile. Even when you were the female Chief Executive of Hong Kong, apparently a few patriarchal assumptions survived intact.

"We understood we were meeting privately with you," Claire continued. She indicated Mrs. Lau's companion with the tilt of her head. "Who is this?"

"This is Albert Chan. He is my Chief of Staff. Albert knows whatever I know. You may speak freely in front of him."

Claire and Tay exchanged a look, and Doris Lau caught it.

"Yes, Albert knows who Emma's father is."

"We were told only you and..." Claire hesitated a moment "...the man who asked us to meet with you knew."

"Clearly, that's not true," Mrs. Lau said. "Both of you know who Emma's father is, and I have no doubt it was discussed among others in your government before they decided to send you."

"The man who sent us here—" Claire began, but Doris Lau interrupted her.

"Oh, for God's sake, just say it. The Vice President of the United States is Emma's father. Albert knows it. All four of us in this van know it. So, stop being coy about it."

Claire glanced at Tay, then shifted her eyes back to Doris Lau and nodded her head. "Yes, ma'am."

"Now, before this goes any further," Mrs. Lau said, "I've got a few questions for you. Are you from the FBI?"

"No, ma'am."

"The Secret Service?"

"No, ma'am."

"CIA? NSA?"

"No, ma'am."

"Army, Navy, Air Force, Marines?"

"No, ma'am."

"Well then, who the *fuck* are you?"

"I'm Claire and he's Sam."

Doris Lau blew out a heavy breath and shook her head.

"If you have any doubts at all about talking to us, ma'am, please telephone the vice president right now. He will confirm we are here at his request and that you may speak to us as you would speak to him."

Doris Lau looked away and waved one hand vaguely in the air.

"I don't doubt that," she said. "I just want to know who I'm dealing with before this goes any further."

"Respectfully, ma'am, no, you don't. I am Claire and he is Sam. The Vice President of the United States sent us here. That is all you need to know. Now, let's get on with finding your daughter, shall we?"

. . .

TONY SOPRANO LEANED forward and folded his thick forearms on the table.

"Perhaps it would be helpful before we begin," he said, "if I explained—"

"No, sir," Claire interrupted. "I don't know you and having you here now isn't my choice. It is apparently Mrs. Lau's wish that you be present and I will accept that out of respect for her, but I will not include you in the conversation. You can listen quietly, or you can leave. Do I make myself clear?"

Tay studied Tony Soprano while Claire was hammering at him. He was wearing a black suit and white shirt that looked exactly like the black suit and white shirt worn by the driver. Maybe this guy and Fatso went shopping together to buy their clothes.

His hair was jet black, but his hairline had receded so far it was almost at the top of his head. It left a face that was all wide forehead, hard eyes, and large nose. His eyes were deeply set and his eyelids sagged, hooding both eyes in a way which left his face set in an expression of permanent suspicion. There was something almost Mediterranean about his features, and the way he was looking at them with his chin lowered, his mouth slightly opened, and his eyes rolled up to the top of his face completed the picture.

Tay couldn't decide if the look was natural or studied. Maybe the guy was just a thug and looked like it. Or maybe he had seen every episode of *The Sopranos* and had deliberately chosen Tony as his role model. If it was only an act, Tay thought he was making a fine job of it.

"Mrs. Lau," Claire said, ignoring Tony Soprano now that she was finished with him, "the only reason for this meeting is for us to find out what you know about Emma's disappearance. The sooner we can do that, the sooner we will be able to get on with finding her. I have only a few questions and then we'll get out of your hair."

Doris Lau turned her head. She stared out the side window of the van and gave a tight nod.

Tay produced a small notebook and a ballpoint pen and prepared to take notes. He had no intention of writing anything down, but he thought it was a good time to remind Doris Lau and Tony Soprano that Claire was in charge here and he was only a note taker.

"What can you tell us about your daughter's disappearance?"

"Not a great deal, I'm afraid," Doris Lau said, shifting her eyes back to Claire. "A friend of hers telephoned two days ago looking for her. She told me she and Emma had gone to Mongkok together and she had lost track of her at the MTR station. She said she couldn't reach Emma on her mobile and she wanted to know if I had heard from her."

"Had you?"

"No. We hadn't spoken in... oh, three or four days, I suppose."

"I'm sorry, but I don't understand why—"

"Emma doesn't live with me."

"Where does she live?"

"In Pokfulam."

Pokfulam was a very upmarket area on Hong Kong Island, one inhabited by the established and the well-off. It wasn't a place you would expect to find a young woman living on her own.

"Does she live there with someone?"

Doris Lau's eyes hardened and she cocked her head like a dog trying to decide where to bite.

"Why would you ask me that?"

"I'm just trying to learn as much about her as I can, ma'am. Does she live alone? Does she live with a boyfriend? Does she have a roommate to help with the rent? Pokfulam is an expensive neighborhood for a young girl by herself."

"Emma is in her last year at the Li Ka Shing Faculty of

Medicine of the University of Hong Kong. Their teaching hospital is Queen Mary Hospital in Pokfulam so I got her an apartment in the area. There is no rent. I bought the apartment and placed it in her name. Does that answer your question, or do you wish to pry further into my personal affairs?"

If Mrs. Lau's response caused Claire any annoyance, she gave no sign. "May I have the address, please?"

"I'll text it to you."

Doris Lau shifted her eyes to Albert Chan. "Take care of it, please, Albert."

Tony Soprano nodded, but he said nothing.

"So, Emma's in medical school?" Claire prodded.

Mrs. Lau looked back at Claire and held her gaze. "I just told you she is in her last year at the Li Ka Shing Faculty of Medicine," she snapped. "Do you want me to say it again?"

She quickly folded her arms and waved one hand vaguely toward Claire in the same gesture she had used the last time she had allowed her impatience to show.

"I'm sorry. That was uncalled for. Everything seems to be happening at once. I apologize."

"It's unnecessary," Claire said. "I can't even imagine how I would feel in your position."

Doris Lau looked at Claire and something about her was transformed. She appeared gentler now, softer somehow, as if Claire's expression of personal empathy had caused her to abandon the personality she had been projecting and revert to the person she really was. The strange thing was she hadn't moved a muscle to do it. She had simply been one person one moment and a different person the next.

Tay had been right about the Meryl Streep thing. One person with so many different people inside. Right before his eyes, Doris Lau had become someone else without doing anything at all. He wondered which was the real Doris Lau. The one he had seen before, or this one. If he had to guess, he would put his money on it being neither.

JAKE NEEDHAM

Then the moment ended as abruptly as it had arrived, and Doris Lau was again the woman they had seen when they climbed into the van.

"Nevertheless," Mrs. Lau said, "I *am* sorry. It won't happen again. Now let's get back to what you wanted to know."

"Who is this friend who telephoned you about getting separated from Emma in Mongkok?"

"Her name is Sarah McFarland."

"Does she go to medical school with Emma?"

"No, she works at Citibank. In the main office in Central. I think she does something in their investment banking division."

"American?"

"She went to school in California, but she's Australian."

"Can you tell me how to reach her?"

"I'm sure we can get her cell phone number for you." She shifted her eyes to Albert Chan. "Albert, will you deal with that for me, too, please?"

"I'll do it tonight."

He spoke rapidly, shooting a glance at Claire as he did. He looked as if he expected her to reprimand him for speaking, but she said nothing. She didn't even appear to notice he had spoken.

"Does your daughter live alone?"

"Yes."

"Does she have a boyfriend?"

"No, no one in particular."

"Would you know if she did?"

"I feel sure I would."

"Then you are close?"

Doris Lau hesitated. "I'm not sure it would be fair to say we are. Emma is no longer a child. She is a young woman and very much her own person."

"Then you feel confident you know what's going on in her life?"

"Is it possible there are things she doesn't tell me? Yes, of

66

course, that's possible. But if there were someone special to her, I think I would know about it."

"Are you certain?"

"Do you have children, Claire?"

Tay's ears perked up. He stopped pretending to take notes and glanced at Claire.

Did Claire have children? He suddenly realized he had no idea. He didn't even know if Claire was involved in some kind of relationship or if she was, God forbid, married. Well, no, she wasn't married, at least he didn't think so. Then again, he had been wrong about things like that before.

"No, ma'am. No children."

"Married?"

Now it was Claire who hesitated. "No, ma'am."

Tay thought he saw Claire's eyes flick toward him after she answered and then away again, but he might have been mistaken.

"Could we get back to the subject of Emma, please, ma'am? What can you tell us about her friends?"

"Not a great deal, I'm afraid. When we talked, it wasn't generally about her daily life. When you are in medical school you have little time for a daily life."

"Can you arrange for us to look through her apartment? Perhaps we can find something there to point us toward other people we can talk to."

"Emma told me she had given Sarah a key for emergencies. I'll ask her to let you in."

"How are you going to explain to Sarah who we are?"

Doris Lau pursed her lips and thought about it. "Well, Sarah already knows no one has heard from Emma in two days. Perhaps I will just tell her I don't want to involve the police yet because I don't want to embarrass Emma if there's some explanation that's personal. Maybe I could just say you're private detectives? Someone who owes me a favor and will therefore look into this quietly? How would that be?"

"It's fine."

"All right." Mrs. Lau heaved a heavy sigh and didn't even try to disguise it. "Is there anything else?"

"Could you message me a few pictures of Emma? Some which might give me a sense of who she is as well as what she looks like?"

"Yes, of course."

"Just one more question," Claire said. "Why do you think someone has taken Emma? Isn't it possible she just went off somewhere without telling you?"

"Young lady, Emma is the daughter of the Chief Executive of Hong Kong and the Vice President of the United States. My first concern has to be that she's been taken by someone who wants to get to one of us by using her. How could it not be?"

"And you don't think it's also possible she's just gone away with someone and not told you about it?"

Doris Lau turned her head and stared out the window. She said nothing.

"Ma'am?" Claire prompted.

Tay watched Mrs. Lau carefully.

"I wish I could say I do," she said after a moment. "That would make this all very easy. But, no, I don't think it's possible."

It was clear to Tay there was something Doris Lau wasn't telling them. What was not at all clear was what it might be or whether it had anything to do with Emma's disappearance.

"Did she know anyone in Mongkok?"

"Not that I'm aware of."

"Why were she and Sarah going there then?"

"I'm sure Sarah can give you more details, but my under-standing is there's a restaurant there where they often go together."

"Does she have any personal connection to that restaurant?"

"What do you mean?"

"Does she know the owner? Does someone she knows work there?"

"If so, I've never heard her mention it."

"How long do we have before you feel like you must get the police involved in this, ma'am?" Claire asked.

Doris Lau looked down at her hands. She had clasped them in her lap and now Tay saw she was grinding them together as if trying to crush something held between her palms.

"I don't know. I haven't thought about it."

She gave Claire a rueful smile.

"I guess that means I'm putting myself in your hands. Do you think I'm making a wise choice?"

"We're very good at solving problems like this."

Mrs. Lau studied Claire closely. "I hope so."

"You can reach me on the number I used to call you. If you think of anything that might help, please let me know."

Doris Lau nodded and looked away, but she said nothing else.

TEN

"YOU DON'T LIKE her, do you, Sam?"

Tay and Claire stood on the sidewalk behind the Peninsula Hotel and watched Doris Lau's van drive away.

"I don't trust her."

"Do you trust anybody?"

"Not really."

"Sometimes you need to trust people."

"I don't see why."

Claire smiled despite herself.

"There's something she wasn't telling us," Tay continued. "Some part of the story she was leaving out. And if it was important enough for her not to tell us... it's important."

"That crossed my mind once or twice, too, but I couldn't quite put my finger on why."

"Maybe it was because of Tony Soprano."

"Who?" Claire laughed.

"Albert Chan. Mrs. Lau's bulldog. He seemed poised to kick the shit out of us if either one of us said the wrong thing. Didn't he make you think of Tony Soprano?"

"You mean the mafia guy in that American TV show?"

Tay nodded.

"He did have a kind of thug vibe about him, didn't he?" Claire laughed again. "And the smell really capped it off perfectly."

"Smell?"

"His aftershave. It stunk up the whole van. Didn't you notice?"

Tay shook his head. He had carefully sized up both Mrs. Lau and her guard dog, but how they smelled hadn't come into it.

"I love the aroma of aftershave on a man, but that was... nasty. He smelled like a doctor's office."

"I didn't notice."

"Maybe it's a woman thing. We react to stuff like that."

Tay didn't wear aftershave, but now he wondered if he ought to. What did he smell like to Claire? That didn't bear thinking about. Maybe he should buy some.

"Tony Soprano?" Claire chuckled. "Seriously?"

Tay nodded.

"You have a very vivid imagination."

"It's one of my best qualities."

"I was kidding."

"So was I."

T HERE WAS NO reason for them to continue standing there on an empty sidewalk behind the Peninsula so they strolled in the direction of Nathan Road.

"You want to get something to eat?" Tay asked.

"I'm beat, Sam. John and I didn't get in from Washington until mid-day and we've been running ever since."

It hadn't occurred to Tay that Claire had been in Washington with August. He thought she lived in Bangkok, so what was she doing in Washington? Had she been in the meeting with the president and vice president which August described?

He could think of a few hundred questions he wanted to ask Claire, but he asked none of them. He just nodded.

"I need sleep more than I need food right now," Claire continued. "We can start fresh in the morning."

That suggested a whole new line of questioning to Tay.

He could, for example, ask Claire where she would be doing that sleeping since she wasn't staying at the hotel where he was. He supposed it was possible she was staying somewhere else simply because of her history with the Cordis. That's what she had said, and he could understand that.

Then again, maybe that was just an excuse. Maybe she was staying with a lover somewhere and didn't want to tell him. Wherever she was staying, he might embarrass her by raising the subject, or worse he might embarrass himself. So he didn't ask.

"If Mrs. Lau sends you the contact for that girl tonight," he said instead, "the one Emma was with at Mongkok Station, call her and get us set up for tomorrow."

"How do you want to do it?"

"Well, she's supposed to have a key for Emma's apartment, isn't she? Get her to meet us there and we'll look it over at the same time."

"Early start?"

"You know I hate early."

"Yeah, I know. That's why I thought I'd better ask. But we may not have a lot of time here, Sam. Looking for a live body is a lot different from figuring out who's responsible for a dead one."

"That's what I tried to tell August when he pulled me into this thing, but he wouldn't listen." Tay sighed. "Okay, early."

When they reached Nathan Road, Tay waved at the first taxi he saw. It pulled to the curb and stopped, and he opened the back door for Claire.

"If you get something set up with that girl, let me know what it is. It doesn't matter what time."

Claire nodded, then hesitated for a moment before getting into the taxi.

Oh God, Tay suddenly thought, *is she going to kiss me goodnight?*

What would he do if she did? How would she expect him to react? No, of course she wasn't going to kiss him goodnight so he didn't have to worry about it. That was ridiculous.

She didn't.

After a beat, she just reached out, patted him on the arm, and slid into the back seat of the taxi. Then she closed the door, and the taxi pulled away.

Tay wasn't certain whether he was relieved or disappointed.

WHILE TAY WAS watching Claire being driven away, another of Hong Kong's ubiquitous little red and gray taxis pulled to the curb and stopped. The driver honked the horn and peered at Tay with hopeful eyes.

Tay hadn't yet given any thought to what he might do after Claire left and he had no better idea than to go back to the hotel. So, after a moment's hesitation, he got into the taxi.

"Cordis Hotel," he told the driver.

The driver was an elderly man with a long thin face, sad eyes, and silver hair trimmed tight to his head in a military-style cut. He slowly turned his head and looked at Tay the way he might have looked at a duck that had started singing an aria from *Carmen.*

"Nee doh hai been?"

"Cor-dis Ho-tel," Tay repeated with the exaggerated intonation people always used when speaking a language which was not being understood. And then, just in case it might be helpful, he pointed up Nathan Road away from the harbor.

The old man looked puzzled. Not unfriendly, just puzzled.

"Cor-dis," Tay repeated, raising his voice.

Yeah, Tay thought, *that'll do it. Just speak really loudly when some-body doesn't understand you. Works every time.*

He felt like an idiot, but he kept trying.

"Cor-dis," he repeated one more time to the confused looking man. "In Mongkok," he added since he couldn't think of anything else to tell him.

"Ah! *Wong Kok!*" the driver barked. *"Mo man tai!"*

The taxi sped away into the night and, by some miracle of near biblical proportions, it slammed to a stop at the Cordis Hotel less than fifteen minutes later.

According to the meter, the fare was forty-four Hong Kong dollars, but Tay was so grateful he had somehow ended up where he wanted to be he gave the driver a red $100 note and waved away the change. The man looked like he couldn't believe his luck. As far as Tay was concerned, that made two of them.

When he got out of the taxi, Tay stood there for a moment without going into the hotel. It was only about nine. He was more hungry than sleepy and calling room service didn't hold any appeal.

He didn't want to get lost in a strange city, but the hotel was by far the tallest building in the neighborhood. If he kept it in sight, it seemed to him he would be okay. How could he not be?

With that the decision was made, and Tay set off to see what wonders Mongkok might have to offer.

THE FIRST WONDER he encountered was McDonald's. *That'll do just fine,* Tay thought.

The place was crowded despite the hour, but the line moved quickly and it was only a few minutes before Tay was sitting in a red plastic booth with a Big Mac, large fries, and a Coke Zero.

Tay had never been a food guy. He didn't spend much time thinking about food, none at all to be honest, and he believed the only important thing about food was to eat it when he felt hungry so he would not feel hungry anymore. What he ate didn't matter much to him. A Big Mac, large fries and a Coke Zero would do as well as anything.

Tay was just nibbling his last French fry and finishing his Coke Zero when he heard a strange warbling sound. At first, he thought it was an alarm going off somewhere in the restaurant, but no one else seemed to notice. That was when it occurred to him the source of the sound was the iPhone August had given him.

He often wondered why telephones didn't just *ring* anymore. Now that telephones were digital devices instead of plastic boxes with a bell inside, it was possible to use all sorts of sounds to replace the traditional ring, but Tay had never believed you should do something merely because you could. He certainly didn't think replacing the ringing of a telephone bell with five seconds of warbling that sounded like a canary with gas was a particularly worthy contribution to human civilization.

Tay fumbled the phone when he pulled it from his pocket and it hit the booth's plastic seat, bounced once, and fell on the floor. He held his breath when he picked it up and turned it over. But he had gotten lucky. The screen hadn't cracked, it wasn't even scratched, and everything else looked intact, too.

He poked at the screen to accept the call.

"Hello?"

"What the hell was that?" Claire asked. "Are you in the middle of a fight or something?"

"I dropped the phone."

"Accidentally, or intentionally?"

"A little of each, to be honest."

Claire chuckled. "Look, Tony Soprano texted me a number for Sarah McFarland and I called her. She does have a key to Emma's apartment. She's meeting us there tomorrow at nine."

"Did you get Emma's address?"

"She lives in the building called Residence Bel-Air in Pokfulam. From a quick Google, I'd say it's a pretty spiffy place."

"*Spiffy*? I don't think I've ever heard anyone under sixty use the word *spiffy* before."

"Is that your way of asking me my age?"

"Not unless you *are* over sixty."

Claire chuckled again. "Look, Pokfulam is a long way away from Mongkok. In morning traffic, God only knows how long it would take you to get there by taxi. I'm going to organize a car and driver and I'll pick you up."

Tay wondered if that meant Claire was staying somewhere close to Mongkok. He thought again about asking her where she was, but he didn't.

"Be in the lobby at eight," Claire said.

"Eight? It'll take us an *hour* to get there?"

"Including a stop for coffee, yes."

A FTER TAY RETURNED the iPhone to his pocket, he sat there and replayed the conversation in his mind.

He was glad Claire had gotten in touch with Sarah McFarland. He was also glad they would talk with Sarah in the morning and look around Emma's apartment at the same time. But that wasn't the part of the conversation he was focused on now.

Was it his imagination, or was Claire being... well, a little bit flirtatious? First, the goodnight kiss that almost was, and now a bantering, slightly flirty telephone conversation? No doubt it was just his imagination working overtime.

Don't be an old fool, Tay reproached himself.

Whether it was or wasn't his imagination, just thinking about the possibility left him feeling a little wound up and he didn't feel like being stuck in his room at the hotel. He would look for a place to buy a pack of Marlboros, then he would smoke one, or two, while he strolled around Mongkok and got a feel for the place.

Just walking around the neighborhood and smoking a couple of cigarettes couldn't get him into any trouble, could it?

76

ELEVEN

MONGKOK IS KNOWN for three things. It is said to be the most crowded place on earth. It is the hub of the Hong Kong sex trade. And it is the stronghold of the Chinese triads.

About ten years ago, a massive complex called Langham Place opened in Mongkok. It had a couple of million square feet of shopping and offices, its own MTR station, and the ultra-modern Cordis Hotel.

That will clean up the neighborhood, a lot of people said. *That will drive away the sex trade and end the control of the triads*.

Didn't happen.

Now most people say it will never happen.

Mongkok is only three stops north of Tsim Sha Tsui on the Mass Transit Railway. In Tsim Sha Tsui, luxury boutiques, exclusive jewelry stores, and futuristic electronics shops line the streets, but it might as well be on another planet for all it has in common with Mongkok. You won't find luxury boutiques in Mongkok. What you'll mostly find there are grimy storefronts selling the basics of life to a massive crush of working-class Chinese.

You don't go to Mongkok if you're looking for Chanel or

Tiffany or Hermès or Louis Vuitton. You go to Mongkok if what you need is the Chup Kee Tool and Hardware Store, the Jam Hong Diesel Injection Service, Wah Keung Screws and Fasteners, or Hings Rubber Products.

You won't find any tourists in Mongkok. Not unless they're lost.

But if you're in Hong Kong on a summer night when the darkness is heavy and liquid and you find yourself at loose ends, jump on the MTR and head for Mongkok. Go see for yourself. It's a ride worth taking.

Get off at Mongkok Station and walk to the Ladies Market. Every night as darkness falls, it fills Tung Choi Street for block after block with hundreds of small stands selling cheap clothes, fake perfume, knock-off purses, and all manner of junk you didn't even know existed. Then, just around the corner, find the narrow street with so many stores selling fake Nikes the locals call it Sneaker Street.

The reek of sewage and the stench of ten thousand vehicle exhausts fills the air. Duck shit and gasoline. It's the smell of Hong Kong. It's something you will never forget.

Keep walking.

When you pass the dim doorways of shops, their steel grates closed and locked until morning, listen to the men coughing and women whispering in the shadows. Pay special attention to the staircases brightly lit with pink and white lights. If you can read Chinese, stop and look at the signs posted just outside. They describe the women you can find inside.

Out there in the darkness are more people than you can imagine. You won't see them, but you'll feel them breathing in the night. Old men with their undershirts rolled up to their nipples and cigarettes clinging to their bottom lips. Worn-out women bent from a lifetime of labor. Hard-looking young toughs wearing dirty shorts, shirtless in the heavy heat.

But I wouldn't hang around, white boy. Stand there too long and you'll feel the triad punks easing up behind you.

Move along, *gweilo*. There's nothing here for you.

You thought you had been to Hong Kong when you window-shopped the designer boutiques in Tsim Sha Tsui, rode the Star Ferry, and took pictures of the harbor, didn't you?

Forget all that. *This* is Hong Kong.

AY STOOD ON the sidewalk in front of McDonald's and looked around. He could see his hotel towering above nearly everything else, so he thought he ought to have no difficulty finding his way back if he didn't stray too far. He turned to his left, choosing the direction more or less at random, and walked toward what looked to be a busy intersection not far away.

Most of the shops he passed were open and people jammed the sidewalk. It could have been the middle of the afternoon, but it wasn't. It was close to ten o'clock at night.

Maybe, Tay told himself, Hong Kong was the mythical *city that never sleeps.* He wasn't at all certain what that meant in practice. He had grown up in Singapore, and he had always thought of Singapore as *the city that never wakes up.*

When he reached the intersection, he looked around until he found a street sign. He was on the corner of Argyle Street and Nathan Road, so he knew more or less where he was.

Nathan Road was the central thoroughfare in Kowloon. It ran in a straight line for several miles all the way from the harbor out to Boundary Street.

There had been a time when Boundary Street actually *was* a boundary, one which marked the line between Hong Kong and China. But in 1898, the British Empire used its considerable military leverage against China and demanded more Chinese territory be leased to Hong Kong so the growing colony could expand north of Boundary Street. The area leased to Britain by China became known as the New Territories, and the lease ran for ninety-nine years.

It was the expiration of that lease in 1997 which caused the British to give Hong Kong back to China and flee.

A new treaty with China provided at least a fig leaf of respectability for Great Britain when it absconded and left the people of Hong Kong to their fate. That was the treaty which established the Hong Kong Special Administrative Region of the People's Republic of China and presumably guaranteed legal protections for the freedom of Hong Kong for fifty years into the future.

No one really knew then how that was going to work out.

Now everybody knew.

TAY SPOTTED A 7-Eleven on the other side of Nathan Road. When the light changed, he crossed over and went in.

A buzzer sounded when Tay pushed through the glass door, and the clerk behind the counter glanced over. He was an elderly man, thin and stooped. He could have been eighty, but he could have been forty. Tay knew Hong Kong did that to people. Unlike Singapore, there was no social safety net for the elderly in Hong Kong. You worked, or you didn't eat. No matter how old you were, you worked until you dropped.

Tay looked around and saw a Plexiglas rack on the wall behind the cash register with packs of cigarettes in it. He pointed, and the man looked over his shoulder to see where Tay was pointing.

"A pack of Marlboros," Tay said, hoping the clerk would understand what he wanted.

He did. The elderly man pulled the Marlboros from the rack and dropped the pack on the counter in front of Tay.

Tay had no idea how much the cigarettes cost, but he pulled a red $100 note from his pocket and handed it to the clerk. He rang up Tay's purchase on the register and returned several notes and a few coins along with a book of matches.

"Thank you," Tay said as he scooped up the cigarettes and pocketed his change.

"You. Are. Welcome."

The elderly man remained completely expressionless, but he enunciated each word as if he were an android with an animatronic voice. Maybe, Tay thought, he was.

Back out on the sidewalk, Tay split the cellophane with his thumbnail and tore open the Marlboros. He paused for a moment to enjoy the smell of fresh tobacco wafting from the open pack, and then he shook out a cigarette and lit it. The first pull was always the best, and he took time to stand quietly and savor it.

He shoved the rest of the pack and the matches into his pocket and marched off down Nathan Road toward the harbor.

TAY HAD GONE only a few hundred yards when he heard the sudden roar of a crowd from somewhere. It sounded as if there was a football stadium close by, but he doubted that could be. Not in a place as densely packed as Mongkok.

While he was still wondering about the source of the sound, it came again, and then a short distance ahead of him he saw people coming out of several side streets and walking right into Nathan Road. At first it was a trickle, but then it was a flood. They stood in the roadway and became a human barricade blocking traffic from moving in either direction.

It was a formidable barrier. There were at least several hundred people, maybe more. Mostly young, mostly wearing helmets which looked like construction hardhats, and many carrying open umbrellas, although it wasn't raining.

Tay walked toward the crowd, curious to see what was happening. Was it one of the democracy demonstrations? Or was it just a bunch of people, university students perhaps, out for a good time and being a little irresponsible about it?

All at once the crowd roared again, turned as if on a signal, and surged in his direction. Most of the people had masks wrapped across their faces which rendered them unidentifiable. This was no party crowd. It was a pro-democracy street mob, and a big one.

Tay knew he had no business in the middle of this. He tried to move toward the safety of the buildings lining Nathan Road, but the swirling bodies had him trapped there on the sidewalk. He was sucked deeper and deeper into the crowd.

When most of the mob had finally pushed past him, he saw why everyone had suddenly begun to move. Massed across Nathan Road, about fifty yards in front of him, was a skirmish line of Hong Kong riot police. They stood four or five deep and, like the riot police he had seen from the car coming in from the airport, they looked like invaders from another planet. Seeing them across the road from inside an air-conditioned Mercedes had been frightening enough. Seeing them in the street from fifty yards away was fucking terrifying.

They all wore sinister-looking black helmets with opaque visors closed over their faces and black head-to-toe body armor. Most carried big rectangular Plexiglas shields and long batons which they swung back and forth in front of them. About half the men carried rifles, although Tay couldn't tell if they were crowd-control rifles that only fired rubber bullets or real rifles that fired bullets which were most certainly not rubber.

He had just decided it wouldn't be wise for him to stick around long enough to find out when a dozen or more smoky vapor trails arched up from behind the skirmish line and soared over Tay's head. The crowd twitched as if it were a single living being and emitted a guttural roar. Some people snapped open their umbrellas and pointed the canopies toward the riot police like weapons, although Tay couldn't imagine what kind of weapons they thought they were.

More smoky vapor trails arched into the sky, and Tay

suddenly got it. The cops were firing tear gas into the crowd. The umbrellas were to fend off the falling gas canisters.

What is commonly called tear gas is most often a cyanocarbon known as CS gas. Different people describe its smell in quite distinct ways. Some say it's peppery and has a vinegary odor. Others say it has a warmth to it and a slight smell of gunpowder, like your father lighting fireworks in the backyard when you were a child.

Tay had never before smelled tear gas. Now that he had, he thought there was something about the scent which was lulling, even comforting. It had almost a benign quality to it, as if it wanted you to know it was there purely for your own good.

But it burned like a son of a bitch when it got into your eyes, and it nearly blinded you with your own tears. Which was exactly what it was supposed to do.

A dozen or more canisters now lay scattered on Nathan Road. They spewed out a dense white fog which rapidly enveloped everything. Next to Tay on the sidewalk was a skinny old man with stringy white hair and a lined, weathered face. All at once, he shrieked, and clutched at Tay's arm. Tay made a grab for him, but he slipped away and went down on the pavement.

Tay had hardly registered the old man's collapse when three people stepped out of the mob of demonstrators and surrounded the man to keep him from being trampled. One produced a bottle of water, tilted the man's head back very gently, and poured it into his eyes to wash away the gas.

That was when the gas took Tay, too.

He sputtered and coughed and wiped frantically at his eyes. He stumbled around blindly, searching for escape from both the advancing riot police and the spreading gas. Pushing through the crowd, he moved in what he hoped was the direction of his hotel.

If he could make it back there, he would be fine, wouldn't he? He had no part in this. He was just a visitor to Hong Kong.

A bystander. Someone who wasn't at all involved in whatever was happening.

But then he thought about the old man lying helplessly there on the sidewalk. In a city that was coming apart, just not being involved didn't seem to offer much protection.

TWELVE

TAY WAS LUCKY.

He somehow stumbled in the right direction and a few minutes later found himself in front of the Cordis Hotel. Still coughing, eyes still stinging, but he was there.

As he rode the elevator upstairs, he kept wiping his eyes with his handkerchief. It wasn't too bad, he told himself. He'd live.

When he got to his room, he went to the bathroom and washed his face and eyes with clean water, but he couldn't stop coughing. He had avoided the worst of the gas, but what he caught was bad enough. He couldn't imagine how being hit with the full brunt of it must feel.

Tay walked over to the windows and looked down toward Nathan Road, but everything appeared peaceful from up where he was. There was no sign of the helmeted demonstrators nor the otherworldly-looking riot police nor even the clouds of white gas that had enveloped him. Funny how that worked. From a five-star hotel, the pain and chaos of the streets was invisible.

His coughing was getting worse. He just couldn't seem to make it stop. He fell into a chair and held his handkerchief to his mouth.

Sometimes Tay felt like he was growing older at an alarming

rate. His body was letting him down in more ways than he could keep track of. His knees ached, sometimes his bowels refused to work, he had tinnitus in both ears, and he needed glasses, even if he refused to admit it.

Another fit of coughing wracked his body and left him feeling like someone had punched him in the stomach.

Tay stood up and stumbled to the bathroom where he drew a glass of water from the tap and drank it down. It didn't help. He started coughing again as soon as the water was gone. Tay filled another glass and tried to gargle some of the water thinking it might soothe his throat. When he tilted his head back he nearly choked, so he bent forward and spit into the sink. He took out his handkerchief again and wiped his mouth.

He folded the handkerchief over to return it to his pocket, but he noticed a stain on it so he dropped it next to the sink instead so he could put it in with his dirty clothes later.

When Tay started to fill yet another glass of water, something caught his eye and he glanced down into the sink. Reddish-brown dots peppered the white porcelain.

What the hell was that?

He looked more closely.

Was it blood?

Surely not.

He snatched up the handkerchief he had used to wipe his mouth and examined the stain he had seen on it. It looked like blood. He didn't want it to look like blood, but it did.

He tentatively lifted the handkerchief to his nose and blew gently. When he examined it, he saw red flecks of fresh blood.

Did tear gas make your mouth and nose bleed? Or worse, your lungs? He had never heard of that, but *something* was making his mouth and nose bleed. Since he had just taken in a load of tear gas, surely it had to be the culprit. What else made sense?

Tay took another drink of water, swirled it around in his mouth, and after a moment of hesitation spit again.

There were dots of blood all over the sink. Fewer than before, but they were there. He wanted to tell himself they weren't, but he couldn't. He was looking at them.

Was it really just the tear gas? If it was, then it would go away in a few hours or a day or two at most and that would be that, wouldn't it?

Or was there something inside him bleeding, something that had nothing to do with the gas?

My God, what was happening to him?

T AY HADN'T EXPECTED to sleep very well that night, and he didn't. He drifted in and out of sleep, tossing and turning, his mind fixed on the specks of blood he had seen in the bathroom sink.

The coughing subsided after a while and once or twice he considered getting up to blow his nose or rinse his mouth again so he could see if the blood was still there. He was certain he could taste it, but he was just as certain it might only be his imagination.

He decided not to get up. What good would it do? If there was blood in his mouth and nose, then there was. What was he going to do about it in the middle of the night? So he just lay there in bed and continued to toss and turn.

Instead of sleep coming, Tay felt dread and foreboding consuming him. Dread and foreboding were two of the things he did best.

There was something about the sudden appearance of the mysterious bits of blood in his mouth and nose that felt almost biblical to him, and the more he looked at it that way, the more it bothered him. He didn't believe in the Bible any more than he believed people received messages from the other side, but somehow the two seem to go hand in hand.

As he lay there in the dark trying and failing to sleep, he became more and more convinced the appearance of the blood in his mouth was an omen, but an omen of *what*? Wasn't there a story in the Bible about water turning to blood as a sign from God? He wasn't sure, and even if there were a story like that in the Bible, what really mattered was what it was supposed to be a sign *of*, he supposed, and he couldn't remember.

What nonsense, Tay told himself over and over, but the thought would not go away.

When he registered the first light of the morning seeping around the edges of the draperies in his room, he felt a palpable sense of relief. He'd had no visions during the night. Nothing had burst into flames. He had not begun speaking in tongues. The blood had just been blood. It wasn't a message from the other side.

Tay felt like a complete idiot being relieved something hadn't happened that never could have happened in the first place, but there it was.

WHEN TAY GOT out of bed, he went straight to the bathroom and stood in front of the sink for a long time. After screwing up his courage, he filled a glass with water from the tap, swished it around in his mouth, and spit it in the sink.

Nothing.

No blood at all.

He pulled a tissue from the box next to the sink and gently blew his nose.

Nothing.

His courage rising, he gave his nose a nice big honk.

No blood.

Thank God, he thought.

But then a second thought followed almost immediately. Maybe he only imagined the blood he thought he had seen last night.

No, he hadn't imagined anything. He had seen what he had seen, and he knew what he had seen. He grabbed up the handkerchief he had abandoned the night before and looked for the bloodstain. There it was! It had not been his imagination!

Tay had to smile at himself. How could he be so happy now to see the same thing he had been so unhappy about seeing the night before? It was so absurd he almost laughed out loud.

The blood came from something, Tay knew. Blood didn't just appear in your mouth and nose without a reason, and usually the reason was something not too good. Maybe it had only been a temporary effect from the tear gas he had breathed. Or maybe the tear gas had triggered something in him that was now lying fallow, waiting to reappear when he least expected it and scare the crap out of him again.

Or maybe it really *had* been a sign from the other side sent by his mother.

That was a stupid thought in the middle of the night, Tay berated himself, *and it's an even stupider thought this morning.*

He looked at his watch.

Seven-fifteen.

Claire was picking him up at eight.

He needed to stop obsessing over a few drops of blood and get moving.

THIRTEEN

TUESDAY. DAY ONE. Searching for Emma Lau.

Claire was waiting in the lobby when Tay stepped out of the elevator. She pointed to a dark blue car of uncertain make parked just outside the hotel's entrance.

"That's us," she said.

When they got outside, the driver jumped out and opened the rear passenger door for Claire. He was a middle-aged man of average height and weight and ordinary appearance, wearing a plain white short-sleeved shirt and black trousers. If he had looked any more unremarkable, he would have disappeared altogether.

"What kind of car is this?" Tay asked him.

"It's a Tesla, sir."

"What in the world is a Tesla?"

"Sometimes, Sam, I don't know if you're for real or not," Claire said. "Just get in the damn car."

Tay walked around the car and got in the other side. The driver pulled away and headed in what Tay thought was the general direction of the harbor.

A Tesla? What in God's name was a Tesla?

"I asked him to take us to some place for coffee first," Claire said. "He said there's a Starbucks pretty close by."

Tay was not fond of Starbucks. The place was far too American for him and he thought the coffee tasted like warmed-up dishwater. The way he felt this morning, however, he would settle for anyplace. He would take a cup of coffee from anywhere. He would take a cup of coffee if he had to lick it off the sidewalk.

"I love Starbucks," Tay said, and leaned back against the soft leather seat of the Tesla.

TEN MINUTES LATER they were sitting at a table in a Starbucks which looked exactly like every table in every other Starbucks Tay had ever been in. Tay had a large cup of black coffee the girl behind the counter had told him was Ethiopian Fair Trade coffee. He had no idea what that was supposed to mean, but he had to admit the coffee tasted better than he had expected.

Claire had ordered something with a name so long he thought he might have to extend his entry visa just to give her enough time to complete her order. His personal view of coffee shops was that they should only offer two things: coffee, and not coffee. He saw no reason anybody anywhere should sell something with a name like skinny vanilla soy milk cappuccino no foam, whipped cream, chocolate drizzle.

There was a bakery case next to the cash register and Tay got two chocolate doughnuts to go with his coffee. Claire gave him a look, but she said nothing. She just sipped her caffeinated milkshake and thumbed through her phone in silence.

It wasn't until Tay had finished his doughnuts and wiped his mouth with a paper napkin that Claire spoke up.

"I hope you won't mind me saying this, but you don't look great this morning."

Like he needed to hear that, Tay thought.

His mind shuffled through several possible responses to Claire's comment, all of them doubtless extremely witty, but he decided to keep it simple.

"I didn't sleep very well."

"Any particular reason?"

"Probably jet lag."

"Sam, you don't get jet-lagged flying from Singapore to Hong Kong. The flight is only four hours and there's no time change. "

Tay shrugged. "Some people are more susceptible than others."

For a moment, Tay considered telling Claire about the street battle he had stumbled into last night and the dose of tear gas he had gotten, but he decided not to. He felt like he had been a bit of an idiot for getting caught up in it. He should have realized what was coming and gotten out of the way, and he was reluctant to confess his foolishness to Claire.

But not even for a single moment did Tay consider telling Claire about the blood he had coughed up after he made his way back to the hotel. He had no idea what it meant, if it meant anything at all, so he didn't see any point in talking about it. He would just sound to her like an aging hypochondriac. Which maybe he was, but he certainly didn't want to sound like it.

So Tay just did what he always did when a conversation threatened to creep into uncharted territory. He changed the subject.

"Did Doris Lau send you those photographs of Emma she promised us?"

Claire nodded and pulled out the iPhone August had given her, the one she had used to call Mrs. Lau last night. She held it in both hands and punched away at it with her thumbs.

"I've sent them to you," she said when she had stopped punching. "There are two of them. Just swipe back and forth."

Tay thought he understood what she meant. Barely.

In the picture he saw on his screen a slim and pleasant if not memorable-looking young woman smiled up at him. She was standing on the balcony of what appeared to be someone's apartment. It had a beautiful and doubtless very expensive view over the sea, and Emma was half turned toward the camera as if someone had just called out her name and then taken her photograph when she responded.

She was wearing a white cotton jacket over a green blouse with a high collar. The jacket didn't look stylish to Tay, more like the jacket his dentist had worn the last time he had his teeth cleaned. Perhaps it had something to do with the medical school she attended.

Tay moved a forefinger across the screen and, to his amazement, the other photograph appeared just as Claire had said it would. Emma looked younger in this one and her hair was shorter so perhaps it was an older photograph. She was seated in a high-backed wooden chair that looked like a Chinese antique with an Apple laptop in her hands. She was barefooted and wearing jeans with what appeared to be a man's long-sleeved white dress shirt, the cuffs rolled up over her elbows and the tail hanging out over her jeans.

"This is all she sent you?"

Claire nodded.

"And we don't know who took them or where?"

"We know now what she looks like, but that's it."

Emma was attractive enough, Tay thought, but not striking. She looked like a hundred girls you passed in the street every day, although something about the photos suggested to him she had a certain spirit, maybe even a bit of attitude about her.

Then again, maybe it was just the money he was seeing. Emma came from parents who were both well-off and prominent. When you were young and had everything, it showed.

.   .   .

A FTER THEY LEFT Starbucks, the driver chose a route across West Kowloon and through the Western Harbor Tunnel to Hong Kong Island. He threaded his way through the streets of Sheung Wan, picked up Pokfulam Road, and headed south. They were just passing the MTR station for Hong Kong University when Claire poked at her telephone for a few seconds and then held it out to Tay.

When he took it and looked at the screen, all he saw were three slick-looking high-rise buildings he didn't recognize.

"What am I looking at?" he asked.

"That's where Emma lives. Her building is the one closest to the ocean."

Tay examined the picture and found the building to which Claire was referring. "It looks expensive."

"It is. I checked the website of one of the big real estate agencies and found several two-bedroom apartments for sale in the building around seven to eight million."

"Well, eight million Hong Kong dollars is only..."

Tay paused to do the calculation in his head.

"No," Claire said, "that's US dollars."

"Good Lord." Tay stared at her, open-mouthed. "Seriously?"

Claire nodded.

"Eight million US dollars for a two-bedroom apartment?"

Claire nodded again.

"Must be nice to have rich parents," Tay said.

Claire just looked at Tay and raised her eyebrows.

Tay conjured up a shrug that would have made an Italian weep with joy.

"Okay," he said, "don't make a big deal out of it."

The only child of an American-born Chinese man and a Singaporean-born Chinese woman, Tay had lived the whole of his life in Singapore. His father had been an accountant, a careful man who insisted his family live modestly, but when he died Tay and his mother were shocked to discover they had inherited a small fortune in real estate, one which would leave them both quite well off for the rest of their lives.

Within a year, Tay's mother had moved to New York and acquired what she described as a Park Avenue duplex, although Tay noticed her address was actually on East 93rd Street. When she married a widowed American investment banker who was a senior partner at some investment firm, the name of which Tay could never quite remember, Tay was still at university and he didn't go to New York for the wedding.

He couldn't recall for certain being invited to New York for the wedding, but he supposed it was beside the point. He told himself he would have stayed in Singapore even if they had invited him.

Tay enjoyed the money his father had left as much as his mother had, but in his own way. He wasn't really a spender. He didn't own a car, he didn't travel, and he didn't buy many things. Except for books. He bought a lot of books, but they didn't cost much.

He had used part of the money to redecorate the traditional row house in the Emerald Hill district of Singapore he had also inherited from his father. The rest he had left in the bank.

He could never have afforded a house like his on his cop's salary and he did love that house, so he was grateful to his father for making it possible for him to live in it. He had never thought of himself as a rich kid, but maybe he was.

Whether he wanted to look at it that way or not, he supposed a rich kid was exactly what he was.

CLAIRE HADN'T INTENDED to embarrass Tay, but when she realized she had it became her turn to change the subject.

"How do you want to handle this?" she asked.

"Handle what?"

"Interviewing Sarah McFarland. Do you want me to take the lead again?"

Tay chewed on the inside of his cheek and thought about it. After a moment he said, "That's probably a good idea."

"And do you think it's a good idea because you realize now I'm as good an interviewer as you are, or is it still mostly because I'm a woman?"

Tay just looked at Claire and said nothing.

"Yeah," she nodded. "That's what I thought."

Tay moved on as quickly as he could.

"What do we know about Sarah McFarland?" he asked.

"We know she's a friend of Emma's. Friendly enough to have a key to Emma's apartment. We know she was with Emma in Mongkok when she disappeared. And we know she's the one who called Doris Lau to tell her Emma was missing."

"But what do we know about *her?*"

"Mrs. Lau said she worked for the investment banking division of Citibank. She also said she was an Australian who had gone to school in California. Other than that, we don't know a lot. Not anything, really. She's meeting us in the lobby of Emma's building. I guess we can find out whatever we need to find out then."

"I don't like going into an interview blind," Tay said. "We should have done at least some basic research on this woman in advance."

"And by *we*, you mean *me?*"

Tay said nothing, which answered Claire's question.

"Hey, you're the hotshot detective here," she said. "Give me a hint now and then what I'm supposed to do. I don't pry information out of people for a living like you do."

"Yes, you're more likely just to shoot them."

Claire grinned and gave Tay a thumbs up.

Then she said, "Let me see what I can find out," and went back to poking at her phone with her fingers.

Tay watched and wondered as Claire's thumbs flew over the

keyboard. On those rare occasions when he typed anything into his phone, he poked it out one letter at a time with his forefinger. He didn't understand how people typed so rapidly with their thumbs. He had tried once and the text which appeared was so garbled even he didn't know what it said. He thought this thumbs thing had to be generational somehow, although for the life of him he couldn't see how that could be so.

After a few minutes, Claire looked up with a rueful expression.

"I found her name on the website for Citibank Hong Kong, but she's listed as an analyst and only the higher-ranking people have biographical information. Other than that, I can't find her anywhere. Sarah McFarland is too common a name. There are hundreds of people on Facebook with the same name and I'd have to go through all of them to find out if one of them is her."

Claire bent down and looked through the windshield past the driver.

"We'll be at her building in five or ten minutes. I'll figure it out."

Tay just nodded and said nothing.

FOURTEEN

THE CAR STOPPED in the circular drive at the entrance to Emma Lau's apartment building. The driver got out and opened the rear passenger door for Claire. Tay opened his own door and walked around to join her.

"When Sarah lets us into Emma's apartment," Claire asked, "what are we looking for?"

"I don't know exactly. Anything that might identify friends of hers or suggest where she might have gone. Photographs? Letters? Maybe she has an address book."

"Sam, where have you been?" Claire laughed. "Nobody has written letters or had an address book or kept a stack of photos around in at least ten years."

Tay said nothing. He wrote letters, and he had an address book. He even had a few photographs somewhere. But from the amusement he heard in Claire's voice when she informed him nobody did any of those things anymore, he wasn't about to volunteer that now.

"You've got to catch up with the times, Sam."

She held up her phone and wiggled it at Tay.

"This is how people keep an address book, send letters, and save photographs these days."

Tay figured he was already more than adequately caught up with the times to suit his personal taste. A bit too much, maybe, to be entirely truthful about it. But he said nothing.

"She must have had her telephone with her in Mongkok," Claire went on. "I can't imagine anyone her age ever leaves home without their phone."

Sometimes Tay left home without his telephone. He considered it a minor but most enjoyable act of rebellion against modern life. Of course, he wasn't Sarah's age either. Most people might not believe it, but he did see the difference.

"If we're lucky," Claire continued, "maybe there'll be a laptop or tablet which will have the same cloud access as her telephone. Then the issue will be getting into it since I'm sure it will be protected by some type of security. At least a password, but maybe biometric. Most people use biometric security these days."

Cloud access? Biometric security?

Tay could see he was being towed slowly into deep water. He had no intention of admitting to Claire that he could barely swim, so he just nodded, walked toward the building's entrance, and said nothing else.

T HE LOBBY HAD an opulent feel to it, but Tay thought it was all a bit much.

An enormous glittering chandelier, a gilt-framed oil painting of uncertain provenance, a massive green and white Chinese rug, and two groupings of couches and chairs covered in gold and blue silk. It looked like a fake French Empire look some decorator had copied from *People* magazine.

There was also a polished mahogany counter with a bronze sign that said Concierge. Behind it lurked a rotund man in a white jacket and black bowtie. The man stepped around the counter and said something to Tay in either Mandarin or

Cantonese. Tay could never tell the difference, but it didn't matter since he spoke neither.

"I don't understand Chinese," Tay muttered.

"Ah," the white-jacketed man said, "I thought you were—"

"You thought I *was* Chinese?"

The man flicked his eyes at Claire.

"Do I *look* Chinese?" Tay snapped.

"Don't be too hard on him, Sam. I'm sure he didn't mean anything insulting."

No, of course he didn't, Tay thought.

Why was he in such a testy mood? Because he had been spitting up blood last night and was so worried about it he hadn't slept. Yeah, that might be the reason.

"We're meeting a woman named Sarah McFarland," Claire told the concierge, shouldering Tay out of the conversation before he leaped forward and tried to strangle the poor man.

The concierge quickly inclined his head toward one of the couches across the lobby, then scurried back behind his mahogany counter, no doubt glad of its protection.

TAY AND CLAIRE looked in the direction the concierge indicated and saw a young woman who appeared to be in her mid-twenties. She was wearing a black t-shirt and jeans, and she was sitting on one of the gold and blue silk couches looking back at them over her shoulder. As they walked toward her, Tay let Claire move ahead of him so she would reach the girl first.

Sarah McFarland was not particularly attractive, Tay noticed. That surprised him, although he couldn't think of any reason it should. She was slightly thick-bodied and had the sort of long thin face he had heard someone once describe as horsey.

Her hair was blonde, although of a shade Tay was certain appeared nowhere in nature, and she had it pulled back and tied up in a long, tight ponytail. That had the unfortunate effect of focusing attention on her face and putting the final touches to the whole horse metaphor.

"Are you the people Mrs. Lau sent?" she asked when Claire drew to within a few feet of her.

Her Australian accent was as broad as it was deep.

"Yes, we are," Claire answered. "I'm—"

"You're not the police?" the girl interrupted.

"No."

Sarah McFarland gave Claire a hard look. She flicked her eyes at Tay and then shifted them back to Claire.

"Are you sure? Do you swear?"

"Why does it matter?" Claire asked.

When the girl said nothing, Claire let the silence build for a moment, but when the girl didn't take the bait she moved on.

"We're not the police, Sarah."

"Then who are you?"

"We're the people Mrs. Lau asked to help locate Emma. My name is Claire, and this is Sam."

"Are you spies?"

Claire allowed herself a half smile. "Does Hong Kong have spies?"

"I'm sure it does," Sarah said. "Well, I don't know. But I know Mrs. Lau claiming she hired private detectives is bullshit. She had to be sending somebody official. Why would the Chief Executive of Hong Kong trust two nobodies with her daughter disappearing?"

Tay wasn't enamored with the girl's characterization of them, but he had to admit she had asked a good question. It was the same question he had asked himself several times, and he still didn't know what the answer was.

"We are not members of any law enforcement organization, Sarah. And we are not spies. But we are people Mrs. Lau knows and trusts."

Sarah McFarland shifted her eyes back and forth again between Claire and Tay. She looked like she was trying to decide whether or not to believe them. The assurances Claire was offering Sarah might not be strictly speaking true, Tay told himself, but they weren't strictly speaking untrue either. He guessed they were close enough for government work.

"Mrs. Lau became concerned about Emma after you telephoned her," Claire prodded, "and she asked us to find her. She expects you to give us whatever help you can. Now can we get on with this?"

Tay thought Claire had handled that well. A little steel, a little guilt. It appeared to relax the girl, although Tay still wondered why she seemed so wary of them.

Sarah McFarland shifted her eyes back and forth between them one more time for good measure and then seemed to make up her mind.

"Okay, sure," she said. "I brought the key to her apartment."

She took an ordinary-looking brass key from her pocket and held it up as if Claire and Tay might not be familiar with the concept of a key.

"It's apartment 4110. Do you want to go up now?"

"Please," Claire said.

"HOW LONG HAVE you known Emma?" Tay asked as the elevator purred its way up to the forty-first floor.

The girl looked back over her shoulder and stared at Tay for a moment. She looked at him the way one might regard a large dog that had just asked for directions to a tree.

"A long time," she said after a moment. "Maybe two years."

From Tay's perspective, two years was not a long time, but he supposed for someone in their twenties two years must seem a virtual eternity.

"Are you in school with her?" Claire took over.

"Emma's in medical school. I'm not that smart. I work at Citibank. In the investment banking office."

"I would have thought you had to be reasonably smart to work in investment banking at Citibank."

"Not really," the girl shrugged. "My father got me the job. He's a big client."

Ah-ha, Tay thought to himself, *another rich girl.*

But he kept quiet since Claire was doing the talking now as they had planned. And anyway, he wasn't about to bring the whole subject of family money up again.

"How did you meet Emma?"

"It was at a party. Or maybe a bar." The girl shrugged more elaborately than seemed necessary. "I don't remember for sure."

"Would you say you know her well?"

"I guess so. We go shopping together sometimes or go out at night when neither of us has a date."

"Does Emma date a lot?"

"No, not really." Sarah McFarland paused and then looked back over her shoulder again and stared straight into Tay's eyes. "But I do."

Just then the elevator slowed to a stop. The doors opened and rescued Tay from having to decide what to say to that.

Claire wanted to look at Tay to check out his reaction, but she didn't dare.

FIFTEEN

INSIDE THE APARTMENT, Claire waved Sarah McFarland to a thickly cushioned sofa covered in a blue and yellow striped cotton slipcover. In front of the sofa was a teardrop-shaped coffee table of glass and polished oak that looked as if it belonged in a museum of furniture from the fifties.

The apartment was expensively furnished, Tay saw, but it seemed somehow impersonal to him, like the best suite at a Four Seasons Hotel. He saw no pictures or books or other personal items which might tell them something about Emma. What he saw was money, and not much else.

The centerpiece of the apartment was its view. One side of the living room was all floor-to-ceiling glass and from there on the forty-first floor the apartment had an unobstructed, panoramic view of the South China Sea. Off on the far horizon, shimmering in the haze, Tay could see what he thought might be Lantau Island where Hong Kong International Airport was, although he wondered if that was what he was actually seeing. As if in answer to his unspoken question, an airliner suddenly rose above the wooded hills in the center of the island, banked to the left, and headed south in the direction of Singapore.

Tay stood watching until the airplane disappeared from sight. Maybe, he thought, he would have been smart to be on it.

Behind him, Claire was beginning a conversation with Sarah McFarland and Tay smiled to himself as he listened. Claire had good instincts. Either that, or she was far more experienced at this stuff than she admitted. She began working her way through innocuous preliminaries: where Sarah lived, her telephone number, where her office was, what hours she worked, where she had gone to school, and where her parents were. Casual questions. Circling.

Then Claire began edging closer to the center of things.

"Please start at the beginning, Sarah," Claire said behind him, "and tell us everything you can remember about the last time you saw Emma."

At that, Tay turned away from the windows. He saw Claire had seated herself in a brown leather chair facing the couch. There was a matching chair next to it, so Tay walked over and sat down.

"I already told Mrs. Lau. Emma was just there one minute and gone the next. I don't know what else to say."

"Let's start with the basics then, shall we? What day was it?"

"What *day* was it? You must already know what day it was. It was last Saturday. Three days ago."

"This was in Mongkok Station?"

"Yes. We got off the train and I stopped next to a pillar to look at my phone. It buzzed just as we were getting off the train and I saw I had a text. I typed a reply, just a few words, and sent it."

"Do you remember what time this was?"

"Twelve o'clock?"

"Exactly twelve o'clock?"

"Maybe a few minutes after. I'm not sure."

"What happened then?

"When I looked up from my phone, I couldn't find Emma."

"What did you do?"

"Well, I looked for her, didn't I?"

"I don't know. Did you?"

"Of course I did. Two trains must have come in at the same time because the station was very crowded, but I pushed my way to the exit we usually used and I didn't see her."

The exit we usually used. Tay made a mental note of that. *The exit they usually used for what?*

"I went up the steps to the sidewalk," the girl finished, "and when I got outside I looked all around, but she wasn't there either."

"Is it possible she never got off the train?"

"No, she did. She got off right in front of me. And that was when I stopped behind the pillar, looked down at my phone, and sent a text. It couldn't have taken more than a few seconds. Maybe ten? But when I looked up again, I didn't see her."

"Do you remember what she was wearing?"

Sarah thought for a moment. Tay got the impression she was genuinely trying to recall, not simply pretending.

"We were both in jeans and t-shirts. Well, I mean, you don't wear a ball gown to Mongkok, do you? My shirt was white, but I don't remember what color Emma's was."

"Why were you—"

"Wait," Sarah interrupted. "I remember Emma was wearing a short jacket over her t-shirt. It was red with big shoulders. I thought it was too much for Mongkok, to be honest, but that's what she was wearing."

"Why were you at Mongkok Station in the first place?"

"It's the MTR station closest to Mr. Wong's."

Claire shot Tay a look, but his eyes were on Sarah McFarland so he didn't notice.

"Mr. Wong's?"

She nodded.

"Who is Mr. Wong?" Claire asked.

The girl's face wrinkled in confusion. "How should I know?"

"You just said you were going to Mr. Wong's so I assume —"

"Oh, I see. No, it's not a person. It's a restaurant. It's called Mr. Wong's. I don't know if there is a Mr. Wong or not. It's just the name of a restaurant."

"Had you been there before?"

"A bunch of times. We liked it a lot. We went there sometimes on weekends for lunch, then we would walk around the street markets in Mongkok."

"Did anyone else ever go with you?"

"No, no one else. Just the two of us."

"Did Emma know anyone in Mongkok? Someone she might have gone to see after you got off the train?"

"Why would she have done that? We were going to lunch. She wouldn't have gone somewhere else without telling me."

TAY WAS THINKING about how to push Sarah a little without coming off as too aggressive when a chime sounded somewhere in the apartment.

Tay and Claire looked at each other, and then they both looked at Sarah.

"The doorbell?" Tay asked her.

Sarah nodded.

"Are you expecting someone?"

She shook her head. "Do you want me to answer it?"

Another look passed between Tay and Claire, and then Tay said, "Sure, go ahead."

When Sarah opened the door, they all saw the man standing there with a smile on his face which looked a little tentative. He was in his late thirties, of average height and weight with his hair cut stylishly long, and he wore round tortoiseshell eyeglasses. He was dressed in an expensive-looking gray suit with a white shirt and a nondescript dark tie.

"Uh..." He hesitated. "I was looking for Emma. Is she home?"

"Who are you?"

"Ah..." The man hesitated again and then appeared to notice Tay and Claire over Sarah's shoulder for the first time. He stared at them for a moment and then said, "I could ask you the same thing."

"I asked you first."

The man chuckled at that and his face broke out in a smile.

"Fair enough," he said. "My name is Eddie Yu. I live—"

He turned his shoulders and pointed off down the hallway with one hand.

"—just a few doors down there."

Sarah examined him carefully. "I remember your name. Emma mentioned it to me."

That obviously pleased the man and his smile got bigger.

"Wow," he said, "that's nice to hear. I hope she told you something good about me."

"Not really. She said you kept asking her out, but you're not her type. She thought you were too old for her."

The man stopped smiling.

"Old? I'm just thirty-five." He hesitated. "Okay, thirty-six."

Sarah shrugged, but said nothing.

The man just stood there. He seemed stumped for anything to say after that. Tay couldn't blame him.

"Look," Sarah said, breaking the silence, "Emma's away for a while."

"Are you staying here while she's gone?"

"No, I'm not a house sitter. I'm a friend of Emma's."

The man shifted his gaze past Sarah to Tay and Claire.

"Emma's mother wants to do some redecorating while she's away," Sarah continued when she saw him looking past her, "and she asked me to bring the decorators in and show them around."

Sarah pointed back at Tay and Claire.

"Emma's away for that long?"

"I really don't know. I'm just doing her mother a favor. Now, if there's nothing else, I'll tell Emma you dropped by."

Sarah didn't bother waiting for Eddie Yu to tell her if there was anything else. She just closed the door.

"Creep," she muttered as she walked back across the room and resumed her seat on the blue and yellow striped couch.

"D ECORATORS?" TAY ASKED.

Sarah shrugged. "I didn't think the truth was any of his business and it was the first thing I thought of. Why? Are you offended?"

"Why would I be offended?"

"Maybe you thought I was saying you looked gay."

Claire snickered.

"But you don't," Sarah went on. "I don't think you look gay at all."

Tay was left speechless by the sudden bizarre turn in the conversation and was relieved when Claire spoke up.

"Maybe we should get back to the main subject here, Sarah."

Sarah shrugged.

"Where do you think Emma went?" Claire asked her.

"I don't know."

"You don't have *any* idea?"

Sarah just shook her head and said nothing else.

"Could she have gone off to meet someone she knew?"

"I suppose so, but she wouldn't have just left without telling me where she was going, would she?"

"Maybe she couldn't find you in the crowds in the station."

"She would have called me. MoMo wouldn't have just walked off. She's not like that."

"MoMo?"

Sarah McFarland looked embarrassed and glanced away.

109

"It's just a silly nickname I gave her. The word for *silent* in Mandarin sounds like that. I thought it suited her."

"You think of Emma as silent."

"She's just kind of quiet, you know. Sometimes she seems shy, but she really isn't. She just doesn't talk a lot."

"But you two talk enough she told you about this neighbor she thought was too old for her."

"We didn't talk about him," Sarah shrugged. "It's just something she mentioned one day."

Tay thought Claire was handling the interview just fine, but he was getting antsy. He was unaccustomed to being a spectator in interviews and he couldn't resist jumping in.

"What about boyfriends?" he asked Sarah. "Are you saying this guy from down the hall wasn't a boyfriend?"

"God, no. She never even went out with him."

"Is there anybody you know of? Someone she might have gone away with?"

Sarah shook her head.

"Or maybe somebody who might have an idea where she is even if she didn't go away with them?"

"No, nobody. MoMo keeps to herself. Look, she's a really serious girl. Medical school is important to her and she's a good student. We go out sometimes together, but otherwise she mostly studies."

Tay wasn't sure he believed that. He would have liked to think somewhere there might be a young woman in her mid-twenties you could describe that way, but he had never met one. Never even heard rumors of one.

"Then she lives here alone?" Tay continued.

Sarah nodded.

"Do you know any of her other friends?"

"Not really."

"Maybe some people she goes to school with?"

Sarah shook her head.

"She has to know *somebody* other than you."

"I'm sure she does. I just don't know who it is."

"How about social media?" Claire cut in. "Is she active on Facebook or Instagram or any of the other sites?"

"I don't think so. I've never heard her mention it."

"And I've never heard of a twenty-something girl who wasn't on social media."

Sarah shrugged. "It's not really her, you know? I guess she just doesn't like people very much."

Tay raised an eyebrow. He was starting to like Emma more and more every minute.

"Where do you think Emma is?" Claire asked.

"I don't know. I've thought about it ever since I called Mrs. Lau. I just don't know."

Sarah McFarland looked back and forth between Claire and Tay.

"Do you think she's okay?"

"We have no reason to think she isn't," Claire said.

"But you have no idea where she is so you can't be sure, can you?"

Both Claire and Tay remained silent.

"That's what I thought," the girl said.

They all fell silent and Tay let the stillness stretch out. He knew silence sometimes worked to get someone talking. Most people were uncomfortable with silence and couldn't resist the compulsion to fill it. He had often been quite successful using the technique of remaining silent until whoever he was interviewing became so uneasy they started talking and telling him things they hadn't planned to tell him.

But it didn't work on Sarah McFarland. She just sat there and looked at them and said nothing at all.

SIXTEEN

"LET'S LOOK AROUND the apartment," Tay said to Claire. "Maybe something will jump out at us."

Sarah McFarland said nothing. She just took out her telephone, settled back into a corner of the couch, and begin thumbing through it.

Tay wondered if she was less concerned about her friend MoMo than she had led them to believe, or if it was just reflex for a twenty-something girl to look through her phone when she had nothing better to do.

"Why don't you start in here," he said to Claire, "and I'll start at the back of the apartment and work my way up to you."

"Tell me again what we're looking for?"

"No idea. But Emma's gone somewhere, and walking up and down the streets shouting her name doesn't strike me as a good plan for finding her. We need people and places with which she had some connection. We need somewhere to start looking."

Tay walked down the hallway away from the living room. Framed posters for concerts by bands he had never heard of lined both sides. The posters looked generic to him, like things acquired by a decorator trying to make the apartment look young and hip.

Did people still say *hip* anymore? Probably not. Which Tay figured showed exactly how hip *he* was.

At the end of the hall there were two doorways, one on each side. The door on the right stood open and Tay poked his head in and looked around.

The master bedroom was furnished in the same expensive good taste as the living room. And, like the living room, it lacked any personal touch at all. Decorator art hung from the walls, decorator knick-knacks sat on the tables, and decorator furniture filled the room. There wasn't even a book on the nightstand. Maybe twenty-somethings didn't read books anymore these days, at least not ones made out of dead trees.

Tay opened several drawers in a polished teak chest opposite the bed, but none of them contained anything other than clothing. He had expected to find some jewelry, no doubt pretty high-end stuff from what he could see in the rest of the apartment, but he found none. Not even inexpensive stuff. That struck him as odd, and he made a mental note of it.

He walked over to the closet and looked inside. It was very large, much larger than he expected. The clothing struck him at a glance as what you would expect a girl in her mid-twenties who spent a good deal of money to have. Flicking through the hangers, he saw nothing that grabbed his attention. He looked behind the hanging clothes for any evidence of a safe. He checked the shelves above the clothes, too. He found nothing of interest in either place.

Back out in the hallway, Tay opened the door across from the master bedroom and his hopes of achieving something from the search lifted. The room was a second bedroom Emma had converted into an office and study room. A big wooden table in the center was stacked end to end with books and papers. What pleased Tay most was the silver laptop he saw in the middle of it.

When he took a closer look, he recognized it as a high-end Apple. He opened the lid and pushed at the touchpad to wake it up. A box appeared in the middle of the screen requesting either a fingerprint or a password. Of course it did.

Tay poked through the books and papers on the desk, but they all appeared to be medical school stuff. Several textbooks, what looked like lecture notes, and some drawings and diagrams which meant nothing to Tay. He discovered an Apple iPad used as a paperweight for one stack of lecture notes, but he had no more luck with it than he had with the laptop since it was password-protected, too. At one end of the table was a compact Brother laser printer. He looked in the paper tray. It was empty.

Tay opened the top drawer of the two-drawer horizontal file cabinet behind the desk and flicked through the files without seeing anything of interest. It looked to him as if Emma had filed away all her course notes from every year of medical school, but there was no sign of anything personal there. No letters, no diaries, no photographs.

Tay closed the top drawer and opened the bottom one. It contained nothing except supplies. Two packages of printer paper, some pads, boxes of pens, and a plastic box filled with paperclips, rubber bands, and a stapler.

He checked the closet, but nothing jumped out at him so he picked up the laptop and the iPad and closed the door behind him.

On his way back up the hall, he put his head into the bathroom but saw nothing of interest there either. There was makeup of various sorts sitting next to the sink. He didn't bother going through it since he wouldn't have known what he was looking at and he didn't see what difference it could possibly make, whatever it was. He took a quick glance into the medicine chest over the sink, but he found only generic stuff. No prescription drugs.

Tay returned to the living room just as Claire was emerging

from the kitchen. He looked at her, raising his eyebrows in the obvious question.

"Nothing," she said.

"Anybody could have lived here," Tay said. "Anybody, or nobody."

"At least it looks like you got something," Claire said, pointing to the laptop and iPad Tay had under his arm.

"I don't know how much good they'll do us. They're both password-protected."

"You're joking, right? I'll get them to John. He'll know somebody who can have them open in a jiffy."

Tay kept forgetting. August was a man who seemed able to conjure up whatever you needed whenever you needed it. Whether you wanted somebody to crack the security for a laptop or a private jet to take you to Bora Bora, August was your man. Tay was pretty certain if he needed a tactical nuclear strike on something within the next half hour, August could organize it without breaking a sweat.

Tay stood looking around the living room wondering if he was missing anything. It all seemed so bland and soulless. He couldn't believe any mid-twenties girl lived like this. Emma was the daughter of the Vice President of the United States and the Chief Executive of Hong Kong, and yet she seemed to be totally without a personality. It didn't make sense to Tay.

But he didn't say any of that. All he said was, "All right, Sarah, I guess we're ready to go."

Sarah McFarland looked up from her telephone as if emerging from a trance.

"Did you find anything that might help?"

"I found a laptop and an iPad, but they're both password-protected. You wouldn't know what her password is, would you?"

Sarah just shook her head.

"I didn't think we could be that lucky. We'll take them to

someone who knows about stuff like this and see if he can get us access to them, but we'll bring them back when we're done."

"Yeah, sure. Mrs. Lau paid for them anyway so I guess she has a right to ask somebody to look at them."

Tay would have guessed most young women would be incensed at their parents having someone paw around in their electronic devices to see who they had been in touch with, but what did he know about such things? Maybe Sarah was more worried about Emma than she was letting on.

I N THE ELEVATOR going back down to the lobby, Tay said, "Thank you for meeting us and bringing the key. I hope we didn't cause you any problems at Citibank by making you late to work."

The girl giggled. "I took the day off. My boss doesn't care. He can't fire me anyway so he lets me do what I want."

It must be nice to be spoiled and rich when you're twenty-five, Tay thought, but he wasn't absolutely sure that was true.

"Is there anything else at all you can tell us which might help us find Emma?" Tay asked.

"No, nothing." Sarah McFarland paused a moment, seemed to think, and then added, "I just hope her disappearance isn't connected to those other girls."

"What other girls?"

The elevator came to a stop, the doors opened, and they all stepped out into the lobby.

"What other girls?" Tay repeated.

She looked back and forth from Tay to Claire.

"You don't know about the others?"

They both shook their heads.

"Mrs. Lau must know," she said. "About a year ago the daughter of this major property guy disappeared. You never heard about that?"

"No," Tay said.

"It was a big scandal because the rich property guy never told the police his daughter had been kidnapped or he was paying a ransom so no one knew anything about it until some newspaper started looking into it. Even then, he denied it had ever happened. It was weird."

"You said *girls*. Plural. Are you saying there were other cases, too?"

"There were stories, you know, but I don't know if any of them were true."

"What stories?"

"About other girls who had disappeared. Two, I think? Both daughters from really rich families. They were just... well, gone."

"Gone?"

"Yeah. They disappeared and no one ever saw either of them again."

"Were there ransom demands?"

"I don't know, but everybody said it was the triads behind it so there must have been. They always say the triads are behind stuff like that."

"None of those girls were ever found? You're sure?"

"Look, maybe the stories weren't even true. They were just things I heard people saying. Ask Mrs. Lau. I'm sure she knows. She'd have to, wouldn't she?"

Tay nodded.

"But there is one thing that is kind of weird," she went on. "I'm pretty sure I remember hearing all three girls disappeared from the same place."

"The same place?" Tay asked. "Where?"

Even before Sarah answered, Tay knew with absolute certainty what she was about to say.

And sure enough, right then she said it.

"Mongkok," Sarah McFarland said. "That was the last place any of them was ever seen. Mongkok."

SEVENTEEN

"THAT WAS LIKE trying to eat a taco with a spoon," Tay said as the car pulled away.

Claire laughed. "You didn't like Doris Lau and I take it you didn't like Sarah McFarland either."

"Liking her or not liking her has nothing to do with it."

"So, what do you think?"

"She's lying to us. She's hiding something."

"You thought Doris Lau was hiding something, too."

"She was."

"Do you always think people are hiding something from you?"

"Yes. Because they always are. There's your first detective lesson. Everybody lies. They lie even when they have no reason to lie. You learn to expect it."

"Then you have to find out what they're lying about."

"Not really. It's *why* they lie that usually ends up mattering the most. Not what they're lying about."

The car wound its way along Pokfulam Road and Tay watched the lush landscape slipping by on both sides of the road. It surprised him how beautiful this part of Hong Kong was.

The thickly forested slopes of Victoria Peak fell away into the South China Sea where dozens, perhaps hundreds of ships bobbed at anchor offshore waiting their turn to enter the container port. Most people thought of Hong Kong as a chaotic urban jungle, but there was something peaceful and unspoiled about Pokfulam. It was almost bucolic. If you had to live in Hong Kong, Tay supposed this was the place to do it.

"That's Queen Mary Hospital up on the right," Claire said.

Tay shifted his gaze away from the scenery and took in the jumble of buildings of various sizes, some of them quite large, all crammed together on what seemed a very small site. Even here in the relative peace of Pokfulam, every inch of land that could be built on had been built on. Land was the most valuable thing in Hong Kong.

"Queen Mary is the teaching hospital for the medical school Emma attends," Claire continued. "I'm sure we could find people there who know her."

"And I'm sure ten minutes after we start looking for them, two hundred people will be talking about Emma being missing since they all know she's the daughter of the Chief Executive of Hong Kong. By tomorrow morning, her disappearance would be on the front page of the *South China Morning Post*."

"So, not a great idea, huh?"

"Not a great idea."

Tay shifted his gaze back to the sea and ran the conversation with Sarah back and forth through his mind as if he was listening to a recording.

"Why do you think that girl was so concerned about whether we were the police?" he asked after a few minutes.

"I thought she was just trying to figure out who we were."

"No, it was more than that. She seemed to think she needed to adjust what she told us depending on who we were."

"So, if we were cops," Claire asked, "was she going to tell us more? Or was she going to tell us less?"

119

Tay didn't bother to answer. Which, Claire decided, *was* an answer.

"Do you think she was telling us the truth about those other disappearances?" Claire asked after a moment.

"I think she was telling us what she thought was the truth."

"But why wouldn't Mrs. Lau have mentioned them to us if they really happened? Particularly if they all occurred in Mongkok. She would have to know about them."

"Maybe not. High profile kidnappings in Hong Kong without the police becoming involved aren't uncommon. Sometimes the story leaks and makes the news, but most of the time it doesn't and very few people ever find out."

"I don't understand. If somebody kidnapped your kid, why wouldn't you call the cops?"

Tay turned away from the window and looked at Claire.

"The triads have been at this in Hong Kong for hundreds of years. They have a well-established record of kidnapping prominent people who will pay a substantial ransom to avoid creating a public spectacle."

The car twisted through the Sandy Bay Gap between Victoria Peak and Mount Davis and began its slow descent back into the chaos of Central.

"Then you think the triads kidnapped Emma?"

"I have no idea. We don't even know somebody kidnapped her for certain yet. I'm just saying the triads run the kidnapping business in Hong Kong."

"But, if somebody did kidnap her—"

"Either the triads have her or they know who does."

"And how do you propose we find out which it is?"

"I guess we'll just have to ask them."

"Oh, that's a wonderful idea, Sherlock. Maybe we can just look them up in the telephone book and give them a call? Are they under T for triads?"

"I may not know much about Hong Kong," Tay said, "but

Chinese cities all work the same way. There's always a guy who knows a guy. You just have to figure out who that guy is."

The car began picking its way through the narrow streets in the western end of the central business district. After the lush greenery around Pokfulam with its sweeping views of the South China Sea, the narrow streets of the city, packed with traffic and swarming with mobs of people, were a shock.

Claire clicked her tongue against the back of her teeth and thought about what Tay had said.

"You know, I just might know the fellow we need."

"You know someone who is a member of a triad?"

"No, this guy's an American lawyer."

"Oh joy," Tay sighed. "Not just an American, but an American lawyer."

"You're being sarcastic, aren't you?"

"What gave me away?"

"You know, you might actually like this guy."

"I doubt that." Tay hesitated. "And I'm not sure we should get anyone else involved, anyway."

"You told John detective work required relationships, and you didn't have any in Hong Kong. John said we would loan you ours. So now I offer you one and you're bitching about it?"

"But does it *have* to be an American lawyer?"

"He's more of a troubleshooter than a lawyer. He has a reputation for solving problems other people can't solve because he's very well connected with the right people."

"You're telling me this American lawyer has connections into the triads? *A white guy* with triad connections? I don't believe it."

"A year or two ago he solved a big money laundering problem for some casinos in Macau and to do it he had to make a deal with the triads."

Tay still thought it didn't sound quite right.

"Let me call him and see if he can put us in touch with somebody," Claire prodded. "What do we have to lose?"

"How much would you have to tell him?"

"I'll just tell him I need a reliable and discreet contact in one of the big triads who wouldn't mind answering a few questions for me. I won't have to tell him why I need it. And he won't ask."

"Why wouldn't he ask why... oh, I get it. You're not just some woman he met in a bar. He knows who you are."

"He has a general idea. And he knows the fewer questions he asks me, the better it is. For him."

"Let me think about it. I'm not sure I like the idea of getting anyone else involved until we have a better idea of what's going on than we do now."

Tay pointed at the laptop and iPad he had taken from Emma's apartment. They were lying on the seat next to him.

"Can you get those to August? See if he knows somebody who can get into them and find out if there's something on them that could help us. Emails, messages, search history. Anything really."

"Sure. No problem."

"And one other thing. Can John access mobile phone records?"

"I imagine so. There's not much John can't get if he wants it."

"You have Emma's number and Sarah McFarland's number. Give both of them to him and see if he can come up with the records for around the time Sarah says she last saw Emma. If we can find the time she received the text she told us about, we'll have the exact time Emma disappeared."

"I'm sure he can do that."

"Also ask him to check any activity on Emma's number since she disappeared. That would be too easy, but we need to check anyway."

. . .

THE CAR ENTERED the approach to the Western Harbor Tunnel and swung through the long curve which led to the entrance. Up ahead at the end of the ramp Tay could see the dark oval mouth of the tunnel into which they were being inexorably sucked.

He wasn't wild about tunnels. They didn't have any in Singapore and he was glad of it, but he understood the three tunnels underneath Hong Kong Harbor connecting the island to the mainland were arteries vital to tying the city together. It wasn't so much that he was claustrophobic, not exactly, but when he passed through any of the harbor tunnels he could never quite get out of his mind the vast weight of water bearing down on them from above. For all he knew, there was even a huge ship up there now right above their heads.

The construction of the tunnels didn't help either. The interiors were brown and beige tile with two long strips of dim fluorescent lighting running above the three lanes of traffic. They always made him think of a gigantic men's room. If he was going to die, crushed to death by tons of water and a five-hundred-foot-long freighter, he didn't want to do it in something that looked like a men's toilet.

At least traffic moved well in the harbor tunnels and you were seldom stuck inside any of them for more than a few minutes. And that was exactly what Tay was thinking when the driver braked and the car slid to a sudden halt.

Tay leaned forward and looked through the windshield. All he could see in front of them were three unbroken columns of brake lights.

"I'm sorry, sir," the driver said. "There must be some kind of traffic jam in West Kowloon. Something has traffic backed up all the way into the tunnel."

Tay had never been stationary in one of the harbor tunnels before and, now that he was, he was less than thrilled. He had never been buried alive either, but if he had, he was certain it would feel just like this.

"What do you suggest we do?" he asked the driver.

"*Do*, sir?"

The driver sounded as if he had never before heard the word.

"Yes, *do*. What do we *do* about being stuck here?"

"We wait for the traffic to clear. What else would we do?" The driver barked a laugh. "You're not thinking of walking from here, are you, sir?"

Tay hadn't been, but now he was.

He wondered about the best way to suggest to Claire they get out and walk. Anything was better than just sitting there and hoping for the best while hundreds of tons of water hung up there over their heads. Surely, she would see that, wouldn't she?

But he discarded the idea almost as soon as it came to him. He knew Claire would think he was foolish for suggesting it, and he couldn't bear the humiliation of her seeing him as ridiculous. All men were like that around beautiful women. They would rather die than make an ass of themselves.

Just then the car started creeping forward, and Tay breathed a sigh of relief.

It turned out to be premature.

THEY EMERGED FROM the tunnel into a scene of chaos.

Northbound traffic out of the tunnel crawled into Kowloon at walking speed, but southbound traffic had all been stopped. The democracy protestors had succeeded in completely shutting down at least one side of the harbor tunnel.

The approaches to the tunnel were littered with debris. Boxes, trash cans, pieces of wood, bricks, old tires, and other scraps of urban life cluttered roadways over which hundreds of cars a minute normally flowed into the tunnel to Hong Kong

Island. Now those cars were stopped dead. They were trapped. They could neither move forward into the tunnel nor could they move backward and get away.

The demonstrators had even found an old sofa covered in tufted yellow fabric somewhere, and they had dragged it into the road and positioned it right in the center of the tunnel entrance. Someone had set the sofa on fire, and now the tufted yellow sofa was burning merrily. Clouds of smoke from it drifted back over the gridlocked cars.

But it was neither the debris nor the smoke which blocked the tunnel entrance. It was the sheer weight of human bodies crowded in front of it. There were hundreds of young Chinese, probably thousands, spread across the roadways. They had massed together so tightly between the abandoned toll booths and the yawning mouth of the tunnel they almost appeared to have fused into a single enormous organism.

Most of the young Chinese wore masks and carried open umbrellas, and they wielded their umbrellas in the same way Tay had seen them wielded on the streets of Mongkok. It was almost as if the demonstrators saw the umbrellas as magical talismans protecting them from all harm. The canopies of those hundreds of umbrellas knitted together into a single colorful patchwork tent which arched over the mass of people jammed into the roadway. It was beautiful and frightening at the same time.

The traffic into Kowloon was crawling because riot police had blocked two of the northbound lanes and were forming up there for an attack to disburse the demonstrators. Tay watched two water cannons being prepared for battle. They were hulking beasts, enormous trucks with three massive steel nozzles poking through their roofs, incongruously painted with cheerful red and white stripes. Tay knew there was nothing cheerful about the high velocity torrent of water each of those nozzles was about to unleash against the kids blocking the entrance to the tunnel.

Behind the two water cannons, at least a hundred riot police clad in full body armor were lined up in ranks. Most carried rifles Tay assumed were loaded with rubber bullets. It looked as if the cops were preparing for a direct assault on the demonstrators after they were hit with the water cannons, and that it would come soon. Those kids would be helpless before the onslaught, Tay knew, and there was nothing he could do to help them.

That didn't mean he had to watch, though.

"Get us the fuck out of here!" he snarled at the driver.

Just then a small opening appeared in the wall of taillights ahead of them. The driver saw it, accelerated, and sped away.

EIGHTEEN

"WELL," CLAIRE SAID, "that was exciting."

Tay didn't feel very excited so he said nothing.

"Why don't we go to your hotel, Sam? I'll call John and get him to pick up Emma's laptop and iPad there, and I'll find out if he can get those phone records. Then we need to figure this out. Come up with a plan."

Under most circumstances, Tay would have been delighted at Claire's proposal that they go back to his hotel. Even when he understood the suggestion was entirely innocent, there was still something about the sound of it he liked a lot.

But right now, he had something else on his mind

"Here's the problem," he said. "I want a cigarette, or maybe two cigarettes, and I can't smoke in my room."

"Are you asking me to stand out on the sidewalk with you while you smoke a cigarette?"

"I thought maybe we could go back to the Garage Bar."

"Genius," Claire smiled. "The Garage Bar it is."

. . .

TAY WENT TO his room and got his Marlboros while Claire went to the Garage Bar to find them a table and call August. When Tay walked in, he saw Claire sitting alone at a table. The rest of the place was empty. No customers, no bartender, no waitresses.

The Garage Bar was closed.

"It doesn't open until five o'clock," Claire said.

Tay looked at the empty bar and grunted.

"What difference does it make, Sam? Just more peace and quiet for us. That's how I see it."

"You don't think they'll mind if we sit here?"

"I swear, Sam Tay, sometimes you are *such* a Singaporean you amaze me. Always got to stay within the rules, right? Even when you don't know if there *are* any rules."

"I just thought..." Tay began and then he trailed off since he wasn't really sure *what* he thought.

"I take more of an American approach," Claire said. "If anyone comes around and tells us we can't sit here, I'll just shoot them."

Tay's mouth dropped open. "You're carrying a gun?"

"Sure. Aren't you?"

Tay could feel this conversation getting well out of hand and it hadn't even started yet.

Tay lit one of his Marlboros and took a long, contemplative pull on it. That was the thing about smoking. It gave you someplace else to focus your attention when things started spinning out of control. It allowed you to take the time to figure out a safe response to almost anything anyone said to you. Although, since he was talking to Claire, he was pretty sure he wouldn't have enough time to do that if he smoked the whole pack. He pulled the ashtray on the table toward him and dumped the match.

"Did you reach August?" he asked, changing the subject.

"He's got a guy."

"He's always got a guy."

"And his guy's coming over to pick up Emma's stuff. He's meeting us here."

Tay thought back to his search for the Garage Bar the night before when he met Claire.

"He'll never find this place," Tay said.

Claire chortled. Then her eyes went somewhere behind him and she smiled. Tay hadn't even had a chance to wonder why she was doing that when he heard the man's voice, a boy's really.

"You Mrs. Claire, no?"

"I'm Mrs. Claire, yes."

Tay looked back over his shoulder. The kid looked like he was twelve years old and appeared to be Indian or Pakistani. He was short and very slight, and he wore a New Orleans Saints t-shirt, khaki shorts, and a blue baseball cap that said LA on the front in white letters.

"These are for you," Claire said and handed him Emma's laptop and iPad. "Both are security protected. I just need them opened. Then I'll take it from there."

"Yes, madam," the boy said with a half bow as he accepted the gear. "I will inform Mr. John when I am done."

Then he turned and scurried away.

"So, August produces an Indian computer nerd in... what?" Tay looked at his watch. "Ten minutes?"

"Yep," Claire said. "John always knows a guy."

Tay took a final puff on his Marlboro, then he stubbed it out in the ashtray.

"Did August think he could do anything with the telephone numbers?"

"He said he'd text me whatever he could get."

At that moment, Claire's telephone buzzed.

"You cannot be serious," Tay said. "Is he *listening* to us?"

Claire picked up her phone, glanced at the screen, and smiled. She pressed a few buttons and used her forefinger to scroll the screen.

"The last time Emma used her phone was at 11:03am on Saturday, and that was a call to Sarah's number. There are two unanswered calls after that..."

Claire leaned closer to her screen.

"But John hasn't identified the numbers yet, and there were three texts, none of them significant. She didn't respond to any of them. Then, at 12:27pm, her phone disappears from the cellular system and hasn't come up again since."

"Disappears? Come up?"

"Her phone disconnected from the cellular network and hasn't reconnected since. She probably turned it off."

"Or somebody did."

Claire nodded and went back to scrolling.

"And then we have Miss Sarah's telephone. She's a popular little girl. There are pages and pages here. This will take a while to untangle."

"Check for the time of the text she sent from Mongkok Station on Saturday around noon."

Claire scrolled some more. "Give me a second," she said.

Tay shook out another Marlboro and lit it.

"Take as long as you need," he said. "I'm good."

Tay smoked quietly and watched Claire as she clicked and scrolled through Sarah's telephone records. Sometimes he wondered who this woman was, but then he remembered who she worked for and what she did for a living and stopped wondering. It would probably be better for him not to know any more than he already did. It would probably be *much* better for him not to know even that much.

He was sure Claire had noticed his attraction to her. How could she not? His clumsiness with women was legendary, but she had been nice enough not to embarrass him over it. How was it possible to be as old as he was and still so inept in dealing with women?

Tay sometimes wondered if other men were as clumsy with women as he was. He had decided most probably were, but were too dumb and self-centered to realize it. At least he was smart enough to know what a clod he was, and most of the time he felt like that knowledge was the only thing protecting him from women looking at him as just one more fumbling old fool trying to get them into bed.

"This is strange," Claire said, cutting into his reverie.

"The text Sarah sent from Mongkok Station?"

"Yes," Claire said and looked up at him.

Tay could see in her eyes he wouldn't much like what she had found.

"What?" he asked.

"There wasn't one. Sarah neither received nor sent a single text between 11:00am and 1:00pm on Saturday."

"But she said she lost track of Emma when she stopped and —"

"I know. She lied."

A TALL, THIN man wearing jeans and a green t-shirt appeared from somewhere and walked behind the bar. When he spotted Tay and Claire, he looked them over, but he said nothing to them and just got on with cleaning up the bar and preparing it for opening at five o'clock.

Tay looked at his watch. It wasn't even three yet. He gathered the man intended to take his time with the cleaning and preparing.

"Why would Sarah lie about stopping to read a text and send a reply when they got to the station in Mongkok?" Claire asked.

"Because there was some other reason she didn't stay with Emma after they got off the train."

"Such as?"

"If Sarah already knew where Emma was going, it wouldn't be necessary to stay with her. Maybe they were planning to meet later."

"Are you saying Sarah's story about them going to some restaurant in Mongkok was bullshit? That Emma was in Mongkok for another reason and the restaurant story was just a cover?"

"Sarah was hiding *something*. I'm sure of it. Maybe that's what it was."

"Then what do we do now? Go back and tell her we know and try to frighten her into telling us the truth?"

"We don't know enough to do that yet. If we make a run at her now and she blows us off, we've given up that we know she's lying and gotten nothing for it."

The thin man came out from behind the bar and walked over to them, wiping his hands on a small towel. He had a narrow face, big ears, and hair down to his shoulders. Tay thought he looked more Korean than Chinese.

"So sorry," he said. "Not open until five. I cannot serve."

Claire smiled. "We know," she said. "It's okay if we just sit here, isn't it?"

The man's eyes shifted back and forth between Claire and Tay.

"My friend here," Claire said, inclining her head toward Tay, "has a terrible seizure if he can't smoke a Marlboro every half hour. Starts foaming at the mouth and everything. You wouldn't want to be responsible for that happening, would you?"

The man hesitated. Was this woman making a joke, or did she mean what she said? His wife kept telling him all foreigners were crazy. Maybe she was right.

"Could you ask room service to bring me a sandwich or something?" Tay asked before the man could decide whether or not Claire was serious. "I haven't eaten lunch and I'm starving to death here. Just a club sandwich will be fine. And maybe a beer. A Tsingtao?"

Tay pointed at Claire. "You in, too?"

"I'm in," Claire said and smiled at the bartender. "Same thing for me."

The man glanced back and forth between them again. Maybe they weren't crazy. Maybe they were just foreigners.

"Okay," he said, mostly so he could stop talking to them and flee. "Can."

"Great," Tay nodded. "Thanks."

W HEN THE BARTENDER was out of earshot, Tay said to Claire, "We need to follow up on the triad angle. We're not even certain yet whether someone did kidnap Emma or if she just took off. But now that we know Sarah was lying to us about the text, it makes it sound like maybe she did just take off."

"That doesn't feel right to me."

"It doesn't to me either, but we have to be sure. If Emma was kidnapped here in Hong Kong, one of the triads either has her or knows who does. That's still the place we have to start."

"So, I guess you're about to suggest I—"

"Call your American lawyer friend."

"I can do that."

"Does he have a name?"

"Jack Shepherd."

He should have guessed it would be something like that, Tay thought. Somehow all the Americans he encountered had revoltingly American names.

"Do you think he has enough credit with the triads to get somebody of rank to talk to us?"

"I can ask, but we have to be careful how much we tell him and I don't really want to do a dance like that over a telephone. I think I better get him to meet us somewhere."

"You're saying you expect me to sit down somewhere and talk to an American lawyer? And I suppose now you're going to tell me you expect me to be polite to him, too?"

"I already said I think you'll like him."

"You're an incurable optimist."

Claire snickered and took out her telephone. She scrolled through her contacts list until she found Shepherd's number, but then she hesitated.

"I guess I should use the clean phone John gave me. We shouldn't draw a line from us to Shepherd just in case anybody follows up on any of this later."

Tay nodded, but he didn't say anything.

All this cloak and dagger stuff was way out of his league. If he needed to talk to someone, he just picked up a telephone and talked to them. It never crossed his mind to do it in a way which would keep anyone from finding out later he had done it. Maybe he needed to think about that more in the future.

Claire got out the telephone August had given her, checked Shepherd's number on her contacts list again, and then punched it into the other phone. As she waited for Shepherd to answer, Tay noticed she shifted her body away from him as if to make it more difficult for him to overhear what she was saying.

That's interesting, Tay thought.

He wondered if Claire's relationship with Shepherd was a little less casual than she was letting on. Was it possible there was even a romantic connection there? Good Lord, Tay suddenly thought. Was it possible Claire was staying with Shepherd while she was in Hong Kong? Was that why she wasn't in the hotel where he was?

For God's sake, stop it, Tay berated himself. *Why would it be any of your business even if it were true?*

He scooped up his pack of Marlboros, shook one out, and lit it. He could hear Claire talking as he did, but he focused his attention on his cigarette and blocked out whatever she was saying. That was one of the benefits of smoking. You always had another place to go when you didn't particularly want to be in the one where you were.

Tay might not have heard Claire's side of the conversation, but he registered the *click* her telephone made when she put it down on the table.

"Okay," she said. "He's on his way."

"On his way where?"

"Here."

"Here? You call this guy and he just drops everything and comes running? What are you not telling me?"

"Why, Sam Tay, I believe you're jealous."

"Don't be ridiculous."

"You are," Claire said and pointed her forefinger at him. "And you're blushing."

"I am not."

"You are, too. I can see it, and now you're blushing even more. Ah, Sam, that's so sweet."

Claire gave him a dazzling smile, but Tay didn't notice. He didn't dare look at her. Instead, he gazed off toward the bartender and puffed furiously at his Marlboro.

NINETEEN

THE ROOM SERVICE waiter appeared just then with their food, which gave Tay a few moments to pull himself together.

While the waiter served their sandwiches and their beers, Tay grabbed the black plastic folder off the tray, opened it, and studied the check with single-minded intensity. He stretched his scrutiny out for as long as he dared, then he fumbled the pen out of the folder and signed the bill at the bottom. He couldn't remember his room number without taking out his keycard and checking, so he managed to kill another fifteen or twenty seconds doing that.

Tay was relieved when Claire let him off the hook and made no further comment about the psychotic episode he had just experienced. He considered it an act of mercy on her part, and he made a mental note he owed her one for it.

They made small talk while they ate, mostly about August. Inevitably they got around to talking about the bombing at the Cordis Hotel that was meant to kill Claire and August. Tay remembered the bomb was placed in a room where a former CIA case officer about to defect to China had been staying. But he hadn't been. There *was* no case officer about to defect to

China. The whole thing had been a set-up to kill August and Claire and another guy who was working with them then. And they had walked right into it.

When they finished their sandwiches, they waved over the bartender and asked him to arrange for two more Tsingtaos. This time the guy didn't bother calling room service and just pulled the beers out of a cooler beneath the bar. As they drank, the talk turned to Tay's trip to Washington to help them hunt down the people who had ordered the bombing. They laughed about the days they had spent playing tourist there together.

An hour or more passed in what Tay thought was easy companionship and pleasant conversation. He even started enjoying himself.

And then Jack Shepherd showed up.

"HEY, DARLING," SHEPHERD said to Claire as he threw himself into the empty chair at their table. "How you been?"

He shifted his eyes to Tay and looked him over with undisguised suspicion.

"This is Samuel Tay, Jack. He used to be a homicide detective in Singapore, but now he works with us."

Shepherd gave a very small nod and smiled at Tay, but the smile made him look hard, maybe even a little mean. Tay wondered if he was.

Shepherd and Tay shook hands. Neither of them put much enthusiasm into it.

There was nothing physically remarkable about Shepherd, Tay thought. Average height, average weight, and average age. Somewhere in his mid-forties. He was happy Shepherd hadn't turned out to be a fat guy in an electric blue suit. He couldn't have borne it if he'd had to deal with an American lawyer who was a fat guy in an electric blue suit.

Shepherd's dark hair was a little long and messy for a lawyer, and he was wearing round, rimless sunglasses, a white dress shirt with the sleeves rolled up over his elbows, and black jeans. The effect was to make him look more like an architect on his way to inspect a new project than a lawyer who handled... well, Claire had mentioned a money laundering investigation for a casino in Macau, but otherwise she hadn't been too clear about what kind of things Shepherd *did* handle.

What Tay hadn't expected was for Shepherd to look so beaten up. His nose was crooked as if it had been broken several times, and he had a quality of wear to him, like an old leather suitcase someone had dragged through a lot of airports. Despite all that, or maybe because of it, Shepherd gave off the air of a man who had everything under control. He looked like the fellow you went to for directions when you got lost. Which, Tay reminded himself, was exactly what they were doing, and exactly what they were.

"You didn't tell me you were here with somebody," Shepherd said to Claire.

"I didn't see that it mattered."

"You suppose they got another one of those?" Shepherd smiled again and pointed to Claire's half-empty bottle of Tsingtao.

Tay waved the bartender over and pointed. The man nodded and went off to get Shepherd a beer.

"So," Shepherd said, looking at Claire and knitting his fingers together behind his head. "You and August here to kill somebody important?"

Tay took note that Shepherd seemed to be pretty clear on who Claire was.

"We're looking for a missing girl, Jack. Her father is somebody August knows. She disappeared here in Hong Kong about three days ago and August promised her father we'd find her and get her back."

"A kid?"

"No, but young. Mid-twenties."

"Anybody I know?"

Claire said nothing.

"If you're here, it must mean the cops are having no luck."

"We're here because law enforcement isn't involved."

"Ah, got it now. The daughter of someone wealthy and well-connected. *Very* prominent and *very* well-connected if they've turned out John August and his jolly band."

Claire said nothing, but then Shepherd hadn't expected her to.

"A kidnapping for ransom?" he asked.

"We don't know. It's always possible she just took off somewhere."

"But you don't think so."

Claire hesitated. "No, we don't think so."

"Has there been a ransom demand?"

"Not yet."

All of a sudden Shepherd pitched forward, folded his forearms against the table, and leaned toward Claire.

"Who is it, Claire?"

"I can't tell you. And trust me on this, even if I *could* tell you, you wouldn't want me to."

"You're thinking it's a triad snatch?"

"It's possible."

"And that's why you called me. You want me to hook you up with somebody at a high level in one of the triads who can help you cut this thing short."

"As usual, Jack, you have gone right to the heart of things."

"I don't mess with the triads, Claire. I thought you knew that. I'm a white boy in a Chinese city, so I don't mess with the triads."

"She could be in danger, Jack. She's just a girl in her twenties going to medical school who's got her whole life in front of her. She doesn't deserve to die."

"I'm sorry, Claire, really I am, but let me say this just one more time. I don't mess with the triads."

"You don't? I heard about the money laundering matter you sorted out for the MGM Macau. The word is Pansy Ho was awfully pleased with your work. And I also know about you hunting down the guy who took the Malaysian sovereign wealth fund for billions. Your triad contacts helped you with both those things, didn't they? That was pretty high level stuff, white boy, and you don't look to me to have suffered one bit from asking the triads for help with those things."

Shepherd said nothing.

"We just want you to ask those same contacts to find out if one of the triads has our girl."

"Oh, that's all, huh?"

"That's all."

Claire spread her hands and smiled.

"Ought to be a piece of cake for a player like you, Jack."

"HOW MUCH DO you know about the triads, Claire?"

"Not a lot."

"Most Americans don't know shit about the triads. Maybe they've seen a few kung fu movies so they figure the triads are a bunch of skinny Chinese fellows who strut around in their undershirts with toothpicks in their mouths. Just a bunch of wild and crazy Chinese guys, mostly fictional, and even a little comic. Take it from me, Claire, there's nothing fictional about the Chinese triads. And absolutely nothing about them is even a little bit comic."

Claire nodded, but she said nothing, so Shepherd continued.

"The triads are global organizations, organized crime syndicates composed of nothing but ethnic Chinese men. They operate everywhere in the world with any Chinese population. Their roots go as deep into New York and London as they do into Shanghai and Hong Kong. The largest triads here in Hong

Kong are the 14K, the Sun Yee On, the Wo Shing Wo, and the Wo Hop To, but there are a lot of small ones, too. They're all separate and distinct organizations. Sometimes they work together and sometimes they kill each other, but they're all involved in drug trafficking, extortion, kidnapping, loansharking, smuggling, gambling, prostitution, and most every other form of criminal activity anyone has invented."

"How big are these groups?"

"Big. A guy who knows about such things once told me the Sun Yee On alone has about six hundred high office holders and over thirty thousand soldiers, which makes them bigger than the Hong Kong police force. And that's just one triad. A lot of people claim there are well over a hundred thousand actual triad members in Hong Kong with another hundred thousand hangers-on."

"The Hong Kong government says the triads are no longer active here."

"Nobody even pretends to believe that. Hong Kong is a city of almost eight million ethnic Chinese. It floats on an ocean of cash. Get serious."

"Then what you're telling me here is the triads are a force in Hong Kong and sometimes they still dabble in the kidnapping business, right?"

Shepherd just looked at Claire.

"All I want you to do," she smiled sweetly, "is ask around and see if they've got our girl."

"I'd have to be out of my mind to fuck around with these guys, Claire. Piss off the wrong people and they just cut off your legs and dump what's left of you in the harbor."

Shepherd watched Claire for a moment, then he shifted his eyes to Tay.

"Do you talk?" he asked.

"I do when I have something to say, but it sounds to me like she's doing fine without me."

Shepherd sighed. "That she is."

"You know you're going to do this for me, Jack," Claire grinned, "so stop screwing around and let's get cracking."

Shepherd tilted his head back, closed his eyes, and shook his head.

"That's a good boy, Jack," Claire said.

TWENTY

SHEPHERD AND Tay left the Garage Bar together and walked south on Reclamation Street.

"I don't think Claire was too happy when you told her not to come," Tay said.

Shepherd glanced sideways at Tay. "You don't know her very well, do you?"

Tay didn't much like hearing that, but he figured Shepherd might be right so he didn't argue with him.

"She understood. Bringing a white woman in to talk to Benny would make him so edgy we'd get nothing. We may get nothing anyway, but at least he knows me and you... well, your face doesn't make you stand out. Claire just had to make some noise and pee on the ground so I'd know I couldn't take her for granted, but she understood completely."

Pee on the ground?

Tay had never understood why Americans used so many idioms that referenced bodily functions. Did they have some kind of fixation on that stuff? He said *shit* occasionally. Okay, maybe he said it a lot. But everybody said *shit*, didn't they? It was a perfectly normal word now. And it was a long way from a phrase like *pee on the ground*. That was just plain... nasty.

"So, now what, Shepherd? Are you going to call and ask this Benny guy to see us?"

"You've got to understand how things work here, Tay. Making appointments is a Western thing. You want to talk to a guy in Hong Kong? Show up wherever you expect to find him and talk to him. If he's there, maybe he'll talk to you. Or maybe he won't. But politely asking for an appointment just confuses people and makes them nervous."

Tay nodded, but he did't say anything.

"Didn't Claire say you're a homicide detective? I thought you guys never let people know you're coming. That just gives them time to duck you or dream up a good story. Works the same way here."

"I used to be a homicide detective."

"Used to be?"

"I'm retired."

Shepherd shot Tay a look. "Retired? You don't look old enough to be retired."

"Thank you."

"Don't thank me yet. By the time you get out of Hong Kong, you'll probably look old enough to be dead."

T HEY IGNORED THE traffic light and crossed Shantung Street dodging through the traffic.

"Let me tell you something about Uncle Benny," Shepherd said.

"Wait... this guy we're going to see is your *uncle*?"

Shepherd grinned. "Of course he's not my uncle. That's just a respectful way to refer to an older man here. Don't you use the same expression in Singapore?"

"We did a long time ago, but now it's considered rather old-fashioned."

"That's the Singapore I know and love," Shepherd said.

"Always trying to convince itself it's more up to date than any other city in Asia."

Tay didn't much feel like getting involved in the traditional Hong Kong versus Singapore debate, so he changed the subject.

"How high in the triads is this guy?" he asked.

"I doubt Benny's a triad member at all."

"Then why are we——"

"I met Uncle Benny when a Macau casino guy suggested Benny talk to me about a money laundering problem Benny thought he had. There had been a sudden spike in the funds passing through Benny's foreign currency exchange booths in the tourist sections of Hong Kong. He was happy to have the extra business, but he didn't believe in the Easter Bunny any more than I did. The extra money was coming from some-where, and it would mean enormous problems for him if it turned out to be the wrong place."

Tay just listened.

"After Benny called me, I did a background check before I took him on as a client. You never know who in Hong Kong has triad connections, and that's something you want to know before somebody gets pissed with you and half a dozen triad soldiers show up in your apartment some night swinging choppers."

"Choppers?"

"Meat cleavers. The weapon of choice for most triad soldiers. This isn't Chicago. Firearms are rare. Besides, meat cleavers are cheap, they do the same job, and they do it far more quietly."

Tay winced. He tried to cover it and hoped Shepherd hadn't noticed.

"Uncle Benny came out squeaky clean on the background check," Shepherd continued. "Turned out Benny had taken a small inheritance from his father and run it into a decent sized business empire. His foreign exchange service, a chain of restau-rants, a driver training school, a bunch of apartments, and a handful of modest sized office buildings. I didn't find the slightest evidence of his involvement in anything criminal."

"So why are we going to ask him about a triad kidnapping?"

"Because Uncle Benny knows triad guys. He cooperates with them sometimes, so he has credibility with them. That's the way things work in Hong Kong. If you're in a business which gets the triads' attention, like Benny's foreign exchange booths, you feed the crocodiles and hope they eat you last. Benny is the guy who hooked me up with the contacts I needed to fix the two matters Claire told you about."

Then Shepherd cut Tay about the biggest wink he had ever seen.

"She doesn't know about the other things Benny helped me fix. At least, I hope she doesn't."

"Why does this guy help you? Just because he's a nice fellow, and he likes you?"

Shepherd chuckled. "The last thing you would call Benny is a nice fellow, and I don't know if he likes me or not. But I've done him some favors and saved him a lot of money, and he wants me to keep doing him favors like that. So when I ask for something in return, he'll do it for me if he can. Not all of it maybe, but enough of it to keep me from being too pissed off with him."

"Does he speak English?"

"Benny's English is perfect, but when he's trying to avoid talking about something he pretends it's not. Then he *no under-standee* and *no speakee*, but don't let the old bastard fool you. He has a degree in business from UCLA. He never told me, of course, but I discovered it when I was doing the background check on him. And here's the really funny thing. When I asked him about it, he denied it."

"He denied he graduated from UCLA?"

Shepherd nodded.

"I don't understand."

"I don't either, not really, but every Chinese guy I know lies about his education. They either tell you they have an MBA from Harvard when they dropped out of school at fifteen, or they tell you they never went to college when they have an MBA from Harvard. I've never figured out why they all lie. I guess it's a cultural thing a poor dumb white guy like me has no hope of ever understanding."

They turned left and walked the two short blocks over to Portland Street. Shepherd stopped on the corner in front of the Sun Hing Building.

Tay couldn't believe it.

"The guy's office is in *here?*"

Shepherd nodded.

The building was six stories tall and maybe forty feet wide. The cracked concrete fascia was pitted and stained with long brown streaks of rust from the ancient air conditioning units hanging precariously out of most of the windows on every floor. The ground level sported a noodle shop on one side of the entrance and on the other side was a shop identified with nothing but a giant red neon foot. Tay couldn't even begin to imagine what that was supposed to mean.

"This building is a dump," he said.

"It's the way Chinese businessmen operate here. Making money's what matters. What your office looks like *doesn't* matter. In fact, the crummier your office, the more money people think you're making."

"Then I'm guessing," Tay said, "Uncle Benny must be practically Jeff Bezos."

Shepherd grinned and pushed through the door into the tiny lobby.

THEY TOOK THE elevator to the fourth floor.
It creaked and banged the whole way up, but no doubt it had been doing the same thing for at least fifty years and it was still running, so Tay took comfort from that. The

smell was harder to ignore. Why did so many elevators in Hong Kong smell of dog piss? At least Tay hoped it was dog piss.

When the doors opened, they stepped out into a narrow, dimly lit hallway with half a dozen unmarked doors. Tay followed Shepherd along the cracked green linoleum to the door at the end. Shepherd didn't bother to knock. He just opened the door and walked in.

A middle-aged Chinese man sat behind a scarred wooden desk covered with piles of gray ledger books. Black plastic-framed eyeglasses sat crookedly on the end of his nose. He was wearing a wrinkled white nylon shirt that was unbuttoned and hanging open, revealing even more wrinkled undershirt. He glanced up at them when they came in, but he said nothing and without a word went back to writing in the ledger book in front of him.

Shepherd strode past the man, opened a door behind him, and walked into another office. Tay followed.

"Uncle Benny!" Shepherd spread his arms. "I've missed you, man!"

A thin, wiry man sat at another wooden desk that looked even more beaten up than the one in the outer office. His hair was jet black and short, shaped close to his head in a no-nonsense cut he must have gotten on the street somewhere. His skin was so fair it almost glowed.

Tay couldn't guess how old Benny was, but judging the age of Asians by their appearance never worked out very well, anyway. Tay made him to be in his mid-forties, but he could have been off by twenty years either way.

Ledger books and papers were scattered across the desk and an ancient wooden abacus teetered dangerously close to one edge. Uncle Benny had a ledger open in front of him when they came in and he didn't bother to respond to Shepherd's greeting. He didn't even bother to look up.

Two mismatched wooden chairs sat in front of Benny's desk. Although they hadn't been invited to sit down, Shepherd took one and gestured Tay into the other. They waited in silence. Shepherd appeared to have been through this routine before and seemed content to wait for Uncle Benny to acknowledge they were there.

It was two or three minutes before Benny looked up from the ledger at Shepherd. He flicked his eyes quickly over Tay, then looked back at Shepherd.

"Who this?"

"This is Samuel Tay. I'm helping him with something."

Benny's eyes went back to the ledger.

"Good for you."

"Sam is from Singapore."

"Good for him."

"He has a friend whose daughter is missing here in Hong Kong and he's trying to locate her."

No response from Benny.

"I hate to bother you with this, Uncle Benny, but we need your help here."

"I not know where she is."

Benny gave out with a strange wheezing sound which Tay assumed approximated laughter.

"No, but you may know someone who does."

Benny looked up and gave Shepherd a hard stare.

"Why you say that?"

"Let's not piss around here, Benny. The triads run the kidnapping business in Hong Kong. You know it and I know it. If she's been kidnapped, one of the triads probably has her. You know people. People know you. All we want you to do is ask around for us."

"*Waaaaaaaaaa,*" Benny breathed out. "You think this girl kidnapped by triads?"

"Maybe. Maybe not. That's what we're trying to find out."

"If they not have her, then who?"

"It's possible she wasn't kidnapped by anybody and just took off, but we don't think so. Somebody has her and it's probably one of the triads."

At that, Benny shook his head vigorously. "Cannot help."

"Yes, you can."

"Cannot."

Shepherd cleared his throat, folded his arms, and added a little asshole to his voice.

"Do you still want me to find out who's behind the offer to buy your Causeway Bay apartment building, Benny, or should we just forget about that?"

Uncle Benny stared at Shepherd.

"You fucker," he said flatly.

"That's me," Shepherd nodded. "You want favor from me. I want favor from you."

"Ask other favor. Not this."

"Yes, Benny, this."

"You fucker."

"Yes," Shepherd nodded. "We've established that."

Benny sighed and bobbed his head around, but Tay could tell Shepherd had him.

"Okay," Uncle Benny finally muttered, "tell me about girl."

"All you need to know is she's in her mid-twenties and is a medical student here in Hong Kong. Her family is very prominent."

"And rich?"

"And rich," Shepherd agreed. "What we want you to do is ask around and see if there are any stories on the street about a triad kidnapping a girl like that."

Benny bobbed his head around some more. "I think about it."

"Don't think about it too long. If a triad doesn't have her, we think she might be in danger."

"When she go missing?"

"Three days ago."

"Where she live?"

"Pokfulam."

"And she disappear from Pokfulam?"

"No. She was last seen getting off a train in Mongkok Station."

Benny's eyebrows shot up.

"*Waaaaaaaaaa*," he howled. "You fucker."

"Exactly," Shepherd agreed.

TWENTY-ONE

W HEN THEY WERE back outside on the sidewalk, Tay looked at Shepherd.

"What just happened in there?" he asked.

Shepherd grinned. "Hong Kong's a lot different from Singapore, isn't it?"

"Did Benny agree to work his contacts for you or didn't he?"

"With Benny you can never be sure what he'll do no matter what he says he'll do, but the Causeway Bay deal is important to him. He doesn't want to, but I think he'll make some calls for us. I'll bet I hear something from him tomorrow morning."

Tay nodded.

"What other angles are you working?" Shepherd asked.

Tay shook his head.

"Yeah, that's pretty much what I figured," Shepherd said. "Look, I do think Benny will come through for us tomorrow. Of course, if what he hears when he asks around is that the triads don't have her and no one knows who might, I'm not sure where it leaves you."

"Would Benny lie and tell you that even if he found out who has her?"

"I don't think so. Benny wouldn't want to get caught lying to somebody he needs to keep sweet, and Benny needs to keep me sweet."

"Okay," Tay said, but he didn't sound confident.

"I'll call Claire the moment I hear anything from Benny."

"No," Tay said, "call *me*."

He pulled out the iPhone August had given him and held it up so Shepherd could read the number taped to the back of it.

Shepherd punched the number into his own phone.

"What are you going to do if Benny turns out to be a dry hole?" he asked Tay after he had put the phone away.

Tay considered several upbeat answers, but then went with an honest one.

"I have no idea," he said. "None."

Shepherd gave Tay a tired smile.

"I know how that goes," he said.

Tay dipped into a pocket and pulled out his pack of Marlboros.

"I should ask if you mind, but right now I honestly don't give a shit. No offense."

"No offense taken," Shepherd said and then extracted a cigar from his pocket. "Now and then I feel the need for a little nicotine myself."

Shepherd pointed in the direction of the Cordis Hotel.

"There's a place on the way back to your hotel that has a couple of sidewalk tables where we can smoke," Shepherd said. "I wouldn't mind a beer or some coffee to go with this cigar."

"Let's go. I've had enough beer, but I could use a coffee."

THE PLACE WAS called K Square, and it was on Reclamation Street, a block over and two blocks down from Uncle Benny's office. It was a tiny shophouse with a long bar on one side and a row of narrow tables on the other. From the decor, Tay could tell it harbored serious ambitions of hipsterism.

A tall, bar-style table sat on the sidewalk to one side of the entrance. It offered two stools and an ashtray, which made it pretty much perfect in Tay's view.

They ordered coffees, and Tay shook a Marlboro out of his pack and sat smoking quietly while Shepherd fiddled with his cigar. He pulled what looked like a tiny guillotine out of his pocket, sliced off one end of the cigar, and inspected it. After it passed muster, he lit a match from the box Tay had left on the table, rotated the cigar in the flame for ten or fifteen seconds, and then puffed it into life.

"That looks like a lot of trouble for a little nicotine," Tay said. "All I have to do is take one of these out of the pack and light up."

Shepherd took a long, steady pull on his cigar and blew a stream of smoke across the sidewalk and into the street. They both watched it hang there for a moment, then break apart and drift away.

"But look what you have, my friend." Shepherd took the cigar out of his mouth and pointed with it to Tay's cigarette. "There you sit smoking burning paper and plastic, and here I sit smoking the richest, most sumptuous tobacco leaf that has ever grown out of the soil of this planet."

Tay had to admit the lush aroma of the cigar held a lot of appeal for him. It smelled organic and biologic, like life emerging straight from the earth. For just a moment, its fragrance transported him away from the concrete sidewalks of one of the most crowded places on earth and made him think of empty forests, and damp foliage, and wet leaves crunching under his feet.

A chubby, unsmiling young girl in jeans and a black shirt brought their coffees, banged them down on the table, and then walked off without saying a word.

And just like that, Tay was straight back in the reality of Hong Kong.

"WHY ARE YOU living here?" he asked Shepherd.

"Everybody's got to live somewhere."

"Now you're just being glib."

"You're not the first person to accuse me of that."

Shepherd smiled and drew on his cigar, and they both watched again as the smoke swirled into the air.

"It was just going to be temporary," he went on after the smoke drifted away. "I was a lawyer at a decent firm in Washington DC, then I took a job teaching at the business school at Chulalongkorn University in Bangkok. It was a whim, I have to admit now, but as the saying goes, it seemed like a good idea at the time. After a couple of years, they asked me to leave because the media had linked me with a client who was a little too notorious for their taste. I didn't really mind. My wife had found somebody she liked better and moved to London, so there really wasn't anything in Bangkok for me anymore. A guy I know offered to loan me an apartment here in Hong Kong and I thought, well, why not? That was two years ago now. He hasn't asked for the apartment back yet, so I'm still here."

"You like living here?"

Shepherd shrugged. "Everybody's got to live somewhere," he repeated and laughed again.

Tay drank some coffee. "What's happening to Hong Kong?" he asked.

"It's dying."

"No, seriously."

"I am being serious. Hong Kong is a dying city. It's been dying on the inside for a long time. Now it's dying on the outside, too."

Shepherd drew on his cigar.

"For more than a hundred years," he continued, "Hong

Kong has been a patch between China and the rest of the world. It served everyone's purposes. Hong Kong gave the West a window on China, and it gave China access to the West. It was the perfect intermediary. A little of both, but not all of either. And being an intermediary made it rich. Then the Brits walked away in 1997 and China dreamed up this one-country-two-systems fairy tale to put a happy face on the future, and that was the end for Hong Kong. Everyone tried to pretend it wasn't. Most people wanted to believe things would go on as before and they wanted everyone else to believe it, too, but they knew they wouldn't. They knew it really *was* the end."

"What do you think about these street demonstrations?"

"These kids out there shouting for freedom are on a suicide run, and they know it."

"A suicide run?"

"You understand the concept of face, Sam. Westerners don't, but you're a Singaporean. You must."

Tay nodded.

"For China to lose control of Hong Kong would be no great economic or political loss, but the loss of face would be massive. It would shake China and the Chinese Communist Party to its foundations. They'll never let it happen."

"But what can China do?"

"I think China has just about had enough of these kids running through the streets and spitting in their face, waving American flags and demanding freedom. What can they do? That's an easy one. They'll just crush them."

"The rest of the world wouldn't just stand by and let that happen."

"Oh, bullshit. Don't be naive, Sam. The Chinese border isn't even ten miles from where we're sitting. China could roll an army of tanks right over the border and be here in half an hour. If they kill a thousand people, even ten thousand, what do you think would happen? You'd hear a few days of outraged calls for action from the US and the UK and maybe a handful of other countries, China would tell them all to stop interfering in its affairs, and then in a week or two everyone would stop thinking about what they did and head back to Walmart to buy more Chinese-made crap. You think anybody's going to war with China over crushing Hong Kong? Forget it."

Tay finished his cigarette and stubbed out the butt in the ashtray.

"That's a pretty bleak outlook," he said.

"Fuck bleak, Sam. Hong Kong's doomed. Five years from now it will just be an insignificant piece of the great Chinese empire. China will bury it because they can never forget the Brits built it, and they can't stand that."

"Are you going to stay?"

Shepherd seemed to think about it, although Tay would guess he had thought about it plenty of times before and would think about it plenty of times later.

"I don't know," he shrugged. "I've got nowhere else to go."

"But you still have your American passport, don't you?"

"Oh sure, so I guess I could always move to Omaha. I'm just not sure how that would work out for me after years of working the back alleys of Bangkok and Hong Kong."

Tay looked puzzled. "You want to live in Omaha?"

Shepherd laughed.

"But you could go back to the United States, couldn't you?" Tay persisted. "You could leave Hong Kong anytime you want."

"Yes, I could. And that makes me one hell of a lot better off than most of the folks around here. Look, Sam, I'd love to go back to the country I left when I took the job teaching in Bangkok, but it's gone. In the years I've lived out here, it's turned into something else. The problem is, I'm not sure I like what it's turned into."

All at once Shepherd got to his feet, pulled a wad of Hong Kong currency out of his pocket, and dropped some of it on the table.

"Look, I'm sorry, but this is a conversation I try to avoid having," he said. "It's just too damned depressing."

"I didn't mean to——"

"Don't worry about it. I've got to run, anyway. I'll let you know what I hear from Benny."

And with one more puff on his cigar, Shepherd turned and walked away down Shantung Street toward Mongkok Station.

TWENTY-TWO

TAY FINISHED HIS coffee and lit another Marlboro. He sat smoking quietly and thinking about Shepherd's abrupt departure.

He couldn't imagine he had said anything to cause offense, but it felt as if he might have. They had been having what Tay thought was an ordinary enough conversation when Shepherd suddenly dropped money on the table and bolted. Maybe there was something about the conversation that bothered Shepherd in a way Tay didn't understand. He couldn't have taken off like that just because he didn't want to talk about going back to America, could he?

Oh, forget it, Tay rebuked himself. Trying to work out why people behaved as they did was an occupational hazard for him.

Sometimes, like the cliché had it, a cigar was just a cigar. Sometimes, people did what they did for the reasons they said they were doing it. Shepherd said he had to be somewhere else. Maybe that was all there was to it.

Why did he always assume people were hiding their real motivation from him? Why did he think people were always lying to him about what they did and why they did it? He was no longer a cop. Maybe he ought to work on developing a more trusting view of the world.

Or maybe not.

The iPhone August had given him rang. He considered ignoring it, but decided he shouldn't. This was his super-secret spy phone, wasn't it? It had to be Claire or August, so he answered.

"Hello?"

"Are you still with Shepherd?"

Claire, not August.

"We're all done. I was just about to walk back to the hotel. Is that where you are?"

"No."

Tay waited for more, but nothing more was forthcoming. Claire appeared not to be inclined to say where she was. He started to ask her, but decided it was none of his business and let it go.

"Maybe I should call you back," Claire said, interrupting his reflections.

"Why? Is there something wrong with this connection?"

"I ought to have used Signal to call you so you can tell me what you found out."

What in the world is Claire talking about?

And then Tay remembered.

Signal was the name of the encryption app August had put on their telephones to use for making secure calls. He had thought it was silly when August told him to use it, and nothing had happened since then to change his mind.

"Don't bother," Tay said. "Uncle Benny didn't say much. Just that he would make some calls and let us know tomorrow what he finds out."

"*Uncle* Benny?"

"That's what Shepherd called him."

"What did you think of this guy? Is he going to be any help?"

"He seemed to me to be a bit of a cartoon, but Shepherd claims he's the real deal. Shepherd said he was doing a favor for Benny over a business matter and he thinks it's a big enough favor to get Benny to try to help us. I figured the guy might just be blowing us off, but who knows?"

"Then this Uncle Benny guy is triad? High ranking?"

"Shepherd says Benny isn't triad. But he also says he's hooked in with people who are."

"It doesn't sound like much to me."

"It doesn't sound like much to me either, but Shepherd seems awfully confident it will get us something. Right now, we don't have much to show for twenty-four hours of work. If Shepherd doesn't come up with something, I don't know where it leaves us."

"At least now we know for certain what happened and where it happened."

"We also know both Emma's mother and the friend she was with when she disappeared are lying to us about something."

"You think they're lying about the same thing?"

"No idea."

A small silence fell. Tay didn't break it since he couldn't think of anything worth saying.

"Do you want me to call August?" Claire asked after a minute.

"And tell him what?"

"I guess just to keep him in the loop on the progress we've made."

"Progress? Is that what you call it? We're nowhere, Claire. Tell him that if you really want to, but I wouldn't bother."

Claire remained silent, and Tay felt embarrassed he had sounded so disagreeable.

"Look," he said, "I'm just tired and I'm frustrated we're bogged down. I'm going back to the hotel to think about where we go from here."

After they ended the call, Tay wondered again where Claire

was calling from and what she was doing there. And he wondered why it was she didn't want to tell him.

He knew it was none of his business, but that didn't keep him from wondering anyway.

T AY WAS LESS than a block from the hotel when he heard the noise.

It was a guttural rumble which seemed to deepen and spread even as he listened. Less a sound than a sensation, a disturbance in the air. Tay didn't bother telling himself this time that he might be hearing the crowd in a nearby football stadium. He knew what he was hearing. He also knew the best thing for him to do would be to go straight back to the hotel before he got caught up in another street battle, but he didn't.

There was something about a city turning on itself, consuming itself, that he could not quite look away from. Tay's curiosity had taken him into places he shouldn't have gone before, and because of some of the things which had happened to him on those occasions he knew he should have learned his lesson by now.

Age brought wisdom, some people said. Tay wasn't so sure. Mostly, he figured, it just brought a bad memory.

Tay turned and walked briskly in the direction of the sound.

W HEN HE STEPPED out into the broad expanse of Nathan Road, he saw the crowd a block to the north. A huge mob filled the roadway from one side to the other. Hundreds of people, certainly, maybe many more. Everyone was facing away from him and most of them had their arms upraised, rhythmically pumping them at something he couldn't see while they chanted something in Cantonese he couldn't understand.

When Tay reached the crowd, he edged through it trying to

see what it was that had their attention. Everyone was very polite and made way for him. It shocked him how young the people he saw around him seemed to be. Most of them looked to be not much more than teenagers.

The chanting grew louder as he drew closer to the front of the crowd and he realized it wasn't coming only from the people around him, but also from in front of him and to his left and right. The mob had something or someone surrounded and the chanting was directed at whatever that was. When he got close enough to see between the bodies in the front ranks, his mouth dropped open.

The mob was massed all the way around the intersection of Nathan Road and Argyle Street, which was the crossroads of Mongkok and one of the busiest intersections in Hong Kong. They filled the roadways on all four sides and had brought everything around the intersection to a complete halt. In the middle of the intersection was a force of perhaps a hundred riot police dressed in green uniforms with black visored helmets and body armor. The cops looked to Tay to be nearly as young as the people in the crowd.

The scene made Tay think of an old American movie, one of those Westerns where a wagon train had pulled into a circle to defend itself and a few men with rifles fearfully stared out at the hundreds if not thousands of screaming Indians encircling them. Even if the white guys didn't understand every word the Indians were screaming, they still got the message readily enough. Just like these cops did. Which was why they looked scared shitless.

Right in front of him, one of the cops lifted an orange fabric banner stretched between two poles and waved it at the crowd. Then he rotated slowly, turning all the way around so the banner was visible to the people on all four sides of the intersection.

There were Chinese characters across the top of the banner, but below that the message was rendered in English.

Disperse Or We Will Fire

Fire *what*, Tay asked himself.

Tear gas? Rubber bullets? Or were the cops threatening to open fire on the crowd with live ammunition? Surely not. They wouldn't do that, would they? The crowd didn't feel anywhere near nasty or threatening enough for that to make any sense, although perhaps he would have felt differently if he had been one of those young cops out there in the middle of the intersection.

Whatever the cops were threatening to fire, Tay was badly exposed. This crowd wasn't going anywhere. Which meant, if the cops weren't just bluffing, and Tay didn't think for a moment they were, they would soon open fire with something, and Tay felt like he was standing right on the bullseye. He was fifty feet from the cops and up in the front ranks of the mob. It was hard to be any more exposed than that.

Just then a man, a boy really, ran out of the crowd blocking Argyle Street off to Tay's left. The boy headed straight for the cop holding the banner. When he got within perhaps twenty feet, he stopped and flung an orange parking cone he had picked up somewhere. It bounced harmlessly off the cop's body armor. The cop didn't even seem to notice.

Then another boy ran out of the same area and also headed for the same cop carrying the banner. He seemed even younger than the first boy had, but Tay couldn't be certain since he had a black hoodie pulled over his head and a black bandanna tied over his nose and mouth. What he could be certain of was that this boy was hefting a brick in his right hand.

A cop next to the man with the banner must have seen it, too, because he lunged toward the boy, drawing his sidearm as he did. The cop waved his long-barreled revolver at the boy, screaming in what Tay assumed was Cantonese, but the boy kept coming. When he got within a few feet of the cop carrying the banner, the boy set his feet and threw the brick.

The cop with the handgun fired.

As the crack of the gunshot echoed off the buildings around the intersection, the boy dropped to the pavement. The crowd went silent.

Even those far back in the mass who couldn't have seen for themselves what had happened had heard the shot. For a moment, they told themselves the sound couldn't have been what they thought it was. Then they told themselves it must have been.

The roar rose again, twice as loud as before, and the mob surged from all four directions toward the cops huddled in the middle of the intersection. The cops answered with a barrage of tear gas, and in the tight confines of the intersection the *woomping* sounds from the tear gas guns sounded like mortar fire.

When the gas canisters began exploding around Tay, he had the presence of mind to pull a handkerchief from his pocket, tie it around his nose and mouth, and start pushing to his left toward the relative safety of the sidewalk. A cloud of gas rose all around him and he coughed violently. He closed his eyes, pushed the handkerchief as tightly against his face as he could, and stumbled ahead.

Stay on your feet, he told himself as he caromed from one body to another. *No matter what happens, stay on your goddamned feet.*

After what felt like hours but was actually only twenty or thirty seconds, Tay slammed into something solid and unyielding. He cracked his eyes into slits and saw he had somehow made it to the sidewalk and was up against the wall of a building. Another violent fit of coughing wracked his body. When it subsided, he edged to the right, following the wall along the sidewalk, moving away from the battle as quickly as he could.

He felt the air around him clearing and he knew now he was out of the gas. The crowd was thinner here as well. He quick-walked a little further then stopped and turned and lowered the handkerchief from his face.

Tay thought the cop had looked more frightened than the

kid had, and not much older, but his fear had led him to draw his gun, and he had fired it and Tay had seen the kid go down. There was no coming back from that.

When he looked back at the intersection, he feared the worst, but all he could see were swirling clouds of gas and dark, unidentifiable bodies moving among its waving tendrils as if they were tiptoeing through a forest of trees wreathed with white smoke. It was beautiful, Tay thought, and yet terrifying at the same time.

He began to cough again, and he pressed his handkerchief back over his nose and mouth until it stopped. Then he used it to wipe his nose and mouth and folded it to put it back into his pocket.

When he did, something made him glance down at it. He froze in horror and stared.

The handkerchief was blotched with patches of blood.

TWENTY-THREE

TAY WAS SO upset about coughing up more blood that he stopped on the sidewalk before he went into the hotel and lit a Marlboro. He willed his hand to stop shaking as he struck the match, but it refused to obey him.

It was just the tear gas, he told himself over and over as he stood there smoking on the sidewalk. This had never happened to him before, and it had only happened now on the two occasions he had soaked up tear gas from the Hong Kong street battles.

So that had to be the cause, didn't it? It was just the gas. The Marlboros had nothing to do with it.

As the nicotine performed its usual miracle and restored Tay to a state of relative psychic balance, with that came a stark realization: he was bullshitting himself.

He was coughing up blood. Maybe the tear gas had something to do with it and maybe it didn't, but there might be something seriously wrong. You didn't cough up blood when there was nothing wrong, did you?

He needed to see a doctor. He was in no doubt of that any longer, but he didn't want to tell either Claire or August about the blood and ask them to help him find one, so he wasn't sure what to do. He wasn't going to pick a doctor out of the Hong Kong telephone book, even assuming such a thing as a telephone book even existed anymore in Hong Kong. The only thing that made sense was to get the hell back to Singapore before pieces of his lungs started coming up with the blood.

But there was an obvious problem there. He couldn't just walk off and abandon August and Claire to find Emma on their own. Even if he wanted to, and he didn't, he would have to tell them why he was leaving them in the lurch, and he didn't want to do that either.

The state of his health was a private matter. It wasn't something he felt comfortable talking about with other people. Besides, if he started telling people he had seen a little blood on his handkerchief and speculating about what that meant, they would think advancing age was turning him into a fretful old woman. He couldn't have that.

Tay dropped the butt of his cigarette on the sidewalk, ground it out with his foot, and lit another. Then he pushed the bloody handkerchief out of his mind and thought about what he had just witnessed. The intersection where a mob had surrounded a group of frightened riot police like Indians circling a wagon train in an old Western movie was only around the corner. Yet now here he was, standing on a quiet sidewalk a couple of blocks away having a cigarette, and he could see no sign of anything unusual.

Had a cop really panicked and shot a kid right in front of him? Had that actually happened only a few hundred yards from where he was standing now? Yes, it had happened. Tay had seen it happen.

But standing there on that quiet sidewalk, it felt more like he must have been visiting a movie set. After the cameras had been turned off, the anger and violence had been turned off, too. The city was once again just the city. A place filled with people who had things to do and were getting on with doing them.

Tay smoked his Marlboro and shook his head at the absurdity of it all.

So absorbed was he in his reflections he didn't notice the van when it stopped at the curb next to him. Not until he heard the door sliding open did he glance over, and even then it took him a moment to register what he saw.

Doris Lau was sitting in the captain's chair nearest the open door. She was looking at him, and her face was an empty mask.

"I ASSUME THIS can't just be a coincidence," Tay said when he walked over.

"Actually, it is."

Doris Lau waved a hand toward where Tay had fled the street battle.

"There's a demonstration over at——"

"I was there," Tay said.

Mrs. Lau didn't react to that. Tay expected her to ask him why he had been there, but she didn't. She just nodded, almost as if she had expected him to be there.

Tay thought she looked bad. He had been sitting in this same van with her twenty-four hours earlier, and she looked like she had aged ten years since then. Her face was drawn and gaunt, and her eyes seem to have receded into her head. She no longer looked like Meryl Streep. Not unless Meryl Streep was playing a woman with a terminal disease.

Tay pushed the thought away as soon as it came to him. This was not a time for him to be thinking about terminal diseases.

"I was nearby when I heard about what happened, and I thought I should be here," Doris Lau said. "I saw you there on the sidewalk as we were passing and we stopped. It was almost like an omen that I shouldn't go to the scene."

Tay said nothing.

"Do you know about the shooting?" she asked.

"It happened right in front of me. Is the kid okay?"

It took Mrs. Lau a long time to answer. When she did, she looked away.

"No, he's not okay. He's dead."

A wave of sadness surged through Tay. He had been a homicide investigator for over twenty years, but with all the death he had witnessed, no one had ever been killed right in front of him before. He always arrived later, after whatever spirit gave us life had fled the body and all that remained was an empty shell which would soon turn to dust.

This time, he had seen the boy in life, and he had seen him in death, and he had seen the passage from one to the other take place not twenty feet in front of him. There was nothing he could have done to stop it, of course, but he still couldn't escape the feeling that somehow he had allowed it to happen.

"Do you have a minute?" Mrs. Lau asked. "I'd like to talk to you about something."

Tay nodded and turned to drop his cigarette into the gutter before he climbed into the van, but Doris Lau put her hand on his arm.

"Keep it," she said. "And give me one."

Tay pulled himself up into the van and settled into the chair opposite Mrs. Lau. He took the package of Marlboros out of his shirt pocket and offered it to her.

"Not my brand," she said, "but they'll do. Thank you."

She took a cigarette and Tay returned the pack to his pocket, then he leaned forward and lit it for her.

The door to the van rumbled shut operated by some unseen controller and the driver's door slammed as the driver got out to give them privacy. He seemed to be accustomed to doing that, and Tay wondered how many conversations Mrs. Lau wanted to have on the quiet had taken place in this van.

Doris Lau pushed a button on her armrest and a window on the street side of the van lowered. She took a long pull on the

Marlboro and exhaled through the open window. A truck growled past, and then everything was quiet again.

"Do they give you a lot of trouble in Singapore about smoking?" she asked Tay.

"I think any day now it will be made a capital offense."

"Smoking is still common here. We're trying to discourage it, but a lot of old people just won't give it up. They don't have a lot of pleasure in this life. For many of them, smoking is about the only pleasure they have left."

"It's become a holy crusade in Singapore to stop people from smoking. I blame the Americans. I really do. Sanctimonious crap like this always seems to start with Americans."

"I don't smoke a lot, but sometimes it gives me the moment I need to pull myself back together. This is one of those times."

"I hope seeing me isn't what's responsible for you falling apart."

"No, it's nothing to do with you. It's all this."

Tay didn't ask what *all this* referred to. He didn't have to.

"I feel like I'm the captain of a sinking ship, and I can't do a damn thing to save it."

"Then I'm glad I was here at the right moment to offer you a cigarette."

"They won't let me smoke in public, you know. They say it's bad for my image."

"I don't have an image," Tay said, "so I don't have that problem."

But he was coughing up blood, he remembered. He did have *that* problem.

They sat quietly smoking and Tay waited for Doris Lau to tell him what had caused her to stop when she saw him. He didn't think it had been her need for a cigarette. He didn't even think it was an effort to delay performing a duty she didn't want to perform. Everything about her manner told him it was something else.

And it was.

171

. . .

TAY WAS JUST looking around for an ashtray to dispose of his cigarette butt when Doris Lau launched hers through the open window with a practiced flick of her fingers. Tay got the impression a lot of cigarettes had taken the big dive out the window, but he didn't ask. He just tossed his butt out right behind hers. Then she raised the window again.

"I lied to you about something last night," she announced without preamble.

"I know."

"I thought you might. I got the impression you're a better interviewer than I am a liar."

"Would you like to amend our conversation now?"

"Yes."

Doris Lau paused and Tay waited.

"Emma has been seeing someone. I don't know who and I can't even tell you with any certainty how it is I know, but I do. Perhaps it's just a mother's sixth sense."

"Why didn't you tell us that last night?"

"It was embarrassing. I didn't want to admit in front of Albert that Emma tells me very little about her life these days."

Tay made a mental note to go back sometime to why she didn't want Tony Soprano to know she wasn't having long, personal conversations with her daughter, but for the moment he moved on.

"Do you have any idea who it could be? Someone she goes to school with, perhaps?"

"I don't think so. I think the reason she hasn't told me is it's someone she knows I wouldn't approve of." Mrs. Lau paused and then finished quickly. "Someone much older perhaps. Maybe even someone who's married."

"Do you think that might be why she disappeared? That she's somewhere with him?"

"No, I don't." Mrs. Lau shook her head. "It would be

entirely out of character for her. Even under these circumstances."

"And what circumstances are those?"

Mrs. Lau said nothing.

"There's something else, isn't there? Something else you lied
to me about."

She looked up and studied Tay, tilting her head first one way
and then another. It was a strangely intimate gesture. Tay
thought she was trying to decide whether she could trust him
enough to tell him the truth.

And then she decided.

"I lied about Emma not knowing who her real father is."

Tay considered the implications of that for a moment.

"How did she find out?' he asked. He thought he could
guess, but he wanted to hear Doris Lau say it.

Then she did. "I told her."

"When?"

"About a year ago. She's hardly spoken to me since."

She looked at Tay as if she was waiting for him to pass judgment and hand down her sentence. When he kept his face
empty and said nothing at all, she went on just as he knew she
would.

"You have to understand I had been wracked with guilt for
twenty-five years. Guilt that I had lied to my husband, guilt that
I had lied to my daughter, and guilt that I was still lying to her
every single day."

"So you decided she deserved to hear the truth."

"No, I decided I deserved to *tell* her the truth. Here is my
confession, and it's ugly. I told her, not because I thought she
needed to know or because telling her was the right thing to do.
I told her to relieve my own guilt. I did it for me, not her."

Tay didn't think that was so ugly, but neither did he think he
had the right to judge Doris Lau or her motivations.

"How did she react?" he asked instead of saying what he
thought.

"Not well. That's why we've barely spoken since then."

"Do you think she's told anyone else?"

"I doubt it. She certainly isn't proud of it. I don't see why she would tell anyone."

"Do you think this has anything to do with her disappearance?"

"I've thought about it a lot the past few days."

Mrs. Lau looked at Tay for a long moment in silence.

"I don't see how it could," she said. "I may be wrong, but I don't see how it could."

"Then you don't think she ran away."

"She's a grown woman, a very serious grown woman who's nearly finished medical school. She's not a little kid who packs her dolls and runs away from home because her mother tells her to eat her spinach."

Tay wasn't sure about that yet, but he said nothing.

"I think I've probably said enough for tonight," Mrs. Lau abruptly announced. The van's door rumbled open, which must have been the driver's cue to return to his seat because almost immediately he did.

Mrs. Lau held out her hand and Tay thought she was offering it for him to shake, but then she said, "Give me another cigarette before you leave. I think I've earned it. Don't you?"

Tay held out the pack. "Keep it. I've got more upstairs."

"No," she said with a crisp shake of her head and plucked out a single cigarette. "So far tonight I've only earned one."

Tay wondered what she thought she would have to do to earn the rest.

TAY WAS WALKING across the lobby of the hotel on his way back to his room when his telephone buzzed. He assumed it was Claire, maybe letting him know where she was, but he was disappointed when he looked at the screen.

The text he saw wasn't from Claire. It was from Shepherd.

Benny came through. Meeting at 9 tomorrow morning at the American Club. Just you and me. Claire will understand.

Why were they meeting at some place called the American Club? Surely Uncle Benny's triad contact couldn't be an American, could he?

Tay thought about calling Claire to tell her Uncle Benny had found a contact for them, but he decided just to forward Shepherd's text to her and leave it at that. She could call him if she wanted to talk about it, or about anything else, and if she didn't want to talk, then neither did he.

He stood in the lobby for a moment and fiddled with the phone until he figured out how to forward the text to Claire. Then he walked over to the concierge desk, found out where the American Club was, and arranged a car for the next morning.

TWENTY-FOUR

WEDNESDAY. DAY TWO. Searching for Emma Lau.

When the hotel car dropped Tay at the American Club the next morning, he discovered the club was not some rambling, homey-looking structure surrounded by green lawns and tennis courts, which was how he supposed he had envisioned it. Instead, it was an elegant but business-like suite of rooms spread over the forty-eighth and forty-ninth floors of a soaring skyscraper right in the middle of Hong Kong's financial district.

Tay took the elevator up to the reception area and found Shepherd waiting for him. He was standing in front of a wall of floor-to-ceiling windows with a spectacular view of the harbor.

"Who are we here to see?" Tay asked him.

"And top of the morning to you, too, Sam."

Tay was not in a good mood. Tay was seldom in a good mood in the morning, but this morning it was worse than usual, assuming such a thing was even possible. He had both his mysterious bleeding and last night's conversation with Doris Lau on his mind.

"Who are we here to see?" Tay repeated flatly.

Shepherd looked at Tay and wondered if he needed more coffee.

"Uncle Benny didn't tell me much. He just said he found a guy willing to talk to us and we should meet the guy here at nine o'clock."

"Does this guy have a name?"

"I imagine he does. Benny told me to ask for Mr. Jones, but somehow I doubt that's it."

"He's some kind of a triad boss?"

"I have no idea who he is. Benny didn't say. I suppose either the guy will tell us who he is himself, or he won't."

"Then we may just be wasting our time?"

Shepherd looked at Tay for a long moment without expression.

"I trust Benny, Sam. Hong Kong functions as well as it does purely because of personal relationships. If you have better ones than I do, by all means go talk to them. But if you don't, you need to calm down."

Tay didn't reply. He knew he deserved Shepherd's rebuke, but instead of admitting it he just clasped his hands behind his back and stood looking out the window.

Between where they were and the sprawling expanse of Hong Kong Harbor was one of the ugliest buildings Tay had ever seen. It was about the same height and size as the building they were in, but its gleaming aluminum skin was punctured on every floor by long lines of giant, circular windows which looked like portholes in the side of a massive ship.

"What is that?" Tay asked Shepherd, pointing at the building.

"It's called Jardine House. They built it in the seventies. Back then, it was the tallest building in Asia, but now it's nothing special."

"It's ugly as sin."

"*Sing chin ki szee fat long.*"

"What does that mean?"

"It's what the locals call the building in Cantonese. It translates as something like *House of a Thousand Assholes.*"

Tay's face broke into a grin.

"Perfect," he said. "That's perfect."

"Yeah, I kind of thought you might like it."

Shepherd and Tay were still contemplating the view together when a voice spoke softly from just behind them.

"Mr. Shepherd?"

"That's me," Shepherd said as they both turned around. "Are you... ah, Mr. Jones?"

The man who had spoken appeared to be in his twenties and unremarkable in either height or build. He had a square Chinese face and shiny black hair cut stylishly long. He was wearing an expensive gray suit, a white shirt, and a solid red tie.

The young man smiled, but not in a way that looked particularly friendly.

"This way please, sir," he said without answering Shepherd's question. Then he turned and walked away.

Shepherd looked at Tay and shrugged.

They followed the man through a pair of heavy wooden doors on the other side of the reception area and found themselves in a large dining room with a spectacular view. Strangely enough, it was completely deserted.

"Where is everybody?" Shepherd asked, but the man didn't reply.

They continued following him as he threaded his way among the empty tables, through another door on the other side of the dining room, and down a long hallway with a line of unmarked doors along its right side.

He stopped at the third, knocked softly, and opened it.

"Gentlemen," he said. "Please go in."

. . .

THE ROOM WAS not large, but the wall of windows overlooking the Macau ferry terminal made it seem bigger than it was. At one end was a mahogany sideboard with a silver coffee urn, a half dozen white china cups, and a platter of Danish pastries. In the middle was a round mahogany table surrounded by six high-backed chairs upholstered in dark green leather.

A man was seated at the table with his back to the windows. He appeared to be in his fifties and was tall for a Chinese, well over six feet. He was very large. Not fat, but large. He looked like a college football player who had gone soft in middle age. The man had silver hair cut short and close to his scalp, and he wore a well-cut blue blazer over a pink striped dress shirt without a tie.

Shepherd heard the door click closed and glanced over his shoulder. Their guide had not come in with them.

The man at the table studied Shepherd and Tay for a moment, then rose to his feet.

"Mr. Jones, I presume," Shepherd said.

The man grinned as if Shepherd had just told a wonderful joke.

"That is not my name, of course," he said, "but I thought it was an excellent choice of name for a meeting at the American Club. Do you like it?"

He spoke with slight traces of an English public school accent which marked him as someone who had probably gone to school in the UK in his youth.

"It's a very unusual name."

The man laughed.

"And from the place you selected for this meeting, I assume you must be an American."

"Oh, dear me, no. I'm a Hong Konger through and through. I'm not actually a member here. I just use the club for meetings occasionally. They don't seem to mind."

"Gee, I wonder why that is?"

The man laughed again.

"You are Mr. Shepherd, of course," he said. "They warned me you can be a bit of a wiseass."

"I am Mr. Shepherd, and I am indeed an internationally celebrated wiseass. People either hate it or they love it. In my experience it's about sixty-forty."

Jones smiled at that, but he didn't offer his hand so Shepherd didn't either.

"And then you would be Inspector Tay," he said, shifting his eyes to Tay. "Somehow I expected you to look more Chinese."

"I am no longer Inspector Tay. Now I'm just Mr. Tay. And I'm not Chinese. I'm a Singaporean."

The man seemed to consider both those things for a moment, and then he nodded and took his seat at the table again.

"Help yourself to coffee, gentlemen," he said, "and sit down. Please."

"I'll get it, Sam," Shepherd said. "How do you take yours?"

"Black."

Tay seated himself in the high-back chair opposite their host while Shepherd went over to the sideboard and poured two cups of coffee. No one spoke until Shepherd returned with the coffees and took a seat next to Tay.

"Perhaps we could begin," Shepherd said, "with you telling us who you are."

Again, the man grinned, apparently enjoying the joke.

"I don't see why that's necessary," he said. "What does it contribute to our discussion?"

"It seems only fair," Shepherd pointed out. "You know who we are."

"I do indeed know who you are. You, Mr. Shepherd, are an American lawyer with a reputation here in Hong Kong for being clever and resourceful in solving complicated problems. You are also known for being discreet and reliable, a man you can do business with. If you did not have that reputation, I would not be here."

The man shifted his eyes to Tay.

"And as for you, Inspector Tay——"

"I already told you. I am no longer a police inspector."

"Yes, you did, but I rather like the title, anyway. It gives you an official veneer, which I think you will find useful in Hong Kong. We're suckers for titles here. So, I think I will continue to use it. You have no personal objection, do you?"

Tay said nothing.

"Good," the man continued. "I will assume that means you do not. Now, so far, we've only been able to do a very superficial background investigation of you, Inspector Tay, but it would appear you also have a sterling reputation. Capable, even brilliant. Those are the descriptions we are hearing. And, like Mr. Shepherd here, a man of his word. A man on whom one can rely."

"You seem to have us at a disadvantage here, sir," Shepherd said.

"Yes, I'm glad you noticed. That's exactly what I had in mind."

Shepherd smiled despite himself. "Then at least tell us what you want us to call you."

"Jones will be fine. You can forget the Mr. part. We're all friends now."

"All right, Jones. But I have to say it doesn't actually feel much like we're friends."

"Oh, but we are, Mr. Shepherd. This is me being friendly. The alternative doesn't bear thinking about."

Shepherd spread his hands, palms up. "Then I guess you have the floor, Jones. We are here to listen to whatever you have to tell us."

"Wonderful," Jones said, and he rubbed his hands together as if he were eager to begin.

Then he did.

181

TWENTY-FIVE

"**I** UNDERSTAND A young woman is missing and you gentlemen are attempting to locate her. I also understand she was last seen in Mongkok Station a few days ago."

"That's true," Shepherd said.

"May I ask why you have involved yourselves in trying to locate this woman?"

"No."

The man considered that for a moment, and then he nodded. "Very well. But it is also my understanding you think she is being held for ransom by one of the triads. Is that correct?"

"When someone of prominence disappears in Hong Kong, it's the first thing you think about."

"Has there been a ransom demand?"

"No, sir. Not yet."

"And how do you interpret that?"

"We don't, but that fact alone does not rule out the possibility of a kidnap for ransom, and we need to do that before we can do anything else."

"Are the Hong Kong police involved?"

"No."

The man nodded but made no comment.

"In order to determine if this was an ordinary kidnap for ransom or if there is some other explanation, we asked Uncle Benny to help us establish contact with someone of sufficient rank and standing among the triads that he could tell us for certain whether any triad in Hong Kong has kidnapped a young woman for ransom within the past few days. Are you someone of sufficient rank and standing?"

The man pursed his lips and thought about how to answer.

"If I tell you no young woman is currently being held for ransom by any triad here in Hong Kong," he said at last, "you may deposit that in the bank and write checks on it."

"Then is any young woman currently being held for ransom by any triad here in Hong Kong?"

"Let's leave that question on the table for a moment, shall we? Before I answer, I'd like to ask a question or two of you."

"You can ask," Shepherd shrugged.

"Who is in charge of this search you are conducting? You or Inspector Tay?"

"You should treat Sam as the man in charge," Shepherd said. "My role is only to provide such local wisdom as may be required."

Jones shifted his eyes to Tay.

"Who is this woman you are looking for?"

Tay hesitated. "I'm sorry, but I can't share that with you," he said.

"Yes, I can understand that," Jones said. "If I was searching for Doris Lau's daughter, I probably wouldn't tell anyone either."

Shepherd's mouth opened.

"You're shitting me," he sputtered. "Is that true, Sam?"

Tay said nothing.

"Is this really Doris Lau's daughter we're looking for here?"

"Dear me, Inspector Tay," Jones laughed, "you *have* been keeping that quiet, haven't you?"

183

"I gather not quiet enough. You are very well informed."

"Of course I'm very well informed. You wouldn't want me here answering your questions if I wasn't, would you? Remember the sufficient rank and standing stuff you asked about? I am indeed of sufficient rank and standing."

Tay said nothing.

"Okay," Jones said, leaning forward on his forearms. "Cards on the table. You have been sent here, almost certainly by someone high up in the government of the United States, to aid Doris Lau in her time of need. Her daughter is missing and the United States is worried the Chinese Ministry of State Security has grabbed Emma to put pressure on her mother to crack down on the democracy demonstrators. How am I doing so far?"

Tay said nothing.

"But before anyone starts World War III over a missing girl, you must establish with certainty this isn't just a simple kidnapping for ransom engineered by one of the triads. Do I have that right, Inspector Tay?"

Tay thought about it for a moment and decided he had nothing to lose by telling Jones the truth, particularly since Jones already seemed to know the truth.

"More or less," he admitted.

"Actually, I think I have all that exactly right."

Jones shifted his eyes from Tay back to Shepherd.

"Leave me out of this, Jones," Shepherd said. "I just discovered I don't know shit about what's really going on here."

Jones looked back at Tay.

"You said cards on the table," Tay reminded him, "but those were our cards you just put on the table. Where are yours?"

"Fair enough," Jones said. "Here are my cards. No triad in Hong Kong is holding anyone at all for ransom right now, let alone Doris Lau's daughter. You have my word."

Tay and Shepherd exchanged a glance.

"I guess we couldn't ask you to be any clearer than that," Tay said.

"No indeed, you could not. But I'm not quite done yet. I have a few more cards I think will be of some use to you."

Tay and Shepherd waited.

"I would suggest you get yourselves some more coffee first, gentlemen. When you hear what else I have to tell you, you'll need it."

S HEPHERD PICKED UP their coffee cups, took them over to the sideboard, and refilled them. When he put the cup in front of Tay, he gave him a look.

"I ought to make you get your own fucking coffee for holding out on me."

Tay said nothing and Shepherd hesitated, but then he sat back down and looked at Jones.

"Since I'm doing so well as a waitress here, can I get you a cup, too?"

"That's very thoughtful of you, Mr. Shepherd, but I don't drink coffee. Caffeine gives me the shits something awful."

Shepherd took a sip of his coffee. "More information than I need."

Tay sat and watched Jones. He had a feeling something good was coming.

And it was.

"Five girls, all with wealthy and influential parents, have disappeared in the last eighteen months," Jones announced, "and all of them were last seen in Mongkok. Mrs. Lau's daughter is the sixth."

"Five?" Tay asked. "We only knew about three."

"Now wait just a fucking minute," Shepherd snapped. "What am I? Chopped liver? First, you didn't tell me this was Doris Lau's daughter you were looking for, and now I find out

185

you know three other girls have gone missing in Mongkok and you didn't tell me about them either?"

"It appears I may have been wrong, anyway," Tay said. "Jones says there were five."

"That's not the fucking point. The point is I am trying to help you here and you're holding out on me."

"It was Claire who briefed you, not me. I didn't decide what to tell you and what not to tell you. If you're unhappy, take it up with her."

Jones leaned forward. "Who's Claire?"

"Don't look at me, pal," Shepherd snapped. "Tay's in charge here. I'm just some local yokel he and Claire keep in the dark and dump shit on."

"Who is Claire?" Jones repeated.

"She's a woman working with me," Tay said. "I can think of nothing about her which is relevant to this discussion."

Jones considered that and, after a few moments, he nodded.

"Very well. Then let me tell you what we know about these five girls."

Jones extracted a small notebook from an inside pocket of his blazer. It was bound in black leather and looked expensive. He opened it on the table in front of him and Tay and Shepherd watched him flip pages until he found the one he was looking for.

"The first girl disappeared a year ago July. Her name was Stephanie Wong. She was twenty and lived with her father, who owns a shipping company. Her mother is dead. She went out one day and simply vanished. Several people claim to have seen her on Argyle Street in Mongkok the day she disappeared, but that has never been confirmed. There was no ransom demand, and she was never heard from again."

Jones reached into his jacket pocket and removed a pen, then he turned to the back of the notebook and carefully tore out two pages. He pushed the pages across the table toward Shepherd and Tay and placed the pen on top of them.

"There's more," he said. "You might want to make some notes about the details."

Shepherd folded his arms and said nothing.

Tay glanced at him and offered a half smile. "You're pouting."

Shepherd remained silent and Tay reached for the pen and paper.

"Would you like me to repeat what I gave you on the first girl?" Jones asked.

Tay was already writing and didn't bother to look up. "I think I can remember that far back."

Jones cleared his throat again and turned back to the notebook page he had been reading.

"The second girl disappeared last October, almost exactly a year ago. Her name was Ning Ho. She was eighteen years old and the daughter of Albert Ho, who is a prominent hotel developer. She and her friend were at a restaurant in Mongkok when she got a telephone call and told her friend she had to go. A week later, Mr. Ho received a ransom demand for two million American dollars. He paid the money, but his daughter was never seen again."

Jones glanced at Tay, who nodded. "Go ahead," he said.

"The third girl disappeared on New Year's Day of this year. Her name was Yu Yang, and she was the oldest of the five. Thirty-one. She was with friends attending a party at the Peninsula Hotel on New Year's Eve. Just after midnight, she left telling no one, but several people later claimed to have seen her getting off a train in Mongkok Station. She hasn't been heard from since. Her father is the Executive Vice President of the Hong Kong Shanghai Bank."

"Do you have contact information for the people who say they saw her in Mongkok Station?" Tay asked.

Jones shook his head.

"Continuing then, the fourth girl disappeared the day before Chinese New Year. Her name was Elaine Zhao, and she was a flight attendant with Cathay Pacific Airlines. She lived with another flight attendant in Mongkok and had called her roommate to say she was on her way home from the airport. She never arrived and has not been heard from since. Miss Zhao is the only daughter of one of the wealthiest families in Hong Kong. There are stories claiming the roots of the family wealth are in the opium trade, but these days like every other commercial family in Hong Kong they are property investors."

"Do you have a name and contact information for this roommate?"

Jones shook his head again and then returned to reading his notes.

"The fifth girl disappeared in June. Her name was Huiling Song and she was twenty-three. Her friends called her April, or so I am told, and her father is in the casino business in Macau. She was supposed to meet a friend at a restaurant in Mongkok, but she didn't turn up. No one has heard from her since."

Jones looked up and glanced back and forth between Shepherd and Tay.

"And now we have the sixth girl to go missing. Emma Lau, whom I understand walked off a train into Mongkok Station several days ago and simply disappeared."

Jones closed his notebook with a snap and returned it to his jacket pocket. When Tay finished writing, he pushed the pen back across the table to Jones, folded the two small sheets of paper, and tucked them into his shirt pocket.

"Why are you telling us all this?" he asked Jones.

Jones pursed his lips and seemed to think about the question, although Tay didn't see why it required any great thought.

Jones wasn't telling them all this because he thought Uncle Benny was a great guy and he was always happy to help out friends of Benny's. He had some purpose of his own for providing all of this information to them, and Tay wanted to know what it was.

"When wealthy people or their children go missing in Hong

Kong, the first thing anyone thinks of is that they've been kidnapped by one of the triads," Jones began. "Occasionally, they have been, it's true, but most of the time they haven't been."

Jones peered at Tay as if he was seeking assurance Tay understood what he was saying.

Tay offered a nod. It was all the assurance he could muster.

"In all of these particular cases I have just described," Jones continued, "I assure you none of the triads had anything to do with the disappearance of these young women. Despite that, the mere fact all the disappearances appear to have a connection to Mongkok, which is known to be an area of triad activity, has brought down what I think Americans call *the heat*."

"Do you mean," Tay asked, "the police are pressing you and your associates about your involvement in these disappearances and you want them to stop?"

"No," Jones smiled, "nothing like that. The police here in Hong Kong are seldom involved in disappearances such as these."

"Why not?"

"Private arrangements are generally made."

"And by private arrangements, you mean the payment of a ransom?"

"Not always. For example, here you and Mr. Shepherd sit asking me for information which might help you find Emma Lau and return her to her mother. I would call that a private arrangement, too."

"If the heat you're talking about isn't coming from the police, where is it coming from?"

"The source is the people with genuine power in Hong Kong, Inspector, and that is not the police. If it were just the police, we would not be so concerned."

"Are you telling me some of these people whose daughters are missing have connections to the triads?"

Jones smiled, but Tay saw there was no humor in it. He pushed a white card across the table to Tay.

"We would like to do whatever we can to help you locate and return Mrs. Lau's daughter."

Tay assumed the card was a business card until he picked it up. There was nothing printed on it but a single local telephone number.

"You may reach me at that number anytime, and it is a number on which you may speak openly. Please call me if we can help."

"Who is this *we* you keep talking about?"

Jones smiled, but he ignored Tay's question as Tay knew he would.

"We would be in your debt," he said instead, "if your search for Doris Lau's daughter also resolved these other cases of girls missing in Mongkok."

"Which would take the heat off you and your friends."

"Which would give the parents of these other girls some peace."

Tay wasn't sure whether to believe that was the extent of Jones's interest or not.

"If you want to help them so much, why aren't you out looking for these girls yourselves?" Tay asked.

"Oh, dear me, I haven't the first idea how we would go about doing something like that."

Jones smiled and folded his hands in front of him on the table. For a moment, he looked to Tay like a vicar come to bring comfort to the afflicted.

"For goodness sake, Inspector, we're not detectives. We're criminals."

TWENTY-SIX

"I'M DONE WITH this," Shepherd said when they had left the building and were outside on the sidewalk. "I don't like being lied to."

"I didn't lie to you."

"You didn't tell me the truth either."

"Claire didn't tell you the truth. That's different."

"How exactly is that different?"

Tay wasn't certain it *was* different, so he said nothing and tried to look enigmatic.

It began to rain then, a light mist that seemed to be less falling rain than moisture squeezing out of the humid air and trying to escape.

"I've got a hotel car waiting." Tay pointed at the big Mercedes hovering in a parking zone about fifty yards away. "I'll drop you off."

"That's not necessary. My office isn't very far."

It rained harder. Big fat drops plopping onto the sidewalk and making hollow *thunking* sounds like big globs of spit.

"For Christ's sake, Shepherd, get in the fucking car before we both get soaked."

Without waiting for an answer, Tay jogged toward the car. After a moment of hesitation, Shepherd followed.

T HE DRIVER LOOKED over his shoulder at the two men shaking off rain in the back seat. He flicked his eyes from Tay to Shepherd and back to Tay again. "To the hotel, sir?"

"Let's just sit here a minute. I need to make a phone call."

The rain pounded down then, banging against the roof and windows of the Mercedes with a rhythm you could almost dance to.

"The rainy season's over," Shepherd said. "This shouldn't be happening."

"I guess God lied to you, too."

Shepherd gave Tay a hard look, but Tay was busy with his telephone and ignored him.

Tay placed a call and waited for it to be picked up.

"Claire?" Pause. "I'm here with Shepherd and he's an unhappy boy. He's so pissed off you didn't tell him whose daughter we're looking for or about the other girls who have disappeared he says he's done with helping us."

Tay paused again, listening, and watched the rain dancing on the car's windows.

"No," he continued, "I didn't tell him. It was this guy we met this morning. He told him."

Another pause.

"How the hell should I know where he found out? He's supposed to be some kind of triad heavy, so I guess he just knows. One other thing. This guy says six girls including Emma have gone missing in Mongkok over the last year and a half, not just three, and he gave me some details on each of them."

Tay listened some more, said uh-huh twice, then went on.

"Regardless, you need to apologize to Shepherd or he's

walking, and I don't want him to do that. My suggestion is the three of us sit down and talk."

Tay turned his head and looked at Shepherd, raising his eyebrows in the obvious inquiry. Shepherd said nothing.

"Yeah, Shepherd thinks it's a bloody marvelous idea, too. He's happy to meet anywhere that's convenient for you."

"Now just a minute—" Shepherd began.

"Where are you now?" Tay went on, holding up his free hand to Shepherd like a traffic cop. "That's great. We're just across a couple of streets from you. We're sitting in a hotel car and it's parked right next to the Thousand Assholes Building."

"The House of a Thousand Assholes," Shepherd corrected him.

Tay glanced at him, but said nothing and shifted his attention back to the telephone.

"We'll pick you up at the front of the Mandarin Hotel. Ten minutes?"

Tay punched off the call and returned the telephone to his pocket.

"Claire's at Alexandra House," he said, "right next door to the Mandarin. I told her—"

"I heard what you told her," Shepherd interrupted. "But you didn't ask me whether or not I was willing to talk to her."

"I knew you'd be delighted, so I figured it was a waste of time."

Shepherd looked away, shook his head, and listened to the rain.

"I don't want to go to some hotel coffee shop," he said after a moment. "I guess we could go to my office. It's just up the hill on Hollywood Road."

"Walking past a lot of people wouldn't be a good idea. We need privacy."

"We'll have complete privacy. My office is a walkup above a noodle shop. I don't even have a secretary."

Tay smiled. "You have coffee? Got to have coffee."

"There's a Pacific Coffee next door."

Tay leaned forward and touched the driver on his shoulder. "First to the Mandarin Hotel, then follow Mr. Shepherd's directions to his office on Hollywood Road."

"Yes, sir," the driver said and started the engine.

The wipers came on and began a gentle slapping motion as they tracked over the windshield. Tay settled back into his seat and the car pulled away.

"I've always thought the sound of windshield wipers was very soothing," he said.

"Do you feel soothed right now?" Shepherd asked.

"Yes, I think I do."

"I'm so happy for you."

S HEPHERD'S OFFICE WAS in a neighborhood called SoHo, the local acronym for South of Hollywood Road. Hong Kong's SoHo, like its New York namesake, tried hard to be the hippest and most pretentious neighborhood going. It was a place where a cool new restaurant or a bar either opened or, more likely closed, almost every week.

They got out of the car in front of the Pacific Coffee Company and bought three large coffees and a bag of cinnamon rolls. The rain had stopped, so they sent the driver to find a place to park and walked the fifty yards from there to Shepherd's office.

Claire and Tay followed behind Shepherd as he climbed up two flights to his office. The concrete stairwell was musty and dim and smelled faintly of urine like every other stairwell in Hong Kong.

Despite the stylishness of the neighborhood, Shepherd's office wasn't. It was just a single, averaged-sized room on the second floor of a shophouse above a noodle shop. The shophouse was old, as old as anything in Hong Kong was, and the interior walls were brick with some kind of white glaze over them. The glaze had been troweled smooth on a day long ago and the walls glistened like porcelain. On the north side of the room, three tall windows looked downhill toward the harbor through a forest of newer, bigger buildings.

Perpendicular to the windows, Shepherd had placed a long library table he used as a desk. It was old and battered, but behind it he had a new Aeron chair that looked as if it had cost a pile. The table was mostly bare. There was nothing on it except for a large leather desk pad, two computer monitors, and an old-fashioned-looking landline telephone. Behind the work-table, three horizontal filing cabinets, each five drawers high, sat on the wall. Locking bars had been welded to all three cabinets and formidable-looking padlocks dangled from each bar.

Tay liked the office at once. It had a comfortable, masculine feel to it. It was a place where he could see himself tilting back in the Aeron chair, swinging his feet up on the table, and opening a book he had been looking forward to reading.

He particularly liked the large oil painting hanging in the exact center of the wall opposite the desk. It was at least five feet on each side and didn't depict any recognizable form, or at least no form recognizable to Tay. Instead, it was a riot of primary colors that swirled and swooped and splashed over the canvas in a way which seem at a glance to be random, but on closer inspection formed intricately interwoven patterns.

"That's a wonderful painting," Tay said. "Where did you get it?"

It was the only one of Anita's paintings Shepherd still had. She had taken all the others when she left him, but she had given him this one for his birthday so it was his and he had insisted on keeping it. He had brought it with him to Hong Kong when he fled Bangkok and had hung it in his new office. It didn't take long for him to decide that had been a terrible idea, but he had never gotten around to moving it.

"It's too long a story to tell," Shepherd said. "And I don't know you well enough to tell it, anyway."

195

He settled into the Aeron chair and waved Tay and Claire to the two wooden captain's chairs facing it across the table.

Shepherd smiled to himself. Those two chairs were uncomfortable as hell, which was why he had bought them. He had few visitors in his office, and most of those he had were ones he wished would go away. Those awful chairs generally got the job done.

TWENTY-SEVEN

C LAIRE SIPPED AT her coffee, put the cup down on Shepherd's library table, and folded her arms.

"I'm sorry I didn't tell you everything, Jack."

"Arms folded over your chest isn't a good look when you're apologizing for something."

"I'm not apologizing. I'm explaining. My instructions were to tell no one who Emma's parents were. I was just following those instructions."

"Oh, you were only following orders, huh? And now I'm supposed to say that makes it okay you lied to me?"

"No, but this might make it okay. I'll tell you the rest of it."

"The *rest* of it? Good God, you mean there's *more*?"

Claire nodded.

Shepherd shook his head. "Look, I don't mind that it turns out you're working for Doris Lau—"

"We're not working for Doris Lau. She didn't know who was going to show up until we talked to her on Monday night, and she still doesn't know who we are."

Shepherd leaned forward and looked back and forth between Claire and Tay.

"Then I guess I don't get it. If Doris Lau didn't ask you to find her daughter, why are you involved in this?"

"Emma's father knows August. He went to him and asked him to find his daughter. August turned the matter over to us."

"Oh, bullshit. I know that's not true. Doris Lau's husband was a big-time property developer here, but he died years ago."

"Doris Lau's husband wasn't Emma's father."

Shepherd's eyes narrowed, but he said nothing.

"Emma's father is William Marsh Rice," Claire continued. "The Vice President of the United States."

Shepherd's mouth opened and for a moment he struggled to regain the power of speech.

Claire didn't wait for him to succeed. She plunged straight in and told him the whole story, everything August had told Tay when they met in Salisbury Garden. After she finished, a silence fell. Shepherd just sat and stared at her.

"You have *got* to be shitting me," he muttered after a minute or two.

Claire shook her head, and Shepherd shifted his eyes to Tay.

"Don't look at me," Tay told him. "That's what August told me, too, and Doris Lau confirmed it when we talked to her."

"And she said no one knows, not even the girl?"

"Mrs. Lau claimed she had never told Emma, but she admitted she had told her Chief of Staff. He's apparently her closest political advisor."

"Albert Chan?"

Tay nodded. "You know him?"

"Not personally. But he has a reputation."

"Reputation?"

"The word is he's a nasty piece of work."

Tay nodded and made a mental note to find out more about that. Maybe Albert Chan's reputation wasn't relevant to anything, but he had learned a long time ago you couldn't tell whether something was relevant until you knew what it was.

"There's one other thing and I haven't even had a chance to

tell Claire this yet," Tay added. "I ran into Doris Lau last night by accident."

"You ran into the Chief Executive of Hong Kong by *accident*?"

"Long story."

"I'll bet."

"Anyway, Mrs. Lau admitted she *had* told Emma who her real father was. She said she had done it out of guilt and that it had led to a break between them. She was insistent, however, Emma had been appalled when she learned the truth about who her father was and she wouldn't have told anyone else."

Shepherd tilted back in his chair, knitted his fingers together behind his head, and closed his eyes.

"So, let me make sure I've got this straight now. You're telling me Doris Lau and Vice President Rice have a secret daughter together, one so secret only a handful of people know about her, and you think this girl was kidnapped here in Hong Kong."

Tay nodded.

"But not kidnapped for money."

"We can't be sure yet," Tay said. "That's why we needed to rule out triad involvement before we do anything else. The big fear is the motive was more likely politics than money. To coerce either Mrs. Lau or the Vice President, or maybe both of them, into doing something they wouldn't otherwise do."

"But you don't know who took this girl or what they want either Mrs. Lau or the Vice President to do?"

"No."

"That's pretty much it," Claire said.

Shepherd opened his eyes.

"Holy fucking Christ on a crutch," he murmured.

"That's pretty much it, too," Tay agreed.

· · ·

"LOOK," TAY SAID, "I know you two love all the cloak and dagger bullshit, but I don't give a damn about it. All I want to know is what happened to these six girls."

"You think they're all dead," Shepherd said. He didn't bother to make a question of it.

"If what your triad source said this morning is accurate, girls have been disappearing for a year and a half now. So, yes, I think most of them are dead."

"Most?"

"Emma's only been missing since Saturday, so maybe..." Tay stopped talking and spread his hands. "There might still be time to get her back before whatever's happened to the others happens to her, too."

"If Emma was taken to blackmail either Mrs. Lau or the Vice President into doing something," Shepherd said, "they'll keep her alive until it's done."

"So, what do you think—" Claire began, but Tay held up his hands and interrupted.

"Let's take this one step at a time, but let's take each of those steps as fast as we can. I don't know how much time we have here. Emma's been missing for four days. Every day that passes, our chances of getting her back alive get a little worse."

Tay looked at Shepherd.

"That's why I don't have either the time or the interest to deal with your hurt feelings over what Claire didn't tell you. I need to know right now. Are you going to be part of this or aren't you?"

"Are you asking me—"

"In or out, Shepherd? One of those two words is all I want to hear from you. In? Or out?"

Shepherd looked at Tay for a long moment.

"In," he said.

"You okay with that, Claire?"

She nodded.

"Then listen up. I'm here because I'm the detective. You weren't thinking of this as a homicide investigation when you asked for my help, but it looks now like it might be one. That's an even better reason."

"Reason for what?" Claire asked.

"For me to take charge." Tay looked from one to the other. "I'm the lead on this. Anybody have a problem with that?"

Both Shepherd and Claire shook their heads.

"Then here's what we're going to do," Tay said. "I want the two of you to take the list we have of the other missing girls and find out everything you can about them by tomorrow. Divide them up, research them online, then go out and talk to their parents and friends. Let's see if we can find any kind of connection between them."

"You mean other than the obvious one?" Shepherd asked.

Tay looked at him and waited.

"They all disappeared in Mongkok," he said. "That strikes me as a pretty solid connection."

"But we don't know what any of them were doing in Mongkok," Tay said. "There's something out there that ties all this together and finding it is the quickest way for us to find Emma."

"Are you taking part of the list?" Claire asked.

"No, I'm going to talk to Sarah again, and I'm going to push her hard. She lied to us yesterday. She doesn't want to tell us the real reason she and Emma were in Mongkok and I'm going to find out what it was."

Tay looked back and forth from Claire to Shepherd.

"Everybody on the same page?"

They both nodded.

Tay fished out the notes he had made when Jones was giving him the details about the missing girls and handed them to Claire.

"Let's get to work."

PART 2

NEWTON'S SECOND LAW OF MOTION

*The velocity of an object changes
when it is subjected to an external force.*

TWENTY-EIGHT

TAY STOOD IN front of the receptionist in the Citibank investment banking office, his face arranged in a look he hoped was deferential, even unctuous.

"I'm here to see Sarah McFarland," he said.

"Do you have an appointment?"

"Yes, I do."

"Your name, sir?"

"Harry Lee," Tay said. "From Citibank Singapore."

He hadn't telephoned Sarah to tell her he was coming, much less to ask her if she would speak with him again. In Tay's experience, you learned a lot more from confronting people when they weren't expecting you. If they knew you were coming, it just gave them more time to dream up a good story.

"I don't see your name on my list of appointments," the receptionist said.

"She must have forgotten. Please, just tell her I'm here."

When the receptionist reached for her telephone, Tay walked over and picked up a copy of *The Wall Street Journal* he saw lying on a coffee table. He turned his back to the receptionist and buried his head in the paper.

The name he had given the receptionist was the name of

Singapore's first Prime Minister. He doubted Sarah would recognize it, but he was counting on her curiosity about who this was who claimed to have an appointment with her to get her to come out and see. Tay was on page six of *The Wall Street Journal* and hadn't yet found anything in it which even remotely interested him when he heard Sarah's voice behind him.

"Are you Mr. Lee?"

Tay folded the paper and turned around. Sarah just stood there and looked at him. She was a lot cooler than he expected, which pushed his suspicions into high gear.

"I don't understand," she said after a moment.

"I think you do."

Sarah said nothing.

"Do you want to do this out here, or can we go to your office and speak in private?" Tay continued.

Sarah hesitated, but not for very long.

"This way, please."

THEY SAT DOWN in Sarah's office, she behind her desk and Tay in an uncomfortable chair which faced her desk. This chair was even more uncomfortable than the one in Shepherd's office. Did everyone in Hong Kong give their visitors uncomfortable chairs? Yes, something told Tay they did.

Tay sat there saying nothing at all. He always thought it was best to allow the person he was questioning to speak first. It made them feel in control, which simplified the moves required to sucker punch them when he was good and ready.

"Who are you?" Sarah asked after a moment.

It wasn't a question Tay had been expecting, but he thought it was a reasonable one under the circumstances.

"Yesterday morning you said your name was Sam. Now it's Harry Lee. You *are* a spy, aren't you?"

"I am exactly who I told you I was yesterday. I'm someone

Doris Lau trusts to find Emma. I am not a spy, and I am not from the police. If it matters, my name actually is Sam."

"But you told—"

"I told the receptionist my name was Harry Lee because I wanted you to be curious enough to come out of your office. I thought you might duck if you knew it was me."

Sarah said nothing, and Tay knew he had been right.

"You lied to us about something yesterday," he said. "I want to know what it was."

"I didn't—"

"Let's just save all that, can we?" Tay interrupted. "Emma has been missing for four days now. You are the last person who saw her. You are the most likely person to know where she went when she left Mongkok Station."

"I don't know—"

"I said save it!" Tay snapped. "We're trying to get your friend back before she ends up like the others."

"Like the others? What are you talking about?"

"You told me yourself about other girls who had gone missing and never heard from again. What do you think happened to them? You figure they're just out shopping some-where? They're dead, you silly girl, and I'm trying to find Emma before she's dead, too."

A look of what appeared to be genuine shock spread over Sarah's face.

"No, that can't be."

"Of course it can be."

"Emma only went—" Abruptly Sarah stopped talking. "I can't tell you."

"Why not?"

"I promised Emma I would never say a thing to anyone."

"And you would rather see her end up dead than break your promise?"

"No! That's not what I meant!"

"Then what *did* you mean?"

"I meant..." Sarah hesitated. "I just can't tell you."

Tay took out his telephone, opened the directory, and tapped on one number to dial it.

"Doris Lau, please," he said into the phone. "This is Samuel Tay."

"What are you doing?" Sarah asked.

Tay ignored her.

"Please don't tell Mrs. Lau any of this."

Tay stayed silent.

"Okay, hang up the phone. I'll tell you."

Tay listened to the voice at the other end of the phone.

"Cordis Hotel. How may I direct your call?"

He pushed the disconnect button, returned the telephone to his pocket, and folded his arms.

"Swear to me you won't tell anyone else," Sarah said.

"I can't do that."

Sarah fidgeted in her chair. "I promised her I wouldn't tell anyone."

"You will tell me and you will do it right now."

Sarah rolled her eyes and looked away. "Okay, Emma was seeing someone. Satisfied?"

"In Mongkok?"

"Yes."

"The restaurant story was just bullshit, wasn't it? She was going to Mongkok to meet someone, and she used you to cover for her."

Sarah nodded with obvious reluctance.

"How many times?"

"How many times what?"

"How many times did you cover for her?"

"I don't know. Six? Seven? Something like that."

"Did she ever go there without you?"

"Maybe. I think so."

"Who was this she was seeing?"

"I don't know. She never told me."

"Oh, come on! You don't expect me to believe *that*, do you?"

"It's the truth! All I know is it was somebody older. A lot older, I think."

"How would you know that if you don't know who it is?"

"It was just the impression I got from the way she talked about him. It was somebody important. Somebody she looked up to."

"And he lived in Mongkok?"

"I don't think so. I think he just had an apartment there where they met."

"Then he was married?"

Sarah shrugged.

Tay wondered at how little Sarah seemed to care about that. Did it no longer matter to people of her age whether or not your lovers were married to someone else? If it didn't, then why did any of them ever bother to get married themselves? The issues of honor and decency and loyalty orbiting Sarah's casual shrug pointed Tay at a moral thicket into which he had no intention of venturing.

"Do you know where the apartment is?" he asked her instead.

She shook her head. "I was never there. I would just have lunch, walk around or go shopping at Langham Place, and then meet Emma somewhere when she was ready to go."

"So, you have no idea at all where—"

"Wait! There was one time I was walking back to Mongkok Station from Langham Place and I saw her coming toward me on Argyle Street. She was a block or two away across Nathan Road."

"Which side of Argyle Street was she on?"

Sarah squinted her eyes and seemed to replay the moment in her mind.

"The right side. At Sneaker Street. I remember because she was carrying a bag, and I wondered for a second if she had gone shopping for sneakers."

"Had she?"

Sarah shook her head.

"Then you think the apartment where she met her lover was somewhere around there?"

"Maybe. Or maybe she was walking from somewhere else. I don't know."

"Do you think she could be there now?" Tay asked.

"Where?"

"In the apartment where she met this guy. Wherever it is."

The question seemed to surprise Sarah, and Tay could see she had never thought of the possibility.

"You mean maybe she just moved in with this guy without telling her mother or anybody else where she is?"

Now it was Tay's turn to shrug.

"Emma wouldn't do that," Sarah said. "She's not like that. You'd have to know her to understand. She just wouldn't do that."

"Do you think she might have gone somewhere with whoever this man is?"

Sarah shook her head. "Not without telling anyone. Look, Emma's a very responsible girl. She's very straight."

"You mean straight like going to an apartment in Mongkok to meet an older married man?"

"What bothers you so much about that? That he's probably older? Or that he might be married?"

Tay just looked at Sarah and said nothing. The mockery in her voice saddened him. He had learned long ago there were gaps between human beings that were simply unbridgeable, and it looked like this yawning chasm was one of those.

"So where do you think Emma is?" he asked.

"I don't know."

"No idea?"

Sarah just shook her head and said nothing at all.

. . .

TAY TOOK SARAH through her story again, but nothing changed. He felt certain now Sarah had told him all she knew. It wasn't much, but it was a hell of a lot more than he had before.

Emma had a lover she met regularly in Mongkok. He was older, probably married if he kept an apartment there just to meet her, and he was well-known enough Emma wouldn't tell even one of her best friends his name.

Best of all, he might have narrowed down the location of the apartment where Emma met this man even if Sarah didn't know exactly where it was.

If you divided Mongkok into four quadrants with Mongkok Station at the center, Sarah had seen Emma walking toward her from the southeast quadrant. Still a lot of territory, but only a quarter as much as it could have been.

But what did any of this have to do with the other girls who had disappeared?

Whoever this married guy Emma was involved with might be, it seemed unlikely he had been involved with all the other missing girls, too. So, if Emma's lover wasn't the connection among the six girls, what *was* the connection? He still had no idea.

What Sarah had told him wasn't much, it might even be nothing at all, but it gave him someplace to start.

And right now, Tay would take whatever he could get.

TWENTY-NINE

ALMOST NO ONE remembered the street's real name anymore. For nearly as long as anyone could remember, everyone had just called it Sneaker Street. For block after block, the street was lined with almost nothing but shops selling the latest in sneakers and whatever other athletic gear might be in fashion. Every brand of sneakers you had ever heard of was on display somewhere along the street, together with quite a few brands almost nobody had ever heard of.

Tay told the driver to drop him at the corner of Argyle Street and Sneaker Street. After he had looked around, he would walk back to the hotel. It was only a few blocks.

Tay sent the driver away with a generous tip. He understood most people didn't tip in Hong Kong, but he usually did it anyway. He told himself it was because he empathized with the people who did the lousy, dreary, everyday jobs that kept the world running, but he knew it was really because he didn't want to risk pissing somebody off and then having to deal with that. He was buying peace.

At a glance, Sneaker Street was nothing special. It was narrow and crowded. Throngs of local kids and a few tourists jammed the sidewalks and poked through the shops looking for bargains. Some shops looked as if they had been transplanted straight from a Los Angeles shopping mall, but most were dumps, open-fronted spaces with concrete walls and shoes sealed in plastic and displayed in utilitarian metal racks reaching to the ceiling.

Tay also spotted a few of the tiny local restaurants that could be found in nearly every block all over Hong Kong. Narrow storefronts opening into linoleum-floored spaces with unadorned plastic-topped tables and uncomfortable-looking chairs. There was almost always a window to one side of the entrance filled with the hanging corpses of geese, ducks, and other wildlife Tay didn't try too hard to identify. The animals were all roasted to a bright red, their skin glistening with fat. Big hooks held each of the little carcasses upright, and Tay always imagined them to be peering mournfully at passers-by, eyes full of resignation.

Between the storefronts, Tay saw the narrow, steep staircases that were another feature of most blocks around Hong Kong. There was no wasted space here. Every inch had a value, usually a high one, and he knew up each of those staircases and above every shop, whether grand or modest, were workrooms or living spaces occupied by more people than he could imagine.

Rents were so high in Hong Kong and space was so precious that Tay knew tiny apartments like the ones above these stores were often subdivided into multiple living spaces. Several families might occupy an area not much bigger than a hotel room. He had never been inside an apartment subdivided like that and, looking up at the grimy windows and laundry hanging from metal poles, he decided he didn't want to either.

Tay carried on walking south on Sneaker Street, peering into the shops, scrutinizing the restaurants, and examining the staircases. What was he looking for? He really had no idea. It wasn't like he expected Emma Lau to appear suddenly walking toward him on the sidewalk.

He had always believed in the importance of the feeling he got from putting himself at the place where a violent crime had occurred. It was almost as if he could feel the presence of the people who had been there when it occurred, as if he could look into the past and see what they had seen.

Tay didn't believe in ghosts, but he did believe when human beings died they left a sense of their presence in the spaces they had inhabited in life. He had never entered the scene of a murder without feeling the victim all around him. In the air, on the walls, in every molecule of the place where they had once been alive.

It was as if the dead hung on as long as they could, clinging desperately to the life they had lived until they were dragged away to whatever came next.

If anything came next.

Which Tay doubted it did.

He stopped walking and looked around. Maybe it wouldn't work this time. He wasn't even certain a violent crime had been committed. And even if it had, he had no idea whether it had been committed here.

Regardless, the compulsion remained with him. He needed to put himself in the place where Sarah had seen Emma and let the place tell him what it could.

Now he was here.

And what was the place telling him?

Fuck all, that's what the place was telling him.

TAY CONTINUED SOUTH for a couple blocks, then he turned around and walked north on the opposite side of the street. Nothing changed. He found nothing that offered him any insight. Whatever mystical vibrations might have been around the neighborhood appeared to have taken the day off.

After a half hour of trolling up and down Sneaker Street with nothing at all useful occurring to him, Tay muttered,

"Screw this." He could see the Cordis Hotel towering over the neighborhood a few blocks away, and he turned left on Nelson Street and headed straight for it.

When the light changed, he crossed busy Nathan Road in front of what looked like the mouth of an urban cavern. A river of humanity flowed into the dark opening and disappeared down underneath the streets of the city. Over the entry he saw the red and white symbol of the Hong Kong MTR, and above it was a blue and white sign that said MONGKOK STATION.

To the right of the entrance an elderly man sat on a pink plastic stool. He was on the chubby side and almost bald, but he was neatly dressed in dark trousers, a blue checked shirt, and a gray windbreaker. He held a walking stick in his hands and bounced it rhythmically against the concrete as he watched the crowds surge past him and down into the station.

It was a sight you encountered all over Hong Kong. The elderly, having nothing else to do and no place else to go, set themselves up near a street or along the sidewalk and sat there much of the day watching the life they had once lived pass them by. Seeing it always left Tay with a strong sense of melancholy. He couldn't help but wonder if that was all life would have for him when he drew close to the end.

T AY ALLOWED THE throng to sweep him into the entrance to Mongkok Station and down the stairs.

He found himself in a wide corridor with red tile walls and a yellow concrete floor, and he moved along with the crowd until he emerged in a massive underground space. It made him think of a colossal public toilet: all glistening red and gray tile walls with a polished concrete floor.

Off to his right, people darted up to one of dozens of automatic ticket machines arranged in neat ranks. With an economy of motion he found admirable, they inserted cash, collected a ticket, and moved on quickly. Large green and white signs over their heads directed them toward the various platforms where the trains arrived and departed.

Hundreds of people moved through the enormous space in all directions and all at the same time, yet they somehow avoided colliding with one another. It was a ballet of pure motion that left Tay awestruck. He was standing there staring at it when he heard a loud *whooshing* sound and a train pulled in.

The train's doors all snapped open at the same time and a mass of humanity surged out and rolled across the station from left to right like a tsunami rolling over a beach.

Right in front of him a young girl did exactly what Sarah had said she had done when she and Emma arrived together in Mongkok Station. She stopped behind one of the red-tiled pillars to shelter from the swirl of the crowd and lifted her telephone. She peered at its screen, poked out a message with her thumbs, then lowered the phone and moved on around the pillar toward the exit.

The station was quiet for a moment, then another train arrived, another tsunami of passengers flooded out, and the process repeated itself all over again. Mongkok Station was one of the busiest train stations in the world, and this was how it went day after day, month after month, year after year.

At least now Tay could see how it would have been possible for Sarah and Emma to have become separated in just the way Sarah had described. Possible, yes, but that wasn't what happened. Emma and Claire had separated on purpose, because that was the way they had planned it.

But then Emma didn't come back.

And that was *not* the way they had planned it.

THERE WAS NOTHING mystical here either, Tay told himself. But seeing Sneaker Street and Mongkok Station had raised one question in his mind, and it was one he had not thought to ask before.

If the missing girls were dead, and he felt less and less doubt they were, what had happened to their bodies?

In the seething, throbbing mass of humanity that was Mongkok, there was no place to hide a body. And you certainly couldn't throw one over your shoulder, carry it down the street, and dump it in the harbor.

Had the killer dismembered the bodies and carried them away in pieces? That might be a popular way of disposing of bodies in movies, but not so much in real life. The dismemberment of a body was hard. It required considerable strength, and it made an awful mess.

Tay made a mental note to get Claire to check and see if there had been any reports during the last year or two of unidentified body parts turning up in Hong Kong. He doubted there were. Five girls made for a lot of body parts. It would have been a huge, international story, and he had heard nothing like it.

No, it was something else. It had to be. But what?

If someone had killed those five girls who disappeared before Emma, what had he done with their bodies?

Once more, Tay's eyes swept across the human anthill that was Mongkok Station. Something about the place gave him the creeps.

He looked around for an exit, found one, and trotted up the steps without looking back.

THIRTY

TAY WENT INTO a 7-Eleven on his way back to the hotel and bought a fresh pack of Marlboros. He paid for it and was halfway to the door when he turned around, went back, and bought another. He had a feeling he might need them.

The hotel had placed a shiny aluminum cylinder filled with sand just outside its main entrance. It was close enough to the door to be convenient for smokers and far enough away to keep other guests from complaining. Tay stood beside it and lit his first cigarette of the evening. He was rewarded with the welcoming, energizing buzz the opening hit of nicotine always gave him.

Tay smoked and watched the pedestrians hurrying along Shanghai Street toward whatever the evening held in store for them. He wondered how many were heading for some secret Mongkok love nest where they would meet a beautiful young girl. Not very many, he would wager. Maybe none at all.

While Tay smoked, he thought about what he knew about Emma's disappearance and what he did not know. When he finished his cigarette, he was still thinking about that, so he dumped the butt into the cylinder of sand and called Claire.

"I hope you've accomplished more today than we have," she said when she answered.

Tay didn't think that was a very auspicious beginning for a conversation.

"You couldn't get anything out of other girls' families?"

"We haven't talked to any of the other girls' families. These are all wealthy and powerful people, Sam. They don't answer their own phones. You have to fight your way through an army of assistants and retainers before you can speak to any of them and we haven't been able to do that yet."

"Can't Shepherd—"

"Shepherd is trying to get to them through people they know, but it's taking longer than we hoped."

"I don't think we have a lot of time here."

"Neither do I. We're pushing as hard as we can."

"I've got something," Tay said. "I'm still not certain what it means, but it's something. I've found the connection between Emma and Mongkok."

"What is it?"

"Sarah admitted Emma has been meeting somebody at an apartment in Mongkok. The lunches she and Emma told everyone they were having at Mr. Wong's were just a cover."

"She was meeting a lover?"

"Apparently."

"Does Sarah know who he is?"

"She says not. Older. Married, she's guessing. But she claims not to have a name or know where his apartment is."

"Do you believe her?"

Tay thought about it. "Yes, I think I do."

"So, what now?"

"We know why Emma was in Mongkok, which makes it even more important to find out why the other girls were in Mongkok."

"You can't think they were all meeting lovers there, too, can you?"

"How would I know, Claire? I don't know the first thing about women."

"So you say."

Tay thought he could hear a smile in Claire's voice. At least he hoped that was what he heard.

"It's still a hell of a coincidence they all went missing from the same neighborhood. There's got to be something about Mongkok that connects them. If not their love life, something."

"What do you think it is?"

"I don't have any idea, but somebody does. Push their parents hard. Somebody knows or suspects something. We know now why Emma was in Mongkok. If we can nail down why two or three of the other girls were there, maybe this thing will unravel."

"Jack is working the phones right now to get to as many of the parents as we can tomorrow. We're doing our best here."

"Do it faster."

Claire ignored the implied rebuke. "Anything else?"

"Did you get anything helpful off Emma's laptop or iPad?"

"August got them open and sent the stuff he found to Shepherd. He thinks Jack can make more sense out of the local references than he can, but if Jack has found anything he hasn't told me about it."

"I've got to call him about something else anyway so I'll ask. While I'm doing that, can you do some online research for me? You're a lot better at it than I am."

"Sure. What do you want me to look for?"

"I want you to see if there are any unexplained cases of body parts turning up in Hong Kong over the past year or two."

"Body parts?"

Tay said nothing.

"You think they're all dead." Claire didn't make a question of it.

"None of these girls have ever turned up, either alive *or* dead, Claire. What the hell happened to them?"

"You think someone dismembered their bodies and somehow disposed of the parts?"

"If these girls were killed in Mongkok, I don't understand what happened to their bodies. What do you do with the body in a crowded neighborhood like that? There's no place to dump it and no way to carry it anywhere else. At least not in one piece."

"Wouldn't they have done DNA on any unexplained body parts that turned up?"

"I don't know. Maybe. Maybe not. But if they had, why would they have bothered to compare it to the families of the missing girls? Remember, no one ever reported these girls missing."

"Okay, I see what you mean. Let me see what I can find."

TAY LIT A fresh Marlboro and then called Shepherd. "Claire says you're going through Emma's laptop and iPad."

"Yeah."

"Anything?"

"Not that I've found so far. Her email and messages are all just normal stuff. At least normal for a twenty-five-year-old girl who goes to medical school, I guess. I'm still looking."

Tay took a long pull on his cigarette and thought about whether he should rely on Shepherd's judgment or look through the laptop and iPad himself. But what did he know about what was normal for a twenty-five-year-old Hong Kong girl in medical school? Screw it. There were more useful ways for him to spend his time.

"I've got something else to ask you, Shepherd. How do I get rid of a body in Mongkok?"

There was a long silence from the other end of the phone, one so long Tay thought one of them might have broken the connection by accident.

"Shepherd? Are you still there?"

"Yeah." Shepherd cleared his throat. "Have you killed somebody?"

"Not recently."

"Then why are you asking me about getting rid of a body?"

"Six girls have gone missing over the last year and a half, and we can tie all of them to Mongkok. Emma may still be alive, but the others aren't sitting in an apartment somewhere playing mahjong and watching television. They're all dead."

"You don't know that."

"You think they are all out there somewhere just waiting to be found?"

"It seems to me possible at least some of them are still alive."

"And doing what?"

"There have been cases over the last few years in which the Chinese Ministry of State Security has grabbed people in Hong Kong and taken them back to China."

"Why would MSS be interested in six young women? Do you think they were political dissidents?"

"That's not what I meant. They're all daughters of wealthy and powerful people here in Hong Kong. How better to put pressure on those wealthy and powerful people than to kidnap their children?"

"Why would China want leverage over these people living in Hong Kong?"

"Look, Tay, this city is at war with itself and as far as China is concerned the war can only end one way. Hong Kong has to do what it's told, and it's people like the parents of these girls who decide what Hong Kong does. The people with money make the decisions here. Control enough of them and you control those decisions."

"Have you ever heard of anyone here forced to say or do something because MSS kidnapped their child?"

"No, but then I wouldn't if the plan had worked, would I?"

Tay thought about that for a moment.

"In one case or two, maybe," he said. "But in six cases in eighteen months? That's too clumsy for an organization as sophisticated as MSS."

"You're giving MSS a lot of credit."

"MSS is tough and smart. Kidnapping six young women within eighteen months to put pressure on their parents is neither tough nor smart."

"It is if you get away with it," Shepherd said.

Tay finished his cigarette and thought about it. He didn't buy it, he really didn't. He dumped his cigarette butt in the cylinder full of sand.

"Humor me, Shepherd. I've been walking around Mongkok and it occurs to me that in such a busy, crowded neighborhood disposing of a body without attracting attention isn't easy. Which brings me back to my question. How would I get rid of a body in Mongkok?"

"I don't know. It's something I've never had to do."

"Maybe you know someone who *has* had to do it. Can you make some calls?"

"I can do that."

"My first thought was you'd have to dismember the bodies to get them out of Mongkok, but then you'd still have to dump those body parts somewhere."

"The dismemberment of corpses and the discarding of body parts was your *first* thought? Man, you must have some great nightmares."

Shepherd didn't know the half of it, and Tay wasn't about to tell him.

"I've asked Claire to see if she can find any recent cases of unexplained body parts found in Hong Kong, but I don't think that goes anywhere. Maybe once, but five times with no one knowing what was happening? If somebody is killing girls and making their bodies disappear in Mongkok, he's got to be doing it another way."

"I can call some guys."

"Somehow I thought you could."

A FTER HE ENDED his conversation with Shepherd, Tay went upstairs to his room and ordered a room service dinner of grilled chicken and salad.

As soon as he hung up, he regretted what he had ordered. It sounded bland, boring even, and he was sure it would be. He thought about calling room service back and asking them to send him a cheeseburger instead, but he didn't. He let his order stand as a gesture of virtue and good health.

His meal came sooner than he expected, and it was even more boring than he had feared. What in the world had he been thinking of? Who was he trying to impress with his personal virtue and earnest commitment to healthy eating? The room service waiter? What an empty and ridiculous gesture.

Tay continued flagellating himself over his weakness in ordering the dinner he thought he should order rather than the one he wanted to order while he shoved the room service trolley into the hallway for somebody to collect. He thought then about going downstairs for another cigarette before going to sleep, but he was so tired he didn't think he could manage it.

"To hell with it," he muttered and stripped off his clothes and dumped them on a chair since he didn't have the energy to hang them. He went into the bathroom and put on the fluffy white cotton robe the hotel provided, washed his face, and brushed his teeth.

While he was brushing his teeth, he thought again about how little progress they had made in finding Emma. They knew a lot they had not known before, that was true, but how much closer were they to locating her than they had been two days ago? He didn't feel like they were much closer at all.

This thing was a different animal from the homicide investigations he had conducted for most of his working life. Dead bodies didn't have anywhere to go. You solved the case when you solved it.

But this was a search for someone who was still alive. At least probably. Maybe. But even if Emma was still alive, how much time did they have to keep her that way? He had no idea, although his gut kept screaming at him that it wasn't very long.

Tay finished brushing his teeth and examined himself in the mirror while he rinsed off his brush. He looked old and tired, which he thought might be because he *was* old and tired.

Maybe this hunt for Emma would be the end for him. There would be a last case sometime, wouldn't there? One last hunt and then he was done? Maybe this would be the one. He could see that, maybe, if he found Emma alive. But if he didn't find her alive, he couldn't let this be the end. He sure as hell wasn't going out on a loss.

Tay shook the water off his toothbrush and dropped it into one of the two water glasses. Then he took the other glass, filled it from the tap, and rinsed out his mouth. He spit the water into the sink and reached for the hand towel to wipe his mouth.

He tried to pretend he didn't see the thick streaks of blood circling the drain.

THIRTY-ONE

TAY SLEPT, BUT not well, and not for very long. When he opened his eyes, his room was dark and still. Something had roused him. He didn't know what it was, but whatever it was had left him with an uneasy feeling. When we are disturbed in the empty hours, we often wake with an uneasy feeling. The thoughts that crawl from our imaginations about the things which might have woken us are seldom soothing.

Tay rolled his head to the side until he could see the clock next to the bed. The numbers glowed a dim green: 2:47 AM.

Did the light wake him? He rolled his head the other way and examined the drapes covering the windows of his room. The dull glow of the city beyond them seemed to be more or less the same intensity he recalled from the night before. No, not light then.

He pushed himself up in bed and braced his back against the headboard. Could it have been a noise? He strained his ears into the stillness, but the silence in his room was so complete it was almost a tangible thing. He could even hear the faint hiss of moving air coming from the air conditioning duct. Then not noise either.

What did that leave? What had roused him from a sound sleep?

Tay thought he knew what it was, and he was not happy about it.

Perhaps he had sensed someone was there with him in the room. Perhaps his mother had come to visit.

Which would not be good.

Because Tay's mother was dead.

S EVERAL YEARS AGO, the spirit of Tay's mother had begun turning up occasionally to give him advice. Sometimes her advice concerned his personal life, and sometimes it concerned the cases he was working, but recently things had been looking up. He had not heard from his mother in quite a while and he had even dared to allow himself to feel a little optimism she had gone and left him in peace. Perhaps he had been wrong about that.

Mothers had been giving their sons unsolicited advice more or less since mothers and sons had existed, but most mothers limited their advice giving to the years in which they were alive.

Tay's situation was exactly the reverse. When his mother had been alive, they seldom talked. In fact, after she moved to New York and remarried following his father's death, years had gone by with no contact between them at all. Since his mother died, however, she simply wouldn't shut up.

Tay knew very well his dead mother wasn't actually appearing to him in the middle of the night to give him advice. He was far too rational a man to believe the ghost of his mother was making nocturnal journeys from the other side to give him helpful hints about what the future held.

On the first few occasions his mother had appeared, he was convinced he had simply been victimized by a particularly acute case of indigestion, but eventually he saw there was more to it than that. He came to understand that in the silence of the

227

night his subconscious was making itself heard. As a detective, he had always relied on his intuition to show him the way through the forest, and his subconscious coming to him in his dreams was nothing more than an expression of his intuition.

When it felt as if he were speaking to the ghost of his mother, Tay understood he was not. No matter how real the conversation might feel, no matter how vivid the dream, he knew he was looking in an emotional mirror and speaking to himself.

What seemed to be a conversation with his mother was really the gathering of thoughts and impressions as they bubbled up from the depths of his subconscious and rearranged themselves into patterns and concepts he had not considered during his waking hours. There was no other explanation.

He did not believe in ghosts. It was as simple as that. But he had to admit he found it a lot easier to express that belief on a Sunday morning sitting in his garden with a cup of coffee in one hand and a Marlboro in the other than he did when he was looking at his mother sitting at the foot of his bed at three o'clock in the morning.

In daylight, the idea his mother was manifesting herself from beyond the grave to give him advice was laughable. In the darkness of his bedroom, in the still and empty hours, the idea was far less amusing.

It also bothered him a bit that his mother's occasional appearances seemed terribly real. Tay was not a spiritual man, but sometimes her presence felt so authentic he wondered in spite of himself if it might not actually *be* real. It wasn't, he knew, but still...

Whether his mother was a spirit manifesting herself from the other side, or just a phenomenon brought about by consuming too much chili crab, Tay had to admit the advice she gave him had often proved quite useful.

On most of the occasions his mother had appeared to him, she simply harangued him for a while about one of his personal failings and then disappeared again, which was probably the reason her visits seemed so real. But every now and then, she offered pieces of useful advice on one of his cases. Maybe she wasn't really there, but there was no harm in listening, was there?

He had once read a magazine story about the American actor, Jack Nicholson, in which Nicholson had said something which rather neatly summed up his own feelings on the matter.

I know the voices in my head aren't real, but they have such damn good ideas I listen to them, anyway.

T AY SLID BACK under the duvet and closed his eyes. Maybe it had just been a distant noise that had woken him after all, and his mother had nothing to do with it.

He knew that if his mother *had* been responsible, it wouldn't do him any good to close his eyes. He had tried more times than he cared to remember to ignore his mother's appearances, but it never worked. She wasn't a woman who tolerated being ignored.

"Honestly, Samuel, sometimes I don't even know why I bother."

Oh crap. It *was* her.

Tay knew if he opened his eyes now he would see a light glowing somewhere in his bedroom. His mother's voice usually emerged from a light or sometimes several lights grouped together. Now and then his mother appeared to him in human form, sitting at the end of his bed and chatting away to him like a parent coming into a child's room late at night, but that didn't happen often. And he was damned glad it didn't.

"Open your eyes, Samuel. Don't be such a baby."

"Go away, Mother." Tay clenched his eyes together even more tightly. "Please go away."

"You know you will open your eyes, Samuel. You always do. Just do it now and save us both a lot of time."

"Why can't you ever show up at a civilized hour, Mother? Why do you always have to come at some God-awful hour when I'm exhausted and need to sleep?"

When his mother didn't respond, Tay cracked one eye and looked in the direction from which her voice seemed to have come.

He didn't see the light he expected to see. It was worse than that. Much worse.

The chair that had been at the desk on the other side of the room now stood facing him a few feet from the end of his bed. A figure was sitting in it. In the dim light, the figure's features were indistinct, and he could only make out that it was an elderly woman. But he didn't need to see the figure any more clearly. He knew who it was.

His mother looked almost prim the way she was sitting there, her legs crossed at the knee and her hands folded in her lap. She was dressed in a long blue robe with a high neck and a big collar in a darker shade of blue. The whole getup made it look like she was wearing a choir robe, but he pushed the thought away as soon as it came to him. He was appalled to see the way his imagination was grasping at clichés.

So instead of the normal light show, this was a night for the full body manifestation thing, was it? That couldn't be good.

"How are you, Mother?"

"Why do you always ask me that, Samuel? I'm dead, that's how I am. I was dead the last time you asked me, and I'm still dead."

"I know you're dead. I was just being polite."

"Well, don't bother. It doesn't suit you."

Tay hesitated. He knew asking his mother about the robe was a sucker play, but he just couldn't resist.

"What is that you're wearing, Mother?"

230

She shifted her body, shook out the robe, and crossed her legs in the opposite direction.

"Do you like it? I'm afraid it makes me look fat."

"It's very... uh, ecclesiastic."

"Of course it is," his mother snapped. "What do you expect us to wear? Jeans and t-shirts? This is the afterlife, Samuel. Not a trip to Walmart."

Walmart? What in the world was she talking about?

"I don't know what—"

"Never mind, Samuel. Some things are just too American for your sensibilities."

"Then could we get to the point here as soon as possible, Mother? I really would like to try to get some sleep."

"Patience, son. Try to have a bit of patience. It's a virtue you ought to work on developing."

Tay said nothing. He just waited.

"That girl seems very nice," his mother went on after a moment.

"What girl, Mother?"

"The one you're working with."

"Do you mean Claire?"

"Yes, her. She's very attractive. Does she cook?"

"I have no idea, but she is very skilled at killing people."

"Don't be snarky, Samuel. I'm your mother. I'm concerned about your future. You're not getting any younger, you know. Find a nice girl and get married. You're not going to have many more chances at your age."

"Is that what this conversation is going to be about, Mother? That I'm getting old and need to find a wife while I still can?"

Was this why he was losing sleep, to listen to his mother nag him about not being married? Under normal circumstances it would have made him angry, but what was the point? Since his mother wasn't there in the first place, getting angry with her was unlikely to make her go away.

"No, son, I was just making family conversation. It would be nice if you did the same thing. Showing some warmth now and then wouldn't kill you. It's not killing me, but then again I'm already dead."

His mother made an unpleasant snorting sound which Tay assumed was supposed to be a laugh.

"Why are you here, Mother?"

"Because I have something very important to tell you."

"What is it?"

"Are you listening to me, Samuel?"

"Yes, Mother, I am listening to you."

His mother hesitated, then spoke slowly, almost solemnly.

"You have very little time left."

Tay's body jerked back. He felt like someone had punched him in the stomach.

The spirit of his mother had come to warn him he was about to die, and here he was being ratty with her. He closed his eyes and took a deep breath. He didn't know what to say.

"Did you hear me, Samuel?"

"Yes, Mother, I heard you. How long do I have?"

"I would say two days at most."

Tay let out a groan.

"Couldn't you have been a little gentler about it, Mother? Just blurting out that I have only two days to live is—"

"Two days to live? What in God's name are you talking about, Samuel?"

"You just said I had very little time left, and when I asked how much time I had, you said—"

"Oh, for Christ's sake, that's not what I meant."

"You didn't mean I'm going to die?"

"Of course you're going to die, Samuel. Just not in two days."

"Do you know when—"

"I'm dead, son, not clairvoyant."

"I thought you had universal knowledge."

"I do. It's one of the few advantages of being dead."

232

"Then why wouldn't you know when—"

"I only know those things that can be known. Not those things that cannot."

"Oh, for Pete's sake, Mother, now you sound like a fucking fortune cookie."

"Language, Samuel, language. I'm your fucking mother."

The snort came again. It *was* a laugh.

Tay tried to wrestle the conversation back on track. "If you didn't mean I only had two days to live, then what were you talking about when you said I had only two days?"

"I was talking about the girl you're looking for. Emma."

"What does that have to do with Emma?"

"My God, Samuel, why do I have to spell everything out for you? You must find Emma within two days. Two days! Do you understand what I'm telling you here?"

"Not entirely. Are you saying Emma is still alive?"

"Yes, she is. Very much."

"Well, that's good news. Thank you, Mother."

"You're welcome."

"What will happen in two days if I don't find her?"

"She'll be dead, Samuel. As dead as I am now."

"And this is all coming from your universal knowledge?"

Tay's mother nodded.

"Your universal knowledge tells you Emma is alive now?"

"Yes."

"But that she will be dead in two days?"

"Yes."

"Does your universal knowledge tell you where Emma is right now?"

"That's not clear."

"Well then, does your universal knowledge tell you I'd much rather sleep than have another one of these stupid conversations with you?"

Tay's mother sighed heavily and shook her head. "Here I

233

am trying to be helpful to you, son, and you thank me in such a hurtful way."

"Your Sally the Seer routine is becoming threadbare, Mother. Particularly because you never seem to see anything really useful. Like where Emma is right now."

"Let me just make certain I understand you here, Samuel. Are you saying you don't want my help anymore?"

"The next time you have a message from the other side, why don't you just send me an email?"

"I thought you didn't read email."

"Precisely."

Tay's mother made a clicking sound with her tongue.

"Always with the jokes, huh? Always with the jokes."

"That was not a joke, Mother."

His mother uncrossed her legs and sat up straight.

"I've told you what I came here to tell you, Samuel, so I'm leaving now. It's not as if I have all night to sit around and listen to your insults. I've got places to go, things to do."

His mother had places to go, things to do?

Tay had always assumed one advantage of being dead was that he would be freed of all the trivia of daily life and he could finally live an entirely spiritual life, so to speak, one far removed from the pettiness of earthly existence.

Was his mother telling him spirits still had appointments to keep and letters to mail? Did they have spiritual smartphones running spiritual calendars so they could keep up with all the spiritual trivia of their spiritual lives? How disappointing it would be if that turned out to be true. There really wouldn't be any point to being dead then, would there?

"Just one more thing before I leave," his mother said. "Are you paying attention?"

"Yes, Mother. I'm paying attention."

"Get yourself to a doctor right away. Coughing up blood like you have been is no joke."

"You know about that, too?"

Tay's mother sighed. "Please let's not have that ridiculous conversation again about what I know and what I don't know. Just listen to me. Get yourself to a doctor."

"Yes, Mother. As soon as I get back to Singapore, I'll—"

"No," she snapped. "Do it now. Don't wait."

Tay hesitated. "You think it's that important?"

"Yes."

"But I don't know any doctors in Hong Kong. Do you?"

"Honestly, Samuel, you have to do *some* things for yourself. You're the hotshot detective and you can't find a doctor in Hong Kong? Sometimes I don't know why I even bother trying to help you."

Tay wanted to ask his mother for more details about her pronouncement he only had two days to find Emma, and a few details about her insistence he go to a doctor right away wouldn't go amiss either, but he would feel like a complete idiot asking a hallucination to explain anything.

"Can I go back to sleep now, Mother?"

"Do whatever you want. I'm leaving."

"Thank God," Tay muttered.

Tay's mother gave him a look of exasperation, and shook her head.

Even as he looked at her sitting there at the foot of his bed, her image began to blur and fade into the night. It grew fainter and fainter until all that remained was a single point of light hovering above the chair. The light quivered in the darkness and made him think of a candle flame flickering in a soft breeze.

Then, after a minute, perhaps two, it vanished as if someone had blown out the candle, and Tay was left lying in his bed in the darkness wondering if he was asleep or awake.

He soon decided he was asleep, and almost at once he was.

THIRTY-TWO

THURSDAY. DAY THREE. Searching for Emma Lau.
Tay woke up earlier than usual and he did what he always did on the mornings following one of his mother's nocturnal appearances. He lay very still and hoped the memory of it would fade like a bad dream in the morning light.

It didn't.

So, he moved on to Plan B.

Plan B was to be stern with himself. To remind himself his mother had *not* appeared to him the night before.

It might have been a case of stomach gas, or a manifestation of ongoing anxiety, or a few buried thoughts bubbling up from his subconscious. It might have been any of those things. He didn't know what it had been. But he did know what it had *not* been. It had *not* been the ghost of his mother crossing over from the other side to have a bit of a chat.

With that thought set in mind, Tay braced himself to rise and face the coming day. He had heard stories of people who did it with vigor and anticipation, but he had never been convinced such people actually existed. Tay himself usually faced the coming day with a degree of alarm. Since most of the days which came before had been so deeply crappy, he had difficulty working up any optimism for the new day now dawning.

Tay swung his feet to the floor and envisioned himself tucking into his first cup of coffee. The image was sufficiently invigorating to motivate him to consider standing up. But before he had dispatched the necessary messages required to accomplish that feat to each of the various unresponsive parts of his body, a telephone rang.

A telephone call before he had drunk any coffee? Was such a thing even possible? He was fairly certain the manic tootling of the ring tone he was listening to was the single most irritating sound he had ever encountered anywhere.

Peering at the nightstand beside the bed, he saw it was not his own telephone ringing, but the iPhone August had given him. He also looked at the clock. A few minutes before seven.

Oh crap. No one calls before seven o'clock with good news.

"Hello?"

"Did I wake you?"

Tay had a very long list of occurrences in life which he found profoundly irritating. Well up toward the top of his list were those occasions on which people telephoned you and started talking without identifying themselves. But right at the very *top* of his list were the people who telephoned you and started talking without identifying themselves before seven o'clock in the morning.

"Who the hell is this?"

"It's Shepherd. Who did you think it was?"

"You say that as if I were expecting you to call."

"I thought you were."

Tay had no idea what Shepherd was talking about.

"Are you hungover, Tay? You sound hungover. What did you get up to last night?"

Tay had never been hungover in his entire life and he had no concept of what it felt like, but if it felt anything like getting a telephone call before seven o'clock in the morning when you haven't had even one cup of coffee yet, he figured it was hell.

"Why are you calling me, Shepherd? And in particular, why are you calling me before dawn?"

"It's not before dawn. It's almost seven."

"My point exactly," Tay muttered.

Shepherd ignored Tay's annoyance. He didn't know Tay very well, but he knew him well enough to figure he spent a great deal of time being annoyed, so there was no point in apologizing. After that, it would just be something else.

"When we talked last night," Shepherd said, "you asked me to find out something for you. I did."

Then Tay remembered.

When he had been walking around Mongkok last night, it had occurred to him that disposing of a body there would be difficult. As crowded and busy as the neighborhood was, how could someone who had killed five women in Mongkok have gotten rid of the bodies with no one noticing? He had asked Shepherd to find someone who might have had experience with a similar problem and see what he could find out.

"I haven't had any coffee yet so I'm thinking a little slowly. But I'm with you now. Please, use small words."

Shepherd laughed. "I talked to a guy who was in a little triad dustup in Mongkok several years ago. Three guys swinging meat cleavers attacked a high-ranking member of Wo Shing Wo when he was getting out of his car right near your hotel."

Tay winced. People being chopped up on the street of Hong Kong with meat cleavers? He wasn't going to try to imagine that. Not without coffee. Not without a *lot* of coffee.

"According to the cops, the killers got away, but the word on the street was some enforcers for Wo Shing Wo caught up with the hitters in Mongkok and evened the score. Nobody ever reported them killed, they were just never seen again, so I thought this guy might know something that would point you in the right direction. He did."

"Was it something inventive?"

"How much do you know about funerals in Hong Kong?"

"Absolutely nothing."

"Then bear with me here and let me give you a little background. There are only half a dozen funeral parlors in Hong Kong—"

"Half a dozen funeral parlors?" Tay interrupted. "For a city of over eight million people?"

"—but there are over a hundred licensed undertakers who operate small businesses called coffin shops plus at least another hundred who operate coffin shops without official licenses. When someone dies, either a funeral parlor or a coffin shop is engaged to process the paperwork and arrange for either burial or cremation. If it's an official coffin shop, they process everything themselves. If it's an unofficial coffin shop, they process things through someone else's license and share the payment."

Tay just listened without comment.

"Cremation is more common here since the lack of space makes burial sites so expensive. The funeral parlors and coffin shops don't do the cremations themselves. The cremations are all done at one of six facilities operated by the Hong Kong Food and Hygiene Office."

The Food and Hygiene Office?

"Here's the thing," Shepherd continued. "Those crematoriums just do the cremations. The coffin shops and funeral parlors do everything else. They collect the body, prepare it, place it in a coffin, organize whatever ceremony the relatives want, transport the coffin to one of the cremation facilities, and return the ashes to whoever is responsible for scattering them somewhere."

"You're telling me the crematorium doesn't actually know who or what is in the coffin they receive?"

"You got it. They just cremate whatever the coffin shop brings them. According to my guy, now and then a coffin has an extra body in it, and no one is ever the wiser."

"So, if the killer had a connection with a coffin shop—"

"If the killer had some way of exerting influence over one of the coffin shops, he could get a body collected, stuffed in a coffin with somebody's Uncle Chin, and then cremated. The body disappears into thin air. Literally."

"You're saying the killer could have bribed a coffin shop to cremate the bodies?"

"Money would be one way to get it done. Money works pretty well for most things in Hong Kong. The other possibility is that someone with serious weight puts on the pressure."

"Like who?"

"Say, someone like a ranking triad member or someone in government. Serious weight is even better than money in Hong Kong for getting people to do what you want them to do. Serious weight means there's someone important who owes you and can deliver a future favor when you need it."

"Then it *would* be possible for five girls simply to vanish in Mongkok."

"It worked for the bodies of three triad hitters. No one ever saw a trace of any of them again."

Tay thought about that for a moment.

"I've gone as far as I can without coffee, Shepherd."

"Fair enough. Claire and I are talking to the parents of at least two of the other missing girls today. Maybe we can come up with something to link these girls together."

Tay ended the call and dropped the cell phone back on the bedside table. Then he picked up the room phone, called room service, and ordered a large pot of coffee. He showered while we waited and had just dried off and wrapped up in the hotel robe when he heard the doorbell.

The waiter carried the tray inside and placed it on the desk. Tay signed the check and added a generous tip since August was paying the bill, then sent the waiter on his way.

When he closed the door and turned around, he saw the chair.

. . .

THERE WAS NOTHING special about the chair itself. It was armless with a wooden ladder back, dark wooden legs, and a seat upholstered in a soft-looking brown leather. Tay hadn't used the chair that he recalled, but he did remember when he had checked into the room it was under the desk where the room service tray now sat.

But it wasn't under the desk now.

Now it was more or less in the middle of the room close to the foot of the bed.

Exactly where his mother sat when she came to visit last night.

Had he moved the chair there himself? No, he was certain he hadn't. Was it possible the room service waiter had put it there? No, he had been with the waiter the whole time he was in the room and the waiter had never touched the chair.

So, what was it doing there?

"Coffee," Tay muttered. "Coffee, coffee, coffee."

He walked over to the room service tray and poured himself a cup. Keeping his back turned to the chair, he downed it in a few swallows. Purely medicinal. Get that heart rate up. Stop imagining things that weren't there.

He poured himself another cup. This time he sipped at it slowly and enjoyed the feel of the caffeine buzz spreading throughout his body.

Maybe he had just imagined the chair sitting by the foot of his bed, he told himself. Maybe he was still half asleep and thinking about the dream he had of a visit from his mother last night, and that had made him *think* he saw the chair sitting at the foot of his bed.

He took a deep breath and turned around.

The fucking chair really *was* sitting there at the foot of his bed.

Oh crap.

. . .

TAY REFILLED HIS coffee cup again, carried it over to the bed, and sat down on the end.

He looked at the chair. The chair looked back at him. It said nothing at all.

Was he actually entertaining the thought that the ghost of his mother had appeared in his room last night and moved the chair to where it was now so she could sit in it while she had a conversation with him? God help him, that was exactly what he was doing.

Tay knew it was not possible for a ghost to have visited his room the night before and moved the chair. He understood that. But he hadn't moved the chair, and of course it wasn't possible for the chair to have moved itself, so where did that leave him? He had no idea.

He thought back on the conversation he'd had with his mother during the night. Or rather, the conversation he had *imagined* he'd had with his mother during the night.

His mother had delivered two messages to him. The first was that he had only two days to find Emma. And the second was that he should see a doctor without waiting until he got back to Singapore. He had already decided both messages were only subliminal worries bubbling to the surface of his dreams and that neither message was going to cause him to alter anything he was doing.

But now there was the damned chair. It stared at him and taunted him, and now he was asking himself questions about things he had no intention of thinking about.

Maybe he should take his mother's messages to heart. Maybe he should at least *think* about taking his mother's messages to heart.

Two days to find Emma? Two days would be up on Friday night. That was tomorrow.

But what about his mother's other warning? That he shouldn't wait to see a doctor.

Something in his gut told him the part about having limited time to find Emma might well be true, so he wasn't going to waste part of whatever time was left looking for a doctor in a city where he knew almost no one. Whatever was wrong with him would wait for a few days until he got back to Singapore.

How serious could it be, anyway? Coughing up a little blood didn't mean he was about to die. At least it probably didn't. Most likely it just meant he ought to stop smoking. And he had no intention of stopping smoking so why be in hurry to hear someone tell him to do it?

This is preposterous, Tay reprimanded himself.

Here he was sitting there glaring at an empty chair and weighing the words of a hallucination as if they had been real. No rational human being could possibly do such a thing, but that was exactly what he was doing.

Tay got up, lifted the chair, carried it across the room, and pushed it under the desk.

He would not be mocked by a piece of furniture.

THIRTY-THREE

WHILE TAY WAS getting dressed, he thought about what he knew and what he did not know and what both meant for finding Emma.

Yes, now he knew Emma had been regularly meeting someone in Mongkok, presumably a lover, and he had a rough idea of the part of Mongkok where she had gone. He also knew five other girls of about the same age had disappeared in Mongkok over the last year and a half, but he didn't know whether the disappearances were connected.

Still, it would be one hell of a coincidence if they weren't, at least some of them, so Claire and Shepherd were working their way through the other girls' parents looking for something, anything, that might tie them together. It all added up to a lot more than they had known a few days ago, but it didn't add up to enough to tell him where Emma might be.

Tay's instincts told him he didn't have long to find her. That was just a matter of common sense and had nothing to do with his hallucination from the night before. A hard truth overrode any speculation about the wisdom of ghosts: few people who went missing turned up again after a week. At least not alive. And Saturday would mark a week since Emma disappeared.

Saturday was two days away, and he still had nothing solid to go on. He needed a breakthrough, and he needed it fast. He just had no idea how to get one.

The strongest thing he had was a hint about the part of Mongkok where Emma had been going. There had to be surveillance cameras in the area, Tay knew. There were surveillance cameras in every area now. The police cameras would be a problem since they were avoiding the Hong Kong cops, but the private security cameras were another matter. All they needed to access those was the cooperation of the store owners.

But the more Tay thought about it, the more he realized those cameras wouldn't do him much good. He had narrowed down the part of Mongkok they were looking at, but it was still a sizable area. At least eight square blocks. Maybe more like fifteen. There would be dozens of cameras in the area, maybe even hundreds. And Emma had been gone for five days.

In Tay's experience, fast forwarding a saved video feed sped it up by a factor of only six times. That meant twenty-four hours of video required four hours to review even at fast forward, more when you included the time required to stop and examine it at normal speed when you spotted something interesting. A minimum of four hours for each of the five days meant it would take twenty hours to review the feeds for every security camera.

He would need an army to review all the security footage in the area for the period Emma had been missing, and Tay had himself and Claire and Shepherd. Not an army.

For security video to be any help, he had to narrow Emma's location down a lot further. He had no idea how to do that, but he had to find a way.

Tay couldn't help thinking back to what Shepherd had told him about making a body disappear in Hong Kong. Was Emma already dead? Had somebody stuffed her in a coffin with an old auntie and turned her into a pot of ash at one of the Hong

245

Kong Food and Hygiene Office crematoriums? If they had, no one would ever find out what became of her.

Tay buttoned his shirt, tucked it in, and buckled his belt. He frowned when he saw the hole in which he usually buckled his belt now made it feel snug. Was he gaining weight or just beginning to sag through the midsection? He guessed it didn't really matter. Getting old was crap either way.

He shook his head at the accelerating pace of his inevitable demise and went into the bathroom to brush his teeth.

T AY SHOOK THE water off his toothbrush and rinsed his mouth.

When he spit the water into the sink, he kept his eyes up, not wanting to know if there was blood. But then, at the last second before the water vanished into the drain, he glanced down.

There was blood. A lot of it. More than there had been the night before.

Tay examined his reflection in the mirror. He was a smoker and smokers got lung cancer. There, he had said it, if only to himself. He had spoken the C-word. Not out loud exactly, but close enough.

A common symptom of lung cancer, he knew, was blood in the mucus which naturally came up from the lungs, and brushing his teeth had always brought up mucus. But never before had that mucus been streaked with blood. Now it was. What could be simpler?

He rinsed out the sink, wiped his face on a towel, and walked out of the bathroom.

Was it sensible to let this go until he got back to Singapore? And how long would that be? A couple of days? A week? A month?

What his subconscious had told him the night before about visiting a doctor as soon as possible was sound advice. He didn't need an imaginary visit from the ghost of his mother to know that. This wasn't something to screw around with. He should consult a doctor right away.

But how to do that here in Hong Kong? He couldn't ask Claire or Shepherd to recommend a doctor. He would look like an ass if this turned out to be nothing.

Picking a doctor at random from a telephone book still didn't appeal to him either, even assuming he could find a telephone book somewhere, which he doubted, but thinking about telephone numbers gave him an idea. He wasn't certain it was a good idea. In fact, he was pretty sure it *wasn't* a good idea, but it was the only one he had.

T AY HUNTED THROUGH the stuff he had dumped on the desk until he found the plain white card Jones had given him with a single telephone number printed on it. Then he went over to the nightstand and picked up the telephone August had given him. Using a secure telephone seemed to him to be the correct way to call a Chinese crime boss.

Tay had assumed the number Jones had given him would go to a voice mailbox, he would leave a message, and Jones would call him back. Or perhaps he wouldn't. He was more than a little surprised when he punched the number into the telephone, hit the key to call it, and Jones answered almost at once.

"Good morning, Inspector."

He was also surprised Jones knew who was calling. How was that possible? August wouldn't have gone to the trouble of setting up secure telephones and then left those telephones sending out a caller ID, could he?

"How did you—"

"No, Inspector, there's no caller ID. But you're the only person to whom I gave this number."

Tay looked at the card he was holding in his hand with the number printed on it.

"You had this card printed just for me?"

"No, but you *are* the only person I've given it to."

None of this made a great deal of sense to Tay, but he got the feeling that was the way Jones wanted it, so he dropped the subject and went straight to the reason he had called.

"I need your help with something, Jones."

"Yes, of course."

Tay hesitated. He wasn't sure what to say. He didn't know Jones at all, and he hated telling a stranger something so personal. All he wanted was for Jones to refer him to a competent doctor, and that didn't require holding hands and sharing their feelings, did it?

"I need to see a doctor," Tay said. "I thought perhaps you could recommend somebody and ask him to see me right away."

"Have you been shot?"

"*Shot?* No, I haven't been shot. Why would you ask me if I'd been shot?"

"I assumed that might be why you chose me, of all people, to provide you with a medical referral."

Tay thought about that for a few seconds. "I believe you're making a joke."

"I am indeed, Inspector. And thank you for noticing."

Tay had to smile to keep himself from choking on the irony of asking Jones to refer him to a doctor. The man might be well dressed and well spoken, but he was still a triad gangster. A guy who sent people with meat cleavers out to kill his enemies. And Tay was a policeman. Well, he *used* to be a policeman, and it was hard for him to stop thinking of himself as one even now.

"I'm asking you because, to be honest, I can't think of anybody else to ask."

Tay expected Jones to wonder why he hadn't gone to Shepherd instead of him, perhaps even to ask him, but he didn't.

"Is this an emergency?" was what Jones asked.

"No," Tay answered. "Well, maybe. I don't know."

"I don't wish to pry, but I would be better able to guide you if you would give me some idea why you need to see a doctor."

Tay didn't want to, but he knew it was a reasonable thing to ask of him.

"I started coughing up blood."

"When?"

"A day or two ago." Tay thought a moment. "Maybe three days."

There was a brief silence and then Jones asked, "You're still at the Cordis Hotel?"

Tay didn't remember telling Jones he was staying at the Cordis Hotel. Had he mentioned it and just forgotten? He was reasonably sure he hadn't.

"Yes, I am, but how—"

"Then you know where Langham Place is, don't you?" Jones asked. "The big shopping mall right next to your hotel?"

"Yes."

"There's a Starbucks on the main floor. It's right in front of the pedestrian bridge where you enter the mall from the hotel. Do you know where it is?"

"Yes, I think I've seen it."

"Can you be there in twenty minutes?"

"I can, but is it really necessary? Couldn't you just give me the number of a doctor you recommend and then—"

But Jones had already hung up.

THIRTY-FOUR

T AY WALKED THROUGH the glass-enclosed pedestrian bridge which connected the lobby of the hotel to Langham Place and the mall's massive open atrium that towered at least a dozen floors above his head.

Masses of people crowded the atrium as they did everything in Mongkok, moving in what seemed to be every direction at the same time. It was Hong Kong, so everyone walked fast. No meandering, no dawdling. There were things to do, there was money to be made.

He saw the green Starbucks logo on a pole above the crowds and walked toward it. He was still twenty feet from it when Jones materialized out of the crowd, took his elbow, and began towing him away.

"I've made arrangements for you to see someone."

Jones bent toward Tay when he spoke and lowered his voice.

"He's someone you can trust. A fine doctor. We use him quite a lot."

Tay did not ask who *we* referred to. Perhaps he should have, but he thought he could guess.

"Dr. Patel's surgery is very well equipped. He can do almost anything there short of a heart transplant."

Jones looked Tay over more carefully than Tay thought was necessary.

"The surgery is only a couple of blocks from here," he said. "It would be better to walk if you can manage it."

"Of course I can manage it. I'm not an invalid. I'm not even sick. I just coughed up a little blood."

Jones gave him a look, but he kept moving.

"Dr. Patel is a good friend of ours," Jones said.

There was the *we* and *our* stuff, again but Tay still wasn't about to ask.

"I told him to clear his other appointments for you, Inspector. He'll see you as soon as we get there."

I'll just bet he will, Tay thought.

D R. PATEL WAS the smallest man Tay had ever met. He was standing next to Jones, who was both tall and heavy for a Chinese, and it made Tay think of a jockey about to mount up and take to the track. That made Jones the horse, of course, but Tay kept the thought to himself.

Dr. Patel wasn't much over five feet tall, and Tay would have bet he didn't weigh a hundred pounds. He had dark brown skin, shiny white teeth, badly cut black hair, and he wore the white lab coat which was the uniform of doctors all over the world. Behind his narrow, rimless spectacles were intelligent and knowing brown eyes, and Tay trusted him immediately.

Why were so many doctors Indians? The only two doctors Tay had seen in Singapore in as many years as he could remember were both Indians and he seemed to remember all of their colleagues he had met were also Indians. Tay assumed there had to be, say, Polish doctors somewhere, too, didn't there? Maybe there were, but all of them must stay in Poland.

"I understand you have been coughing up blood, Inspector."

Tay wondered if he ought to correct the doctor's use of his former title, but the whole matter of Tay asking a Chinese crime boss to find a doctor for him was already tricky enough. Why get involved in too many details, huh? Tay let it pass and just nodded.

"When did this start?"

"Three days ago."

"And how did you discover it?"

"The first time was when I breathed some tear gas on the street and started coughing."

Dr. Patel's forehead wrinkled. "You were in one of these demonstrations?"

"I was walking back to the hotel and got caught up in one. It was purely involuntary."

"Have you noticed blood on other occasions or only after exposure to tear gas?"

"I noticed it another time when I coughed and twice when brushing my teeth."

"Do you smoke?"

Tay nodded again.

"How much?"

"As much as I can," Tay said.

Dr. Patel didn't laugh.

Tay cleared his throat. "Maybe a pack a day." He hesitated. "Or a little more."

"How long have you smoked?"

"A while."

"A while? Months? Years?"

"Decades."

"Stop. Now. It will kill you."

"Yes, I seem to recall another doctor told me the same thing."

"And you ignored him?"

"Well, he's dead now, so..." Tay spread his hands.

This time Dr. Patel at least chuckled.

. . .

THE EXAMINING ROOM was a pleasant space.

Sunlight streamed in through two windows and gave the walls a cheerful yellow glow. Jones had taken up residence in a black leather armchair over in one corner while Tay sat on the end of a polished-aluminum examining table with his feet hanging over the side. The table was very low, no doubt to make it easier for Dr. Patel to reach his patients.

Dr. Patel perched on a stool with wheels which allowed him to zoom around the examining table as needed. He peered at Tay through his rimless glasses.

"What is your age?"

"Fifty-one."

"And how is your health in general?"

"Fine."

Dr. Patel propelled his stool closer to Tay and gestured for him to bend forward. He produced a chrome penlight from the breast pocket of his lab coat, flipped it on, and examined the pupils of Tay's eyes. First the right and then the left.

"No other underlying health conditions? Cardiac issues? Respiratory issues?"

"No. Nothing."

Dr. Patel had a stethoscope draped around his neck just like every other doctor Tay had ever seen. He had always wondered if the stethoscope was a sort of badge of office, something awarded to doctors when they graduated from medical school to prove to the world they were now real doctors.

Patel slid the earpieces into his ears, placed the cup against Tay's chest, and listened to his heart. Then he pushed the stool around, placed the cup against Tay's back, and guided Tay through the standard coughing routine. Tay listened for any reaction from Patel to what he was hearing, but there was none. Not an *ah-ha*. Not even an *uh-huh*.

"Any recent surgeries?" Patel asked.

"No."

"You do look to me like you could stand to lose a few pounds."

"Everybody could stand to lose a few pounds."

"Not me," Dr. Patel smiled.

Jones smiled, too.

Tay didn't smile. He was the one who was coughing up blood.

Dr. Patel gave his stool a practiced kick and zoomed back around in front of Tay.

"Well," he said, "let's not fuck around here. Let's get a CT scan and see what we can see."

Now Tay smiled. Somehow he liked being examined by a doctor who suddenly announced, *let's not fuck around here*.

"Where do I have to go to get a CT scan?" Tay asked.

Dr. Patel smiled and pointed to a door on the other side of the examining room.

"You have your own machine?"

Patel nodded.

"I didn't know doctors' offices had CT scanners. I thought they were just in hospitals."

"We're very well equipped. We can do all sorts of things right here without having to send a patient to a hospital. Your friend here is largely responsible for making that possible."

Dr. Patel indicated Jones with a tilt of his head. Tay glanced over at Jones, but he was expressionless.

So, Tay thought, here he was being examined in a private medical facility so well equipped its patients seldom needed to go to hospitals, and Jones had something to do with setting up the facility. That really underlined the *organized* in organized crime, didn't it?

Could Tay permit himself to be treated in a facility operated for the benefit of Chinese gangsters? He certainly couldn't if he were still a police officer. It would be unseemly. But he was no longer a police officer and now he was... well, he wasn't exactly certain what he was now, but he wasn't a police officer. Maybe that changed things.

"Shall we get started?" Dr. Patel asked

Tay decided it did change things, so he nodded.

T HE CT SCANNER looked like a giant white doughnut with a rectangular platform just large enough for a person to lie on. The platform was supported by a sturdy pedestal and aimed straight into the doughnut's hole.

Tay had had a CT scan once before when he had been caught in the coordinated bombings of three Singapore hotels by Indonesian terrorists, but he remembered next to nothing about it. He was heavily sedated and not very much of anything about how it was done had stuck with him.

Jones had gone off somewhere to wait and Dr. Patel had turned him over to a young woman whom Tay thought was a considerable improvement on both of them. She appeared to be in her thirties and wore blue hospital scrubs. She had one of those round Chinese faces that looked like porcelain, and she was much taller than Dr. Patel. Then again, almost everyone was.

"My name is Nan, Inspector Tay, and I will take care of you during your scan."

An incredibly witty response occurred to Tay, but he had the good sense to keep it to himself.

He settled for saying simply, "Thank you."

"The first thing you have to do," she said, holding out a clear plastic box, "is to empty your pockets and place everything in here."

Tay dumped the contents of his pockets into the box, including both the telephones he was carrying. If it surprised Nan to see he was carrying two telephones, she gave no sign. Tay figured she was probably used to people visiting Dr. Patel with their pockets full of telephones.

"Now, please take off your shoes and stretch out on the platform with your head toward the scanner."

When Tay did, Nan gently lifted his head and slipped a small pillow underneath it.

"Are you comfortable, sir?"

"Yes, I am, thank you." Tay hesitated and then added, "Your English is very good."

"It should be," she said. "I've only been in Hong Kong about a year. I'm from Houston."

Nan giggled and lifted her hand to cover her mouth in a gesture so appealing Tay had to struggle not to fall in love.

"This won't take very long and you will feel absolutely nothing. The platform will move you into the scanner and then will reposition several times while it is operating. Please do not move. You will hear a whirring sound and see some lights, but that's about all you will be aware of. After the scan is complete, the platform will move you back to this position, but please remain where you are. The technician must check the images before we can let you go. Sometimes we have to take several scans just to make sure we have everything. Got all that?"

"I do."

"Are you ready now?"

How did anyone get ready for being shoved back and forth through an enormous white doughnut while your body was being riddled with pulses of electrical energy? An insane desire came over Tay to scream out, "*Let's do this!*" but self-restraint was a virtue in short supply these days and Tay always tried to conduct himself as an example to others.

So, he didn't.

He just said, "Sure. I'm ready."

TAY CLOSED HIS eyes and surrendered himself to the scanner.

The whole process took only a few minutes. The platform

moved in and out of the doughnut just as Nan had said it would, and each time it stopped moving there were whirring sounds and flashing lights, but there was no physical sensation at all.

Still, when Tay thought about it, it was strange to realize this Star Trek-like device was doing something which would allow computer software to create a detailed portrait of the interior of Samuel Tay. Tay had never thought much about what his interior looked like, and he didn't much want to begin doing it now.

Whether he wanted to think about it or not, the blood he had been coughing up came from somewhere, didn't it? There was no good news to be had here. Only bad news and worse news. Something was wrong with one of the things inside him and it was bleeding. The only question was whether something small was wrong, or whether it was something big. The difference here between small and big was as great as the difference between life and death. And that was exactly what Tay had no intention of thinking about.

He busied his mind instead trying to compile a list of all the books he had read in the past year while the doughnut whirred and clicked and flashed and went about doing whatever it did. He was still hard at work on his list when the platform moved him back to his original position and Nan walked over and placed a hand on his shoulder.

"Now remember, don't move. I'll check with the technician to see if he has what he needs and then I'll be right back."

Tay knew he was missing a few titles and was working diligently to dredge them from his memory when Nan returned a few minutes later.

"All done," she said. "Can I help you up?"

Tay didn't think he needed any help, but he wasn't about to tell Nan that.

"Yes, thank you."

Nan wrapped her right hand around his forearm and slipped her left hand behind his back to support it as he sat up.

He swung his feet to the floor, and she moved closer to him and lifted with both her hands to pull him toward her. It was a very pleasant feeling, so Tay took his time about standing up.

Nan had left his loafers within easy reach and he stepped over and slipped them on. She brought him the plastic box where he had placed his telephones and the rest of the contents of his pockets and he returned everything to where it had been before.

"What happens now?" Tay asked.

"The technician will process the data into the images Dr. Patel ordered and then send them to the doctor for review. That takes about half an hour. I can get you some coffee to drink while you're waiting. Would you like to follow me to our lounge?"

Indeed he would, Tay thought. He would like to follow Nan almost anywhere. And if the lounge was what was on offer, then he would follow her there.

But he didn't say that either.

He settled for simply, "Thank you."

THIRTY-FIVE

"HOW DID IT go?" Jones asked when Tay sat down in the lounge.

"It went," Tay shrugged.

The lounge was quiet and comfortable with four soft leather chairs grouped around a square coffee table. They made Tay think of the reading chairs you might find in a good library. The chairs were very agreeable and the coffee was pretty good, and he and Jones were the only two people there.

Jones wasn't drinking coffee and Tay remembered him saying when they had been at the American Club that caffeine gave him the shits. He had no trouble remembering that. In fact, he had been trying to forget it ever since Jones had said it.

"Did they tell you how long it would take to get the results?" Jones asked after a minute or two.

"Nan said a half hour or so."

"Nan?" Jones chuckled. "I didn't realize you were such a fast worker, Tay."

That Jones might think him the kind of man who hustled a nurse when she was supervising his CT scan was too embarrassing to acknowledge, so Tay changed the subject.

"Thank you for doing this, Jones."

Jones shrugged and said nothing.

"There's no reason for you to wait," Tay continued. "I'm sure you've got better things to do than sit in a doctor's office to hear the results of my CT scan."

"Not really."

Tay was still trying to decide what to say when his phone rang and took him off the hook.

"Sam, it's Claire. We've made some progress."

"That sounds like good news."

"I'm not sure if it is or not. Jack got us in to see the father of the third girl to go missing. He's Executive Vice President of HSBC and his daughter's name is Yu Yang. She disappeared on New Year's Day of this year. She was at a party at the Peninsula Hotel and someone her parents knew later came forward to say he had seen her in Mongkok Station right after midnight, but then she just vanished."

"He told you she was seeing someone who had an apartment in Mongkok," Tay guessed.

"That's right. Her parents knew about it, but they didn't know who it was. She had refused to tell them because she said she thought they wouldn't approve. He told us he had the impression whoever she was seeing was older and of some prominence. Two of the missing girls both seeing an older, prominent man with an apartment in Mongkok? That can't be a coincidence."

Tay said nothing. No, it didn't feel like a coincidence to him either, but it wasn't yet enough to add up to anything solid.

"Jack has arranged for us to talk to the father of Ning Ho in about an hour," Claire continued. "She was the second girl to disappear. Do you want to go with us?"

"I can't. I'm following up with something that Jones put me onto."

Jones had been pretending to ignore Tay's telephone conversation, but when he heard his name, his eyes flicked over. Tay kept his own eyes down. He hadn't lied to Claire, not exactly, but he hadn't told her the truth either. Making eye contact with somebody while he was struggling to keep his balance between a lie and the truth made Tay uncomfortable.

"Look, I've got to go," Tay said. "Push this guy hard. Particularly if he knows anything similar to what we've heard about the other two girls."

A FTER TAY CUT the connection and returned the telephone to his pocket, Jones remained silent for a polite interval, but when Tay offered no explanation, he spoke up.

"Making progress?"

"I don't know. We're checking on connections between the missing girls and Mongkok and it's looking like more than one of them may have been visiting a lover who had an apartment there."

"Surely not the same man."

"It seems unlikely, but who knows?"

"Even if that's true, how does it help you find Emma?"

Tay shook his head. "I don't know that either, at least not yet, and I'm beginning to worry we may be running out of time."

"You mean there's been some sort of demand made for her return and now you have a deadline?"

"No, nothing like that."

Tay wished he had never brought the subject up. He certainly had no intention of telling Jones he thought they were running out of time because his dead mother had told him so.

"It's just a feeling I have," he mumbled. "Nothing specific. Just a feeling."

Tay felt foolish saying something so brainless, but he knew Jones didn't believe him anyway.

.   .   .

T HEY SAT IN silence for a while after that, and then Jones
surprised Tay by breaking it.

"Is there anything else I can do to help?" he asked.

Tay opened his mouth to offer the usual polite refusal, but
then something occurred to him.

"Can you get a few people to show Emma's picture around
Mongkok? Maybe we'll get lucky and find someone who saw
her, which might get us closer to pinning down a location."

"A few people?"

"You know... maybe three or four?"

"How about fifty?"

Tay nodded slowly. "Fifty would be good."

"Mongkok is a big place," Jones said. "Even if I put fifty
men on the streets, you would have to be very lucky to stumble
into someone who saw her."

"Maybe I can improve the odds."

Then Tay told Jones about Sarah McFarland seeing Emma
coming back to Mongkok Station from the direction of Sneaker
Street.

"She doesn't know Emma was actually coming from
Sneaker Street," Tay concluded. "But it narrows down the area
we need to cover. Instead of dealing with the entire neighborhood, if we can blanket about eight square blocks around
Sneaker Street, we might come up with something."

"Have you checked for cameras?"

"Viewing five days of video for each camera we find would
take a full day, and there must be dozens of cameras. There's
just no time, and I don't have the people."

"Then I'll make it a hundred men, two hundred if we need
them."

Tay was beginning to see some real advantages in having a
working relationship with a Hong Kong organized crime boss.

"When can you get me a picture of Emma?" Jones asked.

Tay took out his telephone and flipped through it until he

found the two pictures Mrs. Lau had given them. He chose the one which appeared to be the more recent and handed his phone to Jones.

"Pretty girl," Jones said.

He handed the telephone back to Tay.

"Send that to me and I'll have people on the street showing it around in an hour. I'll get them to check whatever video they can find, too."

Tay touched the screen with his forefinger, but then he stopped and sat staring at it.

"Do you know how to forward a photograph?" Jones asked when he realized the uncertainly with which Tay was peering at his telephone.

Tay said nothing.

"Give me your phone," Jones said and held out his hand.

Jones tapped at the screen of Tay's telephone for perhaps five seconds and then returned it to him.

"Is that all there is to it?" Tay asked.

"That's all."

"Maybe I should learn how to do it."

"Maybe you should."

WHEN DR. PATEL came into the lounge a half hour later, Jones was working his phone and Tay was sitting and staring into the middle distance.

"We've found a mass in your left lung," Dr. Patel said, and time stopped for Samuel Tay.

Jones lowered his telephone and looked up. First at Patel, and then at Tay.

Tay didn't look at anyone.

He weighed the word Patel had used. *Mass.* He turned it around and around in his mind as if he were examining a computer-generated image.

It seemed to Tay a formidable word, a word that meant *large,* and he pictured something resembling a tennis ball stuck in the middle of his lung. The image was very vivid. The ball was yellow and had WILSON in red letters across the middle.

"A mass," Tay said.

Patel nodded.

"You're saying I have lung cancer."

Tay didn't bother to make a question of it.

"No, I'm not saying that at all. Look, you seem to me to be a very precise man, Inspector. A man who says what he means to say and doesn't say what he doesn't mean to say. I am the same. I'm saying the scan detected a mass in your left lung. Whether there is malignancy in the mass is a completely different question."

"But it's possible."

"Of course it's possible. It's always possible, and it would be possible whether or not we had detected the mass."

"But is it probable?"

"I can't say. The scan doesn't tell me. That's why we do a biopsy."

Tay tried to think about what he was hearing, but he wasn't focusing well. He couldn't even decide what the most important thing to think about might be.

"The word mass," he said after a moment, "makes whatever you found seem very... well, large."

"It's not small. I'd estimate it's about twelve millimeters in diameter. Or about half an inch, if you'd prefer."

Tay tried to envision a diameter of twelve millimeters, but he couldn't get his mind around it.

Patel fished in his pocket, came out with a Hong Kong dollar coin and held it up between his thumb and forefinger.

"It's less than half this size."

Tay focused his eyes on the coin. The image of a tennis ball suspended in his lung flickered out and the image of a coin suspended in his lung replaced it. It didn't make him feel any better.

Patel said nothing else. Tay assumed he was giving him a decent interval in which to absorb the news. He imagined Patel had delivered news like this a great many times in his career and had learned from experience that saying less was generally better than saying more.

Tay glanced at Jones. He was still and expressionless. Tay imagined he would be the same if their positions were reversed. Shifting his eyes back into the middle distance, Tay examined his reaction to Dr. Patel's announcement as dispassionately as he could.

Since he was a smoker, he didn't feel surprised by Dr. Patel's discovery, let alone victimized. Every time some harpy had a go at him for his smoking, he told her the same thing. He had made his choice freely, and he knew it might have consequences. Unhappy ones. He had always known a day like this was a possibility.

What had never occurred to him was that, when such a day did arrive for him, he would share the most profound and consequential moment of his entire life with a Chinese organized crime boss whom he hardly knew. Sometimes life dealt such strange cards it was well beyond anyone's power of imagination to conceive of them in advance.

Tay looked back at Patel.

"What now?" he asked.

"We do a bronchoscopy."

Tay waited for Patel to explain what that meant, and after a moment he did.

"I go in with a bronchoscope, examine the mass, take a sample for biopsy, and then cauterize it. The cauterizing will stop the bleeding, and the examination and biopsy will establish whether there is any malignancy which might mandate further treatment."

"So, now I'll have to go to a hospital."

"Oh my, no. I'll do it here."

"When?"

265

"Right now."

Tay took a deep breath and looked away.

"I'm sure you can understand this is quite a lot for me to absorb all at once, doctor."

Patel nodded, but he remained silent.

"How do you do this bronchoscopy?" Tay asked.

"I just shove a light and a camera down your throat into your lung and take a look around."

Tay glanced at Patel in alarm and saw he was grinning.

"Relax," Patel said. "It's no big deal. We administer a sedative by IV and then we use a local anesthetic to numb your nose and mouth. When the anesthetic takes effect, I place a very thin flexible tube called a bronchoscope into your mouth. The bronchoscope has a light and a tiny camera in its tip, and I work it down the back of your throat, through your vocal cords, and into your airways. Then I retrieve the tissue samples I need for the biopsy through the same tube."

"How long does all that take?"

"Half an hour tops. In and out. Then we'll monitor you here for a couple of hours just to make sure everything's well. If it is, we'll slap you on the ass and send you home. There's no pain and only a minor sensation. Odds are you won't even remember much about the procedure. The sedatives generally have that effect."

"And afterwards you can tell me what I'm looking at here?"

"The tissue I remove has to go to a lab for the biopsy, and I don't like to jump to a conclusion either way until I've seen the biopsy results."

"How long will that take?"

"About a week. We ought to have the result by the middle of next week."

Then Jones spoke up for the first time since Dr. Patel had entered the room.

"Get it done in two days, doctor," he said. "Two days."

"That will be difficult."

"Today's Thursday. I want the result of the biopsy done for Inspector Tay by Saturday. Do you understand?"

"I'm not absolutely certain I can——"

"I *am* absolutely certain you can. And if you need me to speak to somebody to get it done, I will."

"I have no doubt you can be very persuasive, Mr. Jones."

"Neither does anyone else."

Patel cleared his throat and consulted his feet. Then he gave a little shrug and looked at Tay.

"Well," he said, vigorously rubbing his hands together, "shall we get started?"

THIRTY-SIX

THE NEXT THING Tay knew, he was drifting awake in a half-darkened room. He was stretched out on a low couch, fully dressed except for his shoes.

When he concentrated hard, which required considerable effort, he had a hazy recollection of an IV being inserted into his right arm while he lay on the examining table. He had no idea what kind of sedative had been given to him through the IV, but whatever it was he ought to get a couple of gallons to take home because it worked like a son of a gun. He could dredge up nothing at all from his memory about what happened after that.

Had Dr. Patel even done the procedure yet? Perhaps that was the reason he could remember nothing. Dr. Patel hadn't actually begun.

"Well, look who's awake."

It was a woman's voice, although Tay didn't recognize it. But when he heard a rustling noise and she bent over him, he recognized the nurse who had helped him through the CT scan which had led to all this.

Nancy, wasn't it? No... Nan. That was her name. Nan.

"Are we almost ready to begin, Nan?"

When Nan giggled and lifted her hand to cover her mouth, Tay remembered the same gesture coming after something he had said before the scan. He had fallen in love with it then, and now it happened all over again.

"Dr. Patel finished over an hour ago. You must have liked the sedative we gave you."

"Don't tell me what it was. I'd buy all I could find."

Another giggle.

Tay wondered if his ability to amuse attractive women improved under sedation.

He pressed his hands against the couch and began to push himself upright, but Nan placed a hand against his chest.

"Just stay there. I need to check your vitals before you can move around."

Tay allowed himself to drift while Nan fussed around him. She checked his blood pressure, his temperature, and his heartbeat. He had to admit it was all rather pleasant. He tried to remember the last time a woman had fussed over him. Either it was too long ago for him to recall or, more likely, it had never actually happened before.

"Can you sit up?" Nan asked when she had finished.

"Of course I can sit up."

But when he pushed himself upright, Tay's head swam and the world around him rippled in an unfamiliar way.

"I'll get Dr. Patel and let him know you're awake. Don't try to stand yet. Just stay where you are."

Nan needn't have worried. Tay wasn't sure he could stand even if he wanted to, which he didn't. So he sat as still as he could and yawned several times into the half-darkened room while he waited for her to return.

W HEN THE DOOR opened and the lights came on, Dr. Patel strolled in followed by Nan and Jones.

"How are you feeling, sir?"

"A little woozy, and my throat hurts. Could I have some water?"

Nan stepped around Dr. Patel and handed Tay a full glass of water with one of those half-bent straws in it he had never seen anywhere other than in hospitals. Tay took a long pull through the straw and decided it was without doubt the best water he had ever tasted, so he took another.

"Not so quickly, sir. Be measured in all things. Give it a minute or two and then you can have some more. Can you stand up?"

Tay nodded and handed the glass to Patel. He pushed himself to his feet and was pleased to find it easier than he thought it would be.

"Very good!" Dr. Patel exclaimed. "But please sit back down. Stretch out if you like. Let's give it another ten minutes and then, if you still feel fine, I'll send you home."

Tay sat back down on the edge of the couch, but he didn't stretch out.

"What did you find?" he asked Patel.

"I found the mass where I expected to find it. I took a sample for biopsy and then cauterized it. There should be no further bleeding. If there is any, call me immediately."

"That's not what I was asking."

"I know it wasn't, sir, but it's all I can tell you right now. When I get the biopsy results, I'll be able to say more. Could you give me the number on which you'd like me to call when I hear from the lab?"

He had hoped for something a bit more definitive, but he didn't blame Patel for being cautious about coming to any premature conclusions, either encouraging or discouraging ones. If he had been in Patel's position, he was sure he would have been just as cautious. It took Tay a moment to summon up his personal cell number out of the fog, but when he did, he recited it to Patel. Patel wrote it down on a little pad and put it in the breast pocket of his doctor's coat.

"Will you have the bill ready before I leave Hong Kong?" he asked, "or would you like my address in Singapore to send it there?"

Patel chuckled. "We don't send bills here, sir. This is a private clinic. We only serve Mr. Jones and his colleagues, and now his friends."

Tay shifted his eyes to Jones. "I'm not sure I'm comfortable with that."

Jones shrugged. "I'm not sure it matters whether you're comfortable or not, because it's the way it is."

"Well then," Tay nodded, "I guess I'll just say thank you."

"And I guess I'll just say you're welcome."

Dr. Patel smiled again.

"Mr. Jones has persuaded me to be certain we have your biopsy results by Saturday. You'll hear from me then."

"I've organized a car to take you back to your hotel, Inspector," Jones said. "Let me make sure it's here and I'll be right back for you."

THE CAR WAITING downstairs was a black Mercedes sedan. A big one. What else?

The driver was wearing a dark gray suit and a blue tie, and he neither turned around nor said anything as Jones and Tay got into the back seat. When their doors closed, he pulled away from the curb. Jones didn't have to tell him where to go. Apparently, he already knew.

"I should say thank you one more time," Tay said.

Jones looked at him and gave a small nod. "And I should say you're welcome one more time."

They were so close to the Cordis Hotel it only took them five minutes to drive there. When they stopped at the main entrance, a uniformed doorman leaped forward and held Tay's door open.

"Are you going to be okay?" Jones asked.

271

"All I need is a decent night's sleep and I'll be right back at it tomorrow."

"I have men working the area around Sneaker Street with the photograph you gave me. By tomorrow, we will have talked to every shop owner and resident in the area and we will have looked at whatever video we can locate. If we find out anything that might help you, I'll let you know right away."

"Call me anytime tonight. Don't worry about waking me up."

Jones nodded. "Good night, Inspector."

Tay offered his hand and they shook, then he got out of the car and stood watching until it had driven away.

T HE DOORMAN WAS holding open the hotel's main entrance door for him, but Tay shook his head and walked off down the driveway in the opposite direction from the one in which the big Mercedes had disappeared.

He had no destination in mind but being out in the fresh air, or what passed for fresh air in Hong Kong, was making him feel stronger, so he kept walking. He turned right on Portland Street and headed south, away from the busiest part of Mongkok.

The streets in that direction were quieter and life moved at a pace which made Tay think of the reasons he had always had such affection for life in a city.

Old men stood on street corners, t-shirts rolled up over their potbellies, and argued with their friends. Middle-aged women shuffled along the sidewalks dragging plastic bags brimming with food they had just bought in some market. Young toughs strutted the streets, trying their best to look like the hard men they hoped to become someday.

Tay found the very banality of it all to be cheering. Ordinary life was unremarkable and grounded in regularity, and that was exactly why he loved it. Still, he couldn't help but wonder how much more of it remained for him.

When Tay passed a 7-Eleven, he bought a pack of Marlboros, something he had done so often in his life it was now an act performed almost by reflex. It wasn't until he was back outside on the sidewalk that the irony of what he had done struck him.

He had just had a doctor probing into his lungs to examine what he had discovered there, something he insisted on calling a *mass*, and he had removed tissue from the *mass* to test it for cancer. Yet Tay had walked into a 7-Eleven without a second thought and bought a pack of cigarettes. More ordinary life. His ordinary life.

He wondered if the time had finally come for him to quit smoking.

He wondered if it was already too late for it to matter.

He stopped trying to decide.

Tay shook out a cigarette and lit it with the book of matches the clerk had given him. He inhaled deeply, exhaled a long stream of smoke, and watched it swirl away with a feeling of genuine satisfaction. Life held few enough pleasures for him. He wouldn't give up this one, at least not yet.

That was when it occurred to him he needed a drink to go with this cigarette.

And then maybe another cigarette.

He turned back toward the Cordis Hotel and quickened his pace.

THIRTY-SEVEN

TAY SETTLED INTO a comfortable chair at the Garage Bar, ordered a Bushmills and water, and lit a Marlboro. Everything was again right with the world. Well... almost everything.

He still had lung cancer. Or maybe he didn't. But the truth was, in the very depths of whatever passed for his soul these days, he knew he did. He could feel it working in his body right now, chewing away at his lungs.

Tay had never made any effort to view the world through a lens of sunny optimism, and he certainly wasn't going to start now. Maybe being a cop for all those years had done something to him, but he always anticipated the worst in any situation and he was seldom disappointed in his expectation.

He had decided long ago that most people were worse human beings now than they had been a generation ago, and every year they seemed to get a little worse. Tay accepted that was just as true of him as it was of anyone.

He was not as good a person now as he had once been. Not as hopeful, not as forgiving, not as merciful. Every day he became more of an angry, irascible old fart. Did it work that way for everyone as they aged, or had twenty years plumbing the depths of human misery as a policeman taken a toll on him?

Tay found an odd measure of comfort in reminding himself that the seemingly inevitable progress of civilization down the crapper would end soon enough for him. Soon enough, he would depart this life and leave all the nastiness and hatred and rage for someone else to deal with. At least he had no expectation of anything coming afterward, so he wouldn't be disappointed about *that*.

Did he have lung cancer or didn't he? The more he thought about it, the less he cared.

Tay studied the squat, heavy glass tumbler sitting in front of him. Before he drank from it, he lifted it high and examined the whiskey. He hadn't noticed before what a lovely shade of amber Bushmills was. The liquor gleamed in the low light like liquid honey. Had it always been such a beautiful color?

The first sip rolled over his tongue with a burst of flavor he never before remembered experiencing. Brown sugar, red grapes, cooked plums, hints of raspberries and strawberries, caramel, and maybe even a suggestion of molasses. He had never really noticed.

His ears reached out and embraced the music playing in the background. Jazz of some kind, but he knew nothing about jazz. Nothing about music, really. Still, the crisp tones produced by the trumpet grabbed and held him. The notes vibrated with a clarity that rolled through the air as if they were ripples crossing a pond. The purity of the sound amazed him.

Was this what dying did for you? Did the sights and flavors and sounds of life all at once become so much more intense because you knew that soon enough there would be no more sights and flavors and sounds for you at all? If so, it was a gift, and he welcomed it.

. . .

W HEN TAY'S TELEPHONE rang, he did not welcome it. He had no wish to talk to anyone, but he answered it anyway. Mostly out of habit.

"Hello?"

"Sam, are you all right?"

Tay froze. It was Claire, but why was she asking him if he was all right?

Had she heard about the bleeding and the tests Dr. Patel had run to figure out what was causing it? Surely not. No one but Jones knew, and Tay didn't think Jones would have told anyone. Besides, Claire didn't know Jones and he didn't know her, so he couldn't have told her, could he?

Before Tay could come up with a response which didn't sound like pure evasion, Claire started talking again.

"I mean," she said, "I haven't heard from you all day and every time I tried to call I got your voicemail. Have you had your phone turned off?"

"I forgot to charge it last night. Sorry."

It was the first thing that popped into Tay's head, but he took a moment to congratulate himself on coming up with something not completely stupid. He hated lying to Claire, but lying about his phone not being charged wasn't much of a sin, was it? It was just a minor lie, although he knew the purpose of it was to protect him from telling a much larger lie.

Eventually, he would have to tell Claire the truth, but eventually wasn't right now.

He changed the subject.

"Did Shepherd find anything on Emma's laptop or iPad which might help us?"

Claire hesitated. Tay sensed her reluctance to let him off the hook about not answering his telephone so easily, but she did anyway.

"He said it was all normal stuff," she said. "Nothing

connected to Mongkok. Nothing about being involved with anyone."

"Did Shepherd get you in to see the parents of any of the other missing girls?"

"We saw two more today and I don't think there's any doubt now. The disappearances all fall into the same pattern."

"Who did you see?"

"I already told you about the father of the third girl to disappear, Yu Yang."

"Remind me again what he said."

"He knew his daughter was seeing someone who had an apartment in Mongkok. He had the impression it was somebody older, maybe married, but he didn't know who it was."

"And now you've found other parents who say something similar?"

"We saw Ning Ho's father today. She was the second to vanish. He was the one who paid the two-million-dollar ransom. He tried to keep it secret and even denied it when some newspaper got the story. He said she was seeing somebody secretly, too, somebody she said he wouldn't approve of."

"In Mongkok?"

"He didn't know. He only knew she said she was going to Mongkok when she disappeared."

"He hadn't heard anything about the lover being older, married, or prominent?"

"No, but now we come to the mother of Stephanie Wong, the first girl to disappear. She was last seen on Argyle Street in Mongkok, but no one knew why she was there. Her mother says Stephanie confided in her she was seeing somebody, but she was afraid her mother might know him so she didn't want to tell her who it was."

"She might *know* him?"

"She thought Stephanie didn't mean she might know him personally, but only that she might know who he was."

"Huh."

277

"So, including Emma, we can now connect four out of six to Mongkok where it looks very much like they were meeting a lover. None of them knew who their daughter was seeing, but we've got several repetitions of this general impression of older, married, and prominent in describing the lover."

"Maybe that was only an assumption on the parents' part. Maybe they were just trying to explain to themselves why their daughters weren't telling them who they were seeing."

"I don't think so, Sam."

"You're not seriously telling me you think all of these girls were meeting the same man, are you?"

"I know it sounds crazy, but… well, yes. It's beginning to seem like it. Otherwise, we're looking at a whole bunch of coincidences and that's even harder to believe."

Tay wasn't sure what he thought so he asked a different question.

"Did you have time to search for stories about unexplained body parts being found in Hong Kong?"

"I went back two years, but I didn't find anything."

"Huh," Tay said for the second time.

Maybe Shepherd had been right. If somebody was taking these girls and killing them, their bodies were being cremated, not chopped up and disposed of. Tay could think of no other reasonable explanation as to how five, or maybe six, young women had disappeared in Mongkok without a trace.

"What do you want to do now, Sam? Do you want us to try to see the parents of the other two girls?"

Tay's mind was sliding into overload territory. First, there had been the apocalyptic pronouncement from Dr. Patel about this *thing* in his lung he had insisted on calling a mass, and now it looked like they had uncovered a serial killer stalking young women in Hong Kong. And that was all in just the last three hours. Good Lord, what next? What time was the rain of locusts scheduled?

He didn't know what to say to Claire. He needed to think.

"Let me sleep on it."

"We need to push hard, Sam. Emma's only been gone for five days. She may still be alive, but she might not be alive for long."

That was the same thing his mother had told him. She had insisted they only had until tomorrow to find Emma, but he wasn't about to tell Claire *that*.

"I still need to sleep on it," Tay repeated.

Claire hesitated. "Are you sure you're okay, Sam? You just don't sound like yourself."

"I'm fine, Claire. I'll call you tomorrow morning."

A FTER HE ENDED the call, Tay turned off his phone and lit another Marlboro.

What had he stumbled into here? He had been trying to find one young woman who was missing, and he ended up discovering a serial killer no one knew was operating in Hong Kong.

Did that mean Emma was no longer alive? He supposed it was possible she was already dead, but he still didn't think so. He could feel her presence somehow. She *was* alive. He just didn't know how long she would stay that way.

His mother had claimed she knew how long Emma would stay that way, of course, but then his mother was dead, so what did she know? How could the dead have more insight into life than the living? The more he considered that question, the deeper it took him into places he would just as soon not go.

Tay heard female voices rising and falling and he glanced toward them in time to see three young women come into the bar. They all appeared to be local girls in their twenties, and they were stylishly and expensively dressed in that way Chinese women with access to money always seemed to be.

He wondered if their access to money was because of husbands or lovers or families. They could have their own money, he supposed, money earned from employment or starting a company or designing software, but that wasn't anybody's first thought when they saw three stylish, attractive young women enter a bar in Hong Kong. It might not be fair, but nevertheless it was still true.

Just then one of the girls laughed, which caused her to turn her head in Tay's direction. They made eye contact, and Tay smiled automatically, embarrassed to have gotten caught looking at her. The girl didn't smile back. Instead, she regarded him curiously for a moment, as if he were a member of some species the name of which she couldn't quite recall. Then she spun sharply on one high-heel-clad foot, flashed her long legs, and followed the other two girls deeper into the bar.

T AY SMOKED HIS Marlboro and thought about stylish young women and serial killers and lung cancer. One had nothing to do with the other, of course, not until Tay factored himself into the equation. Then they all very much had to do with each other.

It was the natural order of things for everyone to come to the end of whatever they had done and whoever they were. But when Claire had asked him to come to Hong Kong to find Emma Lau, it had never occurred to him that this case might be his end.

After a lifetime spent digging out the truth about the terrible things people did to each other, he would not go out a loser. He would not accept anything for his final trip around the track other than a win. And the only win for him here was to find out where Emma Lau was and whether she was alive or dead.

It was just that simple.

Tay stubbed out his cigarette, dropped some money on the table, and went upstairs to bed.

THIRTY-EIGHT

FRIDAY. DAY FOUR. Searching for Emma Lau.

A loud banging on the door of his room woke Tay. It felt to him like it was very early, and the noise hauled him ever so reluctantly from the soundest sleep he had enjoyed in months. He had to find out what the sedative that Dr. Patel had given him was. He needed to lay in a big supply.

Tay pushed the duvet aside, swung his feet to the floor, and sat on the side of the bed without getting up. He felt like an old Ford that might never start again.

The banging on his door was very annoying. There was nothing nice about being woken early in the morning by some idiot pounding on his door. Perhaps someone would emerge from one of the other rooms on the floor and strangle whoever was doing it.

But nobody strangled anybody, and the pounding continued.

"I'm coming, for God's sake," Tay croaked. "Just stop the goddamned noise."

He pushed himself to his feet, yawned, and tried to shake the sleep from his muddled brain. He failed.

Tay picked up the hotel bathrobe he had dumped onto a chair the night before and slipped into it, then he staggered to the door and jerked it open. Claire was standing there in the hallway, and she looked unhappy. Tay was genuinely puzzled.

"What are you doing here?" he asked.

"You turned your phone off. Or are you going to make another lame excuse and try to tell me the battery ran down?"

Tay thought for a second. Had he turned his phone off? He couldn't remember.

"Even if I did turn it off, what are you doing here so early in the morning?"

"Early? It's almost eleven-thirty."

Tay squinted at Claire. *Eleven-thirty?* How was that possible? Could he have really slept... what, thirteen hours? Perhaps it was even longer, but complex mathematical calculations were beyond him at the moment.

"Are you okay, Sam?"

Tay weighed up the philosophical implications of Claire's question and decided to ignore them.

"I took a sleeping pill," he improvised. "I guess it hit me harder than I expected."

"Well, stick your head under the shower or something. Doris Lau wants to see us a half hour from now. I said we would meet her at noon on the block behind the Peninsula where we met her before."

Tay's brain was beginning to engage, but Claire's announcement knocked it right back out of gear again. Did they have a meeting with Mrs. Lau scheduled for today and he had forgotten?

Claire read his mind.

"No, you didn't forget," she said. "Mrs. Lau called me this morning. I don't know what it's about, but she says she has to see us right now. I figure you've got fifteen minutes to get dressed and then we can make it to the Peninsula in another fifteen minutes."

Tay took that in. After a moment he gave a very small nod and stumbled off to the bathroom.

He really *would* have to find out what kind of sedative Dr. Patel had given him. It was great stuff.

TAY WAS NOT a man who spent a lot of time on personal grooming. Fifteen minutes was unnecessary. He was ready in ten, including checking three times to be certain his zipper was closed.

There was very little traffic on Nathan Road, and Tay and Claire were behind the Peninsula Hotel at five minutes before noon. There was saw no sign of Mrs. Lau or her Mercedes van, which left Claire the time to look Tay over more carefully than he would have liked.

"Are you sure you're okay, Sam?"

"Of course I am. Why would you ask?"

"You just don't seem to be yourself."

Tay wondered if he was that transparent. He would have to tell Claire about Dr. Patel's diagnosis sometime, he knew, but it would not be now.

"It's just the damn sleeping pill," he continued to improvise. "I almost never take them and you can see why."

Claire nodded, but Tay could tell she was a long way from convinced so he moved right on along.

"Mrs. Lau didn't give you any idea what this is all about?" he asked.

"She just said she had to talk to us and it couldn't wait."

Tay thought that over for a moment and then shrugged.

"There's no point in trying to guess." He pointed past Claire to the black Mercedes van with blacked-out windows as it pulled to the curb about fifty feet away. "We'll just ask her."

The driver's door opened and the same large man with a handgun in a shoulder holster who was driving her before unfolded himself from the van and stepped out onto the sidewalk. This time he didn't get aggressive with them. He didn't even glance at them. He just closed the driver's door, walked behind the van, and lit a cigarette.

The van's door slid back, and Tay and Claire walked toward it.

T HEY CLIMBED INSIDE and sat down. The van smelled like it had been sterilized recently with something which contained chlorine. The odor reminded Tay of a public swimming pool.

Doris Lau and Tony Soprano were both waiting for them sitting in the same seats they had been sitting in the first time Tay and Claire had been in the van. Tay knew he should stop calling Mrs. Lau's Chief of Staff by the name of a fictional American mobster, even just to himself, but he had said it so often he had forgotten the man's real name.

And then Doris Lau bailed him out.

"You both remember Albert, don't you? Albert Chan, my Chief of Staff."

Tay still thought the man looked like Tony Soprano, but he didn't want to call him that by accident so he was glad to be reminded he had a real name, too.

"I'll make this fast," Doris Lau said. "I'm calling this whole thing off and sending you back to Washington."

Tay wasn't sure what he had been expecting her to say, but it hadn't been that.

"I've talked to Bill," she added, "and he has accepted my decision."

"Bill?" Tay asked with a puzzled look on his face.

"The vice president," Doris Lau snapped.

"Does that mean you know where Emma is now?" Claire asked.

Mrs. Lau looked at her, then she looked away and shook her head.

"No, but tomorrow I'm turning the matter over to the Hong Kong police."

"I thought you said——"

"I know what I said, but I've changed my mind. From the beginning, Albert said involving you was a mistake, and I've decided he's right. You can both see what's happening in this city right now. If it became known I was working with people sent here by the White House to help me with a private matter, people whose affiliation I don't even know, it would be a disaster for me."

Tay waited. He sensed something more was coming.

"Albert thinks it would be better to put this matter in the hands of the police. After all, we don't even know if Emma is in any danger. She may have just gone off on her own for a while. It's a simple missing persons case and it should be the Hong Kong police who are dealing with it."

"I don't think it's a simple missing persons case," Tay said.

"Why should I care *what* you think?" Mrs. Lau glowered at Tay. "You've learned nothing, anyway."

"We've learned a great deal."

Tony Soprano rumbled to life. "Such as what? You haven't reported any progress to us."

"I'm reporting it now."

Tay shifted his eyes back to Doris Lau.

"Do you want to hear what we've learned?"

She said nothing, but then gave a single crisp jerk of her head. Tay took it to be a nod.

"It appears that——"

"If you have specific facts to relate," Tony Soprano interrupted, "please do so. But it isn't helpful to hear a lot of suppositions."

Doris Lau waved her hand in the air. "It's all right, Albert. Let them say their piece and then go. I just want all this over with."

"At least five girls have disappeared in Mongkok in the last

285

year and a half, all under similar circumstances," Tay began. "Emma is the sixth."

Tay couldn't tell if that surprised Doris Lau or not since she remained expressionless, but he hurried on before Tony Soprano could interrupt him again.

"These girls were all in a similar age range and all from wealthy and influential Hong Kong families. At least three of them were seeing someone who either lived in Mongkok or kept an apartment there for the purpose of meeting them."

"Are you saying Emma was also seeing someone who lived in Mongkok?"

"She was visiting someone there, and she had been doing it regularly. We're very close to finding out who it was."

That was a slight exaggeration, of course. Actually, it was pretty well a flat-out lie. But if this was the last shot Tay had at Doris Lau, he wanted to make it a good one.

"Do you think Emma is still alive?" Mrs. Lau asked.

Tay hesitated. He considered several responses, and then went with the simplest one since it had the additional advantage of being true.

"I don't know," he said.

"But you think the other five girls you told me about are dead."

"Yes."

Doris Lau looked at Tony Soprano. Neither spoke, but something seemed to pass between them.

"Thank you for your efforts, Inspector. I will convey your theory to the Hong Kong police, but nothing you have told me changes my mind. I want you to go no further with this investigation."

"But, Mrs. Lau—"

"We're done here. Good day."

. . .

T AY AND CLAIRE stood on the sidewalk behind the Peninsula Hotel and watched the van pull away.

"What just happened?" Claire asked.

"I think we were told to piss off. In fact, I'm sure we were."

"Something stinks. And I'm not just talking about Albert Chan's aftershave."

"You mean the chlorine smell in the van? That was aftershave?"

"It certainly wasn't Doris Lau's perfume."

"I thought somebody disinfected the van with chlorine bleach."

"They'll have to burn it to get rid of that smell."

Tay made a mental note to check out any aftershave he bought very, very carefully before he wore it around Claire.

"Do you believe what Doris Lau told us?" she asked.

"You mean, that she was afraid of political blowback from us looking for Emma?"

Claire nodded.

"It makes sense. I can see how we would be a problem for her if anyone found out about us. What *doesn't* make sense is she knew that before we met her the first time, and she didn't mention it then."

"So what changed?"

"I don't know. She looked frightened to me. Didn't you think?"

Claire thought for a moment, and then nodded. "Maybe."

"I can't see why she would be, but I'd like to know."

"My bet is it has something to do with Albert Chan. Did you see how he was pulling her strings? It was like watching a ventriloquist and his dummy."

Tay considered that. "Do you think there's a connection between them other than him being her Chief of Staff?"

"You mean a personal connection?"

"Yeah, do you think they're..."

Tay hesitated, scrambling for a way to avoid the word which had nearly tumbled out.

"...having relations," he finished hastily.

"*Having relations?*" Claire laughed. "Did you just say *having relations?*"

Tay didn't trust himself to speak so he just nodded quickly.

"I swear, Sam Tay, no one else has used the phrase *having relations* in at least fifty years. Are you asking me if I think they're fucking?"

Tay looked away. He was afraid he might be blushing and he knew Claire would never let him live it down if he were.

"No, I don't think they're *fucking*, Sam. Don't ask me how I know it, but I don't sense that kind of connection between them. If he's got a hold over her, it's something else."

Tay had always trusted his own instincts about the people he dealt with, but in this instance he would have to go with Claire's. He supposed it wasn't fashionable to say so these days, but he had always believed women had a better understanding of the relationships between men and women than he did. Who was he kidding? His goldfish had a better understanding of the relationships between men and women than he did. And he didn't have a goldfish.

"What do you want me to do now?" Claire asked.

"Call Shepherd. Have him meet us at the hotel as soon as he can get there. I'm not sure how much time we have left."

"Do you want me to call August and tell him Mrs. Lau wants us to piss off?"

Tay gave Claire a long look.

"Why, I do declare, Samuel Tay, I think you're about to go all cowboy here."

"Fuck a bunch of cowboys," Tay said. "Call Shepherd."

PART 3

NEWTON'S THIRD LAW OF MOTION

For every action in nature, there is an equal and opposite reaction.

THIRTY-NINE

"SHE TOLD YOU to forget about it and just go away?" Shepherd asked. "Seriously? She said that?"

Shepherd was sitting in the desk chair in Tay's hotel room, the same chair where Tay had imagined his mother sitting two nights before. Tay would have preferred for Shepherd to sit in the room's brown leather easy chair over in front of the windows, but Claire had appropriated it.

It was a little disconcerting to Tay that Shepherd had pulled the desk chair over to where he was sitting on the end of the bed since it put Shepherd in almost exactly the same spot where Tay's mother had been sitting. Or would have been if she had actually been there. Which she wasn't.

Tay tried to put the whole matter of chairs and positions in the room out of his mind since he had no intention of telling either Shepherd or Claire about his mother's nocturnal appearance or about the advice she had given him, or rather the advice he imagined she had given him. Not even the part about them only having until tonight to find Emma alive.

Especially not that part.

"Why would Mrs. Lau tell you to drop the search?" Shepherd asked.

"Her Chief of Staff appears to have convinced her the political blowback from her working with Americans to find Emma would be damaging if anybody found out."

"I'm sure he's right," Shepherd shrugged. "This place is coming apart. The kids in the streets are holding up America as the shining temple of liberty and freedom. China doesn't like that, and the political establishment here doesn't like whatever China doesn't like. Americans aren't popular with the powerful in Hong Kong these days."

"That's one of the advantages of being a Singaporean," Tay said. "Nobody cares about us one way or another."

"Then what did you tell Mrs. Lau?"

"I was vague," Tay said.

"Which means, I gather, we're going to keep looking for Emma."

"It means *I'm* going to keep looking for Emma. I'd like to have your help, but you have to live here and I don't. If you think that might be a problem for you, I'll understand. No hard feelings."

"I got nothing else to do today," Shepherd smiled. "Nothing else tomorrow either. I'm in."

Tay and Shepherd both looked at Claire.

"Don't be idiots," she said. "Of course I'm in. What's the plan, Sam?"

"To order an enormous pot of coffee and tell you what I've found out that you don't know about yet."

"I've already had enough coffee this morning," Shepherd said.

"Don't be ridiculous," Tay said. "You can never have enough coffee."

"You told Mrs. Lau you were very close to identifying whoever it was Emma had been meeting in Mongkok," Claire asked. "Was that true?"

"I think it would more accurately be described as... uh, something closer to complete bullshit."

"That's what I was afraid of."

"But at least I've narrowed it down. Let me get that coffee and I'll take you through it."

B Y THE TIME the room service waiter had brought the coffee, poured it, and left again, Tay had told them about bracing Sarah McFarland at her office and her admission the lunches she and Emma had been having were just a cover for Emma meeting a lover in Mongkok.

"So, you've got Emma secretly meeting somebody in Mongkok," Shepherd said, "and we've got three of the other girls who disappeared secretly meeting somebody in Mongkok. That can't be a coincidence."

"So now you *do* believe they were all meeting the same man?"

"I believe they could have been," Tay said. "Some pervert sets up an apartment in Mongkok, lures a girl in every few months, does what he likes with her, then kills her. It wouldn't be the first time something like that has happened."

"Then there's a guy out there who's killed six girls in a year and a half?"

"Five girls," Tay said. "Emma is still alive. I'm sure of it."

They all considered that in silence for a few moments, and then Shepherd cleared his throat.

"You said you had narrowed down who took her."

"Not *who* exactly. More like where."

"I don't follow you."

"Sarah saw Emma coming back to Mongkok Station from the direction of Sneaker Street, and that gives us a good focus. If you look at a map, you'll see it's unlikely Emma would have been walking along Sneaker Street unless she had been coming from a fairly small area, maybe ten square blocks. I'm betting she was meeting this guy at an apartment somewhere in those ten blocks, and I think there's a decent chance he's still holding her in the same place right now."

"That's still a lot of ground to cover," Shepherd said. "As densely populated as Mongkok is, there could be thirty or forty thousand people living in an area even that small. And they're all local people who speak Cantonese and don't like outsiders. We're two white folks and one Singaporean, and none of us speak a word of Cantonese. We can't just go around knocking on doors asking people if they've seen Emma."

"You're right, we can't," Tay said. "But I know someone who can. And he's doing it right now."

"I LIKE IT," Shepherd said after Tay explained how Jones was flooding the streets in the area with men showing Emma's picture around. "Send out triad soldiers to shake down the neighborhood. Nobody in Mongkok would dare lie to those guys."

"What about video from security cameras?" Claire asked. "Shouldn't we try to check it, too?"

"There'll be too many cameras for just the three of us to search whatever video there is. Besides, we'd have the same problem asking people to look at security video we'd have getting them to talk to us. Jones said he would tell his people to look at whatever video they could find."

"You know, Sam, this just might work. If Emma has been in that area, we might at least have a chance to find her."

"How long do you think it will take before—"

Tay's telephone rang, and they all stopped and looked at it. Tay walked over to the desk, picked it up, and looked at the screen.

"It's Jones."

"Seriously?" Shepherd asked. "Do you suppose he has this room bugged?"

"Don't be ridiculous," Tay said, but suddenly he was wondering a little about that himself.

Tay answered and after the usual exchange of greetings Jones said, "I think I may have something for you."

"Shepherd and Claire are here with me now so let me put you on speaker."

Tay took the phone away from his ear and looked at the screen, which was when he realized he wasn't quite certain how to put the phone on the speaker. Shepherd got up, walked over, and did it for him.

"Okay, Jones, go ahead," Tay said.

"I have a man at the Adidas shop on Sneaker Street right now who says he's found someone on their video surveillance you should see. He thinks it might be the girl you're looking for. When can you get over there?"

"We're at the hotel now, so... ten minutes? Fifteen maybe."

"The shop is at the corner of Sneaker Street and Nelson Street. You can't miss it. You shouldn't have any trouble communicating with him. His English is... well, I'd call it interesting, but it's good enough for you to get by. I think he learned it from watching American TV shows."

"What was his name?"

"Just call him FL. It's the short version of his Cantonese nickname."

"What's his nickname?"

"Fei Lou."

Shepherd laughed.

"Oh, you know what that means, do you, Mr. Shepherd?"

"Yes, I do."

"Would you care to enlighten our friends?"

"I knew a guy in Macau who was an enforcer for a casino there and everybody called him Fei Lou. I was told the English translation was something like Fat Boy."

"Very good, Mr. Shepherd. But my advice is for you to stick to calling my man FL. A detailed discussion about the origin of his nickname would be most inadvisable. You'll understand what I mean when you meet him."

T HE ADIDAS SHOP was on the ground floor of an old six-story building with peeling white paint, grimy windows, and wheezing air conditioners dripping water on the sidewalk.

The shop itself was slick and modern. Behind glass show windows in polished chrome frames was a display of brightly colored NBA jerseys and flashy-looking basketball shoes. The shop looked like it could be in a shopping mall in Dallas, but it wasn't. It was on the ground floor of a grubby building on a dirty street in Mongkok.

A giant billboard was plastered over the first three floors of the building right above the shop. It featured a pair of thirty-foot-tall black American basketball players springing toward the heavens, no doubt propelled by their Adidas shoes. Just below these two monsters, was Adidas' current tag line.

Me. Myself.

Tay could think of no better illustration of the overweening narcissism of America's professional basketball players than that. But it baffled him why Adidas thought the self-absorption of these chuckleheads was a good way to sell shoes.

Tay had always believed Americans had many admirable qualities: their initiative, their inventiveness, their generosity, their confidence, their willingness to go over the next horizon just to find out what was there. But in some Americans, professional athletes and entertainers in particular, self-confidence had morphed into little more than arrogance and self-adulation. Tay was sick to death of the lot of them, and he suspected many Americans were, too.

"Two outside cameras I can see," Shepherd said as the three

of them stood on the sidewalk across the street looking the place over. "There's one on each side of the windows and the fields of view look like they cover the whole sidewalk in front of the store."

They were less than a block from Argyle Street. The intersection of Argyle Street and Sneaker Street was where Sarah said she saw Emma walking back to Mongkok Station. To get there, Emma would probably have walked right past this Adidas store.

The sidewalk was wide and unobstructed. It looked to Tay like the security cameras would have a clear view of anyone walking by. If Emma had been there recently, Tay would bet one of those cameras caught her head on.

T HE SHOP ASSISTANT was a girl who didn't look to be much past twenty. She had long, glossy black hair that fell almost to her waist and she was wearing gray sweats with white Adidas trainers. Her eyes were brown and large, and Tay could see wariness in them.

Shepherd was the expert on local behavior, but Tay thought perhaps he should take the lead here, anyway. Mongkok wasn't a neighborhood where people saw a lot of tourists. A white man and woman stood out, and not in a good way. At least Tay was Singaporean. That made him a little less unsettling.

"Is there someone here named FL?" Shepherd asked before Tay had decided on the best way to approach the girl.

So much for being less unsettling. Americans might have a lot of virtues, but delicacy wasn't one of them.

The girl's eyes shifted from Shepherd to Claire to Tay and back to Shepherd.

"What?" she asked. "Who you want?"

"FL," Shepherd repeated, speaking louder and over-enunciating in that annoying way all Americans did when they thought they weren't being understood. "We were told to ask for FL."

297

"Back here, buddy!" a voice sounded behind them and they all turned around. "Come on down!"

From an open doorway at the rear of the shop a man was beckoning energetically to them.

When Tay saw him, the first thing that popped into his mind was the famous description some New York film critic had once hung on the American actor, Danny DeVito. *He looked like a testicle with legs.* Tay had always wondered what could make someone think of such a bizarre description for any human being. Now he knew.

FL's body was almost perfectly round. He had very short arms, even shorter legs, and a small, completely bald head. He looked as if he could withdraw all his extremities into his body at any sign of danger, like a turtle seeking safety in its shell.

When Shepherd started toward FL, Tay tucked in right behind him and bit hard on his lower lip. Laughing at the physical appearance of a triad solider didn't seem to him a particularly smart thing to do, and he knew he was right on the edge.

T HE SECURITY SETUP was more elaborate than Tay had expected. The room itself wasn't much larger than a good-sized walk-in closet, but two large flat screen monitors sat on a long table against one wall with a keyboard between them. On the floor beneath the table, Tay saw an impressive stack of computer equipment which he assumed powered the monitors.

The image on the right-hand monitor was divided into four separate quarters, and Tay saw the output from a different camera displayed in each quarter. The top two quarters showed what looked like live views of the sidewalk from the two outside cameras Shepherd had spotted, and the lower two quarters showed views from cameras inside the store. The left-hand monitor had a still image of the sidewalk frozen on it. Tay gathered it was connected to the computer system and used for viewing video saved to the system's memory.

298

"I speak English good," FL grinned.

Shepherd nodded. Tay and Claire looked away. They appeared to be studying something just outside the orbit of Pluto.

"I learn English on television." FL grinned some more. *"Come on down!"*

Shepherd nodded again. He didn't appear to trust himself to speak.

FL threw himself into a black swivel chair in front of the two monitors. The chair shuddered and Tay thought he could hear it groan. There were no other chairs in the room, so Tay, Shepherd, and Claire gathered around behind him and remained standing.

FL pulled out his telephone and displayed the picture of Emma that Tay had sent to Jones.

"This is girl, yes?" he asked.

"That's her," Shepherd nodded.

FL scooted the chair over until it was in front of the monitor displaying the frozen image of the sidewalk. He lifted his phone and held up the picture of Emma, then tapped one fat finger on a woman in the frozen image who was all but obscured behind other pedestrians.

"This her, I think."

He moved his finger to the keyboard, poked at it, and the figures in the image began to move very slowly. As they did, there were brief glimpses of the woman to whom FL was pointing.

Tay, Shepherd, and Claire all leaned closer to the monitor.

FORTY

THE VIDEO WAS of outstanding quality, but slowed down the way it was the images came in jerky bursts. Tay felt more like he was flicking through a stack of still photographs one after another than watching a video.

He saw right away the woman FL had identified could be Emma. The age was about right, the general body type was right, and the hair color and shape were like they were in the photograph, but there was no single moment when her face was clear enough to say for certain it was Emma.

And there was another problem. Sarah had said Emma was wearing jeans, a white t-shirt, and a short, stylish red jacket when she disappeared at Mongkok Station. This woman was in black pants and a cheap-looking, dark green coat. Could Emma have changed clothes somewhere after she disappeared at Mongkok Station? Possible, Tay thought, but it didn't feel likely.

"When was this taken?" Shepherd asked FL, almost as if he had been reading Tay's mind.

FL tapped his finger in the lower right-hand corner of the monitor, but all Shepherd saw were Chinese characters followed by the number 1307.

"Monday," FL explained. "In afternoon. At 1:07pm."

"Can you run it back?" Shepherd asked. He waved his fore-finger back and forth a few times to illustrate his question. It was the kind of exaggerated gesture people make when they're not certain they're communicating in a common language.

FL looked annoyed.

"Talk," he said. "No wave hands. I speak English good."

"Sorry."

FL poked at the keyboard again and they all watched as the video went into reverse and then started forward again. The woman FL had identified appeared from the far edge of the frame, moved along the sidewalk past the shop, and then disap-peared again, but Tay couldn't find a single moment with a clear view of her face.

"What about the other camera, FL?"

"Only show behind."

Which made sense. The other camera pointed in the oppo-site direction. If this camera had picked up the woman walking toward the shop, the other one would have picked her up walking away.

"Let's see it anyway," Tay said.

FL rotated his head very deliberately and focused on Tay for the first time. He didn't appear to like what he saw very much, but after a moment he shrugged and poked at the keyboard again.

The monitor they were watching went blank and then another image appeared, this one looking in the opposite direc-tion down the sidewalk. FL ran the image forward at high speed, stopped, ran it back a bit, and then stopped again.

"She there," he said, tapping his finger against the monitor.

Sure enough, it was the same girl, her back to the camera and moving away from the shop.

"Let it run," Tay said.

The girl who might have been Emma moved forward at about half speed and they all watched as she walked past two women standing in the middle of the sidewalk. The women

301

looked as if they were shouting at each other because of the way they were waving their arms. The woman closest to the girl swung one arm wildly and it banged into her shoulder. The girl snapped her head toward the woman and gave her an annoyed look.

"Stop!" Tay shouted. "Right there!"

FL stopped the video, then moved it back and forth a few times until the woman's profile was at its clearest.

Tay took out his own phone, found the photograph of Emma, and held it up next to the image on the monitor. They all leaned in and stared.

"It's not her," Claire said.

"No, I don't think it is." Tay moved his telephone closer to the frozen picture of the woman. "Look at the ear. It's a different shape."

"It not her?" FL asked, disappointment in his voice.

"No," Tay said. "I'm afraid not."

FL sighed and clicked a key on the keyboard. They all watched as the woman who was not Emma walked away and disappeared in the distance.

"I sorry," FL said.

"It's not your fault," Shepherd soothed. "It could have been her. I thought it was when I first saw her, too."

"Not give up. I look more."

The video continued to run on the monitor, and Tay watched as pedestrians flowed past the shop by the hundreds. This was Mongkok, and people jammed the streets and sidewalks practically around the clock. It seemed hopeless to think anyone would have enough sheer luck searching through video to find the single moment when the one girl they were looking for walked past a specific spot. That was just too much to hope for.

"Wait!" Tay shouted. "Stop! Go back!"

Everyone looked at him.

"Did you see her?" Claire asked.

"There was something," Tay said.

He leaned forward and gestured to FL, moving his hands back and forth in the same way Shepherd had before.

"Can you play it back again?" he asked.

FL looked over his shoulder and gave Tay the same annoyed look he had given Shepherd.

"Speak! Speak! I English good."

"Yes, sorry. I was just asking if you could go back and run the last minute or so again?"

"Can."

Tay watched as the video went into reverse, ran for a few seconds at high speed, and then move forward again.

After twenty seconds, he leaned forward and tapped the screen with his finger. "Stop!"

Tay's finger was on a man who had cut diagonally across Sneaker Street and stepped onto the sidewalk a few yards past the Adidas shop.

"I know him," Tay said.

"Who is it?" Shepherd asked.

"I don't know."

"That's not much help then, is it?"

Everyone stared at the man, now frozen on the screen in the moment of stepping up onto the sidewalk. He looked to be in his mid-thirties and was average in almost every way. Average height, average weight. His hair was stylishly long, and he wore round tortoiseshell eyeglasses he might have chosen to make himself look older. He was neatly dressed in an expensive-looking blue blazer with a white shirt and pressed jeans.

"I know who it is," Claire said.

Everyone looked at her.

"It's Emma's neighbor. The guy who came looking for her when Sam and I were with Sarah at Emma's apartment."

"You're right," Tay said. "That's exactly who it is."

"So, what's he doing here?" Claire asked. "When you live in Pokfulam, you don't come to Mongkok to take a stroll. It would take you at least an hour to get from there to here. Maybe more."

"Do you remember his name?"

Claire pursed her lips and thought, but then she shook her head. "I can't remember."

"A man who lives fifty feet from Emma turns up an hour away from the building where they live and in exactly the place where she disappeared? That's more than just odd."

"Do you think he was involved in Emma's disappearance?"

"I don't know, but we need to find out everything we can about this guy."

"Sarah knew him. At least she knew about him. We could call her."

"Didn't she say this guy had been hassling Emma, but Emma wasn't interested?"

"That doesn't make him a kidnapper," Shepherd said, and they both looked at him. "If I went around kidnapping every woman who wasn't interested in me, I wouldn't have time to do anything else."

FL laughed. Neither Tay nor Claire bothered to join in.

"And what about the other women who disappeared?" Shepherd continued. "You've got no reason to connect this guy to any of those other women."

Tay reached out and tapped his forefinger against the man frozen on the monitor. "Then you think this is just a coincidence?"

"This is actual life, Tay. Not a movie. Coincidences *do* sometimes happen."

THEY PLAYED THE video through several times, and each time they watched until the figure disappeared from sight.

Tay put his hand on FL's shoulder. "Can you play it one more time? And slow it down just before he disappears?"

They all leaned forward and watched the screen as the man walked away from the shop at normal speed.

"Now slow it down," Tay said, and FL tapped at the keyboard until the video was moving at about one-third speed.

"That's good," he said.

They all followed the man as his head bobbed in slow motion through the densely packed crowd on the sidewalk. When he reached the end of the block, he turned left and disappeared.

"That's it then," Shepherd said. "He just walks down and turns left on Argyle Street."

"I don't think so."

"Sure he did. We all just saw him do it."

"He turned left *before* he got to Argyle Street. I think he went into the building on the corner. Can you please run it again, FL?"

FL backed up the video and ran it forward again, slower this time.

"I think you're right," Claire said. She leaned forward and pointed at the screen with her finger. "Look how he slows down after he turns. He's going in a door somewhere before he gets to Argyle Street. Not around the corner."

"Maybe we *have* got something here," Tay said.

"You really think it's possible this guy took Emma and still has her stashed here in Mongkok?"

"I don't know. I just think it strange. Here we are looking for Emma in this video and suddenly a guy who lives down the hall from her turns up."

"Then what about all the other missing girls?" Shepherd asked. "Are you saying Emma found herself the object of a serial killer's interest, one who coincidentally lived just down the hall from her, *after* he'd already taken five other women? That's hard to buy."

"It's what we've got," Tay said.

"I know you think we're running out of time," Shepherd went on, "but don't jump on the first coincidence you run into."

"Does it look to you like he turned onto Argyle Street?"

"Maybe not. But even if he went into some building instead, I don't think you'll find Emma stashed there."

"We need to walk down there," Tay said, "and have a look for ourselves."

I T WAS ONLY about a hundred yards down Sneaker Street to where it intersected with busy Argyle Street.

When they got to the spot just before the corner where the man had seemed to disappear, Tay stopped, put his hands on his hips, and looked around. Two stores occupied the whole ground floor of the corner building. One was a Yonex sports shop, and the other was a bakery.

"I don't get it," he said. "Where did he go?"

"There's your explanation right in front of you," Shepherd said. "Obviously the man came to Mongkok for a bag of croissants."

Claire and Tay both looked at Shepherd, but neither one laughed.

"I sense you're both getting a little tired of my wiseassery, aren't you?"

"A bit," Tay said.

"Okay, I think I can understand that. But at least let me try to redeem myself."

Shepherd pointed to a doorway between the two stores. It was narrow, dark, and a little grimy.

"He went in there."

"How do you know?" Claire asked.

Shepherd hesitated. "You understand I know all sorts of things about Hong Kong, don't you? Not all of the things I know come from personal experience, and if I tell you about certain places, you shouldn't assume what I know about them comes from going there myself. Sometimes it comes from what people have told me about those places."

"What in the world are you prattling on about, Jack? If you have something to tell us, just say it."

Shepherd pointed at the doorway. "That's the entrance to the King Hing Building."

"What's the King Hing Building?"

Before Shepherd could answer her, two middle-aged Chinese men emerged from the doorway Shepherd was pointing to. They were laughing and slapping each other on the back as they turned right down Sneaker Street. Behind them, three more Chinese men came out of the same doorway, all of them much younger but looking equally happy. They turned left into the crowds along Argyle Street and disappeared.

"There you go," Shepherd said. "That's a good example of the King Hing Building."

"I'm completely lost," Claire said.

"I'm not," Tay said. "It's a whorehouse, isn't it, Shepherd?"

"We use a more gallant term in Hong Kong," Shepherd smiled. "We call places like this working girl houses, and this is the biggest one in the city."

Tay and Claire just waited. They knew Shepherd wouldn't leave it at that.

"I can give you a few details if you like," Shepherd said, "but based purely on gossip, you understand. I deny all personal knowledge."

Tay and Claire waited some more, and after a moment Shepherd went on just as they knew he would.

"The entire building above the shops is filled with two hundred or more rooms, each one of which has a single girl working out of it. Men come in, and walk either up or down through the building going from one door to another. If the girl is busy, the door will have a sign on it saying so. If the door doesn't have a sign, men knock, the girl answers, and the men decide if they like what they see. When they do, they go in. When they don't, they move on to the next door."

"That's awful," Claire said. "How utterly dehumanizing."

"I've always thought of it as a wonderful metaphor for life," Shepherd shrugged. "You knock on a door, take a quick look, and either walk in or move on."

Claire shook her head. "You're a profoundly cynical man, Jack."

"It's sort of like the wiseass thing. People either hate it or they love it."

"I know," Tay said. "You figure it's about sixty-forty."

"Do you think he could have Emma stashed in there some-where?" Claire asked.

"Not a chance. There's more traffic in and out of the King Hing Building than across the Star Ferry. If you want to hide someone in Hong Kong, the King Hing Building is the last place you'd pick to do it."

"Then you're saying there's no way Emma—"

"Emma's neighbor wasn't in Mongkok to visit a place he had Emma stashed, Tay. He was just here getting his pipes cleaned."

"Getting his pipes cleaned?" Claire muttered. "*Getting his pipes cleaned?*"

"Yeah, you know, dipping his wick, buttering his biscuit, rummaging in the root cellar, putting the banana in the fruit salad, filling her out like an application, getting his—"

"You're disgusting, Jack. What are you, twelve years old?"

"Give or take," Shepherd said. "Want to ride the bologna pony, baby?"

Claire spun on her heel and stalked off.

FORTY-ONE

THE THREE OF them walked west on Argyle Street toward the Cordis Hotel, but Tay didn't know if they were actually going to the hotel or if they were just walking in that direction. Looking at the moment either literally or metaphorically, Tay had absolutely no idea where they were going from here.

"I got nothing," he said. "My head feels like it's full of fudge."

"Yeah, that was disappointing," Claire said. "I thought we were onto something there. We'll just have to put it out of our minds and start fresh tomorrow."

"I don't think tomorrow's good enough. I think today was our last chance to find her alive."

Claire peered at Tay and shook her head. "I just don't get why you keep saying that, Sam. There's been no contact from anyone about Emma. Where in the world did you come up with this deadline of today for getting her back alive?"

Tay was so tired and sick at heart he almost told Claire about his mother and her occasional appearances to give him advice, but he didn't. Honesty had limits. He would rather

Claire thought of him as depressed than crazy, and taking guidance from ghosts was a long way over the line into crazy town.

Shepherd put a hand on Tay's shoulder. "You've done your best, Sam, but this was a moon shot from the beginning. Maybe it's time for you to let it go and make a graceful exit."

"And how do you think I ought to go about that?"

"Doris Lau asked you to stop looking for Emma and said she was going to turn the matter over to the police. So let her."

"Maybe she said she was going to turn it over to the police, but it's bullshit and you know it. She won't do any such thing."

"Oh, come on. You don't think she would just walk away and abandon her daughter out there somewhere, do you?"

"That's exactly what I think she'll do. How about the parents of the other five girls who have gone missing? How many of them went to the police?"

Shepherd looked away and said nothing.

"Nobody in Hong Kong wants to be the one who points the finger at the wrong people," Tay snapped. "Are the triads responsible? Maybe Beijing? Keep your mouth shut and your head down. That's how you get along here."

"That's a little harsh."

"Is it? Tell me how I'm wrong. Tell me which parents went to the police and demanded an investigation. Tell me which parents said they would take on the world to find their child."

"I understand what you're saying, but—"

"Look, Shepherd, if you want out, just say so. But I'm going to keep on looking."

"How do you propose to do that? I thought you just told me you had nothing, and you thought you were out of time."

"Jones has his soldiers all over this part of Mongkok showing Emma's picture around and looking for her on surveillance video. If she's been anywhere around here in the past week, I'm willing to bet they'll find her."

"And what if she *hasn't* been anywhere around here? What if the girl who covered for her on her trips to Mongkok was mistaken or lying when she told you she'd seen her on Sneaker Street?"

Tay took a deep breath and let it out. "Then I really do have nothing. I'll just have to admit I fucked up and go home. But that time isn't here yet."

"Have you told Jones that Mrs. Lau wants you to stop looking for Emma?"

Tay said nothing, which Shepherd thought answered his question well enough.

"How about August? Have you told him?"

Tay kept walking.

"And you must have led Mrs. Lau to believe you would honor her wishes. You didn't just tell her to stick her instructions in her ear, did you?"

"What's your point?" Tay snapped.

"I just wanted to make sure I understood. You're lying to a Chinese organized crime boss, you're lying to your own boss and through him to the Vice President of the United States, and you're lying to the Chief Executive of Hong Kong. All this so you can keep searching for a girl you don't know, have never met, and don't have a clue how to find. Does that pretty much cover it?"

"Yeah, pretty much."

"So, what am I missing here?"

"That if this is going to be my last case, I'm sure as hell not going to go out by walking away from it."

Claire stopped walking. She grabbed Tay's elbow and pulled him toward her.

"Why would this be your last case?" she asked.

Then Tay realized what he had said.

If he couldn't tell Claire about his mother's occasional visits and the deadline she had told him he had for finding Emma, he sure as hell couldn't tell her about the bleeding, his visit to the doctor, and the biopsy.

"You've been acting very weird, Sam. Is there something

wrong? Something you're not telling me?"

Tay hated lying to Claire, he really did. He didn't have many friends, and he thought of Claire as one of the few, although he had no idea how she thought of him. Still, he hated telling her the truth about what was happening to him even more than he hated lying to her about it. The comment about this maybe being his last case had just slipped out. He shrugged it off as well as he could.

"I'm just getting old and tired," he said. "I've always thought of the work I do as being who I am. I don't know where the end of that work is, but it can't be much longer. This case might be it."

"Why don't I believe you?" Claire asked.

"Because you're a deeply cynical person who doesn't trust anybody?"

"No," Claire said, pointing to Shepherd. "That's him. Not me."

None of them seemed inclined to add anything to that so the three of them simply stood there together on the sidewalk alongside Argyle Street.

They were like boulders in a river. Around them flowed hundreds of ordinary Chinese going about their business or hurrying home to their families or just trying to survive for another day. They paid Tay and Claire and Shepherd no more attention than the water pays the rocks. They just moved on and left them behind.

And, after a bit, Tay and Claire and Shepherd moved on, too.

C LAIRE AND SHEPHERD tried to persuade Tay to join them for a drink or even an early dinner, but he refused. He knew they meant well, but he didn't need the drink and he didn't need the food and he certainly didn't need the company.

What he needed was a cigarette.

After they left, he walked to the same 7-Eleven where he had bought his other packs of Marlboros. He had a couple of half-used packs upstairs in his room, but it was a lot easier just to buy a fresh pack than to make the journey up thirty-seven floors and then back down again thirty-seven floors and out to the sidewalk to smoke. He was already on the sidewalk and for a few dollars he could stay there. It sounded like a bargain to him.

As soon as he came out of the 7-Eleven, he slit open the pack and lit a cigarette.

Before he shoved the pack into his pocket, he took a close look at it and shook his head. Printed on both the front and back of the pack were graphic, grotesque photos of people hideously disfigured, presumably from smoking cigarettes, and most of the rest of the space was covered with hysterical health warnings in both Chinese and English. The anti-smoking do-gooders in America had infected the entire world. They were relentless, but why had everyone surrendered to them without a fight?

Where were the health warnings on liquor bottles or prescription drugs or junk food? There weren't any, of course, and there never would be. It was his vice they had selected to throw under the bus. It was his vice they had designated as fall guy for the virtue peddlers. All the rest of the unhealthy crap on which people spent untold billions of dollars every year had been awarded a free pass. It was all so damned unfair.

He walked south on Shanghai Street. Going no place in particular. Just strolling along, smoking his Marlboro, and lamenting the unfairness of the world.

There would be plenty of time later to think about Emma and whether she had come to her end here in Mongkok. Plenty of time to think about himself and if he was at his own end here as well. He just wanted to finish this one cigarette in peace before it all flooded back and took him over again.

Then he heard the chanting, and he noticed the sound of it was growing louder.

. . .

THERE WERE AT least fifty of them, Tay saw when they
rounded a corner about a hundred yards to the south and
headed straight for him down the middle of Shanghai Street.

They looked as if they were mostly young, but they were
wearing black clothing and facemasks so it was hard for him to
be certain. A few of them even wore yellow hardhats of the type
worn by construction workers. There appeared to be more or
less an equal number of men and women in the group, and two
sturdy looking boys a few strides to the front of the others waved
American flags on metal poles.

They had come from the direction of Nathan Road, and
Tay assumed the riot police must have formed up somewhere
over there to prevent the demonstrators from blocking traffic.
Like water flowing through the streets, the kids had squirted in
another direction and now here they were on Shanghai Street
coming directly toward him.

The entire group of them were half jogging to a rhythmic
cadence, like a platoon of soldiers running together in basic
training. As they jogged, they chanted.

Liberate Hong Kong
The revolution of our time
Liberate Hong Kong
The revolution of our time
Liberate Hong Kong
The revolution of our time

A motley crew of chubby middle-aged men wearing yellow
high-visibility vests jogged on both sides of the kids. They
looked like a bunch of highway workers on a break from filling
potholes, but they weren't. They were the press pack, and there
were more of them than there were demonstrators. All of them
frantically waved cameras and microphones seeking a picture or

a sound bite that might make the evening news somewhere in the world.

Tay stood and smoked and watched the demonstrators with the circling flock of press coming straight at him. It wasn't a school of sharks surrounded by a pod of fish. It was a school of fish surrounded by a pod of sharks.

When Tay heard the scuffling of heavy boots behind him, he didn't even have to turn around to know what it was.

T HE RIOT POLICE knew how to flow like water, too. A squad of at least forty of them had filtered over from Nathan Road and formed up into a human barricade stretching all the way across Shanghai Street. Tay glanced around and saw they were only about a hundred feet behind him.

Like all of the other riot police he had seen in Hong Kong, they were a frightening sight, and he gathered they intended to be. Military-looking uniforms in army green, black helmets with plastic visors so heavy they looked like they could stop bullets, balaclavas covering their faces up to their eyes, black body armor strapped over torsos, and plastic shields strapped around their legs.

Some of them carried short-barreled weapons that looked like shotguns. Others waved thick batons the size of baseball bats. And others thrust out scarred Plexiglass shields to protect the rest of the squad, although Tay couldn't see what they were protecting the squad *from* since the kids had nothing to attack them with but their bare hands. Half a dozen of the riot police raised their weapons and began firing at the same time. Not live rounds, but pepper balls. They thumped out of the guns, soared above Tay's head, and smashed into the street in front of the advancing demonstrators and their attending pod of press.

When the broken balls began releasing their clouds of noxious pepper gas, Tay dropped the butt of his cigarette to the sidewalk and ground it out with his foot. Was pepper gas flammable? He had no idea, but he didn't want to find out the hard way.

Tay smiled a little when he realized the riot police had targeted the press more than the demonstrators. The cops understood it wasn't the kids who were their biggest problem. It was the reporters who spread images around the world of the population of Hong Kong rising against its masters in China.

As street battles went, this one wasn't much. There didn't seem to be a lot of passion on either side. These combatants looked like they were just going through the motions. Everything about their clash seemed old and tired. Tay knew exactly how that felt.

Still, as much as he enjoyed watching the agents of the world's media choking on pepper gas, he figured he had better get the hell out of there before he got caught in the middle again. Street battles in Hong Kong didn't cut any slack for non-combatants.

He had stopped on the sidewalk in front of a Wellcome supermarket and there was an alleyway next to it which appeared to lead to a loading dock in the back. He melted into the alley, followed it behind the store, and then on into another alley which took him out to Nathan Road.

There traffic moved as usual, old men and women shuffled along the sidewalks with their shopping, and young triad toughs shouldered through the crowds as if they owned the neighborhood, which they more or less did. There were no chanting demonstrators, no ferocious-looking riot police, and no clouds of pepper gas.

The *revolution of our time* seemed, for the moment at least, to be limited to Shanghai Street. Nathan Road didn't appear to give a toss whether a revolution was occurring a couple of blocks over or not.

Tay lit a fresh Marlboro and walked back to his hotel.

FORTY-TWO

SATURDAY. DAY FIVE. Searching for Emma Lau.

Tay was dreaming he had died, and he was shocked to discover what came after death wasn't all that bad.

A ringing noise started up from somewhere and he kept seeing himself going to the door to find out who it was, but there was never anyone there. That made no more sense than most of the things that had happened in his life, which was when he started to wonder if there was really much difference between being alive and being dead.

Eventually Tay realized he wasn't still asleep, and he also realized that it was his telephone that was ringing, not a doorbell in some life-after-death dreamland. Not the fancy super-secure phone August had given him this time, but his personal telephone.

He had left it across the room on the desk the night before so he pushed himself to his feet and stumbled toward it. The room's blackout drapes were so effective he could see almost nothing and he had no idea if it was morning or still the middle of the night. Halfway across the room, he hooked one foot around a leg of the desk chair, stumbled, and went down on one knee.

"*Shit!*"

For a moment, he couldn't imagine what the damned chair was doing sitting out there in the middle of the room, but then all at once he remembered.

The night before, he had put it there.

He had placed it in the very spot where his mother sat the night she had visited, or rather the night he had imagined she had visited, because he had been hoping to lure her into returning. Or at least lure himself into imagining she had returned. He had a few questions about the future, both Emma's and his, and he had been rather hoping his mother might answer them for him.

Moving the chair before he went to sleep had been a foolish gesture, and now it had a truly pathetic air to it. Worse, it hadn't worked. If it *had* worked and his mother had answered his summons, maybe the gesture wouldn't feel so desperate.

Then his telephone stopped ringing before he could get to the desk and answer it.

Of course it did.

T AY PULLED HIMSELF to his feet and somehow made it to the blackout drapes without falling over anything else. He jerked them open and the bright sunshine momentarily blinded him. What time was it anyway? Had he overslept?

He grabbed up the phone from the desk, activated the screen, and checked the time.

Nearly ten o'clock? How could that be?

Then he registered the missed-call notification on the telephone's screen. Dr. Patel had called. He must have the results of the biopsy.

Tay peered at the telephone as if it might speak to him at any moment and tell him what the result was. It didn't. He would either have to call Patel back or it wouldn't tell him. The phone couldn't care less.

He called.

"Dr. Patel? I'm sorry I didn't pick up when you called. I was..." Tay hesitated "...in the bathroom."

Well, what else was he going to say? Was he going to explain to Dr. Patel he had gotten out of bed and fallen over a chair he had put out for his dead mother to sit in if only she would have been good enough to visit during the night and tell him the future? Not bloody likely.

"No need to apologize," Patel said. "Look, I won't beat about the bush, but I don't think you'll be happy about the news I have for you."

Oh Christ, he was going to die.

He knew it. He had known it all along. He supposed he had known it from the first moment he had coughed up blood. The only question now was how long he had. Was it years? Months? Oh God... was it only weeks?

"I've never had this happen before," Patel went on before Tay could say anything, "but the biopsy returned an inconclusive result."

Inconclusive?

What the hell did *that* mean?

He was just working up to feeling good and sorry for himself and now... well, *what?* Was an inconclusive result better than being told he had cancer? Or was it worse?

"I don't understand," Tay said.

"Well, to tell the truth, neither do I. As I said, it's never happened before. Regardless, it just means we have to do it again."

Tay had expected to have an answer one way or another today. He had been counting on it more than he realized until right at this moment. But now he had... well, nothing. All he knew he had not known yesterday was he had to do it all again and wait some more.

"You mean I have to come back in and—"

"Oh dear me, no," Patel cut in. "We still have enough tissue

319

JAKE NEEDHAM

from the procedure we've already done. The lab just needs to run the test again. I wouldn't even have told you, but Mr. Jones was adamant that you get the result by today so I thought I should call. I apologize, but now it will be tomorrow before we have a result from which I can give you a diagnosis."

After making a few predictably soothing noises and apologizing again, Patel ended the call.

Tay was glad of it. There was nothing else to say and continuing to talk about whether he might be dying of cancer when no one as yet knew for sure would have served no purpose other than to fuel his growing depression.

Tay returned his telephone to the desk and sighed. Then he picked up the room phone and ordered coffee. He told them to hurry. He also thought about asking them to bring him toast or something else for breakfast, but he really had no appetite so he let it go. Had he heard somewhere that loss of appetite was one symptom of cancer? God help him, he thought he had.

When the coffee came, he drank one cup straight down, then he poured a second cup and sipped at this one more slowly. Thank God for coffee. Against all the odds, he actually started feeling quite decent.

Then the phone rang again.

His first thought was that Patel was calling back to tell him he had made a mistake and they did have a result from his biopsy after all. But then he realized that it wasn't his personal cell phone that was ringing.

This time it was the secure one August had given him.

"HAVE YOU HEARD from Dr. Patel yet?" Jones asked as soon as Tay answered. "It's none of my business what the test results showed, but it is my business whether he got them to you this morning like I told him to."

"He just called. He said the biopsy was inconclusive."

Jones hesitated. "Inconclusive? What does that mean?"

320

"That's precisely what I asked. I gather it means they have to run the test again, although he doesn't need to take a new tissue sample to do it. He says now it will be tomorrow before he can tell me the results."

"I don't understand."

"Neither does Dr. Patel. He said it had never happened to him before."

"Do you want me to talk to him?"

"I don't see what good it would do. Besides, I'm in no hurry to hear when I'll die. Tomorrow will be fine. Or even the next day."

There was a brief silence, after which Jones said simply, "Very well."

Tay had to admit he had rather liked Jones right from the beginning, as unseemly as it might be for a Singapore cop – okay, ex-cop – to admit he liked a guy who was after all a Hong Kong organized crime boss. But now he *really* liked Jones.

No effort wasted on empty words of comfort. No time squandered on meaningless platitudes. Just...

Very well.

When there's nothing useful to say, say nothing. It's a man's response to another man's time of fragility.

"I may have something for you on the girl you're searching for," Jones went on when Tay said nothing more. "One of my men found a woman who says she's seen her, although it was almost a week ago. She thinks it was last Saturday or Sunday, but she's not certain."

Emma had disappeared on Saturday so that could fit.

"Where do I find her?"

"I don't think she speaks English, and neither does the man who located her. Let me meet you there."

"Fine."

"The woman is the manager of a Café de Coral. It's on the second floor of a building at the corner of Sneaker Street and Dundas Street."

Even Tay knew Café de Coral was a sort of Chinese McDonald's. It was a local fast-food chain that dished up things like Hainan chicken rice, sweet and sour pork, and roast duck with rice. There were hundreds of them all over Hong Kong.

"Shall we say in an hour?" Jones asked.

"That's fine."

"I'll meet you in front of the building and we'll go up together," Jones said and ended the call.

TAY GOT THERE a little early. Jones was precisely on time. Of course, he was.

Sixty minutes after Jones said he would be there in an hour, a black Mercedes pulled up at the curb and Jones got out of the back. Not fifty-nine minutes later, not sixty-one minutes later. Exactly sixty minutes later.

Jones nodded without speaking. Tay took the hint and silently followed him up the stairs to the second floor of the building and into Café de Coral.

It was an unexpectedly pleasant space. Bright and cheery with a wall of glass looking down over the passing crowds on Sneaker Street. It was still the lunch hour, and the place was busy. Not jammed, but busy. Hong Kong people worked hard, and dawdling over lunch wasn't something they did. Food wasn't an experience, it was fuel, so they ate quickly and efficiently and got back to work. There was money to be made.

Tay waited near the door while Jones walked over to a big, hard-looking man sitting with a middle-aged woman at a table against the wall. The man had a square face and a nose that looked like someone had broken it more than once. He was wearing a white nylon shirt hanging out over a pair of black pants and he jumped to his feet when Jones approached the table. He didn't actually salute, but his body looked like it wanted to.

They spoke for a moment, and then Tay saw both the hard

man and the woman look in his direction. He considered waving, but decided it was unlikely anyone would see the humor in that so he just looked back at them.

The hard man said something to Jones, then he inclined his head, turned, and walked toward the stairs. As he passed Tay, he gave him the obligatory hard-man glare that was part of the repertoire of every triad solider Tay had ever met. Tay held the man's empty black eyes until he was forced to look away, which the man seemed to find disconcerting.

Jones was now talking to the woman at the table. She wore a blue skirt with a white top that looked to Tay like some kind of uniform. She was pleasant-looking and round-faced and had on heavy black eyeglasses that made her look as if she wrote book reviews for *The New York Times*. Tay did not think she did.

After a moment, she pointed at another table, one about twenty feet away and up in front of the windows. Two young Chinese men sat there shoveling down their lunch with the usual dispatch. Jones walked over to them and spoke a few words. Both men quickly rose to their feet, abandoned the rest of their food, and double-timed their way past Tay down the stairs. A restaurant employee appeared the moment they left, cleared away the dishes, and cleaned the table.

Jones looked back at the woman and pointed to the now empty chairs around the table by the window. Then he looked at Tay and beckoned for him to join them.

Being a Chinese crime boss, Tay could see, meant getting whatever you wanted whenever you wanted it. And you never even had to say you were sorry.

FORTY-THREE

"SHE DOESN'T SPEAK English," Jones said when Tay walked over and sat down.

Tay would have to take Jones's word for it, but he wasn't so sure. In his experience as an investigator, a lot of people didn't speak English when they thought it might get them in trouble. When they decided it wouldn't, they often spoke English just fine.

Jones hadn't introduced them, but Tay needed to find a way to establish an independent connection with the woman regardless. Whatever she saw and however she described it through Jones, Tay would still have to decide how credible she was.

"I am Samuel Tay," he said, offering his hand to the woman across the table.

She responded with a shy smile and bobbed her head, but said nothing. She took Tay's hand and shook it quickly, efficiently.

Tay took out his telephone, found the picture of Emma he had sent to Jones, and held the screen up for the woman to see.

"Is this the girl you saw?"

The woman nodded her head vigorously and pointed over

Jones's shoulder toward the street. There was no hesitation in her nod or her gesture. She seemed in no doubt.

"What made you notice her?"

Now the woman looked confused. Her eyes flicked back and forth between Tay and Jones.

"*Nǐ shénme yìsi?*" she asked. "*Nǐ shénme yìsi?*"

"I appreciate your concern with judging this woman's credibility yourself, Inspector," Jones said, "but I think this will be smoother if you let me handle it. Trying to question a witness when you don't have a language in common is likely to turn into a bit of a mess, don't you think?"

Tay shrugged and spread his hands, conceding the point.

Jones spoke to the woman in what Tay assumed was Cantonese, the woman replied, then Jones spoke again, and the woman replied again.

"She says," Jones began, "she was on her break and sitting at this table when she saw—"

"When was this?" Tay interrupted.

Jones translated the question and then the woman's reply.

"It was last Saturday. Between two and three in the afternoon."

Emma had been last seen at Mongkok Station in the early afternoon, and Mongkok Station was only about a ten-minute walk from here. But Tay said nothing. He just nodded.

"May I go on?" Jones asked.

"Yes, of course."

"She was sitting here on her break having her lunch and looking out at the street when she saw the woman in the photograph. She noticed her because she was very attractive and much better dressed than most of the women you see in Mongkok. The woman was wearing a jacket she remembers because she liked it a lot. It was bright red and had very wide shoulders."

Tay sat up straight. He felt as if he had touched a live wire. That was exactly how Sarah McFarland described what Emma was wearing when she disappeared. Maybe this woman really *had* seen Emma.

"Ask her what the girl was doing when she saw her."

Jones translated. It seemed to Tay the woman's answer was long and rather detailed. Jones listened to her, nodding, and then turn to Tay.

"She was on the sidewalk on the other side of the street. She had two plastic carrier bags and the way she carried the bags made them look as if they were heavy. It appeared to our witness the bags were filled with food from a market. She says she saw bok choy or some other leafy looking vegetables in the top of one bag."

"Could she tell where this girl was going?"

Jones translated again and listened to the answer again.

"She went into the building across the street."

Tay's mouth opened and his eyes jerked to the street beyond Jones's shoulder.

On the other side, across from the restaurant, he saw two very tall high-rise apartment buildings. One was faced with gray tile and the other with salmon-colored concrete, and each of them must have contained several hundred apartments. Between them was a much smaller building, not much more than a narrow shophouse about twenty feet wide. It was only five floors high and had a dirty white concrete façade cracked and pitted with age.

"Which one?" Tay asked, holding his breath.

"The one you want it to be," Jones smiled. "The small white one."

Tay breathed out. This was almost too good to be true.

"Did she see anything else? Was anyone with this girl?"

Again, Jones translated, waited for the answer, and then turned to Tay.

"She wasn't with anyone, but our witness says she did notice something strange. When this girl went into the shophouse, she put one of the bags down by the gate at the bottom of the stairs, walked up, and then came back to collect it. Our witness thinks perhaps the bags were very heavy, and the girl didn't want to carry both upstairs together. She says she was afraid the other bag would be stolen before the girl came back down to get it."

Tay stood up, walked to the window, and took a long look at the shophouse. On the ground floor he saw a slick-looking space with a shiny gray fascia surrounding a large plate-glass window. Above the large window was a sign which identified the business as a dental surgery.

The four floors of the building above the dental surgery appeared to contain apartments. Those floors were not slick looking. They all had small, grimy windows and air conditioning units poking haphazardly out of the walls. Visible pipes and wiring ran up the face of the building, evidence of the constant renovation and reconstruction old buildings required, but also evidence no one cared very much about how that renovation and reconstruction looked as long as it was cheap.

The two floors at the very top had laundry flapping from poles beneath the windows, but the two floors in the middle were dark and quiet. Access to the apartments appeared to be up a narrow staircase behind a gold-painted gate just to the left of the dental surgery.

"How long did it take?" Tay asked without turning.

"What do you mean?" Jones sounded puzzled. It was a note Tay had not previously heard in his voice.

Tay turned from the window, walked back to the table, and sat down.

"How long did it take her to come back for the second bag of groceries?"

"Of course," Jones said. "Why didn't I think of that?"

He spoke rapid Cantonese to the woman, who responded succinctly.

"Not long," Jones said. "Maybe half a minute. Not more."

Tay nodded and looked back at the building. She couldn't have gone higher than the second floor then, most likely not higher than the first floor. Unless she carried the first bag up to a landing, left it there, and then came back for the second because she shared their witness's fear someone might steal it.

He thought about it a little longer and decided he doubted that. If she left the bag there in the first place, she must have been confident it was safe. No doubt it was simply heavy, too heavy to carry up the stairs together with the other bag.

So, she had gone to the first or second floor. Most likely the first.

It was almost too good to be true.

An hour ago, he'd had nothing. Now he had everything. Well... almost everything. Maybe.

An hour ago, he hadn't even known for sure Emma was anywhere near Mongkok. He knew she was last seen in Mongkok Station on Saturday afternoon, but that was it. Now he had a credible sighting of Emma about an hour later carrying groceries into an apartment not far away from the station. There had to be at least a million apartments in Hong Kong, and now he had narrowed Emma's destination down to two of them. Probably down to one.

"Ask her if she's seen the same girl again since then," Tay said to Jones.

When Jones translated, the woman immediately shook her head and made a sharp guttural sound. Jones didn't need to translate that for Tay, and he didn't bother.

Okay, the woman hadn't seen Emma leave and she hadn't seen her since then, but it didn't necessarily mean she was still in there. Tay simply had no way to tell whether or not she *was* still in there, not for sure, but with every atom in his body he knew she was.

That was the way every investigation went. First, you didn't have much. Then you had nothing at all. Then you had everything. It had happened the same way for him over and over in his career. He chastised himself for losing faith. He should have known it would happen again that way this time, too.

He had found Emma!

It was almost enough to make him forget he had lung cancer.

Almost.

"I OWE YOU one," Tay said to Jones.

"Then you think this is the girl you're looking for?"

"The timing is right and your witness's ID from the photo feels right. The most important thing is that the description of her clothing is exactly right. She would have no way of knowing what Emma was wearing if she hadn't actually seen her."

Tay paused.

"Yeah, it's her," he said. "It's Emma. That's why I said I owe you one."

"I understand why that troubles you, Inspector. If I were in your position, I wouldn't want to owe me one either. But don't let it bother you. I won't come back to you and ask for a favor in return. I did this because it was the right thing to do, not because I wanted you to owe me."

"Then I will just say thank you."

"And I will just say you're welcome."

Jones hesitated. "I assume now you will search the building for her," he said.

Tay assumed so, too, although he hadn't thought it through yet. What else would he do? He nodded his head.

"If you want me to get a few men together for you, I can—"

"No, I've got it from here," Tay interrupted.

He might not yet be certain about what he would do, but he was sure what he would *not* do was mount an all-out assault on the building at the head of a band of triad soldiers. He couldn't see that working out well for anybody.

"I'd like to stay here for a while if it would be all right. I need to bring in Shepherd and Claire, and we'll have to watch the building for a while before I can decide when and how we should go in."

"Consider this table yours for as long as you like."

Jones said something in Cantonese to their witness. She jumped up from the table, half bowed to Jones and then to Tay, and scurried away.

Jones held out his hand to Tay, and they shook.

"Thank you again for asking Dr. Patel to see me," Tay said.

"It was my pleasure. I hope he will have good news for you tomorrow."

Tay said nothing. He just nodded.

"I hope we will see each other again someday," Jones added.

Tay folded his hands on the table and looked down at them.

"I think that's unlikely," he said.

"As do I," Jones nodded. "Goodbye."

He stood, turned away without another word, and trotted down the stairs to the street. Through the window, Tay watched him get into the black Mercedes waiting at the curb below.

As the Mercedes pulled away, the restaurant manager returned with a pot of tea and a round ceramic cup. She poured Tay a cup of tea, left the pot on the table, and disappeared.

Tay leaned toward the window as he drank it and silently studied the little white shophouse on the other side of the street.

FORTY-FOUR

TAY CALLED CLAIRE and told her where he was and asked her to get there as quickly as she could. He also asked her to call Shepherd and get him there, too.

While he waited for them, Tay sipped tea and watched the street. An elderly woman, stooped and bent, shuffled along pushing a rickety cart piled high with Styrofoam boxes. A young girl wearing baggy blue pants and a long-sleeved blouse printed with enormous yellow flowers stood waiting to cross the street, sheltering under a black umbrella which she maneuvered to keep the sun off her face. Three adolescent boys in shorts and t-shirts with big backpacks slung over their shoulders pushed and shoved each other along the sidewalk like adolescent boys did all over the world. One of Hong Kong's ubiquitous red and white taxis pulled to the curb, and a tall man wearing a tan suit who looked to be Indian or Pakistani got out carrying a leather brief-case and strode away.

It was all such an ordinary scene that it somehow surprised Tay.

Didn't those people realize what had just happened? He had located the missing daughter of the Chief Executive of Hong Kong and the Vice President of the United States, and she was right inside the building everybody was passing without a second glance.

No, of course they didn't realize it. That's how life is. We each live in our own world and know next to nothing about what is happening to anyone other than ourselves. The most extraordinary events can be occurring almost within arm's reach, and yet we pass them by as if they don't matter. Which, to us, they don't.

Sometimes when Tay walked by people on the street, he wondered what misfortunes and afflictions and heartbreaks they were hiding behind those empty faces. We might all share this small planet, but we all live our lives separately and bear the sorrows of life by ourselves. We come into the world alone and we leave it the same way. In between, we just do our best to outwit the loneliness and prevent it from taking us. Tay had been a solitary man all his life, but he was not really lonely, at least not often. It was one battle he felt like he had won.

Tay drank more tea and watched the little white shophouse across the street.

The dental surgery seemed to do a fine business. A steady flow of people came and went. But above the dental surgery, he saw no sign of life in any of the apartments other than the laundry hanging on the fourth and fifth floors.

He was pretty sure Emma didn't do laundry.

On the first and second floors, the apartments were dark and quiet. Curtains covered the windows and the air conditioners were still. Despite that, Emma was there somewhere. Tay knew it in his bones. He would make book on it.

I T DIDN'T TAKE Shepherd and Claire long to turn up. Shepherd was there in half an hour, and Claire was five minutes behind him.

As soon as they sat down at the table, the manager brought a fresh pot of tea and two more cups. They both sat drinking tea while Tay told them what he had learned. They listened without interrupting.

When he finished, Claire inclined her head to where the restaurant manager hovered in the back.

"This is the woman who saw her?"

Tay nodded.

"And you're sure it was Emma she saw?"

Tay nodded again.

Shepherd pointed out the window to the shophouse. "She's over there? You're saying she's just right over there?"

"She was a week ago."

"A week ago," Shepherd repeated, shaking his head. "She could be anywhere now."

"She could be, but she isn't."

Tay pointed his own finger at the little white shophouse.

"She's there."

"And this you know exactly how?"

Tay lifted his shoulders and let them fall in a small shrug. He had no idea how he knew, at least no idea that would make any sense to Shepherd, but he knew.

"Then let's knock on some doors," Shepherd said. "There's no point in just sitting here and trying to guess whether she's there or not."

"It's not that easy. Remember, six girls of similar ages, all from prominent families, have disappeared in the last eighteen months. Every one of them went to Mongkok and then just vanished."

"What are you saying, Tay? That we'll find all their bodies over there across the street?"

"No, I'm inclined to believe the story you heard from your contact. I'm guessing the first five were cremated, or at least one body would have turned up somewhere."

"Just the first five?" Claire interrupted. "You seem awfully sure Emma is alive."

"I know she was yesterday. I'm not sure she is today."

333

"What in the world are you talking about, Sam? How could you possibly know that?"

For the second time Tay considered telling Claire the truth about his dead mother passing along occasional guidance from the other side. He might have done it, too, but Shepherd sitting there changed everything.

Telling Claire a bizarre tale about nocturnal conversations with his dead mother seemed almost imaginable, but telling Shepherd was another matter altogether. A woman might understand, Tay thought, even see it as suggesting a spiritual side to his personality they had never before noticed, but another man would have a completely different reaction.

Another man would just think Tay was screwy.

Not telling Claire the truth left him with nothing to say, so Tay just tossed out another small shrug and said nothing.

"WE HAVE TO think about how to do this," Tay said.

Shepherd gave him a hard look. "I don't see what's so complicated about it."

"We can't just go in banging on doors with no idea what's over there. There are four floors of apartments, but how many apartments are there on each floor? One in front and one in back? Maybe another one in between them? And is there some kind of back entrance? Is it possible Emma and whoever else is there have been going and coming through another door without anyone seeing them?"

"You don't have to worry about any of that," Shepherd said. "There are shophouses like this all over Hong Kong, and all of them are the same. The floors are small. I've never seen more than one apartment on each floor. And there's no back entrance because the back of the building shares a common wall with the building behind it. There's not much space in Hong Kong, and every foot of ground is worth a fortune. No one wastes it on back entrances."

"Then the only entry is the front?"

"The only entry is through the gate at the bottom of the stairs next to the dentist office. You can be sure of that."

The gate was metal with closely spaced vertical bars. Around the handle was a solid plate of the same color as the bars.

"There's not even a fire escape?"

Shepherd shook his head.

"What do people do in case of fire?"

"They burn to death. We may not have much space in Hong Kong, but we've got plenty of extra people."

Tay couldn't tell for certain whether Shepherd was serious or had just switched back into wiseass mode. He wasn't even sure he wanted to know.

"I wonder if we could slip in, have a quick look around, and get out again without being noticed?" Tay asked.

"How long have you been sitting here looking at that building?"

"An hour, maybe a little more."

"And have you seen anyone go in or out of the gate?"

Tay shook his head.

"So," Shepherd shrugged, "there's your answer. We would have to be damned unlucky to stumble over anyone. If we do, we'll just kill them."

Now Tay was sure Shepherd was doing his wiseass thing. At least, reasonably sure. Probably.

"Look," Shepherd said, "let me go over there and take a look at the gate. It's probably locked, but none of these old shophouses are very secure. Let's find out if we *can* get in before we start trying to decide if we want to."

Tay glanced at Claire.

"That makes sense to me," she said.

"Okay, Shepherd," Tay said. "Look at the gate, but don't hang around too long. White guys are way too conspicuous in this neighborhood."

. . .

W HEN SHEPHERD LEFT, Tay refilled Claire's teacup
and then his own.

"What is it you're not telling me, Sam?"

Tay thought about it for a moment. His mother's visit and
the warning she had given him about having to find Emma by
Friday? His coughing up blood and his diagnosis of a mass in
his lung?

Where to start? Shepherd would be back long before he
could explain either of those things to Claire, let alone both, so
he just shook his head.

Claire didn't want to push him. "Okay," she said, "I guess
you'll tell me when you're ready."

Tay wasn't certain he would ever be ready, but he didn't say
that. He just pointed through the restaurant's windows to the
street, where they both watched Shepherd dodge through the
traffic and step up on the opposite sidewalk about ten feet past
the dental surgery.

Shepherd turned to his left and ambled past the surgery's
front windows, seemingly captivated by the view of the reception room just beyond them. He stopped walking just past the
surgery and looked around. When it was clear no one was
paying the slightest attention to him, he turned toward the gate.

Shepherd's back was to them then and they couldn't see
what he was doing, but within a few seconds the gate swung
open. Shepherd looked up at them and grinned.

" H OW DID YOU do that?" Tay asked when Shepherd
returned.

"I picked the lock with a paperclip."

"Seriously?"

"Don't be ridiculous," Shepherd laughed. "I reached

through the bars and turned the lock from the inside. You can do that with half the shophouses in Hong Kong."

"All right," Tay said, "since I've got the least conspicuous face here, I'm going over alone to have a look around."

"Forget it," Claire said. "You're not armed and I won't let you walk into a building unarmed and by yourself when there could be some guy in there who's already killed six people."

"Then I'm going, too," Shepherd said. "I don't want to sit here alone. I'm afraid of the dark."

"It's the middle of the afternoon," Claire pointed out.

Shepherd just shrugged.

"I need to keep this low-key," Tay said. "Taking two white people with me doesn't qualify as low-key in Mongkok."

Claire and Shepherd just looked at him.

"Okay," Tay shrugged. "Let's go. But try not to look any whiter than you absolutely have to."

FORTY-FIVE

THEY CROSSED THE street, Tay walking about twenty feet in front so they wouldn't look as if they were all together.

When Tay reached the gate, he saw Shepherd had left it unlocked. He slipped through and waited on the other side until Claire and Shepherd caught up with him.

The stairs were narrow and steep. Concrete with worn black plastic treads on each step. The first flight of stairs led up to a large landing which seemed to have no purpose since there were no doors opening onto it. Then the second flight went up to another landing where there was a single door. Painted on the wall in fluorescent green right next to the door was the numeral 1.

The door was wood and painted the same shade of green. It didn't look flimsy, but it didn't look sturdy either. Tay bent and examined the handle. It was a simple key-in-handle lock set, not a dead bolt.

They continued up the stairs walking as softly as possible and passed similar doors on similar landings, these with the numerals 2, 3, and 4 painted next to them in the same green color. On the last landing at the top of the stairs there was a metal door with nothing painted next to it that looked sturdier than the doors below it.

Tay tried the handle. Locked.

"Roof access," Shepherd said. "Has to be."

They started back down again.

Tay stopped at the door marked 4, put his ear against it, and listened. When he straightened up, he shook his head. It was unnecessary for him to repeat the ear-against-the-door thing at the door marked 3 since the sound of Cantopop, music which mixed Cantonese opera and Western pop music into a raucous local stew, was blaring from behind it.

At the door marked 2, Tay heard no sound, but as he bent closer to the door Shepherd reached past him, put his palm against it, and pushed. It swung open.

"You could see the bolt," Shepherd said. "Somebody didn't close it all the way."

The reason for that was clear when they looked into the apartment. It was empty.

Tay took a couple of steps inside and glanced around. No furniture anywhere. He bent down and ran his hand over the floor. When he looked at his palm it was covered in dirt.

"It's been vacant quite a while," he said, wiping his hand on his pants.

"Do you think Emma would have been able to get to either of the apartments above here and back down for the rest of the groceries in the time our witness saw her do it?"

Tay shook his head.

"That leaves door number one," Shepherd said. "What do you want to do?"

"I don't know."

"If you honestly think she's in there, we've got to go in," Shepherd said. "What's the alternative? Just drink tea and watch the building?"

Tay hesitated.

"Okay," he said after a moment. "Let's see if we hear anything to tell us if the apartment is occupied."

"And if we don't hear anything?" Shepherd asked.

Tay didn't answer. He would cross that bridge when he got to it.

Tay moved down the stairs, placing his feet in the center of each plastic pad and making as little noise as possible. Shepherd stayed right behind him. Claire closed the door of number 2 as quietly as she could and followed.

T HEY STOPPED OUTSIDE the door with the 1 painted next to it and listened.

Nothing.

Tay bent forward and placed his ear up against the door. He closed his eyes and concentrated for fifteen or twenty seconds, then straightened up and shook his head.

"What do you want to do?" Shepherd stage-whispered.

Tay knew what he wanted to do. He wanted to go in and find out if Emma was in there. He just wasn't sure it was the right thing to do.

If Emma was inside, they knew nothing about the circumstances under which she was being held. Or maybe she wasn't being held. Maybe she was just in there getting ready to prepare dinner for her lover. Well, he doubted that.

And if she *was* in there, who else was in there with her? Was it just the man who took her, or did he have other people with him? Besides, how in the world were the three of them going to rescue Emma if there was *anybody* in there with her?

He wasn't armed, and he assumed Shepherd wasn't armed. Claire doubtless was armed, but if whoever was holding Emma fought back then one gun might not be enough. Or it might be too much. The last thing he wanted was a shoot-out with Emma caught in the middle. Nothing would be worse than Emma getting killed in their rescue attempt.

Tay knew his own weaknesses well, and his very worst was overthinking everything. He wasn't a good candidate to become an action hero since he reflexively weighed and balanced every conceivable factor before he made any decision. He did it even at those moments when he knew he should just stop thinking and do something.

Like this one.

"Oh, for fuck's sake, Tay," Shepherd snapped, taking him off the hook. "You are such a goddamn Singaporean."

Shepherd reached out with his left arm and moved Tay to one side. Then he leaned back against the wall, raised his right foot, and slammed it into the door right next to the knob.

The door was old and even more fragile than it looked. It blew in like it was made of cardboard.

CLAIRE SLIPPED PAST Shepherd and was the first through the door. She stayed low and kept her right hand under the back of her shirt, up near the waistband of her jeans.

Claire went to the right, so Shepherd went to the left. Tay went straight in, moving in a half crouch. He felt a little foolish doing it, but it was what Claire and Shepherd did so he did it, too.

All three of them froze in those positions and listened, but there was no sound from anywhere. Either there was nobody in the apartment, or their slam-bang entry had scared the shit out of whoever was there, and now they were afraid to move.

The apartment was dreary. The door from the hallway opened into a living area furnished with a couch upholstered in ugly green fabric and two brown vinyl-covered easy chairs. On the cheap-looking chrome and glass table between them, Tay saw a white Starbucks cup and a folded newspaper.

Tay moved over to the table. The Starbucks cup was empty. He touched it with his hand. Cold. The newspaper was the *South China Morning Post*. Tay checked the date.

"Somebody's been here recently," he said. "It's yesterday's paper."

There was a strange smell in the air. Tay straightened and tried to work out what it was. He sniffed at it, but then he lost it.

Shepherd side-stepped to a half-open door on his left. He ducked his head, took a quick in-and-out peek, and then a longer look.

"Kitchen," he said. "Clear."

Claire began moving up the hallway that ran off the living area in the opposite direction. Her hand stayed under her shirt near the small of her back and she kept low and close to the wall.

The first door along the hallway was open. She did a one-eyed peek.

"Bathroom," she said. "Clear."

The next door was closed. Claire put her ear against it, listened for a moment, then stepped back and jerked it open.

"Closet. Empty. Clear."

Only one door left. The one at the end of the hallway.

Claire slid all the way to the right side of the hall and saw the door was standing open about six inches. To have the widest possible field of view through the small opening without touching the door, she got so low she was almost duckwalking.

About a foot from the opening, she stopped and moved her head back and forth to see as much of the room as she could. Tay watched her hand moving under the back of her shirt and he imagined her fingers clenching against the butt of a handgun and then opening again without drawing it.

Then abruptly she stood straight up and plunged through the door.

"Back here!"

Shepherd and Tay glanced at each other and quick-stepped down the hallway. The moment Tay entered the room and saw the figure rolled up in a threadbare blanket and lying across the bed, he knew it was Emma.

Claire sat on the edge of the bed and gently pulled the blanket away from Emma's face.

"Is she..." Shepherd trailed off without finishing, but it was clear enough what he was asking.

Claire put two fingers against Emma's neck and searched for a pulse. Tay held his breath.

"She's alive! Pulse is weak and slow, but she's alive!"

Claire pulled out her telephone. "I'll call 999."

"Wait!" Tay said, and Claire looked at him. "Try Doris Lau first. If you can reach her, she'll get people here faster than we could."

Claire nodded. She scrolled through her phone, found the number, and punched the call button. Then she stood up and walked past Tay and Shepherd back down the hallway.

The two men moved over to where Emma was wrapped up in the blanket. Neither one had any idea what they could do to help her, and they stood looking down at her, shuffling awkwardly from foot to foot. They could hear Claire on her telephone in the other room, but they couldn't make out who she was talking to or what she was saying.

Tay sat down on the edge of the bed and took Emma's hand. It felt cold and clammy. Could Claire have been mistaken? Maybe she just thought she felt a pulse. Maybe Emma wasn't alive at all.

He held his forefinger underneath her nose searching for air movement. At first, he felt nothing, but then he shifted his finger closer and felt a tiny disturbance. He looked up at Shepherd.

"She's breathing. It's shallow, but she's breathing."

"I don't know what to do other than call for help," Shepherd said. "I'm just a lawyer. I have no fucking idea how to help her."

Tay didn't either. He had never felt so helpless.

At the sound of footsteps in the hallway, they both looked around.

"Mrs. Lau will get emergency medical people here right away," Claire said. "Five minutes."

"I'll wait for them on the street," Shepherd said. "To bring them straight up here."

After Shepherd left, Tay stood up. He reached down and tucked the edge of the blanket back around Emma. It was a pathetic gesture, he supposed, but he couldn't think of anything else to do.

"There's something else," Claire said. "Mrs. Lau is close. She's coming, too."

T AY AND CLAIRE were standing there together watching Emma when Tay got another whiff of the same smell he had noticed in the living room.

He lifted his head and tasted the air like a dog sniffing for danger.

"What?" Claire asked.

The odor was familiar, and it was far stronger back here than it had been in the living room, but Tay still couldn't quite place it. It seemed so familiar, but...

"Do you smell that?" he asked Claire.

She sniffed the air and a puzzled look slid across her face. Then she sniffed it again.

"What *is* that?" she asked.

"I'm not sure, but there's something familiar about it."

"It makes me think of a doctor's office."

And then at exactly the same moment they both realized what they were smelling.

"I think it might be—"

"That's exactly what it is," Tay interrupted. "There's no doubt in my mind. That's what it is."

"Well, I'll be a son of a goddamned bitch," Claire muttered.

FORTY-SIX

T HE STAIRS WERE too narrow to bring the gurney up.

The EMTs took the cushion off so they could use it to bring Emma down when they were ready to transport her and Shepherd carried it up for them. That left their hands free to lug their heavy equipment cases.

One of the EMTs was a tough-looking middle-aged man. He was heavily muscled with tats peeking out the front of his open-necked blue shirt and crawling up both sides of his neck. The other was a small woman wearing rimless glasses who looked like she could have been a nun. Tay doubted she was.

The man pulled a stethoscope from one of the pockets of his blue jumpsuit and looped it around his neck. He got down on his knees next to the bed and lifted the blanket away from Emma. She didn't move. While the man used the stethoscope to listen to her heart, the woman produced a blood pressure cuff and wrapped it around Emma's forearm.

The man pulled a small flashlight out of another pocket and lifted Emma's eyelids, first the left then the right. He muttered something to the not-a-nun in Cantonese. Tay didn't understand what he said, but from the look on his face it seemed obvious it wasn't good news.

Just then Doris Lau rushed into the room and went straight to where the EMTs were bent over Emma. If she saw Tay, Claire, and Shepherd, she gave no sign. She just dropped to her knees next to the muscled man with tats and laid her hands on Emma's cheeks. The man started to say something, no doubt to tell her to move back, but he glanced at his partner first and she gave him a very faint head shake.

C LAIRE NUDGED TAY. The two of them slipped out into the hallway and Shepherd followed.

"She's been drugged," Claire said, keeping her voice low. "Heroin or scopolamine maybe. Something to keep her docile and unresponsive."

"Do you think she's been—" Shepherd began, his voice equally low, but Tay cut him off.

"Of course, he rapes them."

Shepherd took a breath and exhaled heavily. He didn't know what to say.

"I don't know how it began," Tay went on, "but he's discovered how much he likes it. He's getting better at it. It's all very well planned now. He gets their confidence, brings them here, drugs them, and keeps them until he's tired of them. Then he kills them and disposes of their bodies."

"But you still don't have any idea who's doing this, do you?" Shepherd asked.

"I know exactly who's doing it," Tay said.

"Are you serious?" Shepherd looked dumbstruck. "How long have you known?"

"I just found out."

"Well, for fuck's sake, don't keep me in suspense. Who the hell is it?"

"I'm not sure you want to know."

"Like hell I don't."

"You should trust me here, Shepherd. You're better off not knowing."

"That's bullshit."

"You live in Hong Kong. You're part of what happens here. And this won't end well."

TAY WAS STILL trying to decide how much to tell Shepherd when the three of them walked back into the living room and found Albert Chan sitting on the ugly green couch.

Chan was slumped in one corner, his legs stretched out and crossed at the ankle and his arms folded tight against his chest. His eyes shifted from Tay to Claire, flicked over Shepherd, and then came back to Tay.

"Doris and I were in a meeting at the Mongkok Police Station when you called," Chan said. "She insisted on coming immediately."

This was the first time Tay had ever seen Chan anywhere other than in the back of Mrs. Lau's Mercedes van and he studied his face. It was an ordinary enough face for a somewhat heavy middle-aged man with a receding hairline and droopy jowls, but something in Chan's eyes held him. They were dark and small and empty and slanted slightly downward. They gave his face an air of barely restrained menace. He looked like he was only moments away from springing to his feet and kicking the crap out of somebody.

"You're the ones who found Emma?" Chan asked when Tay said nothing.

Tay nodded.

From the bedroom down at the end of the hall they could hear the voices of the two paramedics murmuring to each other and Mrs. Lau choking back sobs.

"You haven't asked how she is, sir."

Chan watched Tay with a wary look, but he said nothing.

"Why is that?"

"Why is what?"

"Why haven't you asked how Emma is? Is it because you already know?"

"How would I know that?"

"Because you're the one who drugged her and left her here. When were you planning to kill her? Today? Tomorrow? Or did you think she was already dead?"

Chan looked almost amused. "You're mad, Tay. I am the Chief of Staff for the Chief Executive of Hong Kong, and you're nobody. Just some retired ex-cop from Singapore. Be very careful how you talk to me."

"You know I'm right, sir."

"And you know who Emma's mother and father are. If you try to smear me with a crazy story like that, you little shit, I'll bring down the governments of two countries, and then I'll bury you just for the fun of it."

"What about the other five women, sir? Did you drug and rape them right here in this apartment, too?"

Chan just looked at Tay, his face empty.

"Did you kill them and bully someone in a coffin shop into putting their bodies into coffins already scheduled for cremation?"

Chan kept looking at Tay.

Tay just waited.

He thought Chan might say, *what the fuck are you talking about, Tay?*

But he didn't.

Instead, his face crinkled into a sneer that caused an iciness to bloom at the back of Tay's neck and spread quickly all the way down to the base of his spine.

If Tay had any doubts Chan was the man responsible for the disappearance of all six young women, and he had very few, that moment erased them.

"I don't have to listen to this crap, Tay. You have no way to connect me to Emma or to any of the other women."

"You wear a very distinctive aftershave."

"What the hell does that have to do with anything?"

"The odor remains in the air for a long time wherever you go."

The look of puzzlement on Chan's face turned slowly into a broad smile.

"That's it, Tay? That's your evidence I'm responsible for killing six women? You think you smell my aftershave in this apartment?"

"Five."

"What?"

"You killed five women. Emma is very much alive."

Chan's smile faltered. "I don't believe you," he said after a moment.

"What did you give her? Heroin? Scopolamine? Maybe you didn't give her enough. When she wakes up, you're finished."

Now it was Tay who had a small smile on his face as he watched Chan calculate and recalculate the odds. Apparently, he decided they favored him.

"Fuck you," Chan said. "You've got nothing. A smell in the air that might be my aftershave? A drug-addled young girl who probably won't remember her own name even if she does wake up? That's the evidence you're going to use to get me arrested?"

Tay took a breath and let it out. "It's not much, is it?"

"They'll laugh you out of Hong Kong, Tay. Your pal the Vice President will be ruined for nothing."

"Yes, sir," he said, "Maybe you're right. Maybe it's not enough to have you arrested."

Chan spread his hands and unleashed a nasty grin.

"So, what are you going to do now, hotshot? Try to slander me by selling the story to some newspaper? Beat me up? You've got nothing, Tay. You *are* nothing."

"Is this our guy, Sam?" Claire asked.

349

When Claire spoke, everyone looked at her. Until then, she had been leaning against the wall with her arms folded, listening to the conversation between Chan and Tay and saying nothing.

Tay knew what Claire was asking him and he understood what his answer would mean, but he thought about Albert Chan's sneer when he had asked him about the other five women and he answered Claire without the slightest hesitation.

"Oh yeah, it's him," Tay said. "We may not have the evidence, but there's no doubt in my mind. It's him."

Chan's eyes swiveled back to Tay and the menace on his face became a cloud of malevolence that looked as if it might engulf them all.

ONE MOMENT CLAIRE was leaning on the wall and the next moment she was standing next to Chan with the barrel of a small black pistol pressed into the hollow behind his right ear.

Tay didn't know much about guns, but from this one's small size he figured it had to be a .22. A .22 was almost useless for self-defense. It fired such a small caliber round you could barely stop a squirrel with one. In fact, a .22 was only good for two things: shooting paper targets at a range, and killing people with a close-up shot to the head.

Cops sometimes called the .22 the hitman special. All the best hitters used them. A single, low-velocity .22 round fired into the skull at close range didn't have enough power to pass through and come out the other side. Instead, it just ricocheted around inside and pulverized the target's brain as completely as if somebody had run it through a blender.

The .22 was also quiet. Add a decent sound suppressor, and Tay had been told the sound of the shot wasn't much louder than a hand clap. Claire had come prepared. He could see the sound suppressor screwed into the muzzle. Tay was anything but surprised by that. Claire had done this a few times before.

She pulled the trigger before Chan could react. The noise of the shot was exactly like the hand clap Tay had always heard about. The sound of the semi-automatic's slide cycling was louder than the explosion of the bullet leaving the barrel.

Despite how little noise the .22 had made, Tay shot a look down the hallway to the bedroom. The murmuring of para-medics' voices and the heartbreaking sounds of Doris Lau's sobs continued just as they had before. If anyone had heard the shot, they gave no sign of it.

When Tay turned back to the living room, Chan was on the floor, his last sense of consciousness draining away. Claire spun the suppressor loose from the barrel of the .22 and slipped it into her pocket. She wiped the grips of the pistol on her shirt and then knelt down and curled Chan's fingers around it. After holding his hand in place for a moment, she dropped his hand and the pistol onto the floor.

They fell a few inches apart. Just as they would have if Chan had been holding the pistol and shot himself.

Claire turned away and walked out the apartment's front door with Shepherd right behind her.

Tay threw one more glance down the hallway toward the bedroom, then he trotted down the steps to the street behind them.

O UTSIDE ON THE sidewalk the arrival of the ambulance had attracted a small crowd.

Maybe a dozen people were standing around on Sneaker Street in ones and twos, peering at the building's gate waiting for something to happen.

When a white man and woman came out of the building, a few people glanced at each other with puzzled expressions, but then a guy who looked sort of Chinese came out right behind them and he didn't attract any interest at all.

Shepherd and Claire went to the left and Tay went to the

right, and within seconds all three of them had vanished into the crowds thronging the streets of Mongkok.

It was almost as if they had never been there on Sneaker Street at all. Certainly not on that Saturday afternoon in October.

FORTY-SEVEN

T AY HAD DIFFICULTY getting to sleep that night. It was not because he was unsettled over what had just happened, but rather because of his foreboding about what was yet to happen.

He had killed Albert Chan. Claire might have pulled the trigger, but he had called the shot. He had done it without a second thought, and he would do it again. He had no pangs of conscience over it. None at all.

Claire's suicide scenario wouldn't survive even the most casual scrutiny, of course, but Tay was certain there wouldn't be any. Rugs all over Hong Kong were already lumpy from all the crimes swept under them over the years. What difference would one more body make?

The Chinese were a practical people. Why ask questions you didn't have to ask? Why demand answers that would only embarrass people who had the power to make your life miserable? The corpse of Albert Chan would become part of Hong Kong's large collection of things no one wanted to remember. And that, Tay thought, was just as it should be.

In the years he had spent as a policeman, he had learned that justice was a malleable concept. When he was younger, he had focused resolutely on enforcing the law and doing so even-handedly and without favor. There was justice in that, to be sure. At least there was most of the time.

But his focus had shifted somehow. Now he thought less about enforcing the law than he did about doing what was right. Sometimes it was the same thing. Sometimes it wasn't.

Albert Chan was a powerful man with impeccable connec-tions, and he was a careful man who had left no obvious trail connecting him with what he had done. Tay knew that if he gave the Hong Kong police what he had discovered, they wouldn't have been able to touch Albert Chan. He doubted they would have even tried.

Oh, some people might have had suspicions about him, but the outcome would have been the same. Albert Chan would not have paid for what he did. Five young women were dead and one was in hospital, and Albert Chan would have walked away.

That was not just, and it was not right.

Tay had been given an opportunity to correct the moral balance of the universe, and he took it. He had no regrets.

If that had been the only thing on his mind, he would have slept like the proverbial baby.

It was the other thing that kept him awake.

TAY WAS NOT a man who believed in much, but somewhere deep in whatever passed for his soul these days he had a strong sense all life operated in a sort of cosmic equilibrium. The universe giveth, and the universe taketh away.

Today, they had found Emma Lau, and they had found her alive. Yes, he and Claire and Shepherd had worked hard to do that, but Tay knew their success was not entirely their own doing. They had found Emma as much through sheer good fortune as they had through cleverness and hard work.

Finding Emma Lau had been a gift from the cosmos, and he doubted the cosmos was likely to give him another gift when Dr.

Patel got the biopsy results. The universe giveth, and the universe taketh away.

Perhaps, Tay had decided somewhere deep in the empty hours of the night, that was a fair enough deal all around.

He had expected his mother to make another appearance, and he was disappointed she hadn't. She had been wrong about him only having until Friday night to find Emma alive. It wasn't until Saturday that they found Emma, and she was very much alive despite his mother's dire prophecy. Tay had been looking forward to reminding his mother of that. Perhaps this would put an end to the ridiculous idea he was receiving messages from the other side through his dead mother.

Stomach gas and nightmares were part of the human condition. They were not a window into the future no matter how much one might wish them to be, and his mother was not traveling back and forth over the line dividing life from death to tip him off about what the celestial infiniteness had in store for him.

He had always known that. He had always understood that. But yet, sometimes in the silence of the night...

No matter. It was settled now. The message his mother claimed to be delivering from the future had been wrong. And what was the value of tapping into the infinite wisdom of the universe if it turned out to be full of shit?

Toward dawn Tay slept, but it was such a harsh and unhappy sleep he almost wished he hadn't.

S UNDAY. DAY SIX.
When he woke, it was late. He ordered his usual pot of coffee from room service. He had no appetite, so coffee was all he ordered. When the coffee came, he sat and drank it looking out the windows over the city, beyond West Kowloon to the far reaches of the harbor.

Dr. Patel had said he would have the biopsy result today, but Tay supposed *today* could mean almost anything. This morning, this afternoon, tonight, or maybe even another regretful message that the result was still inconclusive, whatever that would mean. Regardless, he didn't fret. He just kept his mind as empty as possible and waited for the telephone to ring.

Tay had had three cups of coffee and was wondering if he could drink another without beginning to levitate, when his telephone rang. He walked over to the desk, scooped it up, and answered without looking at the screen.

"Are you okay this morning, Sam?"

Claire, not Dr. Patel.

"I'm fine." Tay thought about saying more, but decided not to, so he repeated himself. "I'm fine."

"I'm going to the hospital this morning to check on Emma. Do you want to go?"

That gave Tay a moment of pause.

"Don't you think it might be better if you didn't go?" he asked.

"Why? What do you mean?"

"An unknown white woman turning up and asking about what is surely the hospital's most prominent patient will raise some eyebrows."

Claire said nothing.

"Mrs. Lau knows we were there in that apartment and the two EMTs know, but they don't know who we were and they won't know unless Mrs. Lau tells them. And she's not going to tell them."

Claire still said nothing.

"Keep your head down, Claire. I know you mean well, but don't stir things up."

"I could always just call Mrs. Lau, I suppose."

"I think that would be better."

"It sounds to me like you probably want to go back to Singapore right away."

Tay hadn't really thought about that, but now that Claire

raised the subject he knew that was exactly what he did want to do.

"Yes," he said. "Today, if you can arrange it."

"Sure. Just tell me when."

As soon as Dr. Patel calls to tell me when I'm dying, Tay thought. But that was not what he said.

"I'm not certain. This afternoon sometime."

"I'll put a plane on standby from... what? Two o'clock?"

"Fine."

"Just get a hotel car to take you to the Business Aviation Center at the airport when you're ready. A plane will be waiting for you."

Tay had to admit the private jet thing was becoming awfully appealing. He still didn't much like traveling, but there was something undeniably cool about having an airplane standing by just for him whenever he felt like leaving.

"Thanks for your help, Sam. I've already filled August in on everything. I'm sure he'll be in touch."

Tay would much rather it was Claire who would be in touch, but he didn't think that was the right thing for him to say just then, so he didn't say it. Instead, he just said, "Let me know how Emma is doing."

"I will."

And there they ended the call.

Tay went back to drinking coffee, looking out the window, and waiting.

FORTY-EIGHT

D R. PATEL CALLED a half-hour later.

This time Tay looked at the display before he answered. He wanted no more surprises.

"Good morning, Dr. Patel."

"Good morning, Inspector Tay."

In the moment of silence that followed, Tay could feel his entire life compressing into a single point of light.

"The biopsy found no sign of malignancy. The mass is a benign hemangioma. You have nothing to worry about."

And the point of light expanded until it filled Tay's entire being and consciousness, and he could see nothing else but that light. His throat was so dry he had to clear it twice before he could speak.

"I don't know what to say, doctor."

"Say you'll stop smoking."

Tay wasn't prepared for that. To be told he was going to die, yes, but not to be told he had to stop smoking.

"That's part of the treatment?"

"Not really. It's just good advice. There's no treatment required."

"No treatment at all?"

"Only reassurance."

"Then you don't have to operate to remove this..."

Somehow, he still couldn't bring himself to use the word *mass*.

"...thing from my lung?"

"Hemangiomas such as yours are quite common. Once we've confirmed it's benign, life goes on as before."

There was more conversation after that, but none of it mattered. Having just received a reprieve from his impending execution, Tay was weightless.

When Dr. Patel continued to talk, Tay did his best to make appreciative noises and grunt in all the right places, but he had nothing else to say to Dr. Patel, and Dr. Patel really had nothing else to say to him.

The only thing that mattered was the message. And Dr. Patel had already delivered the message.

Samuel Tay was not going to die. At least not right away.

Tay brought the conversation with Dr. Patel to a conclusion as soon as decency allowed. His life had now been extended to an unknowable point somewhere in the future. He wanted time to himself to savor that.

And he wanted to go downstairs for a cigarette.

TAY DROPPED HIS telephone on the desk and pulled on a shirt and a pair of pants. He had just slipped his feet into a pair of loafers without bothering to put on any socks and was reaching for his cigarettes and matches when his telephone rang again.

He froze and stared at it.

Was Dr. Patel calling back to say it had all been a mistake? That he had been reading the wrong biopsy report?

Tay had never been a man who saw the future through the lens of optimism, but at this moment every pessimistic gene in his body assembled into a single mass and seized him around the throat.

Surely not. The universe was a cruel place, but it was not *that* cruel.

Tay reached out and picked up the phone with all the caution of a man wrapping his hand around a poisonous snake. For a moment he could not even bring himself to look at the screen, but then he did.

Claire, it said.

And the breath he hadn't even realized he was holding released with an audible explosion.

"Hello?"

"Sam?"

"Yes, Claire."

"She died, Sam."

For a moment, Tay didn't understand.

"What?" he asked.

"Emma died this morning," Claire repeated.

And just like that, the entire world went into reverse.

TAY DIDN'T FEEL like standing on the sidewalk outside the hotel and smoking a cigarette anymore. Instead, he decided to walk for a while. Stepping out of the lobby, he headed down the hotel's driveway to Reclamation Street and turned left.

Hong Kong might not be a Christian country, but Sunday morning still brought a stillness to the city. Tay walked south past the builders' supply shops, the electronic parts stores, and the whorehouses, all closed, and thought about what Claire had just told him.

His mother had been right after all when she said he had to find Emma by Friday night or she would die. Or his mother's ghost had been right. Or his stomach gas had been right. Whatever.

Well, crap.

What was he supposed to think about those messages from the other side now?

At Dundas Street, he turned right and walked past the Sunrise Aluminum Company and the Soi Leun Hardware Company, and then he came upon the Tung On Street Garden. He stopped there and watched a line of four elderly women dressed all in black standing doing graceful tai chi moves in the garden.

Tay had felt in the depths of his soul it would be either Emma or him. Only one of them would make it through. He had been right about that, but he had been wrong in his conviction he would not be the winner of the lottery. Even, perhaps, that he should not be.

Two hours ago, he had known as well as he had ever known anything that he was condemned, a dead man waiting only on the formal confirmation of his demise, but at least he knew he had saved Emma. And that seemed to him a fair enough trade.

One hour ago he learned he had been spared, and he decided that the forces of cosmos had decreed, against all the odds, that both he and Emma each deserved a little more life.

Now everything was back to front.

Now everything was upside down.

Now everything was inside out.

Now he was saved and Emma was lost.

Emma, a young woman with her life in front of her, was gone. Samuel Tay, a man in late middle-age with most of his life behind him, was still there.

Tay had learned a long time ago that in this life there was no negotiation. You took the deal you got.

The universe giveth, and the universe taketh away.

. . .

TAY SHOOK A Marlboro out of the pack and lit it. He drew the sweet smoke into his lungs, savored the fierceness of it, and exhaled in a single long breath.

Up ahead, an elderly man in baggy black pants and a grimy white undershirt shuffled along the sidewalk toward Tay. A few feet before their paths crossed, the man stopped and pointed to the cigarette in Tay's mouth. Tay smiled and started to shake a cigarette out of his pack for the old man, but then he stopped.

He handed the man the entire pack, clapped him on the shoulder, and walked on by.

The breeze kicked up a notch and swirled away pieces of paper from the sidewalk. Tay felt its coolness through his shirt.

There was a meanness in the air, a reminder that even in Hong Kong the chill of winter always came. It arrived whenever it was ready, not whenever *you* were ready. Nothing any of us could do would ever change that.

The sky was a gloomy, monotonous gray. It was the color of grief. It was the color of sadness.

Sunday morning coming down.

Two people are working the case.

One of them has been dead for a decade.

For over thirty years, a man named Harry Black lived quietly in a small town on the Gulf of Thailand. Then while walking on the beach on his eighty-sixth birthday, he's shot and killed by a sniper firing from half a mile away.

Why would someone send a highly skilled sniper to kill an insignificant old man? Maybe he wasn't really as insignificant as everybody thought he was.

Inspector Samuel Tay was once Singapore's best-known homicide detective, but he's no longer a cop. He was too much of a maverick for straight-and-narrow little Singapore and his bosses forced him into an early retirement. When a guy who once did Tay a big favor asks him to look into Harry Black's murder, it's his chance to get back in the game.

Tay's mother wants to help. Tay has always had a somewhat fraught relationship with his mother, but he figures they get along pretty well now, particularly considering she's dead. Tay doesn't believe in ghosts, of course, and when his mother shows up in the dark of night to give him advice about his cases, he knows perfectly well that her appearances aren't actually real.

But here's the thing. Some of her advice is so good he can't help but listen to it anyway.

This time, Tay's mother warns him that he's fishing in dangerous waters. 'I'll help you, Samuel,' she tells him, 'but you are about to expose secrets that will fundamentally alter the way people see the world. No one is ever going to thank you for what you're doing.'

That sounds pretty overwrought to Tay, and besides, his mother isn't really there, so why should he believe her?

Harry Black was just an old man who lived in complete obscurity for the last thirty years of his life. What secrets could he possibly have known that were so important somebody might have murdered him to keep them hidden?

But that also raises a really awkward question Samuel Tay needs to think about.

If he discovers the secrets someone killed Harry Black to bury, why wouldn't they kill Tay to silence him, too?

THE INSPECTOR SAMUEL TAY NOVELS

 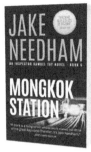 

 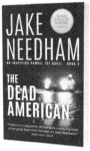  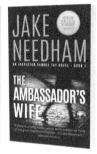

They steer a tight ship in squeaky-clean Singapore. No dissent, no opposition, no criticism. Disneyland with the death penalty somebody once called it.

Samuel Tay is a little overweight, a little lonely, a little cranky, and he smokes way too much. He's worked almost his entire life as a senior homicide detective in Singapore CID, and he's the best investigator anyone there has ever seen.

Problem is, the senior officers of CID don't much like Tay. His father was an American and there's something about him that's just a little too American for most Singaporeans. Tay knows they'll get him someday, and eventually they do.

That's when a whole new world of unexpected possibilities opens for Samuel Tay.

THE AMBASSADOR'S WIFE - Book 1

THE UMBRELLA MAN - Book 2

THE DEAD AMERICAN - Book 3

THE GIRL IN THE WINDOW - Book 4

AND BROTHER IT'S STARTING TO RAIN - Book 5

MONGKOK STATION - Book 6

WHO THE HELL IS HARRY BLACK? - Book 7

THE JACK SHEPHERD NOVELS

Jack Shepherd was a well-connected lawyer in Washington DC until he tossed it all in for the quiet life of a business school professor at Chulalongkorn University in Bangkok.

It was a pretty good gig until the university discovered the kind of notorious people Shepherd had gotten involved with in his law practice. That was when they suggested he'd probably be happier somewhere else.

These days, Shepherd lives and works in Hong Kong where he's the kind of lawyer people call a troubleshooter. At least that's what they call him when they're being polite.

Shepherd is the guy people go to when they have a problem too ugly to tell anyone else about. He locates the trouble, and then he shoots it.

Neat, huh? If his life were only that simple.

LAUNDRY MAN - Book 1

KILLING PLATO - Book 2

A WORLD OF TROUBLE - Book 3

THE KING OF MACAU - Book 4

DON'T GET CAUGHT - Book 5

THE NINETEEN - Book 6

"THE BIG MANGO is a classic!"
-- Crime Reads

$400 million is in the wind, ten tons of cash, the result of a bungled CIA operation to grab the foreign currency from the Bank of Vietnam when the Americans fled Saigon in 1975.

A few decades later, the word on the street is that all that money somehow ended up in Bangkok and a downwardly mobile lawyer from California named Eddie Dare is the only guy left alive who might still have a shot at finding it.

Eddie knows nothing about the missing money. At least, he doesn't think he does. But so many people claim he's got an inside track that he and an old marine buddy named Winnebago Jones decide to head for Bangkok anyway and do a little treasure hunting. What do they have to lose, huh? Their lives, as it turns out.

From the Big Apple, to the Big Orange, to the Big Mango. You have to admit it has a kind of nutty logic to it. Bangkok is about as far from California as Eddie can go without sailing completely over the edge of the world.

Although, at times, he wonders if that isn't exactly what he *has* done.

THE BIG MANGO

available in both ebook and paperback editions

MEET JAKE NEEDHAM

Jake Needham is an American lawyer who became a screen and television writer through a series of coincidences too ridiculous for anyone to believe. When he discovered how little he actually liked movies and television, he started writing crime novels.

Jake has lived in Asia for over thirty years and has published fourteen novels that have collectively sold nearly a million copies. He has twice been a finalist for the Barry Award for the Paperback Mystery of the Year and once a finalist for the International Thriller Writers' Award for Ebook Thriller of the Year. He and his wife, an Oxford graduate and prematurely retired concert pianist, live in Bangkok.

Every month or two, Jake sends out one of his famous *Letters from Asia* to those readers who have asked to receive them. He often talks about the real people, places, and things that appear in his novels in fictional form and sometimes lets his readers know about new books he has coming soon or suggests books by other writers that he thinks they might like. If want to be one of those readers who receive Jake's letters, go to this web address and give him the email address you'd like for him to use:

www.JakeNeedhamNovels.com/letter-to-readers

MONGKOK STATION © 2020 by Jake Raymond Needham

Cover © 2020 by Jake Raymond Needham

Ebook edition ISBN 978-616-497-612-2

Trade paper edition ISBN 978-616-497-613-9

Made in the USA
Las Vegas, NV
26 June 2024

91531593R00225